BY THE SAME AUTHOR

Novels

Lunch with the Generals
Lunch with Mussolini

Short Stories

Dead Fishy
Psycho Cat

DEREK HANSEN was born in England, raised in New Zealand and now lives with his wife and two children in Sydney, Australia. Derek turned to writing novels after a career in advertising and met with instant success.

Sole Survivor

DEREK HANSEN

HarperCollins*Publishers*

HarperCollins*Publishers*
77–85 Fulham Palace Road,
Hammersmith, London W6 8JB

The HarperCollins website address is:
www.**fire**and**water**.com

A Paperback Original 1999
1 3 5 7 9 8 6 4 2

A catalogue record for this book
is available from the British Library

ISBN 0 00 651268 2

Set in Bembo

Printed and bound in Great Britain by
Caledonian International Book Manufacturing Ltd, Glasgow

BOOK ONE

One

~~~~~~~~~~

Red O'Hara woke at first light convinced that he should be dead and ashamed that he wasn't. There was nothing unusual about this. Every day began the same way. He pushed aside his mosquito net and glanced quickly around the bare wooden slat walls of his bedroom. He needed to confirm that he was safe in his bedroom and not back in hell. He rose and walked to the window to begin another day of discipline and routine, to realize the objective the doctors had insisted he set himself.

"Progress will only come through setting objectives and achieving them," they'd said smugly, cleverly transferring the blame for their own lack of progress onto him. One day Red had surprised them by obliging. He wrote a single word in large childish letters and taped the sheet of paper to the wall above his bed.

"Survive," was all it said.

His doctors had encouraged him to write more but in the end had to make do with what they'd got. They didn't think survival was much of an objective, but to Red it had seemed like an insurmountable mountain. They thought survival was the means to an end. Red thought it was the means of avoiding one.

The window had no curtains. The bush and isolation guaranteed Red's privacy. Barely two hundred people lived on the whole of Great Barrier Island, and only three were sufficiently antisocial to live on the northern end in the wilds around Wreck Bay. Both his neighbors kept their distance.

The sun was still well short of the horizon as Red slipped into his routine. Exercise, breakfast, housework, shower. Only then could he face up to the other duties his survival demanded. He allowed himself a few moments of deep breathing to calm his mind before easing slowly into his stretches. Anyone watching would have been thoroughly perplexed. His movements were fluid and graceful, but almost impossibly slow and stylized. The early light revealed a body without an ounce of fat on it. But if his ribs were clearly defined so were his muscles, and what they lacked in mass they more than made up for in tone. Red lived a hard, spartan life and it showed.

He finished his exercises yet still made no move to dress. His skin was tanned, leathery and desensitized from years of exposure to sun and the elements. Red was forty-four years old with the body of a younger man and the skin of one years older. The sun had bleached his Celtic red hair and beard so that they turned gingery at the tips. He wore both long but never untidily. Regulations had been unequivocal about that. His eyes were his most remarkable feature, and not just because they were unnaturally bright. The whites dazzled like retouched teeth on toothpaste posters, and the irises had the green hue of a troubled sea. They were the eyes of a great seducer, though Red showed not the slightest inclination to use them that way. Only rarely did anyone feel their intensity.

Breakfast was fish rice, and that rarely varied either. Red's kitchen typified the man. Everything was in its place and spotless. His pots and pans hung on meat hooks from a rail above his wood-fueled cast-iron stove. The old Shacklock with its water cistern had been freshly scrubbed, and the green and cream enamel gleamed. He used it nine months of the year to cook his meals, heat his water and warm his home, a cottage little bigger than a holiday bach. He never used the Shacklock in summer, when it sat cold and idle. Instead, he lit both rings on his propane stove, put on the kettle for a cup of tea and a pot for his rice. He opened the door of his fridge, grabbed a jug of powdered milk, a bowl of fish stock in which to boil his rice, and a small steamed snapper. He closed the door quickly to keep in the cold. Once the rice was on, he broke the steamed snapper into small pieces, laid it in a bamboo steamer and placed it over the simmering rice to warm through. Archie sat on his rug beside the cold stove and whined in anticipation. There was a strong chance that no one else in the whole of New Zealand sat down to a breakfast remotely like this.

While the rice cooked, Red had another ritual to perform. He opened his screen door and walked along the veranda to the end railing, where the hill sloped abruptly away to the sea and not even his grandfather kauri tree came between him and the rising sun. Sunrise still disturbed him even though he knew he had nothing to fear. Not anymore. No Kimigayo anthem, no standing on parade, no forced labor, no beatings. Once the sun burst free from the sea he returned to the kitchen. Another day, another challenge had begun.

He divided the rice meticulously between two bowls, shared the flesh of the snapper equally, but laid the fish head on Archie's portion. Red liked sucking out the eyes and the cheeks, but so did Archie, and it was the border collie's turn. Red was never anything but scrupulously fair.

"Good to the grain," his mates in the camp used to say, even though the rice they shared was often green or rotting. They liked it when Red served, and there were never any arguments or fights when he did. Red and Archie always had breakfast on the veranda except when rain or high winds made it too uncomfortable. Red ate at a table he'd fashioned from timbers salvaged from the old mine battery at Oreville, while Archie had his bowl on a square of linoleum. Fish was a delicacy neither of them tired of, though the overriding sentiment that governed Red's appreciation was gratitude. He was grateful that there was something filling and life sustaining to put in his bowl. Anyone who'd ever been forced to go without would understand.

After breakfast came the clean-up. The dishes had to be scrubbed immediately, along with pots, pans, countertops, sink and little square of linoleum. Cleanliness meant hygiene, and hygiene was another key to survival. After the dishes, Red stripped his bed and folded the blankets and sheets according to regulations, and set them in a neat stack at the foot of his bed. He completed the housekeeping by chasing a broom around the floors and then a mop around the kitchen area. He did this every day.

11

His shower followed. In summer he used a watering can suspended from a beam that ran between his shack and the laundry and was fed from a hose that ran from his water tank. The water was cold and bracing even in midsummer. Red wasted neither time nor water in washing his body and hair. He scrubbed himself vigorously with Sunlight soap, which the makers had intended for laundry use. It was cheap, lasted and did the job.

Once he'd showered he released his chooks—his five hens and rooster—from the chookhouse, threw them rice and scraps he'd deliberately saved from dinner and breakfast, and gathered their eggs in exchange. He checked his vegetable garden next. There were no locks on his doors or windows, yet his garden was securely fenced in with heavy chain mesh, which was also sunk into the ground so that no animal could burrow beneath it. A heavy bolt held the gate closed, and an equally heavy lock secured the bolt. Pieces of cloth and milk-bottle tops fluttered from strings that crosshatched the plot to keep birds off. Red opened the gate and worked his way between the lines of vegetables, searching for weeds and snails. Neither stood a chance of escaping detection.

Red's final task was to attend to his wall calendar. Keeping track of the days was important because it had always been important. It was important in Burma, where they'd made their own calendars, each a log of survival, charting the time between the present and home and family, and promising one day a reunion. Keeping a calendar up to date was proof of survival and a declaration of defiance. The twenty-fifth day of February 1966 was consigned to history with the stroke of a pencil. Through rigid routine, discipline and the sameness of his days, Red achieved his objective. He survived. He believed he had defied the predictions of his doctors and had his life back under control. Red lived a simple life of self-delusion.

Red had risen from his bed knowing he had two jobs to do that day. He kicked away the wedge that held the laundry door slightly ajar, so that a breeze could flow through, and entered the cool, dark room. He had a favor to ask and he hated asking for favors. He also had a sick man to see, something else that impinged on his day. But he'd learned about obligations in Burma, and obligations to the sick were sacrosanct. Two bush safes, light timber frames encased in fine mesh, hung from a rafter. In one were eight smoked snapper, all around six or seven pounds. In the other were row upon row of sprats and piper, split up the middle, salted and sun dried. The fish weren't only for himself but to give. Years on the railway had taught him the value of the gift. You could never doubt the stamp of a man who willingly gave his food to others. Red helped himself to two smoked snapper and set off along the pathway to the Scotsman's bach, Archie trotting along at his heels. It was barely seven-thirty but Red knew Angus McLeod would be up and about. He also knew he wouldn't be welcome. And neither would Archie.

Two hundred yards down the trail, Red left the path and threaded his way through the ferns, tea trees and pungas to the big old grandfather kauri. He liked to touch the giant trunk, to feel its age and let it know that it was safe. No one would ever take this tree, survivor of centuries and of ruthless logging. Archie waited and watched. There was nothing odd about what his master and mate was doing. It was something else he did every day.

Red made his way farther and farther down the slope before branching off to the right where the trail forked. Up in the canopy he could hear fantails and tiny goldfinches and, occasionally, catch glimpses of them. The pathway turned crimson as it wound around a clump of pohutukawas that had found shelter and shed their blossoms beneath the ridge of Bernie's Head. They'd been doing this for six or seven hundred years before Bernie had thought to share his name. Red walked on uphill until he came to the clearing and paused. The old Scot was cantankerous at best and loathed visitors.

"Hello, Angus!" Red called, and waited, keeping the Scot's vegetable garden between himself and the house. He looked along the lines of vegetables and had to fight back the urge to pluck out the young weeds he saw growing there. There shouldn't be weeds. And there should be a proper fence, not just a sagging run of chicken wire. Red had tried to fix both one morning when he'd called by to drop off some fresh snapper, and had copped an earful for his trouble. Still, it wasn't right and it troubled him. He'd seen men beaten senseless for less.

13

"It's you. What is it you want this time?"

"I'm going round to Fitzroy."

"I see. Wait there. I'll get my list."

As the old Scot turned back into his shack, a bundle of fur barreled down the steps and bounded over toward Red. Archie whined with excitement.

"Stay, Archie," said Red. "Hello, Bonnie. Say hello to Archie." Bonnie purred like an outboard motor and rubbed herself up against Red's legs. What cat wouldn't love a man with such a fishy air about him? Bonnie purred and rolled and also rubbed up against Archie, who bent his nose down to greet the cat Maori-fashion. Both cat and dog were black and white, as if neither owner could afford color. Bonnie responded without fear. They'd met before, and Archie had a fishy aura about him as well.

"I don't encourage that. I'll not have Bonnie bringing in fleas."

Red glanced up into the humorless face on the veranda above.

"All we're bringing is smoked snapper."

"Don't you be smart, now! If you're intending one of those fish for me then I thank you for it." The Scot stepped down from the veranda and skirted around the vegetable plot. "Here is my shopping list."

"Here's your fish." Red took a deep breath. This was the part he hated. "I need to borrow some diesel."

The old Scot glowered but had little option. Besides, the madman was saving him a trip. Even so, Red had to learn not to use him as a convenience. "This is not the first time. Can you not monitor your levels more closely?"

"I had to rescue birds."

"Aye, well." Angus had also rescued birds from Japanese longlines and moderated his tone. "Mind you replace it, now."

"I will."

"In full, mind."

"Yeah."

"See you do. And for God's sake, man . . ."

". . . make yourself decent." Red finished the sentence for him. "Heel."

14

Red turned and Archie followed so abruptly that Bonnie, who had been rubbing herself against the dog's front legs at an angle of roughly thirty-five degrees, toppled onto her side and rolled down the slope after them. Bonnie was like a football covered in fur, kept fat by the old Scot not so much from affection but to deter her from catching the native birds. Bonnie, birds and children in general—though rarely in the specific—were the only creatures on earth the old Scot cared a damn about.

Red retraced his steps by the pohutukawas and their carpet of decaying red needles, and began to climb back up the trail to where it split below the grandfather kauri and the gray soil gave way to yellowish clay. He'd made the trip up to Bernie's every day for the past month and sometimes twice a day. The old man needed help. Red always brought Bernie food, cleaned and cooked. Lately he'd had to bed-wash him, but Red was no stranger to that. Bernie was always affable and grateful, but he was just filling in time before he died. Red had seen that happen before, in Burma.

He walked up to the shack's front door and shooed the chooks off the veranda. He knocked loudly on the frame. The groan from within noted his arrival. An empty sherry jug lay on its side on the kitchen counter, keeping company with the previous night's soiled dishes. Red opened the door of the old kerosene fridge. The shelves were spotless because Red had cleaned them the day before, and empty except for a quarter pound of Anchor butter, a jar of homemade plum jam and a jug of milk. Red took out the milk and butter and set them on the kitchen table alongside the smoked fish. He wandered into the bedroom. The room stank, bitter and vinegary. He opened the window.

"You okay?"

Bernie groaned and tried to sit up. He wheezed as he tried to draw breath. Phlegm caught in his throat, and he doubled over the side of the bed, head down, helpless in a fit of coughing. Red held him and beat firmly on the back of his ribs until Bernie finally coughed up a dense gob of mucus onto the floor. Bernie's face had turned crimson, and his forehead was bathed in sweat. He shivered. There were pinkish bubbles in among the mucus. Red pulled the blankets back over the old man and laid his head back on the pillow.

"Okay?"

"Yeah. Sorry, mate."

By the bed was a roll of toilet paper, which Bernie tore up and used to spit into during the night when the coughing took hold. Red took some to mop up Bernie's latest contribution. He went out to the back door, where he'd left the mop and pail the day before, half filled the bucket with water and Janola disinfectant and returned. He collected the sodden lumps of toilet paper, took them out and threw them into the kitchen waste bin, knowing he'd have to put a match to them later. Then he mopped down the bedroom floor. He couldn't help himself. Infections bred and spread in filth, and he couldn't allow it. The Aussies had known that and wasted no time getting organized, but the British soldiers had learned the hard way. Maybe it was the heat that got to them, or maybe they just hadn't understood. They'd died of dysentery, diphtheria, cholera, malaria, typhoid, gangrene and septicemia, but Red suspected they'd died as much from ignorance. They'd died where the Aussies had survived, died in greater numbers at any rate.

"How about a cuppa?" Bernie had propped himself up on his elbows and was shuffling his pillows around behind him as a back rest. "Man could die of thirst around here."

Red nodded. He never knew with Bernie how much was real and how much was put on for his benefit. He knew that Bernie had lived for years on a disability pension because of a back injury suffered on a building site in Auckland that prevented him from engaging in any further manual labor, the only type of work he was qualified to do. But when Red had first come to the Barrier, he'd seen the old reprobate haul his timber half-cabin boat up onto the beach single-handed, and chop through manuka scrub as well as any Maori work gang. He'd also put in a vegetable plot, carted buckets of topsoil over the hills from the floodplains, planted rose bushes and fruit trees. Rumor had it that there was nothing wrong with his back, either, when he'd gone down to Thames to visit one of his old girlfriends. But, in truth, Bernie looked as bad as Red had ever seen him and possibly even worse. The pink bubbles were not a good sign.

16

"Want some poached smoked snapper?"

"Nuh."

"You're going to eat it anyway." This was a conversation they had every day, and it always ended the same. Red took the mop and pail and put them outside the back door. He scrubbed his hands, as thoroughly as any doctor preparing for surgery, before putting the fish on to heat through and making tea.

"You gunna let your mate in?"

"Okay. Archie . . ."

The dog needed no second invitation and galloped into the bedroom. By the time Red had poured the tea and stirred in Bernie's two spoonfuls of sugar, the fish was ready. He flipped it onto a plate and took it in to the old man.

"Don't give any to Archie." Red went back out to the kitchen for the two cups of tea. Archie was licking his lips when Red returned.

Bernie ate without speaking but certainly not in silence. He'd lived alone so long virtually all of the social graces had slipped away. He chewed with his mouth open, smacked his lips and frequently stuck a finger in his maw to guide his food toward the few remaining teeth that were still operational. He also had the habit of scratching himself whenever parts needed scratching, in company or otherwise. Not surprisingly, he never thought Red's nakedness worthy of mention. Bernie wasn't too fussed about clothes himself. He'd eaten half of the fish before his cough started up again. Red took his plate.

"Drink some tea."

The old man grabbed the cup and gulped a couple of mouthfuls. He handed the cup back to Red and sank back onto his pillows. He'd begun to sweat again.

"Mate, I'm knackered."

"You'll be all right."

"Nuh . . . not this time. Had enough anyway."

"You've been saying that for years."

"Yeah, but I mean it."

For once Red was inclined to believe him. Bernie did look knackered. "You'll feel better after a wash."

"You can give me a wash, but I won't feel no better."

17

"We'll see. Give you a shave, too."

"No! Sit, mate. Got something I want to tell you."

Red sat back down on the edge of the bed.

"Wrote a letter last night. Yeah, knew that would surprise you. You still going round to Fitzroy?"

Red nodded.

"Yeah, well, I want you to witness the letter and take it with you. It's there on the tallboy."

Red reached over, picked it up and read it. It was Bernie's will. The writing was hesitant and spidery, and the lines curved away to the right. For all that, it was clearly legible.

"Dear Rosie, I'm dying," it said, "and I thought I'd leave my bach and things to you. The bach isn't much, just two bedrooms, living room, kitchen and bathroom, but it's been a good home to me. It's yours if you want it. Forget about it if you don't, 'cause it isn't worth much. Garden's got some nice roses, though. Thanks for being my friend. Hope you grew up good-looking. Yours sincerely, Bernard Arbuthnot." Rosie's name and Green Lane Hospital were written at the top of the sheet of paper. Red stared at the letter, unable to come to terms with the contents.

"Met her when I had TB and a bit of an alcohol problem. Her dad treated me for the booze. What a bugger he was, but she was nice. He wouldn't know a cop was up him till he blew his whistle. She came with him sometimes, a bit of a tomboy. She used to sneak me in a bottle of beer. They never could work out where I got it from. What's the matter with you?"

"You're leaving your place to a woman?"

"Yeah. She was a good girl, that one. Real cheeky."

"A woman?"

"Yeah!" Bernie cackled. "Thought that would get ya! Oh, she was a beauty, hair as black as any Maori's, and wicked black eyes. Always up to mischief. Stole fags for me, too. One day I suggested to her that an occasional nip of scotch wouldn't go astray, so she started filling up an old cordial bottle for me. Trouble was, she knew that if she filled the whole bottle with scotch her father would realize someone was nicking it, so she had this idea. She filled it with a drop from every

18

bottle they had. Mate, I'd never had a cocktail like it. Had everything in it! Bloody Pimm's and chartreuse, bloody crème de menthe, and that bloody eggnog stuff. Had whisky, rum, gin, vodka and I don't know what. The only way I could drink it was in my coffee. They took it off me before I was halfway through. My singing gave me away." He burst out laughing, stopped when he started to choke.

"You reckon this will find her?"

"Who knows? If it does, it does. Long time. I told her, though, told her every time she came in that I'd remember her in my will."

"Reckon she'll come?"

"If she does, she does."

"Wish you hadn't done that, Bernie."

"Aw, ya never know. Ya might thank me one day, a pretty woman and a good-looking bloke like you." He started laughing again. "Never know, do ya?"

"I'll get your things from the bathroom."

"Not yet." Bernie coughed and gestured to Red to sit down. "Something else. I want to be cremated."

"Why?"

"I want you to toss my ashes into the ocean, out past Aiguilles Island where I used to fish. Used to dive there a bit, too. My secret possie, my secret spot. On the rise where the shells are."

"What shells? Paper nautilus?"

"Nuh. Army shells." The old man was cut off by another bout of coughing. Red handed him the toilet paper just in time. "Where they dumped the old munitions after the war." Bernie's face had gone from wax to scarlet beneath a sickly sheen of sweat. All the talking was taking its toll. "Christ! I just might decide to kick the bucket to-day. Nobody's supposed to know about dumping the shells, but they used to take me out with them when they wanted to do a spot of fishing on the sly." He began to laugh, but his laughter quickly turned to a rattling cough that snapped his breath. Red rolled him over and stuffed some more toilet paper in his hand. Bernie coughed and hawked and sank back exhausted on his bed. The smell of his sweat rose bitter and pungent. That was what had stunk the room out. Still, Red had smelled worse, a lot worse.

"Tell me later."

"Might not be a later." Bernie slowly drew in deep breaths until his breathing was back to normal. Red noticed tears in Bernie's eyes, but that could just have been from the effort of talking. "I'll give you the markers. Line 'em up and you're right over the rise."

"I didn't know there was a rise."

"Neither did the army. It's like a small island that never quite made it to the surface. I got them to drop the shells on it because I thought I might go back later and salvage some for scrap. Now listen carefully."

Red listened until Bernie had finished.

"Now you can give me a wash, if it makes you happy. And Red, when you go to Fitzroy, do you think you could leave Archie here?"

A normal man might have welcomed the prospect of an attractive young woman coming to share his lonely neck of the woods, but all Red could see was disruption to his daily life. Women didn't belong. They didn't belong in the camps and they didn't belong at Wreck Bay. His day had begun like any other, yet suddenly Bernie had pulled the rug from under him. His whole world hung in the balance. Bernie's letter threatened change, the thing Red feared most. Change brought risk, the risk that he'd no longer be able to cope. The Japanese fishermen threatened change, challenged his existence by stealing his fish and by destroying the ocean bottom so no fish would ever return. He could fight them but he couldn't fight Bernie's letter. There was nothing he could do about it, nothing at all. He was powerless and bound by duty. He could not deny a dying man the right to leave his few possessions to whomever he chose. The wishes of a dying man were also sacrosanct.

Red couldn't get Bernie's letter out of his mind. He thought about it constantly as he stopped off at his shack to grab a pair of shorts and a sweater, and made his way down to the beach. He thought about it as he fitted his forty-four-gallon drum onto the jib arm at the end of the jetty and loaded it onto his boat. He worked hard to stop himself thinking, but still the thoughts persisted. What would a woman do at Wreck Bay?

The double-prowed lifeboat was immaculate, its clinker hull kept brilliantly white. According to hearsay, it had once swung from davits on the ocean liner *Oronsay,* though some claimed it was from the *Orsova.* Somehow it had ended up in the hands of the whaling company, and Red had taken it over when the station closed down. It had been fitted out with a Cummins diesel that was more powerful than need be and something of a glutton for fuel. But Red could squeeze economy out of it, never feeding it more revs than the hull or conditions could use. Diesel was expensive.

Each resident of Wreck Bay kept a drum at the jetty and another at their house. They drew diesel off into four-gallon tins for the long haul up the hill to fuel their generators, and used hoses and gravity to refuel their boats. Red filled a four-gallon jerry can from the Scotsman's drum and funneled the contents into his fuel tank. He repeated the process twice to be on the safe side, then filled his emergency can. That was sixteen gallons he owed, and a debt he'd pay in full. Red was good to the grain in all his dealings. He checked to see that his freshwater tank was full and his life jacket where it should be, and cast off. It was strange motoring out of the bay without Archie standing up on the bow, telling the gulls where they were headed. It didn't feel right. It was not how things were done.

Red was always cautious before putting to sea because there was little chance of hailing another vessel if he got into difficulties. Although Great Barrier Island was only fifty-five miles by sea from Auckland, New Zealand's largest city and main port, it might just as well have been five hundred and fifty. Only twenty-five miles long north to south and ten miles at its widest, there was little reason for anyone to visit or live there once the logging had finished, the mines had petered out and the whaling station had closed. There were few roads and few guest houses to encourage visitors. The locals either worked farms or caught fish and crayfish for a living. Nobody got rich.

Red was fortunate that the land around Wreck Bay on the northeast coast was too rugged and too poor for commercial cultivation and had proved too inaccessible for the loggers. The forbidding cliffs that lined the coast did not encourage visitors, either. As a result the entire northern end was left to the seagulls, terns and gannets. Only Wreck Bay provided shelter, and the three bachs were well sited to avoid the worst of the storms. It was possible to live there if you were sufficiently bloody-minded.

Red motored due north toward Aiguilles Island off the northern tip. With the tide almost full and the seas slight, he decided to take the narrow channel south of the island. Normally, even on a moderate swell, the surf pounded in on Aiguilles Island and Needles Point like heavy artillery, which was fair warning for all to give it a wide berth. He slipped through the channel and increased speed, swept around past Miners Head and across the mouth of Katherine Bay. Seagulls and gannets began diving on a school of kahawai. Even though a catch was guaranteed, Red was far too preoccupied to throw out a lure. Leaving Archie behind had unsettled him, but even worse was the prospect of a woman coming to live at Wreck Bay. It had taken him long enough to adjust to the Scotsman's arrival.

His keen eyes picked out the dorsals of two mako sharks, circling around the periphery of the feeding school. He knew what the predators were waiting for and it wasn't for kahawai. They were just a sideshow. The sharks were patrolling, waiting for the massive schools of migrating snapper, part of a never-changing cycle. Red had the utmost respect for never-changing cycles. He glanced up to the bow compartment where he'd stowed Bernie's letter, carefully protected inside his oilskins. Red also had the utmost respect for letters. He'd seen dying men survive because of them. He found it hard to reconcile the fact that letters, which could do so much good, could also do so much harm. He tried to imagine what would happen if the woman came. But why would any woman, perhaps even a beautiful one, want to come to Wreck Bay? Red didn't know much about women, but he knew enough about Wreck Bay to know that it held nothing for them. Even the hardy Barrier women couldn't imagine why anybody—male or female—would want to live there. If they couldn't handle it, how could a city woman? The letter worried Red all the way from Wreck Bay to the Port Fitzroy wharf.

• • •

The store at Port Fitzroy was aptly named the Last Gasp. It was opened originally as a holiday canteen to service the summer yachties. The owner, Col Chadwick, maintained he called it the Last Gasp, not just because of its remoteness, but because of the objections and obstructions of the other residents who were opposed to change of any kind as a matter of principle, particularly since they hadn't thought of opening a store themselves. Once opened, the store instantly became indispensable to the point that the locals would have fought to prevent it closing. Col gave up his crayfishing to become full-time shopkeeper. The Last Gasp sold everything Red needed—except alcohol, because the shop wasn't licensed. Col ordered in Bernie's jugs of sweet sherry anyway, on a nod-and-a-wink basis.

Red waited outside the store until Col had time to attend to him. The locals thought that was just another of Red's eccentricities. They still recalled the time he'd come ashore without remembering to put his pants on. But the fact was Red got claustrophobic in the little store with its crowded shelves. If anyone else came in while he was there he found it unbearable. The locals also still talked about the time he'd had one of his turns in the store. He waited outside until two visitors, guests of Fitzroy House, had left.

"G'day Red."

Red shook hands with Col Chadwick and handed over his two shopping lists. "And two jugs."

"How is the old bloke?"

"Not good. He wants this letter to go off to Auckland."

Col raised an eyebrow. Bernie had written a letter? "Okay. Anything else?"

"Need a hand with the diesel."

"No problem. I'll just fill your orders and walk down with you." Col trotted off with the orders. He glanced down at the envelope. Rosie Trethewey, Daughter of the Professor, Green Lane Hospital, Auckland. The handwriting was Red's. "Jeez," said Col to himself. "Helluva address."

Red fretted for Archie. It was hard to stand around without a dog. It wasn't right. They were a team, and splitting up only weakened them both. But the sick man needed company and that was all there was to it. Archie—his Aussie mate in Burma—would have stayed, he was certain of that. Archie had never let anyone down, never refused anyone. Red decided to walk on ahead to his boat and unload the empty drum. The simple mechanics of the job brought the woman back into his mind. How would she get by handling drums of fuel? How would she handle a boat and rounding Aiguilles in a blow? Old Bernie had done the wrong thing by them, no doubt about that. He hoped fervently Bernie had also done the wrong thing by the woman and she'd be smart enough to realize.

Red's boat was an oddity on the Barrier, where all boats, with the exception of the visiting yachts, were working boats of one kind or another and bore the scars of their trade. A wise man never had a picnic downwind from a beached fishing boat. Red used his thumbnail to scratch off seagull droppings. Wherever there were seagulls there was no place for idle hands. He hated idleness in the same way he abhorred dirt and untidiness. There was always something that needed attending to. He'd seen blokes stop working one day and be dead the next. The two went together.

"I'm amazed you even let your boat get wet." Red looked up to see Col on the wharf above him, a carton of supplies under each arm. "Reckon I could eat my bloody dinner off it. I'll have to go back for the sherry."

They manhandled a fresh drum of diesel over to the edge of the wharf, secured it, swung out the jib arm and lowered the drum gingerly onto the deck. Red jumped aboard and untied the ropes.

"You seen the Jap longliner yet?"

Red looked up sharply at Col. "Tuna? I freed some birds."

"Nah. Snapper. I've been getting reports of a Jap longliner sending its dories in to within one or two miles of the shore, night after bloody night, all the way up from Mount Maunganui. He's following the bloody snapper, ripping out millions of the buggers. He's been working the Coromandel Peninsula for the last week. They reckon he was off Whitianga a couple of nights ago. He's not like the others. This bloke doesn't use lights. Bastard's ripping out the fish. Just wondered if he'd made it up as far as you."

"Tell the fisheries?"

"Reckon. Rang the fisheries but they already knew about it. Apparently the navy's been informed."

"They doing anything?"

"Dunno. They sent a Sunderland flying boat down around Great Mercury Island. Didn't come up with nothing."

"I'll keep an eye out."

Col smiled. He knew Red would, too, and it would serve the Japs right. He was still chuckling as he made his way back up to the store to fetch the two jugs of sherry. Red might not be able to do anything about the snapper the Japs had already stolen, but he'd give them something to think about if they tried to steal fish from his patch. Col tried to put himself in the place of the Japanese fishermen in their dories when a raging, naked Red descended upon them. What on earth would they think?

Two

It was pitch dark when Shimojo Seiichi, the skipper of the *Aiko Maru, gave the order to lower the dories. He hadn't come six thousand miles to pull up* six miles short of his objective. The nor'easter had freshened, and the helmsman battled to keep head-on to the sea. The crew was grateful for the rehearsals their captain made them do blindfolded every month, for they worked without lights. The sliver of moon had been and gone, and the stars might as well have been hidden behind clouds for all the light they gave. The four dories edged slowly away from the unlit *Aiko Maru* in a staggered line astern. The skipper watched until they were swallowed up in the darkness. He couldn't help feeling apprehensive about fishing so close to New Zealand's major naval base, and home of the Sunderland flying boats. If the navy got wind of their presence and dispatched a Sunderland, it would be upon them within twenty minutes. Then there'd be nowhere to run and nowhere to hide. But the potential rewards justified the risk. They were right on the navy's doorstep and about to steal the rice from their mouths. That would be something to boast about later, in the bars around the docks at Kitakyushu.

The wind whipped the tops off waves and showered the crouching dory crews with spray, stinging eyes and leaving a bitter salt taste on lips and tongues. But it was the lot of all fishermen to taste the sea. Almost to a man, the crews came from fishing families. Their fathers had tasted the sea, and their fathers before them, though none had

26

ever ventured far from their little fishing villages and rarely out of sight of land. Now they were living their fathers' dreams six thousand miles from home, catching more fish in one voyage than their forebears had caught in their entire lifetimes.

Their course took them west of Aiguilles Island where they could fish in the relatively calm waters of the lee. They didn't use spotlights this near to shore, in case they alerted unfriendly eyes to their presence. Instead they slowed so that any change in wind or sea would be more apparent. Once they felt the softening of the sea and wind, they slowed even further, and moved in closer as quietly as the dories' twin outboards would permit. The greater darkness of Great Barrier Island loomed up in front of them. Once they were within half a mile of shore, and two to three miles west of Aiguilles Island, they took up position and began fishing in their prearranged staggered pattern. By the light of hooded lamps, they released the end buoys. As the buoys drifted away into the darkness behind them, they counted off the knots in the line until they'd released one hundred yards. Then, creeping slowly forward so as not to foul the props, they attached the weights that would hold the fishing lines to the sea bottom. The crew of each dory began to bait and lower the one-and-a-half-mile lines of double-barbed hooks, each set eighteen inches from the next. They worked with practiced hands and enthusiasm. Half a mile from Aiguilles Island they lowered the last of the baited hooks, the lead weight and head buoy. One after another the dories turned westward to return to their start position to lay the second of their four lines two hundred meters out to seaward from their first. Away to the east, the new day was yet to dawn.

At first light they began to retrieve their lines. They caught the end buoys with their boat hooks, turned and wound the lines twice around the winch drums. The lines tightened as the winch took up the strain. The men looked at each other, smiling, shouted to the other crews. The lines sang from weights far greater than those they'd lowered a few hours earlier. *"Tairyo!"* they shouted. Good catch!

They stared into the depths of the water, straining to catch the first glimpse of color. It was there, flashing pink and silver and sometimes gold in the pale light. The lead weights came up over the side and were expertly detached. The first snapper came aboard to be un-hooked and thrown into fish boxes before they were aware they were even out of the water. Fewer than half of the hooks came up empty and less than ten percent with by-catch. Fish after fish piled on top of each other, spilling over the fish boxes.

"*Tairyo! Tairyo!*" the crews shouted, as they hauled in the snapper that justified the risk they'd taken, that ensured their end-of-trip bonuses, that brought profit and esteem to the company, that brought glory to them all. The crews worked as fast as they could and needed no urging. The fish flashing red in the water flashed gold in their pockets. Still the fish came up, some over twenty pounds, most over six. *Tairyo! Tairyo!* Lengths of line where mako sharks had stripped both fish and hooks provided the crews' only rest. The superstitious fishermen saw this loss as a good sign. The spirits of the water would approve of them sharing their catch.

The sun broke free of the ocean as they neared the heads of their second longlines. Eager hands tossed more ice over their haul and made room for the fish from their third lines. So many fish! The gods had smiled upon them. Some of the younger fishermen laughed at the superstitions and devotions to the old gods. But the gods had not let them down and they only had to look at the overflowing fish boxes to know who had the last laugh.

As the crew of the lead dory began to retrieve the head buoy of their third line and work their way back to the end buoy, the sun edged above Aiguilles Island, bathing them in its brightness and im-pressing urgency upon them. Their line sang with the weight, crack-ling around the winch drum. They stared intently into the depths, looking for the first flash of color, the blaze of red that would confirm that this catch was as good as the last. Perhaps it was the grinding of the winches or their concentration on the catch they were steadily hauling up from the sea bottom, but they were slow to hear the speed-ing motor. When the sound registered, they turned as one toward the source. But the morning sun blinded them. They covered their eyes with their hands to peep through the slits between their fingers. Then they saw it, their nightmare, and cries burst from their lips. There was a bow wave dead abeam, coming out of the sun on course to ram them and cut them in half. But that was not what chilled their blood. It was their fathers' and grandfathers' fears and superstitions come alive before their eyes. It was the drawings shown by other fishermen whose terror they now shared. The local *kami* had turned on them for their theft, and a Red Devil riding a boat of pure white foam was upon them, hair ablaze, breathing fire from its nose, its whole body fringed by the flames of damnation, seeking vengeance.

The helmsman screamed in warning. His crew, who had many times fled both plane and patrol boat, did not hesitate. No sooner had a knife flashed when the dory's twin props bit into the ocean, throwing the bow high, scattering fish and ice across the deck, and almost hurling one man overboard. The other dories saw the lead dory cut and run and did likewise. They rose instantly onto the plane despite their heavy loads and raced across the water. The helmsman risked a glance astern and saw that the Red Devil had fallen behind. Nevertheless he held the throttle wide open, determined not to slacken off until they'd reached the sanctuary of the mother ship. Then he would have to face up to the loss of fish and lines. Then he would have to justify his actions to his captain.

The skipper of the *Aiko Maru* saw his dory crews cut and run and sounded the alarm. The longliner was waiting just beyond the six-mile limit. He scanned the radar but could pick up nothing that would indicate a patrol boat or Sunderland. None of the lookouts had spotted anything, nor had the representatives ashore radioed in to say that the patrol boat at Devonport had slipped out during the night. Yet the skipper knew his crews would not run without good reason.

The number four and number three boat had cleared the six-mile limit when he heard a lookout call down on the intercom. He raced to the window and looked astern. He strained his eyes to see it, then spotted it, low and hugging the coast, using the land mass of Great Barrier to hide from his radar. Where were the number one and two boats? Half a mile astern and closing rapidly. They were safe. Just. Shimojo Seiichi breathed a sigh of relief that the last working day of their tour of duty would not end in disgrace, but he was curious. How had his dory crews known about the Sunderland?

Three

*R*ed *throttled back as the more powerful dories left him in their wake,* *hands shaking from rage and helplessness.* "Bastards!" he screamed. "Bloody bastards!" His boat was no match for the Japs' outboard motor–powered dories and he knew it. Even at half throttle their motors could leave him floundering in their wake. His fists clenched in frustration and his shoulders shook. He tried to pull back from his anger because he feared the consequences. But he was too late. Already his chest was tightening, his throat contracting. His breath came in sobs and he could feel the panic coming on again. He began to battle for breath, to fight the panic rising inside him. Cold sweat prickled his body, his hands turned clammy and the shaking intensified. Blood pounded in his temples and roared in his ears.

"Bastards . . ." he cried desperately, but there was nothing he could do. It had happened often enough before and he knew there was nothing he could do. His vision blurred and he was back on the railway with his mate Archie, and the Big Bash Artist and imminent death. He could feel the heat and heavy, water-laden air. Taste his fear and helplessness, too weak to cry out, too weak to stand. His hand went up to Archie. For help? For comfort? Reaching, reaching, for his mate and protector before the bullet's hot passage ended his life. Archie could not save him this time, nothing could. He saw the little man with the long rifle and prayed that he would pull the trigger and end his suffering. Pull! Pull now! But it always ended the same way, and there was nothing he could do to change it.

He knew the moment would pass and begged God to let it pass quickly. But it would never pass completely. The shadow would remain, never entirely out of his mind, never far away, always poised to haunt and claim him whenever it chose. His burden, his guilt, his nemesis. A thunderous roar filled his ears, and the air around him pulsed and beat down on him in waves. He squeezed his eyes tightly closed. Archie was barking. Barking. Barking. Cautiously he opened his eyes, momentarily disoriented. He cowered down as the monster passed directly overhead. It took him a few moments to comprehend, to clear his mind and realize the enormity of the thing he had done.

"Nooooo . . . !"

He watched the lumbering seaplane swoop low overhead, knowing how the aircrew would be cursing him. He smashed his fist into the helm console. The Japanese had won again and it was all his fault. He watched the big Sunderland turn in a slow arc and pass once more over the Japanese longliner. It banked toward him no more than two or three hundred feet above the water so that he could clearly see the cameras mounted in the forward dome where the nose guns would normally be. It was also close enough for him to see the gloved fist shaking at him from the copilot's window.

He collapsed backward onto his seat in despair. They'd set a trap for the Japs, and he'd sprung it prematurely. Dear God! His hands still shook from the attack he'd had, and he still felt light-headed. Dear God! Would there ever come a time when he was not at war with Japan? He spotted a buoy floating off to starboard, seized upon it as his salvation. There was work to be done and he needed it. Work was his sanctuary. So long as he could work he could keep control. There'd be time for recriminations later.

Red began the task of hauling in the miles of abandoned longlines. Without a winch to help him, the work was slow and backbreaking. He knew the lines would be heavy with snapper because he'd planned to fish there himself. He threw the dead and neardrowned fish into his fish boxes and set free all those he found that were still in reasonable condition. He could afford to release the live fish because he knew the proportion of dead ones would increase the farther he worked out from shore. The snappers' air sacs would rupture in the haul up from the deeper water. The dead fish from the first line half filled his boat despite the fact that he'd thrown forty to fifty percent back. The efficiency of the Japanese fed his bitterness.

It took him all morning to retrieve the remaining lines, setting free the few survivors and throwing the remainder overboard for the sharks and stingrays, the octopi, crabs and the crayfish. The second line had filled his boat, but Red wanted the remaining lines out of the water where they could do no more harm. The slaughter and waste appalled him.

He regretted the fact that he hadn't brought ice with him, because now he had no option but to motor straight around to the fish processing plant at Okupu. He couldn't allow the fish he'd kept to add to the waste, but he was also concerned about Bernie. It would be evening by the time he got back, and the old man would have been on his own all day. Red wondered briefly if the Scotsman had thought to take Bernie something, then dismissed the thought. There was a better chance of the sun rising in the west and the Japanese fishermen becoming conservationists. He fired up his diesel and set off to Okupu, fish piled high in his boxes, keeping cool under soaking-wet sugar sacks. The longlines were piled high in the bow. Nothing was wasted. He wished he'd left Archie behind again to keep Bernie company.

"That you off Aiguilles this morning?"

Red looked up into the smiling face of Jack Lampton and discovered the bad news had preceded him.

"Whole island's talking about you."

Red threw him his bow line. The low tide meant that Red would have to manhandle the fish boxes high over his head to lay them on the jetty. Given the weight of them and the fact that his back hadn't yet forgiven him for his earlier exertions, he knew it would be no easy task.

"Navy wants a word with you, too."

"Give us a hand with these boxes."

"Hang on. I'll get you a cray tank. Off-load them into the tank and we'll haul them up with the winch." The fish factory wasn't really set up for fish but for crayfish—the delicious red crays they sent to the mainland whole, and the giant packhorse crays, which they tailed first. But Jack had the means to help the snapper fishermen and make a few pounds for himself in the process, so he did. He was a young man in his early thirties, married with two small kids, and determined to make a go of the factory, even though everyone said it would fold soon enough, which is what usually happened to business ventures on the Barrier. He looked at the load of fish as Red transferred them into the steel cray tank. "You've been busy."

"Japs have been busier. There were four dories, Jack, four lines apiece, and they were using those double-barbed hooks. They hardly ever missed. Snapper won't stand a chance if they keep this up."

"Bastards."

"I freed the live ones and took all the dead fish I could, but I had to throw ten times as many away. Kingfish, kahawai, gurnard, trumpeter, trevally and blue cod as well as snapper. Would've given you a yell, but by the time you got there the sea lice and crabs would've ruined them. It's just not right!"

"Bloody waste," said Jack. "But you did what you could, that's the main thing." He could hear the tension rising in Red's voice and knew it was time to hose him down. "You did good, Red, letting the live ones go. I'll get you another tank and chuck this lot in the freezer till I get some ice."

The two men worked diligently for half an hour, until the boat was unloaded. Then Jack reminded Red of his obligation.

"Are you going to call the navy?"

"Suppose."

"Just get Kate on the exchange. She knows the number and name of the bloke you have to talk to."

Red walked into the half-partitioned corner of the corrugated iron factory shed that constituted the office. He lifted off the handset and cranked the handle. He waited anxiously. Only four lines connected Great Barrier Island with the mainland, and there was usually a queue. For once Kate answered almost straight away.

"Yes, Jack."

"It's Red."

"Hello, Red, have you got any pants on?"

"No."

"Oooohhhh . . ."

"I have to call the navy, Kate."

"All right . . . keep your hair on." He heard Kate giggling. "Stay there, Red. I'll call you back."

Red hung up and stood by the phone. The mess on Jack's desk distracted him, and he couldn't help himself. He gathered the scraps of paper into a pile and weighted them down by putting Jack's pad over them. The dregs in Jack's coffee cup had evaporated, leaving a caked crust. He reached over to the washbasin in the corner, rinsed the cup, filled it and left it to stand in the bottom of the basin. He straightened the calendar, and crossed off the last two days of February, which Jack had omitted to do. The phone rang.

"Red here." Red could feel a tingling grow in the pit of his stomach and his neck muscles tighten.

"Lieutenant Commander Michael Finn."

Lieutenant commander. Red could feel his throat begin to tighten. "You want to speak to me, sir?"

"No, I bloody well want to kick your arse! What the hell did you think you were doing? Do you know how many strings we had to pull to set up that ambush? Do you know what it costs to get a bloody Sunderland airborne?"

"Please don't shout." Red lined up Jack's ruler parallel to his pad.

"Jesus H. Christ!"

The fist in Red's stomach tightened. His hand trembled. There were too many memories beating on the door inside his brain. Screaming officers, screaming guards, and a body that couldn't obey. His voice shrank to a whisper. "Don't shout. You don't have to shout." Perhaps some of his desperation reached down the line to the naval officer, because his attitude changed.

"Sorry. My turn to apologize. I guess we're on the same side, Red, but we've got to find some means of keeping out of each other's way."

Red waited for the officer to continue. He laid Jack's ballpoint pen and his pencil neatly alongside the ruler.

"What I mean is, we've got to work together, pool information. You with me?"

"Yes, sir."

"Any chance you could come over to Devonport?"

"No." Red gathered up Jack's wayward paper clips and returned them to their home in a little plastic bowl.

"What if I sent a boat for you?"

"No. I have a boat."

"Don't like cities?"

"No." Red closed his eyes. "I don't like cities."

To say Red didn't like cities was colossal understatement. He couldn't stand the cars, the noise, the crowds, the milling and disorderliness. He'd had to leave Auckland when he'd become too frightened to go outside his own front door.

"Do you want me to come to you?" The officer worked hard to keep the exasperation out of his voice and only partially succeeded.

"You coming alone?"

"Alone, but with a crew. If you want, they can stay aboard the patrol boat while I come ashore."

"Okay." Red was beginning to feel more confident. "I took their lines."

"I guess that's something. I'm sorry for shouting. Don't feel too bad about this morning. You weren't to know. But look, if we can get something worked out together, we could really nail the bastards next time. You're in the ideal position to help us. Have you got a number I can ring you on?"

"No. Call Col at Port Fitzroy and leave a message. He'll know what to do. Good-bye, Lieutenant Commander."

Red hung up too quickly, before the officer had a chance to respond. He stood silently in the gloom of the shed while he gradually calmed down. He'd fulfilled his obligation. His duty was done. If the lieutenant commander needed to find him he knew where to look. More than anything Red just wanted the whole thing to blow over. Like the hermit he was, he just wanted to crawl back into his shell.

Red motored home as fast as he could and copped a soaking in the process. He grabbed a spray jacket from the storage locker and huddled in close to the console and splash guard. Archie had crawled up under the bow deck, safe from the flying spray and wind. The wind was the problem, working on his wet skin and chilling him to the bone. He knew he had no need to run so fast, knew he was also wasting diesel, but he had things on his mind. Unwelcome things. When he wasn't worrying about Bernie, either the woman or the lieutenant commander would sneak into his thoughts, and he couldn't find sufficient distraction. There was no place for either of them at Wreck Bay. He turned the corner around Needles Point and felt the wind and sea swing behind him. The temperature jumped ten degrees immediately, and his entourage of seagulls, blown from their station astern, wheeled indignantly as they tried to regain formation. They knew about the fish. Red had kept one box of snapper, which Jack had generously iced for him, and left nearly fifteen hundred pounds of fish behind to be sent to the co-op. Enough to pay his bills for months.

The calmer water gave Red the chance to work. He began gutting and filleting his fish, splitting the big fish up the back and saving them for smoking. The gulls feasted raucously on the guts but he kept the heads and frames to make stock and fish soup. Nothing was wasted, ever. He killed the motor as he reached Wreck Bay, and let the boat's momentum carry him up to his mooring. He knew that he should make Bernie his first priority, but there was still work to be done and a logical order for doing it. His boat needed cleaning and there was no way he could leave it while one speck of fish blood or guts remained to harden in the sun and stain the paint. He scrubbed the decks and gunwales till they were spotless, dried them with cloths, then fastened the storm cover into place. The sun had dropped behind the ridge by the time he began the steep climb up through the bush to Bernie's. When he reached the pohutukawas he automatically took the left fork, which would take him by the Scotsman's cabin. Angus was waiting for him, a grim, brooding presence framed in the doorway.

"I saw you come in. What is it you want?"

Red glanced up at the veranda, the demarcation line beyond which he'd never set foot, not in the Scotsman's time anyway. "I've brought you some fish."

"Aye, I thought as much. It's why I never went fishing myself."

Angus took the fish and watched as his faithless Bonnie smooched up to Red. "Is there something I can give you in return, some gherkins, perhaps?"

"No. I have to get on up the hill to see Bernie."

"How is he, the old man?"

"Why didn't you go up and see?"

"Don't you lecture me! He's entitled to his privacy as I am to mine."

"He needs help," Red shouted back in a flash of anger. "And he's entitled to that!" He wasted his breath. Angus had gone indoors and slammed the screen door shut behind him. Red turned and made his way back down to the pohutukawas. The muscles in his back had stiffened in the cold of the return journey and ached under the load of fish and the steepness of the climb. He felt bad about leaving the old bloke on his own and worse for not leaving Archie. But he couldn't go without Archie's company two days in a row. Red put the fish box down where the track forked to Bernie's and left Archie to mind it. He took a couple of medium-sized snapper fillets with him up the trail to the shack. He called out as he approached, but there was no answer. He pushed open the screen door.

"Bernie?"

Red felt his way in the darkness, found the matches on the table and lit the hurricane lamp. One of the jugs of sherry was missing off the table, so the old man had obviously got up at some time. Red wandered into the bedroom and found Bernie lying on his bed, dead to the world, the half-empty jug alongside amid gobs of toilet paper. Red knew he'd get no sense out of the old man that night, and that there was no point in cooking him a meal. He reached down to pull a sheet and blanket over him so that he wouldn't get a chill in the night. His hand brushed Bernie's cheek. It felt cold, unnaturally cold. He held the lamp closer to the old man's face. His eyes were half open but they'd long given up seeing. Bernie had died alone, and there was nothing Red could do about it.

Red took the lamp back out into the main room and sat down at the table. He'd failed a dying man. He put his head in his hands and let his tiredness and dismay wash over him. Archie had to see Bernie, too, so that he'd understand. Red went to the door and whistled. The dog sensed what was afoot the second he stepped into the shack. Instead of trotting in to see Bernie, he stole in, nose quivering. He sniffed along the length of Bernie's arm to confirm his suspicions and retreated to the door, pausing to look reproachfully at Red.

Red forced himself to his feet. He hadn't wanted the responsibility of caring for Bernie but the responsibility had found him anyway. He opened Bernie's cupboards and grabbed as many preserving jars as he could find, relics from the time Bernie bottled the fruit from his plum, peach and nectarine trees. He opened the freezer compartment in the top of Bernie's fridge. It was filled with trays of ice kept for icing his catch. Bernie had never entirely discounted the possibility of taking his boat to the rise one final time. Red took the trays out and shook the cubes onto the bench. He filled as many jars as he could with ice and sealed them. He carried the jars into the bedroom and distributed them evenly around Bernie's body. He pulled the blankets up over him to trap in the cold air, found two more in the wardrobe and tossed them over the bed as well. He tidied up the floor around the bed, put the top on the half-empty jug and put it away in a kitchen cupboard. He pulled the curtains closed. Bernie had liked to sleep late and had curtains to block out the morning sun. The curtains would help keep the shack cool. Red began to feel better. He'd done his duty. The bach was tidy and Bernie was taken care of. He half-filled a tin with chicken pellets and went out to round up the chooks. There was nothing else he needed to do. Once the chooks were safely in the henhouse he could go home and slip back into his routine. At least until morning. He picked up the two pieces of snapper and turned down the hurricane lamp.

Another day was drawing to a close, a day in which he'd had to confront Japanese poachers and the navy, a day in which Bernie had died and cleared the way for the woman to claim her inheritance. His world was changing, but at least he still survived.

Four

~~~~~

Rosie Trethewey was not happy. When she'd left for work that morning, summer had been in full cry. The sun had beaten down from a cloudless blue sky, and for once, though only briefly, she was glad the judge had taken away her driving license. But the walk up Shelley Beach Road to the bus stop had soon tested her antiperspirant and found it wanting. Her cotton dress had darkened beneath her arms and clung to her back. Then she'd cursed the judge and the smug policemen who'd picked on her and booked her for speeding. Even the judge had expressed surprise that her Volkswagen could go as fast as the police had claimed it had. But that was Rosie. She only had two speeds, flat out and stop.

The afternoon had brought clouds, low and threatening, and sent temperatures plummeting. She'd shivered in windowless offices while the air-conditioning thermostats struggled to figure out what was happening and failed. She'd spent the day talking to groups of women, trying to divine their innermost thoughts and attitudes toward toilet cleaners and bathroom disinfectants. Up until then Rosie had thought that skid marks were something immature men in fast cars left on roads. She'd learned differently and wished she hadn't. But the job of a market researcher was to research markets, and there was a market for toilet cleaners, just as there was for most other things. She had no control over what products she was given to investigate. Nevertheless, it had been an unedifying day and was no way to spend a life.

"You'll have to find something else to do," Norma insisted whenever she moaned about it. Norma was her friend and meant well but, Christ on a motorbike, what was there left for her to do?

The rain had held off until the bus deposited her at the top of Shelley Beach Road, then the heavens had opened. Typical. The only certain thing about the weather in Auckland was that it would change. Rosie began to run but quickly realized the futility of it. She was going to get soaked no matter what she did. She walked head-on into the wind and driving rain as it howled in off the harbor. The thin cotton stuck fast to her body like a second layer of skin, defining her figure in intimate detail. Rosie didn't care a damn. There was no one dumb enough to be out in the rain to see her, and even if there had been, she was in no mood to care. She was more concerned with the cold and her hates. Walking briskly helped fend off the chill from the wet and wind, but there was nothing she could do about her hates. She hated the judge who wouldn't let her drive her car, and she hated the police. It was their fault she was cold and wet. She hated buses. She hated her job. She hated her flat. She hated her father, her ex-husband, stupid women who had nothing better to do than waffle on endlessly about toilet cleaners and skid marks as if they were making some worthwhile contribution to the sum total of human knowledge, and she hated dresses that rode up and bunched at the crotch.

"You waste too much energy on negative thoughts," Norma kept telling her, but Norma was younger, better looking and had a boyfriend who was loaded. It was easy for Norma to give advice. Nature had given her everything except depth.

Her flatmate hadn't closed their letterbox properly the day before, and all the mail was saturated. She cursed the office wally who told her to keep the windows of her VW open a half inch to let air circulate. Now rain circulated. Too bad. She stepped off the driveway onto the path that wound through the overgrown garden to the once-grand two-story home that had been converted to flats. Leaves tipped water over her as she brushed past unpruned bushes. The downspouts were blocked, causing the gutters to overflow and a sheet of water to cascade off the roof right in front of the steps leading to the front door. She groaned aloud. There was the whole front of the house, but of course the gutters had chosen to overflow by the front door. She'd complained to the landlord.

"Plumber's coming to fix it next week," she'd been told, but next week never arrived and neither did the plumber. She hated the landlord, cheap old bastard, and she hated the real estate agent who'd signed her up to a two-year lease. She opened the door to her flat and paused, wondering how to circumnavigate her beloved kelim rugs that lay scattered across the dark-stained timber floors. Then she thought of her flatmate, who'd simply barge in regardless, and gave up. She'd long given up protecting her things against flatmates and considered herself lucky if nothing was stolen when they moved out.

She closed the door behind her, switched on the light because the flat was gloomy even on a bright day, and began to strip off her wet clothes. She thought of leaving them in puddles on the floor as her flatmate would, but thought better of it. It was smarter to leave one big puddle to wipe up than half a dozen smaller ones. She slipped out of her clothes. Wet, cold and naked, she didn't feel a bit beautiful, but she had the sort of figure that turned men on, particularly the one watching from the window of the house next door. She groaned at the indignity, gathered up her bundle of wet clothes and strode into the bathroom. She didn't even bother giving her voyeuristic neighbor the finger as she normally did. It bothered her that the man never seemed to blink.

One good thing about the flat was that they never ran out of hot water, not even when her flatmate took his usual half-hour shower. She always flatted with men and still harbored the hope that one day she'd find one who was clever with his hands. In a practical way. But she was always the one who had to change washers on leaky taps, hang curtains and fix doorknobs. Yet the men were better than the women she'd shared flats with in her younger days, who spent forever putting on makeup and no time at all doing housework. She'd begun to relax and let the steaming bathwater do its soothing work when she noticed her towel missing. How many times had she warned her flatmate not to use her towel? But he had. Again. And once again he'd left her towel in his bedroom. She gritted her teeth and clenched her fists. Perhaps the bastard was working in partnership with the voyeur next door, because she'd have to run the gauntlet once more. Had she left the light on? Of course she had. She hated her flatmate. He had to go. Enough was enough. She lay back in the bath and tried to relax. Perhaps the bloke next door had finally gone blind through self-abuse. That was a thought that comforted her and brought a glimmer of a smile, but only briefly. There was no escaping the reality. She was thirty-four years old, trapped in a grubby bathroom in a grubby flat by a grubby little man next door. What, she wondered, was she doing with her life? The sound of a key turning in the lock on the front door dragged her away from her reveries. Her flatmate had come home.

"Hi!"

She heard him call out and drop his valise. She'd grown tired of telling him to put the bloody thing away, so now it lived just inside the front door. She heard a clump, a step, another clump. He was taking off his shoes. He'd be halfway across the kelims, probably dumping his shoes on her indigo blue Kazak, which he thought didn't show the dirt.

"Where are you?"

"In the bath, you bastard, waiting for you to come home and replace the towel you nicked this morning."

"Sorry. Just get out of these things." She heard his belt buckle scrape on the polished floor. Trousers down. His bedroom-door handle rattled. Coat hung. "Shit!" Slipped taking off socks. It was all so familiar and predictable they might as well have been married instead of just flatmates. Rosie never slept with flatmates, because that created too many complications; she preferred to think of them as no more than rent-sharers. She heard him open her bedroom door, open a cupboard and close it.

"Here he comes," she said softly, slipping as deeply into the bath as she could, wishing she'd been more liberal with water and soap. But it was the old story. Too little, too late, too bad.

"Here's your towel. Got a dry one."

"How very clever of you." He hadn't knocked. He hadn't discreetly opened the door a whisker and thrown the towel through the gap. No, he'd just marched straight in and stood ogling her.

42

"Anything else?"

"John, I am a woman. You are a man. I am naked and you are staring."

"Sorry." He made no move to go.

"John, leave me the towel. Put it on the rail. And then please go next door and punch Merv the Perv's lights out. And when you've done that, ask him to do the same to you for the same reason."

"Jesus, Rosie. Here's your bloody towel. Don't bother to say thanks." He left and closed the door behind him. Rosie didn't move. She knew better. The door pushed open again. "Want a cup of tea?" John looked vaguely disappointed.

"Yes, please. Now do be a good boy and piss off."

"Did you get any milk?"

"Why would I get milk? There was plenty when I left this morning."

"I used it on my cornflakes."

"John, when you're drinking your black tea, get the paper and look through the flats-to-let section."

"What do you mean?"

"Exactly what it sounds like. Piss off. Out of my bathroom. Out of my flat. Out of my life. Take as long as you like, but if you're not gone in one hour you'll find all your stuff out on the street."

"You can't do that. It's raining. Where will I go?"

"John, you're still staring. Don't stare at me. One, I can throw you and all the rubbish you flatteringly call your things out onto the street. You know I can. We know each other well, and you know I've done that before. Two, I don't care if it's raining. Three, I don't care a damn where you go. Just go." Fixing him with the look he'd come to fear, she sat up. He saw her breasts clearly, which is what he'd wanted to see all along, but more than that he saw she meant business. He went.

Rosie sat at the kitchen table with her head in her hands. John had gone by taxi, but not without argument, not without some of her things as yet undiscovered, and not without asking if he could borrow her car. She was alone again, and wondering if she should cry. The flat was cold and damp and there was no milk. Tomorrow she'd have to begin writing up the report based on the findings of the group discussions she'd conducted. What, she wondered, was the benchmark for removing skid marks, and did anyone really care? There was nothing to eat except limp vegetables, a can of baked beans that John had left behind because he'd put it in the wrong cupboard and a butterscotch-flavored Gregg's instant pudding, which needed milk. Crying seemed the preferred option when she heard knuckles do a drumroll on her door.

"Come in, Norma, it's not locked."

"Hi," said Norma brightly. "Guess what? You and me are going out to dinner. Loverboy's had to fly down to Wellington on business. I stopped off at the Bistro and reserved a table."

"Don't tell me," said Rosie. "John rang you to see if he could sleep the night at your place."

"How'd you know?" Norma seemed genuinely puzzled.

"Doesn't matter. It's good to see you, I need a friend and I'd love to go out to dinner with you because there's nothing to eat here."

Norma hung her raincoat on the back of the door and flopped down on a chair opposite Rosie. "What happened?"

"Nothing, everything, the usual, what the hell does it matter? In a funny way I'll miss him. Sometimes I think I'm the most useless creature on earth, then I come home and John's here and suddenly I feel reassured."

"Negative thoughts," said Norma.

"I've earned them," said Rosie.

"There's never any excuse for negative thoughts. You're brainy, your whole illustrious family is brainy, and they're all wonderfully successful."

"Except me."

"Except you. You don't even try." Norma stuck a Du Maurier in her mouth and lit it. She had the knack of talking while her cigarette sat glued to her bottom lip.

"What do you mean?" Rosie wasn't protesting but complaining. She was due a good moan, and moans were only good if there was someone to hear them. "I tried. I still try. Trouble is all I ever wanted to be was a beatnik, make pottery and love everybody and throw

44

pink rose petals in the air. Instead I became a doctor and went off to save the world. They sent me to India, which was full of sick people, but didn't give me any medicines to save them. Instead of curing them, I joined them and had to be evacuated home. It's all been downhill since then."

"Stop feeling sorry for yourself. I've got a bottle of wine in the car. We could drink it now and get another to drink over dinner. What's this?" She spotted the sodden pile of letters and idly peeled them apart. Bills, more bills and a large envelope with Green Lane Hospital printed across the bottom. Norma raised her eyes questioningly. When she shook the envelope something slid around inside it.

"Probably notification from the VD clinic. That would just about be my luck."

"Better open it and see," said Norma.

"You get the wine, I'll open the envelope. Probably need a drink by the time you get back."

Norma grabbed the umbrella Rosie hadn't bothered to take to work with her and dashed out. Rosie picked up the envelope from the hospital and weighed it in her hands speculatively. A fund-raising brochure? A letter from her father? No, he'd know better than to write to her. She could imagine what it would say. "Please find enclosed my written disapproval of the way you are conducting your life." But perhaps for once the old boy might have got it right. She tore the envelope open and picked up the letter that fell out. She chuckled at the address. "Care of the Professor." Well the professor had done the right thing and forwarded it on, or at least his receptionist had. She turned it over and looked at the return address, printed neatly on the back though somewhat blurred by rain. "Red O'Hara, Wreck Bay, Care of Col Chadwick, Port Fitzroy, Great Barrier Island." Her first thought was that she'd won a holiday. She wondered if it was raining on the Barrier.

She pulled a knife out of the cutlery drawer and slipped it beneath the flap. Gingerly she opened the envelope, careful not to damage the contents. She spread the letter and will out on the table and read them.

"Who the hell is Bernie Arbuthnot?" she asked out loud. The

name rang a bell, albeit distant. She thought back to when she was a child, accompanying her father on his weekend rounds. She vaguely recalled an old tubercular alcoholic who gave her sweets in exchange for stolen bottles of her father's beer, and told her rude jokes. She couldn't remember his name but guessed it was him. "Bernie, you old bastard," she said.

"Who's a bastard?" said Norma as she shook out the umbrella at the door. "You haven't got a dose, have you?"

"Norma, Green Lane Hospital doesn't have a VD clinic. It has my father instead. Tell me, what do you know about Great Barrier Island?"

"Not much. You can see it away on the horizon on a clear day. Yachties go there, and that amphibian plane flies there. Why?"

Rosie told her.

"God Almighty! You wouldn't even consider moving there, would you? I mean you'd be mad. No one lives there, well no one with any sense. There's nothing there."

"I don't know," said Rosie. She didn't know much about Great Barrier Island, either, but the idea of owning a house and doing nothing but make pottery and grow roses suddenly appealed. Outside, the wind gusted, causing the rain to beat a violent tattoo on the window. She picked up the letter and reread it. Maybe it was a sign, or divine intervention, or simply a stroke of luck out of the blue. A new life beckoned, a better life, a simpler life where she wouldn't hate everyone and everything around her. She could picture herself at her wheel, shaping the clay, a smile on her face and contentment oozing from every pore. She looked around her flat and thought of a future documenting skid-mark removers and house-training flat-mates. Norma shoved a glass of claret into her hand.

"Rosie, I'm telling you, don't even think of it. You're not the type."

"It couldn't be any worse," Rosie said softly, optimistically. She took a generous swallow of wine. Somewhere inside her the mischievous young girl who'd wanted to be a beatnik awoke from her slumber.

•   •   •

There was a time when Rosie would have simply walked out of her flat and her job and hopped on the Grumman Widgeon amphibian that flew people out to Great Barrier Island. But age and experience had curbed her impetuosity. The last thing she needed was another disappointment. So the following morning she bought a map of the Barrier and studied it. The first thing she noticed about Wreck Bay was that it appeared uninhabited, the second was that there were no roads that went anywhere near the place, and the third that it was surrounded on three sides by what appeared to be steep and rugged hills, all of which, according to the artist who drew up the map, were covered in dense bush and scrub. There were no trails in or out that she could see. Strangely, she didn't find any of this the least bit off-putting. On the contrary, she found it intriguing. She knew someone did live there or, at least, had lived there. Bernie had lived there and grown roses. Among the bushes and birds. Gazing out across an ocean that stretched unbroken halfway across the world to Chile. Bernie had managed to live there. How old would he have been, she wondered? She'd thought he was old way back when she was a child. If an old man could live there, so could she. Rosie leaned back in her chair and sipped at her tea and tried to imagine what life at Wreck Bay would be like. No corner stores to run to for milk or bread. No supermarkets. No television or phones. No cars. No electricity. No doctors, apart from herself, and that didn't count. No voyeuristic neighbors. No neighbors.

No neighbors?

Rosie felt the first tinge of doubt. Surely someone else would live there. She knew she couldn't handle the loneliness of being all alone. Then she thought of the man who'd left his name on the back of the envelope, Red O'Hara, Wreck Bay. She almost cried with relief. She could be alone but not alone. She picked up the map of Great Barrier Island once more and gazed at the bite out of the northern end. She was staggered that somewhere so close to the bustling city of Auckland could be so remote. Wreck Bay made Easter Island seem like Club Med.

Norma thought Rosie had finally flipped when she applied for two weeks' leave and booked a flight on Captain Fred Ladd's amphibian.

"I'm off as soon as I've presented my findings on toilet cleaners," she said.

"You're mad," said Norma. All she could do was wonder at the change that had come over her friend. She played her last card. "There are no blokes over there, none that you'd want to go to bed with at any rate, and you're not cut out for celibacy." Her cigarette bobbed indignantly.

"It's only for two weeks," said Rosie. Her face lit up and she burst out laughing. "I know it'll be tough, Norma, but I think I'll survive."

Five

"Come in, come in." Lieutenant Commander Michael Finn rose from behind a swamp-green metal desk that looked like it had been built from a Meccano set. His office walls shared the same bilious color, and the only relief came from a window overlooking the naval docks that was partially screened off by drab, apple-green venetian blinds, and a painting of the light cruiser *Achilles* engaged in battle with the German pocket battleship *Graf Spee*. He'd heard about Red and half expected him to walk in naked. If he had, Red would not have surprised him more.

He wore a gray, pin-striped, double-breasted suit jacket with wing lapels that might have been popular before the war, but had been studiously avoided by fashion ever since. It was at least two sizes too big but helped hide the frayed blue shirt beneath. His trousers were black and stopped well shy of his ankles. It didn't help that his shoes were brown. Col had done his best and scratched around for clothes for Red to wear but had had to make do with what had been left behind by guests at the hotel. The lieutenant commander had seen Guy Fawkes effigies on bonfires that were better dressed.

"Sit down, sit down!" he said.

Red sat. If someone had shot his legs out from under him he couldn't have sat down faster. He looked for somewhere to put the package containing the little urn that held the last mortal remains of Bernie Arbuthnot, finally choosing the corner of the lieutenant com-

49

mander's desk. He couldn't help but notice that the blotter was square to the desk, ruler parallel alongside and pens neatly in a cup. He wrongly assumed that the lieutenant commander was responsible for the orderliness.

"That your friend?"

"Sorry." Red grabbed the package off the desk and looked for somewhere else to put it.

"It's okay, it's okay," said the lieutenant commander quickly. "Leave it there, it's okay."

Red's hands shook as he placed the urn of ashes back onto the desk. His responsibilities toward Bernie hadn't ended with the old man's death. Someone had had to farewell the old boy and nobody else had rushed to put their hand up. The Great Barrier Island community had chipped in for the cremation and to fly the three of them to Auckland on the amphibian. They'd been given a discount to make up for a shortfall in funds on the grounds that a dog didn't really constitute a person as far as fares went, and Bernie could travel as cargo.

Red and Archie had sat in the little chapel until the coffin had descended. The experience had made Red think of the prayers they used to say over the graves of fallen comrades in Burma and the tears he'd shed over the mate for whom Archie had been named. "Yea though I walk through the valley of the shadow of death." Nobody had warned him that the valley was so long and the shadow so deep.

"I appreciate the fact that you've come to see me."

Red looked up, startled. He'd agreed to the arrangement so that the lieutenant commander wouldn't send a patrol boat to Wreck Bay but wished fervently that he hadn't.

"Should I offer condolences?"

"A cup of tea, please, sir. Some water for Archie."

"No problem. Here, let me take your coat."

If the man had released Red from stocks he could hardly have been more grateful. Lieutenant Commander Michael Finn smiled. It wasn't every day people dropped in to his office dressed like pimps with a dog and a fresh urn of ashes. He hung Red's coat on the back of his door and stuck his head into the corridor. "Gloria! Could you do me a tea, a coffee and a bowl of water please? Yeah. Bowl of water.

Ta." He turned and crouched down to let Archie sniff his hand. He ran his hand sharply up and down the dog's spine. "Like that, do you?" Archie shuffled and made it plain that he did. The lieutenant commander concentrated on the dog and deliberately ignored his owner. Red was on the verge of hyperventilating, and the officer wanted to give him time to settle and relax. He found the spot above Archie's tail that all dogs like having rubbed and stole a quick look at Red. The man looked like he was going to bolt out through the door at any moment. "Do you think we should have a beer for your mate later?"

"Sherry."

"What?"

"He drank sherry."

"Then we'll have a sherry for him." Mickey grimaced. "No. Perhaps not. Beer or nothing."

Red forced a smile. He looked around the little office. It wasn't as bad as he'd thought it would be. At least it had a window so he could look outside if the walls started closing in. The lieutenant commander wasn't as formidable as he'd feared, either, and showed no sign of shouting at him. He was a big bear of a man and seemingly ill at ease with his size. His limbs flopped haphazardly as if their owner only exercised occasional control. But their looseness also suggested that at one time the lieutenant commander might have been an athlete. They were near the same age, but while Red didn't have an ounce of fat on him, the lieutenant commander had a few pounds too many and had the least military bearing of any officer Red had ever met. He hadn't expected a lieutenant commander who got down on his hands and knees and patted dogs, and he found that reassuring.

"Red—you don't mind me calling you Red?—would you please call me Mickey." He gave Archie one last pat and stood. His uniform had crumpled into familiar folds. The crease in his trousers zigzagged as if unsure of the way to his shoes. "I've been called Mickey ever since I started school. My parents hated it, and I hate it. But when they named me Michael Finn, what the hell did they expect?"

Red snorted, an attempt to laugh by a man who had forgotten how. Mickey's charm was beginning to bite and had a pleasantly familiar ring, like the laconic good humor of the Aussies. A young woman in naval uniform interrupted them with the tea, coffee and Archie's bowl of water. She appeared very young to Red, almost too young to be in uniform. But then, they'd all been young once.

"Third Officer Gloria Wainscott, my ever-so-efficient assistant. Red O'Hara."

Red rose awkwardly to his feet and held out his hand uncertainly. He wasn't sure that shaking hands with women was the right protocol. Women made him uncomfortable and brought back memories.

"Pleased to meet you, Mr. O'Hara." The young woman blushed, disconcerted. Red was staring at her. No, not at her. It was as if he was staring through her, past her to some distant spot only he could see. Gently but firmly she pulled her hand from his grip, and drew the only other free chair up toward the desk. The lieutenant commander gave her a quick glance and cut in.

"Red, is it okay if Gloria joins us? If you prefer . . ."

"No, it's okay," said Red, anxious to please and get the interview over. He ran a finger around the collar of his shirt, pulled at it until the top button gave.

"Right," said Mickey. "Take your tie off before you choke. While we have our tea, just let me fill you in. Some of this you'll know already but it won't hurt to hear it again. Up until January this year our territorial waters extended only three miles from shore. That's not a lot of water to protect unless you've only got four patrol boats to protect it, which is all we had. Despite the blurb our publicity department put out, we did a lousy job. So lousy that at the beginning of the year the government extended our territorial waters to twelve miles, on the theory that if we can't catch poachers inside three miles, we can catch them inside twelve. When the navy pointed out that they'd actually increased the area of water we had to patrol by four hundred percent, they solved the problem by giving us two more patrol boats. Bit like sending school prefects out to control the mafia."

"You're still better off," said Red quickly, unsure whether he was allowed to comment.

"True. Except that Japan refuses to recognize the twelve-mile zone and has appealed to the International Court of Justice. It's just a delaying tactic, of course, because our people in Japan know that five prefectures there are about to follow our example and impose their own twelve-mile limits. In the meantime, the Japanese are grabbing all the fish they can and coming down heavy on our guys in trade negotiations. Japan is a major buyer of our wool, so their *kanji kaisha* —their champion negotiators—simply linked the needs of New Zealand sheep farmers with the needs of Japanese fishermen. The result? They run rings around our blokes, and our government agrees to license a limited number of longliners to fish as close as six miles from the coast. Give us twelve miles and our Sunderlands stand a chance. Give us six and the Japanese skippers laugh at us."

"What do you want me to do?" asked Red.

"I'll get to that. How's the tea?"

"Fine."

"What the government fails to appreciate is that we're up against the most sophisticated and aggressive fishing fleets in the world. Everybody's heard about the cod wars off Iceland, but believe me that's just a sideshow. We've got the Japs, and they've got the best fish finders in the world, the best techniques, the biggest nets, the longest lines, the most dedicated crews, and they've got radar that can find us, often before we can find them. Their dories are faster than anything we've got except the Sunderlands, and the flying boats can only photograph poachers but can't catch them.

"We've also got the Russians, who tend to fish out deeper but are not averse to a bit of poaching, either. Their mother ships are equipped with electronic surveillance gear so they can do a bit of intelligence gathering on the side, which, of course, also means they can keep better tabs on us than we can on them. Then there are the Taiwanese, the Chileans and even our friends the Americans. At any time there can be as many as twenty to thirty foreign boats harvesting the waters around New Zealand. Against this armada we have six Fairmiles. Six pathetic Fairmiles." Mickey Finn stopped talking and took a long sip of coffee. Red shifted uncomfortably in his seat.

"What about the Sunderlands?" Red asked.

"Ahhhh . . . our ace in the hole. A dozen Sunderlands patrolling night and day and a government with balls, and our problem would sail peacefully over the horizon. At least beyond the twelve-mile limit. But we never have more than one Sunderland up at a time and we're lucky to get that. They're not ours, they belong to the air force, Number Five Squadron, so we have to rely on interservice coopera-tion. They're not bad, the blokes out at Hobsonville, and the aircrew are as committed to nailing the Japs as we are. But it makes things dif-ficult. For example, I can convince my superiors that an intercept is in order, but they in turn have to convince their opposites in the air force. And those blokes have heavies breathing down the phone at them, as well. The Aiguilles operation was ours. We'd planned to in-tercept that Jap bastard before he reached the Coromandel Peninsula. By the time I'd convinced our guys, and our guys had convinced their guys, and somebody from both services had put their gold braid on the line, two weeks had passed, and you know what happened then. The air force got egg on its face and flipped it neatly onto ours. Christ, you should've been here. The phones were on meltdown. Your unfortunate intervention is only going to make it harder for us to get a Sunderland next time."

"Sorry."

"Don't worry about it. That's history. We have to accept that the current system doesn't work, and we have to get a whole lot cleverer. It's no good you or the fisheries ringing us with sightings of poach-ers, because by the time we do anything about them they're long gone. They're too fast and too smart. Our only chance of success lies in targeting the most incorrigible poachers, learning how they oper-ate and then setting a trap for them. To do that, we need an informal network of dedicated observers to keep us informed. That's where you come in."

Red leaned forward expectantly, his nervousness forgotten. Mickey found himself pinned by the most startlingly intense eyes he had ever seen. He forced himself to continue.

"You may have read recently that the navy was throwing addi-tional resources behind solving the problem of poaching. I am those resources, or should I say, Gloria and I are those resources. We have been assigned to the fisheries protection squadron to gather intelli-gence and formulate strategies to counter incursions by foreign vessels. I have some control over the operations of our patrol boats, but in reality I can't actually do anything without informing my superior, Staff Officer Operations, who in turn reports to Commodore Auckland. This particular Staff Officer Operations is a button polisher and social climber. Rumor has it that he's never actually set foot aboard a boat. It's also fair to say that nailing poachers is not the navy's highest priority. Nor is it necessarily the government's. There are plenty of people in power who don't want us to catch the Japanese, fearing the effect incidents might have on our trade relations. They're worried the Japanese might stop buying our beef or our wool. The government talks big but isn't prepared to back its words. Yet despite this, we believe we can have some impact. With your help."

"What do you want me to do?"

"Gloria will draw some binoculars and a radio from stores. We want you to report every sighting you make of foreign fishing boats. What can you get out of your boat? Eight knots?"

"Twelve."

"Do your best to get a solid identification, but call us anyway. If you don't get the name, hopefully someone else will. You won't be alone in this. We're setting up a network of spotters up and down the coast."

"What happens when you catch poachers?"

The lieutenant commander's shoulders sagged. "You want to tell him, Gloria?"

"If we're lucky enough to surprise a foreign vessel fishing in close, we still have a need to gather evidence so we can mount a successful prosecution. If we can get close enough to photograph a mother ship taking dories back on board, identify it and hopefully gather some of their longlines, we can put together a case. Similarly if we catch a trawler at work or hauling aboard nets filled with fish. Then we can make an arrest and use the fish they caught as evidence of poaching. Even so, we have to make the arrest within the twelve-mile limit or, in the case of the licensed longliners, the six-mile limit."

"Once they're in international waters there's not a lot we can do," cut in Mickey. "If we can't get them into court we can't fine them. Instead we send a complaint to their embassy and the vessel is usually withdrawn temporarily from New Zealand waters. I say temporarily advisedly, because give them a couple of months and they're back again and up to their old tricks. By the way, do you know what the maximum fine is for a skipper of a boat caught poaching? Tell him, Gloria."

"Fifty pounds, and twenty pounds per crewman. Technically, they can take out thousands of pounds' worth of fish, all at the risk of a fifty-pound fine."

"That's ridiculous," said Red. He could feel his anger rise and fought to suppress it.

"Gets worse," said Mickey. "The way the laws are written, the only thing our courts can get them on is fishing without a license in an unregistered boat. That's the irony. They can invade our waters, and the only thing we can do is fine them for not having something they're not allowed to have in the first place."

"So why do you bother?" asked Mickey.

"It's my job and someone has to do it. Look, the fines themselves mean nothing. It's the time the boats and crews lose in port, waiting for the case to be heard. Meanwhile our fearless prime minister sends an official protest note to Japan, which usually results in the vessel being withdrawn back to Japan in disgrace. That costs the fishing companies a lot of money. That's the big stick we wave." Mickey leaned back in his chair and opened his arms expansively. "We don't pay, the hours are long and the conditions lousy, but will you join our little band anyway? Be our eyes and ears?"

"If you think it'll help."

"Good man! So look and don't touch from now on?"

"What if the dories are fishing in close?"

Mickey took a long look at Red and surrendered to the inevitable. "Check with me first. If there's no operation planned I guess there's no reason why you shouldn't rip into them. But be careful. We don't want anyone getting hurt. I guess if that bastard Shimojo Seiichi tries another crack in close it won't hurt if you keep him on his toes."

"Shimojo Seiichi?" The name came easily to Red's lips, his accent near flawless. It had been so long ago yet still seemed like yesterday.

"He's the skipper of the *Aiko Maru,* the longliner you frightened off."

"Shimojo Seiichi," Red repeated softly, committing the name of his enemy to memory. "When do I get the radio and binoculars?"

"Gloria?"

"Might take a while, sir. You've promised quite a few lately."

"We'll do our best." Mickey stood. "Now how about that beer for your mate? I come off duty in five minutes." He picked up the package on his desk and handed it back to Red. "Guess you'll be lonely up there now."

"Yeah," said Red. "With any luck."

Mickey Finn put Red and Archie on a tender that was taking officers' wives across the harbor to the Admiralty Steps. Red carried two packages, the second one containing his jacket and tie, which Gloria had offered to wrap up in brown paper. She'd guessed correctly that Red would rather be cold than wear the dreadful jacket again. The flight back to Great Barrier wasn't due to leave for another three hours, so Red decided to walk to Mechanics Bay, where the amphibian was based. He knew there was no point trying to find a taxi driver who was prepared to carry a dog. He tried to ignore the thunderous diesel trucks and their foul-smelling exhausts as they hauled cargoes on and off the wharves. He glanced up at the steel bows of the giant cargo ships. Everything was *Something Maru.* It hadn't been so very long ago when every ship in port had boasted British registration. What had happened? How had everything gone so wrong? He turned his attention to Archie to calm him down. The dog was spooked by the trucks and forklifts whizzing around him, and pulled at the rope leash Red had made for the visit. They couldn't get out of Auckland fast enough.

He thought about the lieutenant commander. He seemed a good man, the type that did well in Burma. It buoyed Red to know that others felt the same way about the Japanese fishing fleet as he did and wanted to do something about it. It gave him hope. The lieutenant commander's young assistant troubled him, but he knew he'd get over it. Despite the fact that she had light brown hair and hazel eyes, she

57

made him think of Yvonne, and he'd managed not to think of her for such a long time. She made him think of what he'd lost, what the Japanese had taken from him. He could never forgive. They were always one step ahead, always taking away, always destroying. His hands began to shake. Two Japanese sailors heading ashore walked out through the wharf gates ahead of him. He automatically checked his stride so that he wouldn't walk in front of them and stopped.

"*Konichi-wa,*" he said, head bowed. "Good day." Twenty-two years had passed but nothing had changed.

"*Konichi-wa!*" the sailors replied, surprised that someone spoke their tongue, and even more surprised that it was a quivering tramp with a dog. They laughed and walked on. Just past them a newspaper boy was selling an early edition of the *Auckland Star*. The headlines trumpeted the good news: Japanese wool buyers had pushed prices to a new high.

The flight back to Tryphena, at the southern end of Great Barrier, took thirty minutes, five minutes longer than scheduled, because Captain Ladd had spotted a whale and its calf and swooped low to show Red. They'd managed to get close enough to see the barnacles growing on the mother. There'd been a time when whales were a common sight, but the whaling station at Whangaparapara had put paid to that. The Japanese weren't to blame for everything.

Red decided to call into Fitzroy on the way home to refill his tanks. He slipped through Man-of-War Passage on the south side of Selwyn Island with barely twenty meters of water either side. Both shores were fringed with giant pohutukawa trees, which had insinuated their way into every niche in the rocks and seemed to thrive in the barren ground. Once around Selwyn Island he found shelter from the prevailing winds, the southwesterlies, which were the bane of the island and the reason why Port Fitzroy was so popular with yachties. Up on the ridges, the surviving kauris and totaras shook their heads as if warning all sailors against taking to the sea. Red was glad he had his sweater, work trousers and parka. He was going to need them.

Col was waiting for him on the wharf and tied off his painter. Red handed back the borrowed jacket, trousers, tie and shoes and accepted two four-gallon tins of diesel in exchange, which Col had filled and ready.

"How'd it go?" asked Col.

"As Bernie wanted."

"Think I'd rather be planted myself."

"What difference does it make?"

"My way, the worms get a feed. Oh hell. I forgot. There's a letter for you up at the shop. Help yourself. I'll go fetch it."

A letter. Red couldn't remember when anybody had last sent him a letter. His spirits sank. There'd been a time when letters promised hope, life and an afterward. It hadn't even mattered if the letter had been written to someone else. News from home had been proof that the rest of the world still existed, still cared. But letters had since come to mean something else, and he didn't relish receiving them. Red had no reason to expect this letter to be any more welcome. Maybe some government department wanted to move him off his land. After all, there'd been talk of turning the north end of the island into a reserve. He sought diversion in work, but the fuel poured too slowly into his tank, and all that was required was patience. Why couldn't the world leave him alone? Archie sensed his distress and nuzzled up close.

Col returned and handed him the letter. Red examined it cautiously and distastefully, as if it might explode. The envelope was white and his name and address typewritten. The name of a market research company was printed in orange on the back. He didn't even know what a market research company was. It made no sense to him.

But it would soon enough.

Six

*A*ngus McLeod was as happy as he'd ever been. He stirred and thought briefly about pulling his bedcovers up over his head to try to block out Bonnie's insistent meowing. It was time for breakfast and both of them knew it. The first rays of the morning sun had pierced his window and lit upon his bed, warming and seductively indolent. He had no reason to rise other than his ingrained sense of discipline, but that was reason enough. Angus was one of those dour Scots to whom happiness always carried with it a suspicion of sin and was never acknowledged without due caution.

He followed Bonnie to the door of his refrigerator. The shiny new Kelvinator was one of two additions to a rather primitive kitchen. The other was a new Stanley woodstove imported from Ireland. Only the Kelvinator looked out of place, a proud and incongruous acknowledgment of progress alongside a chipped enamel sink with two brass taps, a kauri countertop, table and chairs.

"Here you go, you spoiled thing," he said as he gave Bonnie a saucer of fish pieces. "Look at you now, fatter than butter, like a sheep with the bloat." He slipped a couple of pieces of hakea into the Stanley's firebox and opened the flue to boost the flame. With nothing to do but wait until the hob had heated sufficiently to boil water for his tea and fry his fish, he strolled out onto his veranda to greet the day. Like so many of his countrymen, Angus had left home with the solemn hope of re-creating it in some other part of the world. It wasn't until he retired from the New Zealand police force five years earlier at the age of sixty that he finally realized his objective. He gazed over a landscape that was as wild, rugged and inhospitable as his birthplace on the slopes of Mount Conneville on Scotland's far northwest coast. Of course his bach was a castle compared to the crofter's hut that had been his home, with its thatched roof, cold stone walls and pounded-dirt floor. And the vegetation bore no resemblance other than that it clung to the poor soil in equal desperation. But he'd found heather upon the slopes, not the true heather of Scotland but a species he'd grown up calling ling. Still, it was heather enough for him to collect and dry and hang in bundles from the kitchen's exposed beams. It helped make him feel at home.

Angus took advantage of the morning sun to eat his breakfast out on his veranda, where he could look down over the treetops to his boat moored in the bay below. Now that he was up, he was anxious to get to work. Angus had two secrets. The first was that he wrote children's books. He did his best to conceal the fact because he didn't think it was a fitting occupation for a retired police officer. It concerned him that others might interpret it as weakness or a softening on his part, and he couldn't allow that. Nevertheless, his writing gave him great pleasure and satisfaction. If he'd had a chat with Rosie's father, the psychiatrist would probably have concluded that Angus was compensating for the childhood he'd never had.

He noticed Red's boat back was on its mooring when a wind shift brought it into view. So the madman had returned. A few years earlier he would have arrested him for indecent exposure or for causing a public nuisance and had him locked away in the Carrington Road mental institution. He didn't doubt that Red meant well, but equally it was clear all was not as it should be inside his head. Insanity troubled Angus, it was something beyond his ken. He was just about to sit down at his typewriter and return to the story of the boy who tamed the fierce griffin and saved his village, when movement caught his eye. It was the madman and his dog, coming up the trail toward his house. He looked for Bonnie, thinking he could throw her inside before they arrived, but she had also spotted the visitors and run along the veranda rail to greet them. He felt a surge of anger build up as he waited for Red to appear through the tea-tree arch that marked the head of the trail.

"What is it you want this time?" he snapped. "Can you not leave me alone for five minutes?" His eyebrows bristled and his face flushed with indignation.

"We need to talk," said Red.

"We need do no such thing! Away with you, now. Stop pestering me!"

"Angus, we need to talk." Red had learned to be patient with the belligerent old Scot, but controlling his temper had not come easy. There'd been a time when his temper had cost him his freedom, when he'd exploded for no reason and could do nothing to control it.

"If it's about the old man, I've nothing more to add."

"How can you add to nothing?" Red's hands began to shake. "Don't you play smart with me! I contributed to his funeral."

"You should have contributed to his life." Red felt his patience slip and his anger flare. He didn't want to talk about Bernie, but now that Angus had raised the subject there were things that had to be said. Responsibilities that had to be faced. "You had a duty to attend his funeral."

"I don't attend funerals."

"He was your comrade."

"He was no comrade of mine. He was my neighbor; an acquaintance and distant at that!"

"No!" Red began to shout back, his voice growing shrill. "He was your neighbor and your comrade. He would have stood by you if you'd needed help. Bernie would never have turned his back on you like you did on him. You had an obligation."

"I have obligations to no man. I did not want him as my friend. I did not want him as my neighbor. I don't want you as my neighbor and I certainly don't want you as my friend." Years as police spokesman had taught Angus how to use words to maximum effect, and his precise Highland accent turned them into bullets. He watched them strike home with satisfaction.

"Like it or not, we're neighbors, and neighbors carry obligations."

Red stuck doggedly to the beliefs that had been shaped in Burma and had enabled men to survive.

"I don't want neighbors. Can't you get that through your thick skull? I don't need you. Now, would you kindly get off my land and take that mangy animal with you."

Red took a deep breath to calm himself. He couldn't leave without raising the matter he'd come to discuss. Angus glowered at him, and he glowered back. Finally Red turned away. He looked at Archie and Bonnie, one purring and the other wagging his tail. How could natural enemies like a cat and dog get along so well while their respective masters were at each other's throats? "I didn't come here to discuss Bernie," he said softly. "I came to tell you about the woman he left his bach to."

"What!" Angus nearly tripped off his veranda.

"Bernie wrote a will and left his bach to a woman."

"To a woman!" Angus could hardly conceive of a greater blasphemy. "How do you know about this will?"

"He asked me to witness it."

"Then you're a bloody fool, man! A bloody fool!"

"What would you have had me do, Angus? Deny a dying man? Lose his letter overboard? Is that what you would have had me do?"

"Don't you mock me!" Angus wrung his hands in frustration. "Bonnie, get inside!" Bonnie took no notice. "A woman, you say? Here? At Wreck Bay? Was the old man mad?"

"She sent me a letter. She wants me to pick her up from Fitzroy next Saturday."

"You're not going!"

"No choice!"

"Of course you've choice, man! Have you lost your senses altogether?"

"Angus, if I don't fetch her she'll just pay someone else to bring her. The question isn't whether I pick her up, it's what do we do when she gets here."

"Dear God, a woman here at Wreck Bay!" A thought occurred and gave cause for hope. "She's not young, this woman? Perhaps she's one of Bernie's old flames?"

"From what Bernie told me I'd say she'd be in her mid-thirties."

"Oh dear God . . . Married, perhaps, is she?"

"She's coming alone."

"Dear God in heaven."

"Angus, think about it. There's nothing here for her. We've got to stick together and make sure she understands that."

"Aye, we'd better talk. You'd better come up here. I suppose I should offer you a drop of tea. Make sure your dog stays down there, mind."

"Archie goes where I go."

"Ah, suit yourself!" The dog was the least of his worries. Angus walked slowly back into his kitchen to put another hakea stick on the flames and the kettle back on the hob. "Dear God, a woman here! A young woman, at that!" He'd found paradise and peace, a hiding place from the dream that he'd finally accepted could never be. But it seemed the dream had sought him out once more and brought with it all the pain of despair and abandoned hopes that he thought he'd left behind forever. His brain struggled to comprehend the scale of the disaster. He couldn't allow it to happen. *They* couldn't allow it to happen. Whatever it took, they couldn't allow the woman to come to Wreck Bay.

The two men sat together on the veranda, uncomfortable with their closeness, plotting and concocting schemes neither man was capable of executing. They discussed wrecking Bernie's bach, but neither man was a vandal. They thought of draining his water tank, but abandoned that idea for the same reason. They thought of laying baits to encourage the native rats to move into the bach, but they didn't like the idea of encouraging the kiore, either. They decided they could do nothing but allow the isolation and deprivations of Wreck Bay to speak for themselves, confident that they would not so much speak as shriek. Let her face the prospect of hauling four-gallon tins of diesel all the way up the hill from the beach. Let her face the prospect of carrying bucketfuls of soil for her garden over the hills from Whangapoua. Let her face the prospect of taking a boat single-handed around Aiguilles Island in hostile weather to fetch supplies. Let her learn the vagaries of cooking on the decrepit Shacklock

Orion slow-combustion stove. Let her suffer the deprivations of life without shops, cinemas, bright lights or a friendly voice. Let her fend for herself. Wreck Bay was wildly beautiful but promised a hard life to anyone who chose to occupy its shores. The two men resolved not to make it easier for her.

They parted not as friends but as reluctant allies, each committed from self-interest to a common cause. Red took the track down to the beach to prepare his boat and set off with Archie for the rise beyond Aiguilles Island to honor his dead mate's wishes. Angus had declined Red's invitation to join him and help in the scattering of Bernie's ashes. Instead he sat unmoving, head in hands, trying to find the strength to confront and dismiss his fears. If any prayers had passed his lips they would've been reserved for his own salvation, not Bernie's.

Angus was not one to admit failure, yet he had failed to accomplish the one thing he believed made sense of his existence. He'd never wanted riches, fame, possessions, nor particularly a wife. He'd learned to expect nothing and to be given less. But it had never seemed an unreasonable expectation to one day have a boy child in his image. A son to indulge as he had never been indulged, to love as he had never been loved, to shape and mold and make beneficiary of his experiences and wisdoms. A son who would love and look up to him. If marriage had been the price, he would have paid it stoically, but there would never have been the slightest doubt as to whom the boy belonged. The boy would have been his, and he felt the lad's absence from his life as keenly as a blade. This was Angus's second secret.

Angus had come to terms with his disappointment, and the woman threatened his acceptance. Her presence would remind him of his failure and, worse, perhaps rekindle his hopes. He could not allow it, not allow it! Waves of anguish washed over him so bitterly that he groaned in despair, startling Bonnie, who'd settled on his lap. He looked up at the dense wild bush surrounding him, his home by choice and hiding place from necessity. What would happen when he could no longer hide?

Seven

Little Barrier passed away beneath the port wing, but Rosie hardly gave it a second glance. She was too busy concentrating on the pilot's description of her new, antisocial neighbors.

"They're a funny pair," said Captain Ladd. "Particularly Red. You can be sitting talking to him and suddenly get the feeling that you're talking to yourself."

"Bit rude."

"No, it's not like that. It's just that his mind goes off on leave without notice. You can see it in his eyes. One minute he's home, next he's off somewhere. Heard he got a hard time from the Japs during the war."

"What's he like, I mean physically?"

"Red? Mid-forties, wiry as a whippet, quite good-looking, according to the girls in the office. Red hair, beard, regular features, and eyes that make them want to drop their knickers—so they say, anyway." He laughed. "They've all had a go at chatting him up and got nowhere. He just gives them his thousand-yard stare."

"His what?"

"You'll know it when you see it."

"Think I know what you mean. He sounds promising, anyway."

"More promising if you were a dog."

"What?"

Captain Ladd told Rosie about Archie.

"What about the other bloke you mentioned?"

"Angus? Mid-sixties, retired, ex-police inspector. Remember a police spokesman on television with a James Robertson Justice accent?"

"Vaguely. Big, bristly, gray eyebrows that seemed to have a mind of their own?"

"That's him. Always looked like he'd just stepped in a cow pat and his eyebrows want to get away from the smell. If he ever smiled, nobody I know was there to see it."

"Sounds like a barrel of laughs."

"Like I told you, Rosie, it's hardly a fun neighborhood. Tell you what, we're ahead of schedule. If you like I'll give you a sneak preview. Might change your mind." Captain Ladd banked left away from Fitzroy and dipped the nose toward Motairehe ridge. Rosie stared through the Lexan, eager for the first glimpse of her new home.

"Oh, Christ," she muttered as she saw the wilderness beneath her. In her first flush of optimism after reading Red's letter, she'd imagined there'd be rolling green pastures dotted with Persil white sheep and goats, with the odd Jersey cow thrown in for fresh milk. Instead she saw three drab-looking bachs in tiny clearings that the surrounding bush threatened to engulf at any moment. If this was her Garden of Eden it was high time they sent in the gardeners. She thought back to the old man whose legacy had brought her. If an old man could make a go of it, so could she. It was an argument she'd often mounted to harden her resolve, but from the front seat of the Grumman Widgeon she began to question her conviction. How on earth can anyone live down there, she wondered?

"Not much here, is there?" Captain Ladd interrupted her thoughts. "I think that's Red's place just below us, old Bernie's place is over there on the next ridge, and ex-Inspector McLeod's place . . . down there. See it?"

Rosie saw it all right. The amphibian glided down the slopes and leveled out barely one hundred feet over the water. She caught her first glimpse of Wreck Bay's three sandy beaches and their ancient pohutukawa sentinels. This was better. Captain Ladd began a slow, banking climb for the return pass.

"All three moorings have boats on them, so you'll have a bit of a wait at Fitzroy."

"Odd. I told Red what time I was arriving."

"I did warn you not to expect them to roll out the red carpet."

"Look! Someone's waving." Rosie returned the wave. Down below them, Angus cursed louder and shook his fist even harder. "Maybe you're wrong."

The pilot looked at her and bit his lip. Years of looking at the world from an eagle's point of view had taught him how to interpret what he saw. Never in his wildest dreams would he have interpreted Angus's raised fist as a wave. He rolled his eyes. She'd learn.

"Look. There! By my place."

Captain Ladd was a bit taken aback by the unexpected use of the possessive and peered out of his side window. A man, a dog and half a dozen chooks were standing in front of Bernie's bach, looking up at them.

"Hell's bells, does he normally dress so formally?"

The pilot laughed. "Apparently." Both man and dog stood motionless as the plane passed overhead and left them behind.

"Well, you could say he wore a lovely smile. And at least I know he's a genuine redhead."

Captain Ladd laughed. But he couldn't help wondering what sort of happy elixir his passenger had taken. He'd seen no trace of a smile. No sooner had they recrossed the ridge than the amphibian began its descent into Port Fitzroy. Rosie settled back in her seat as the ripples beneath her took form and substance and became waves. The aircraft bounced once as Captain Ladd had predicted, slowed, then began a sweeping one-hundred-and-eighty-degree turn back toward the wharf.

"Can't run up on the beach here," he said. "Just too muddy. You'll have to wait for someone to come out and collect you." The amphibian motored gently up to a vacant buoy, where the pilot tied off. "Well, what do you reckon?"

"Not what I expected. There's no one here."

"Oh, there are a few buildings dotted around. By Barrier standards this is pretty crowded. What did you think of Wreck Bay?"

Rosie laughed, but it was more a nervous laugh than good hu-mored. "Well, it does make this place look crowded."

"Think you'll give it a go?"

"That's what I'm here for."

"Any second thoughts, give me a call. If the conditions are right, I could probably put down in Wreck Bay and run up onto the beach. Up there you can begin to feel that the world's forgotten all about you. But remember this. You're just twenty-five minutes away from civilization. That's all. One call and I'll come and get you. You've got my number. Otherwise I'll see you in two weeks."

"Thanks, Fred."

"One more thing. Deep down both those blokes up there are good, decent men. Just might take you a while to find the good bits. They're not used to strangers, and they're certainly not used to hav-ing a lady around. But if you get into strife they won't let you down. Things aren't necessarily as they might appear."

"They never are, Fred. Thanks for the warning. But has anybody warned them about me?"

Captain Ladd burst out laughing. His passenger had pluck. But nonetheless she was asking too much. If she got through her two-week trial run he thought she might last two months. Maybe three, because he could sense her stubbornness. He decided to give her three months before she called, but call she would. "Here's your trans-port."

Rosie looked at the tiny clinker dinghy being rowed out to meet them, bucking in the small but steep chop. Both she and her bags were about to get wet, but she guessed that was something she'd have to get used to. She wished she hadn't bothered going to the hair-dresser's. She reached across and kissed the pilot on the cheek. "Thanks, Fred. And thanks for showing me my new home."

"How'd you like the snapper?"

"Great, Col."

"Glad you like it, because over here we eat snapper like people over there eat lamb chops." Col gestured vaguely westward.

Rosie smiled. "Over there" was where she'd just come from. "Over

69

here" was Great Barrier. "Up here" was Fitzroy. "The other side" was the east coast. Col had invited her into his home to have lunch and told her to put her things in the spare bedroom. Then, as gently as they could, he and his wife, Jean, had let her know that she might be needing it for a few days.

"Things don't run to schedules up here," Jean told her. "If anything, they're worse over the other side. Tell 'em to be here Saturday, you probably won't see 'em till Monday. They won't come even if they intended to come before they were told to be here. They won't come even if they're low on fuel and supplies. There's something about the Barrier makes people contrary, and those blokes on the other side are more contrary than most. Ask somebody to do something, they'll go out of the way to do the opposite."

Once she'd eaten lunch, Rosie decided to go for a walk along the road that followed the shoreline to the community center, a hut the army had left behind at the end of the war. She needed to escape from all the advice she was getting and absorb something of the Barrier for herself. She needed time to gather her thoughts. As she strolled down the corrugated, loose-gravel road, the first thing that struck her was the silence. She'd never heard it before. There were no vehicles, no planes overhead, no blaring radios, no people. She stopped and listened. By concentrating she could hear the wind in the trees high up on the ridge tops and, away to her right, the waves slapping against oyster-encrusted rocks. But nothing else. The sun beat down on her as if she had its whole and undivided attention. It felt eerie and oppressive. She'd just managed to convince herself that the silence was beautiful and restful when she was startled by a sudden rustling of dry leaves. A banded rail poked its head out of the thicket to take a look at the intruder, then boldly crossed the road in front of her. Rosie had never seen one before and tried to catch its attention.

"Here chook-chook-chook!" she said, and immediately felt foolish. She was a city girl, and that was the only way she knew to attract a bird's attention. She looked quickly around to make sure nobody had heard her. Farther on, the road dipped down toward what appeared to be an iron sand beach. She jumped again as a ruckus broke out in a pohutukawa tree on her left, and a black bird chased away two mynahs that had strayed onto its territory. Rosie held her breath. A tui! She'd never been so close to a tui before, and the bird seemed to know it. It strutted up and down on a branch right above her head, displaying its arrogant puff of white throat feathers, and rocking from leg to leg so that the feathers she'd taken to be black occasionally flashed deep blue and emerald. After a few minutes the tui became bored and flew up to a higher branch where it was no more than a dark silhouette against the sky. Rosie exhaled deeply. She hadn't realized she'd been holding her breath. So this was Great Barrier. The view from the plane didn't do it justice. It changed once you could smell the bush, hear the birds and taste the sharp, mineral freshness in the air. Her spirits lifted again, now that she'd begun to take in her surroundings, and lifted once more when she noticed the clay bank on the high side of the road. She realized she'd seen clay earlier. From the plane. Yes! A great bank of it as the amphibian had skimmed across Wreck Bay, and it was right by the beach with the jetty and moorings. At least one part of her speculations was accurate. Where there was plenty of clay, there was the potential to make pottery.

She strolled down to the iron sand beach, where she found an old bleached tree trunk to sit upon. She looked out toward Selwyn Island, where the last yachts of summer clustered in its lee. Her earlier apprehension had vanished and had been replaced by cautious optimism. She no longer minded that Red wasn't there to meet her. She'd get her own back on the bastard one way or another. She'd teach him not to keep a lady waiting. Not this lady, at any rate. But optimism founded on finding clay and sighting two native birds no farther from her than she was used to seeing common sparrows was, to say the least, premature. Her introduction to Great Barrier Island was far from over, and it would be some time before she'd start teaching Red any lessons. He had a few lessons to teach her, and they'd not be ones she'd enjoy.

The sun had dipped behind Selwyn Island by the time Rosie returned to the Last Gasp. She'd kept an eye on the bay but had seen no boats come in. Col was waiting for her and called her into his shop. He showed her a box of supplies.

"I hope you don't think I'm presumptuous," he said, "but I'm blowed if I know what old Bernie was living on those last few months. All he got from me were jugs of sherry and occasional tins of stew or soup. I know this is just a look-see and you're only planning on staying a couple of weeks, but I reckon you'll need everything I've put in here. You better take this gas cylinder and four-gallon tin of diesel, too, in case your generator's dry. Bill's on top. Cash or check. Reckon your checks would be all right."

"If you believe that you'd believe anything." Rosie smiled as a look of uncertainty flickered across Col's face. She pulled her checkbook out of her handbag, looked at the bill and began writing.

"Your neighbors have post office savings accounts with me. I just draw what they spend. They top it up when need be."

"Sounds a good system."

"We've taken the liberty of making you up a bed. If Red was coming today he'd have come by now. The trip around the top's no fun at night, particularly when there's a bit of a wind. Missus is making up a stew. You're welcome to join us."

"Only if you let me pay you something."

"Thought you said your checks were no good? Nah. You're a customer. We like to show a bit of hospitality toward new customers. Particularly if they look like being regulars."

"Thanks for the vote of confidence."

"Ahh . . . the boys are all right deep down. Got hearts of gold. You just have to prospect pretty deep."

"In that case, couldn't I have just borrowed some diesel instead of carting that tin in with me?"

"They're not borrowing sort of people. Like I say, hearts of gold but you've got to dig deep."

"So there's no point asking for a cup of sugar, either?"

"You've got it. I gather they share their surplus. You know, if one catches more fish than he needs, or grows too many tomatoes. Sometimes Red brings us lovely fresh smoked snapper, but I'd never think of asking him for any."

Rosie looked at the bulging box of supplies. Alone but not alone. Isn't that the way she wanted it?

•   •   •

Col and his wife, Jean, were mystified how anybody could make a living talking about toilet cleaners. Rosie laughed along with them. Her hosts hadn't pried exactly, but their questions made it clear they wanted to know more about her, if only to figure out why on earth she'd even consider living at Wreck Bay.

"How do you get to be a market researcher?" asked Col.

"If you're anything like me, you get there the long way," said Rosie. "My family expected me to be a doctor, and for years I was one. Even worked as a psychologist and social worker. But, in all honesty, medicine's not my calling." She laughed. "I don't actually know what my calling is. I've been a teacher, medical reporter, librarian, waitress and picked apricots down in Otago. I even went back to university and got an arts degree."

"You're a doctor?" said Jean in awe.

"Was," said Rosie. "I did have grand ideas of curing the sick, but do you know what a doctor's surgery really is? It's a complaints department. All people do all day is come in and complain."

"All the same . . ." said Jean.

"Leave Rosie be," said Col. "Her dinner's getting cold."

Rosie battled her way through a mountainous plate of stew and homegrown vegetables. She was trying to find a way to avoid the jelly-and-custard dessert, when someone knocked on the door.

"Now who the hair oil could that be?" said Col.

Rosie had a sinking feeling she knew. Her jelly shivered as Col walked off down the hall.

"Buggeration, Red!" said Col in amazement. "What are you doing here this time of night? Are you out of your bloody mind?"

Red wasn't. In fact he had a very clear idea of what he was doing, even though he knew what he was doing wasn't right. "If you'll just pass me her things, I'll put them in the boat."

"Good evening, how are you?" Col waited for a response but his sarcasm was lost on his visitor. "Hang on a sec and I'll come with you."

"It's okay, Col, I can manage."

"The hell it's okay! Come in and meet the lady."

"Just pass me her stuff, Col."

"Jesus, Red. Here, you take this." Col shoved the box of supplies at Red. "Hang on. This tin of fuel, too. I'll get her bags."

Red put the box under his left arm and picked up the jerry can with his right hand. He turned and walked away without another word. Col caught him up at the wharf.

"Hell you playin' at, Red?"

"She asked me to pick her up, I'm picking her up."

"She's a nice lady, Red. She doesn't deserve this sort of treatment. She'll be chucking her guts over the side before you clear Selwyn Island. What the hell's got into you?"

"Earliest I could get here."

"Bullshit! You could've waited till tomorrow. But no. I can see your game. I know what you're up to. Get her sick, get her frightened, get her out of your life. Just so long as she doesn't get a fair go."

"Just pass the stuff down to me."

"No! Damn you." Col's anger started to get the better of him. "You can just shove off. I'll bring her around myself tomorrow, or I'll get someone else to. You can shove off."

"Okay. If that's what you want."

"Hold it. What's going on?"

Red looked up as he was about to cast off and saw Rosie for the first time. He couldn't make out much detail in the gloom, but at least she wasn't wearing a dress.

"Red, this is Rosie Trethewey."

Red climbed back onto the jetty. He reluctantly held out his hand. "Pleased to meet you."

"Like hell." Rosie walked right past him, ignoring his offered hand. She sensed his surprise. Well, what did he expect? That she'd just roll over like one of her brothers' silly wives? "What's up, Col? What's this about you taking me around tomorrow?"

"I wouldn't send a dog out there on a night like this." "Out there" apparently meant open water. "I was just suggesting to Red that he's left his run too late, and that I'd find someone to take you around to Wreck Bay tomorrow."

"I don't know that we should do that, Col. Red's taken the trouble to come and pick me up, so we should let him. As for sending a dog out there, well, if it's good enough for Archie—I assume those eyes down there belong to Archie—then it's okay by me."

"You're out of your mind." Jean had wandered down to put in her twopence worth.

"Maybe. But this bloke here obviously wants to show me how hard life on the Barrier can be for a poor, defenseless woman. Let him have his moment of glory. Never know, I might surprise him."

She already had, but Red couldn't let on. He and Angus had their plan, such as it was, and they were determined to stick to it. He didn't enjoy what he was doing but accepted the necessity.

"Jesus, Rosie, you're as mad as he is."

"I heard that was the qualification for living here. C'mon, Col, pass me something." Rosie jumped nonchalantly down into the boat. Her legs were wobbly and her hands shook. But she was determined to show Red she could be just as stubborn and unyielding as he was.

"Leave it to Red and me. He knows where to put things to keep them dry. Relatively speaking, of course. Now, have you got any foul-weather gear?"

Rosie shook her head.

"Jean, you better go get your spare set. And Rosie, you better put on another sweater as well. You might feel warm in here but you won't out there. And if you feel like throwing up at any time, just throw up in the boat or down the back of Red's neck. Don't lean over the side or you might get thrown out. You don't mind if she pukes her dinner up all over your lovely white boat, do you, Red?"

"I've brought a bucket."

"He's brought a bucket! How bloody considerate. I told you he was a gentleman. Now Rosie, sit on the motor housing directly behind Red. The windshield will give you some protection from the spray, and you won't get thrown about so much."

Rosie did as she was told. Already she was regretting her bravado. The wind was singing through the rigging of the boats on their moorings, sharp and discordant like a school orchestra tuning up. If the wind was like this in the sheltered harbor, what would it be like "out there"? A sudden shudder made her reach for the gunwale. All the talk about puking had already made her feel queasy. She remembered once helping crew a friend's yacht from Auckland to the Bay of Islands and being violently seasick for all but the first hour of the journey. She remembered how she'd dropped to her knees and begged God to let her die. She wondered if it was too late to take Col up on his offer.

"Here's Jean."

Rosie looked up at the torch's beam flickering down the road toward them. Oh well, she'd played her cards and couldn't back out now. She shouldn't have opened her big mouth, but she hated it when any man assumed weakness simply because she was a woman. She was beginning to hate this chauvinistic bastard when she remembered that hate also was something she was trying to get away from. She put on the heavy oilskin coat. It smelled of dead fish, and the sleeves were too long. She covered her head with the oilskin hat, pulling it down hard so that the wind couldn't get beneath it, and tied the cord under her chin. Rosie was glad it was dark and nobody could see her. She thought she must look like one of the Three Stooges.

"Good luck!"

"Thanks."

Col threw the painter down to Red. "Look after her, you bastard, or you'll have me to reckon with."

"See you," said Red noncommittally and turned the bow into the channel. It might have been Rosie's imagination, but the wind seemed to freshen immediately.

Col hadn't been wrong. Red groaned as Rosie reached for the bucket as soon as they cleared the lee of Selwyn Island. She needn't have bothered. The combination of wind and tossing sea made the bucket an impossible target. He began to have second thoughts himself. He'd expected the going to be rough, but nowhere near as rough as it was. The sea would test the fillings in their teeth until they'd rounded Miners Head, and still be uncomfortable until they'd cleared Aiguilles Island. At least they weren't in any danger. His boat was more than a match for the seas, and his Cummins diesel was boringly reliable. He thought he ought to say something to reassure his passenger, then thought better of it. That would defeat the object of the exercise. Get her sick and get her frightened. Then leave her on her own. It sounded good in theory, but putting their plan into practice was something else. What he was doing just wasn't right. It went against everything he'd learned in Burma. It was one thing to be unhelpful, something else to be deliberately cruel. Yet what he was doing was cruel and indefensible. He heard Rosie retch violently once more and gritted his teeth. It was wrong but it was necessary. Wrong but necessary! Acknowledging the necessity didn't make him feel any better. He sensed Archie up under the bow deck, gazing back at him reproachfully, and felt doubly guilty. Guilty and disgusted with himself. At least he should have left Archie at home.

Once they'd rounded Aiguilles Island, Red began to feel more at ease. He stayed close in to the shore, out of the wind where the black surface of the water was barely ruffled, so that his passenger could recover. A quarter moon sat low on the horizon, touching the shore with a wan and watery light. Rosie had stopped throwing up, possibly, Red surmised, because there was nothing left to throw up. His boat was a mess, but he accepted that he only had himself to blame. He smiled grimly. That was another of Col's predictions that had proved accurate. She'd thrown up her dinner, lunch, breakfast and the previous night's dinner as well. But she hadn't moaned or groaned or uttered a word of complaint. He respected her for that. He felt he should break the silence.

"You okay?"

"Why wouldn't I be?"

"We're just coming into Wreck Bay."

"What? So soon?"

Red couldn't help himself. He smiled. In the darkness with his back to her it was okay to smile. She'd never know.

"And wipe that smile off your face."

Red stiffened.

"Don't think you're clever, mister. That was nothing. Until you've puked out on Pernod you don't know what puking's about."

Red's face flushed with embarrassment. There was something about her that reminded him of Yvonne. His mind drifted back to the Alexandra Hospital in Singapore when the Japanese came. He recalled the nurses standing up to the Japanese soldiers, defying them by shielding their patients, and having their faces slapped for their audacity. They never voluntarily took a backward step. He could sense that Rosie was from the same mold, somebody who wouldn't take a backward step either. It hadn't done the nurses any good. Ultimately, it wouldn't do her any good. He slipped the gear shift to neutral and let the boat glide gently on its own momentum up onto the beach.

"Hop ashore and I'll pass your things out."

Rosie got slowly to her feet, praying that her legs could still support her. It had been a long time since she'd felt so sick and been so scared. But she was damned if she'd give him the satisfaction of knowing. She walked gingerly along the length of the boat, transferring her weight from hand to hand along the gunwale. Her legs threatened to buckle under her. She knew that if she jumped down onto the beach she'd just fold up into a heap. She needed time to pull herself together. Up ahead, two eyes watched her every move.

"Hello again, Archie." She pushed past Red and was gratified to hear the dog's tail thump, thump, thump against the bow planks. "What sort of a man takes a dog out on a night like this?"

"Archie goes where I go."

"Who's talking to you?" She reached as far forward as she felt she could without toppling over and let Archie sniff her hand. "It's a good thing dogs can't talk, because I do believe he'd say things you wouldn't like to hear."

Red ignored her. What did she know about Archie? "Got a torch?"

"A torch?"

"So you can see where you're going."

"Right." The moment of truth had come. She sat her bottom down on the bow deck and swung her legs over the side. She peered into the darkness to try to judge her height from the sand. A straight drop was out of the question. She twisted, put both hands firmly on the side of the boat and jumped. Her legs buckled as she hit the beach, but her hands held her upright. She straightened. "Give me the box of supplies. Col probably put a torch in there."

"Probably?"

It was Rosie's turn to flush with embarrassment. It simply hadn't occurred to her to bring a torch. What had she expected? Street lighting where there were no streets?

"Let's hope he probably put batteries in as well."

Rosie took the box from him and carried it up the beach. She started to rummage through, wishing to hell she'd thought to go through the box when Col had given it to her. Any smart person would have. She heard one of her bags thud into the sand behind her and rushed to get it before an incoming wave beat her to it.

"Here's another."

She reached up and grabbed the second carryall.

"How are you going with the torch?"

"Give me a chance!" she snapped.

Give her a chance. Yes, Red thought, he should give her a chance. But what if he did and what if she stayed? Oh Christ! Old Bernie had a lot to answer for. Red waited until she'd dumped both bags by the box of supplies. As much as he wanted to, he couldn't let up on her.

"Don't forget the diesel."

"Who could forget the diesel?"

Red reached for the jerry can, not daring to smile. "While you're here, I've got something else for you."

"What?"

"My clothes."

Red peeled off his oilskins and handed them to her. Then his woolen sweater, shirt and trousers. He was determined to do things the way he always did, woman or no woman.

"What am I supposed to do with them?"

"Just keep them dry. Now let me push her out. C'mon, Archie." Red jumped naked onto the sand, followed by Archie, and began to push his boat off the beach sternforemost.

"Where are you going?"

"To the mooring."

"Oh."

Red grimaced. There'd been a touch of anxiety in her voice when she'd thought he was leaving her all alone. It was enough that their plan worked without having to feel the hurt it caused. He started the motor and ran up to the buoy. The deck was slippery

79

with vomit, and it seemed no part had been spared. His instinct was to clean up the mess immediately, but the trip had been hard enough, and he couldn't bring himself to leave her standing alone on the beach while he did. Reluctantly he let things be, knowing he'd have to beat the sun up in the morning and get back to his boat or it would stink to high heaven. He tied off the mooring rope, jumped over the side and swam ashore. When he reached the shallows he stood and waded the rest of the way. A torch beam caught his crotch and held it unwavering.

"Nice penis," said the voice behind it.

"If you want me to help carry your things up the hill, would you mind not shining your torch in my eyes."

"Strange place to have eyes." Rosie turned the torch away so that it shone on her bags. She picked up Red's trousers and held them out to him. "Your eye shades."

"I'll put them on when I'm dry. Leave the jerry can here and pick it up in the morning. There's diesel up there. In the end, Bernie couldn't be bothered running the generator. You carry the bags and I'll carry the box of supplies."

"Then lead on. Do you need my torch?"

"No. I know the way. C'mon Archie." He set off up the track at his normal brisk pace.

Rosie followed, trying hard to keep up with the shape in front of her, the smaller of the bags and torch in one hand, the larger bag in the other. The track shone smooth and white in the torch's beam, well worn and friendly. Then it began to steepen and crisscross with roots. She couldn't keep up no matter how hard she pushed herself and fell farther and farther behind. She tried to picture the beach and her bach as she'd seen them from the amphibian. She gasped as her legs gave way and she stumbled. "Bastard!" she muttered. But curses didn't make her stronger or the track less steep. She vomited, then lay down on the track unable to continue. She'd vomited up every last ounce of energy as well.

"Red! Wait!" she called weakly.

Red put down the box of supplies and turned back. "Stay, Archie." At last she'd cracked. Now he could afford to show some kindness.

Not too much, but enough to make him feel better about what he'd done. He found her sitting on the track with her back to him. Her shoulders slumped, her head in her hands. He thought she was weeping and was stricken with guilt. He'd seen men slumped that way before, their spirit broken and no longer able to drive their weary, wasted bodies. He'd been the same way himself.

"I'll take your bags."

"Thanks, Red. How much farther?"

She sounded tired, but her voice didn't waver as it would have if she'd been crying.

"About halfway."

Rosie closed her eyes. How would she possibly manage when she could hardly take another step?

"Need a hand up?"

"Mister, I need a crane, closely followed by a taxi. But no, I'll manage." She dragged herself to her feet. "How about slowing down a bit?"

Red grunted noncommittally. He slipped his arms through the handles of both bags, flipped them over his shoulders and set off back up the track, moving noticeably slower than before. He paused briefly to pick up the box of supplies and kept walking. He could hear her plodding along slowly behind him, stopped and waited for her. "This is where your track branches off. Not far to go now." He listened for a reply, but Rosie was too weary to give one.

As they neared Bernie's bach, Archie ran ahead to see if he could surprise a careless bush rat. Red heard him suddenly crash into the undergrowth, so at least he was on the trail of one. "Here we are."

Rosie looked up wearily and saw the dark, looming shape of the bach and the welcoming glow of a lamp within.

"Didn't think you'd want to arrive to a dark house."

"Red, you surprise me. You really do." Without thinking she reached forward and briefly put her hand on his arm to acknowledge his kindness. It was a nothing gesture, but it totally unnerved Red. That was something Yvonne used to do. It aroused memories he kept hidden in the dark, buried parts of his mind. The nights when the touch of her hand and the comfort of her nearness were his only

81

medication. He remembered his gratitude and the love that grew from it. All gone. Wasted. Destroyed by the Japanese. Then the pain came and he felt himself hurtling headlong into a flashback. He jerked forward as if reacting to the starter's gun. Work could drive her from his mind. Work could give him back his control. He took the veranda steps two at a time and pushed the door open, threw the box down on the table and the bags alongside it, then raced back out the door. Don't think! Don't think! Don't think!

"I'll start the generator." Not a statement, nor a shout. More a plea.

Rosie didn't move. Her mouth hung open in surprise. Her hand still reached out in front of her. She wondered what had suddenly got into the man. Perhaps she'd just hit him with a massive dose of static electricity. Maybe it was her vomit breath. Or maybe—just maybe—she was the first woman who'd ever touched him. Christ, don't tell me, she thought. All this way and the bastard turns out to be queer. But weariness overcame speculation, and she dragged herself up the steps and into her new home. She slumped wearily into a chair and looked around her. It didn't occur to her to turn up the brightness of the propane lamp. The place looked clean, though, which surprised her. Dying old men weren't noted for their housekeeping. A generator coughed, and the bare bulb above her head flickered into life. She was wrong. The place wasn't clean, it was spotless. Scrubbed to within an inch of its life. Even the gold and silver flecks in the tacky Formica countertops shone. Fresh flypapers hung from the ceiling. The screen door creaked open as Red returned.

"Looks like you've been busy."

Whatever devils had got into Red had gone back into hiding. He looked away, embarrassed.

"The flowers are a nice touch."

"Thought I'd better check the place out before you arrived. Make sure the water was all right and the generator worked." Red felt guilty about the work he'd done around the house and was beginning to regret the fact that he'd done it. Angus would never have agreed to it and would be furious if he ever found out. But Archie would've approved. Whenever they heard more prisoners were moving up to the camp, they always did their best to prepare huts for them, dug latrines and organized whatever food they could. Invariably, the new troops arrived hungry, exhausted and in no shape for work. It wouldn't have been right to leave them to fend for themselves. Survival depended on helping each other.

"I appreciate what you've done, Red." Rosie looked down at the tabletop, weighing up what next to say. The contradictions in the man staggered her. He'd made it clear she wasn't welcome, then laid out the welcome mat, having vacuumed and fluffed it up first. The absurdity of sitting there having a normal conversation with a stark bollocky, naked man who was a virtual stranger added to her confusion. Nothing made sense. "I think if I'd walked into a mess here tonight I wouldn't have bothered to unpack my bags." She looked up quickly to catch Red's reaction, but he'd already turned away from her.

"Kettle's on," he said, and began to put on his clothes.

Rosie took a good look at Red while they drank their tea. Fred Ladd had been right on a number of scores. He was certainly wiry, pleasant to look at and totally devoid of small talk. But there was no sign of the thousand-yard stare or anything that would make her want to drop her knickers. Even in the dull light she could see his eyes had a brightness, but they were as lifeless as a dead fish's. He stared silently into his tea like a fortune-teller into her crystal ball. She guessed he was trying to come to terms with whatever had spooked him.

"Well, are you going to show me around?"

"Sorry!" Red shot up like a startled bird.

"No hurry, take your time." Rosie laughed to ease the tension, but her gesture was ignored. He took her on a tour of the house, slowly reverting to the cold and distant person who'd picked her up from Fitzroy. Red had remembered the game plan. He introduced her to the kitchen, living room, two bedrooms and bathroom. She smiled when she saw the way the blankets were folded neatly at the foot of the bed. Only soldiers and nurses folded blankets that way. The bed sagged slightly in the middle but looked comfortable enough. At that point, she would have given anything just to curl up in its hollow, but there were things she needed to know. He introduced her to the outside lavatory, which operated on the big-drop principle. It was enclosed in weatherboard for privacy, and for ventilation, the bottom and top two planks were omitted on three sides and the door cut to match. Red had dropped a couple of buckets of soil down the toilet to try and smother the odors, but had met with only limited success.

"Needs a new hole dug," said Red. "That'll take some digging." He flashed her torch around the vegetable garden. "Needs weeding and new topsoil," he volunteered. "Ages since Bernie did a trip down to the flats for more soil. Needs fencing and a secure gate. Henhouse could do with a clean. You've got half a dozen chooks, but they don't all lay." He led her back inside. "The whole place needs fixing and painting," he said, "particularly the gutters." Rosie realized Red was about to provide a whole catalogue of things that needed doing, all of which were calculated to discourage her.

"All it needs is love, Red," she said. "And all I need right now is sleep. I need to wash and clean my teeth and rinse my mouth out. My breath could melt asphalt. Perhaps you can come back tomorrow and show me how the stove works."

Red hesitated. The temperamental old stove was one of the cornerstones of their plan. "Do one thing for her and we'll be running after her for the rest of our lives," the old Scot had said. "There'll be precious little peace then." In his heart, Red knew that Angus was right and that their plan was sound. But old Shacklocks could be tricky to operate. They'd agreed to drop her in at the deep end, but just how deep did it need to be? Surely just having to rely on an old woodstove for cooking, heating and hot water would be enough to discourage any woman accustomed to limitless electricity. Surely it couldn't do any harm to show her how it worked. But he wouldn't cut firewood for her. He'd draw the line there.

"I'll come around sometime tomorrow," he said, and turned to leave.

"Red, before you go."

"What?" What else did she want? Surely she wasn't going to start making demands on him already.

"Thank you," she said. And reached up to kiss him lightly on the cheek.

Eight

～～～

*O*nly *one person at Wreck Bay greeted the new day with enthusiasm, and it wasn't Angus. He rose early and made porridge to ward off the* cold. He hadn't slept well because he was worried about the woman, and he wasn't ready to start writing because he was worried about Red. Change was in the air, and he was consumed by a feeling of unease. The thing that concerned him most was that he didn't trust Red to stick to their agreement. Some people were just born to do good works, and it was a condition he knew to be incurable. But it could be managed if one was diligent enough. Aye, he thought, and when it came to diligence there were few better than he. He'd almost had to take a gun to stop Red from leaving too early to collect the woman from Fitzroy. He'd forced Red to see that it made sense to pick her up when it was cold, dark and wet. To let her know right from the start that life on the Barrier didn't come any harder than at Wreck Bay. The sooner she was forced to face the truth, he'd argued, the sooner she'd be gone. Red had acquiesced but was plainly unhappy about it. The man was soft, no doubt about it, and that was cause for worry.

Angus poured himself a cup of tea, wandered out onto his veranda and automatically looked over the bay. The madman was already up and cleaning his boat. The fool was obsessive! He looked up at the sky to see what sort of day would be forthcoming. Clouds and more clouds tumbled down the hillside, big and puffy, roiling and boiling, charcoal hued and swollen with rain. He almost cackled with glee.

When he concentrated he could hear the roar of the wind in the treetops high up on the ridge. It was going to pour down, nothing surer, and provide precisely the sort of welcome he wanted for the city woman. Soaking wet and no hot water. He rubbed his hands together gleefully as he contemplated her discomfort. Shut indoors with no television and no telephone. And no food other than what she'd brought, unless . . . unless the madman gave her some fish. The thought caused his brow to furrow. Damn the man! That was exactly the sort of fool thing the man would do. He looked up once more at the sky to see if he'd have time to get down to the beach and back before it rained. It was time for words, no doubt about it.

In every respect, Red's day had begun as any other except for one thing—he couldn't keep the woman out of his mind. She'd interrupted his sleep and intruded into his consciousness. She'd kept him company over breakfast. Accompanied him on his rounds of garden and chookhouse. The only time he'd escaped from her was during the discipline of his exercises, when he'd emptied his mind and looked inward as he had been taught, calming himself, strengthening his body and keeping the many parts of his fractured mind together. But when he'd finished, she was there waiting patiently for him. He'd resented that. She disturbed and unsettled him, made him feel guilty for having to do things that went against his instincts. The woman did not belong. She had no right to come where she was clearly not wanted. He set off for the beach the instant he'd brought his calendar up to date.

The stench of her vomit as he cleaned out his boat didn't upset him. He'd grown accustomed to the smell of vomit and human feces while helping out in the camp hospital, helping the men dying of cholera and dysentery, washing fouled sheets and Jap-happies, the loincloths the men wore after their trousers had rotted away. He'd looked after men dying from injuries inflicted by swinging boots and rifle butts. He'd scraped tropical ulcers and putrefying sores. He'd lanced boils. Vomit didn't upset him, but it was unhygienic, and hygiene was important to survival. He couldn't help wondering if Angus's embargo on help extended to the woman's toilet. Perhaps he should help Rosie sink a new hole. Whenever newcomers arrived at the camps, those already there always helped dig new latrines.

"You! You out there!"

Red looked up from his work. Angus was waving to him from the beach, lean and angular in khaki shirt and baggy, knee-length khaki shorts.

"What do you want?"

"Come ashore. We need to have words."

"I'm nearly finished." Red continued cleaning the boat in his usual methodical way. He thought about topping up his fuel tank but hadn't used enough on the run back from Fitzroy to justify it. He rinsed his brush over the side and put it away. He picked up a bucket filled with fresh water and a clean cloth and began to wipe all the interior surfaces so salt wouldn't build up.

"C'mon, man, I haven't got all day!"

Red wiped down the console and his seat. He wiped down all the metal around his controls. Things rotted in saltwater and salt air as quickly as they rotted in the jungle, unless they were properly cared for. He tossed the dregs over the side, stowed the bucket and went forward to the bow locker where he kept his storm cover.

"For heaven's sake, man! Can you not do that later?"

Red could see that Angus was getting agitated. He couldn't understand his impatience. Neither of them was going anywhere. There was work to be done and an order for doing it in. He fastened the cover off at the stern cleats, checked to make sure that all of the clips were secure and dived into the water.

Angus watched the madman swim toward him, Archie dog-paddling by his side, and looked around to see where Red had left his clothes. Unless the madman had buried them, he hadn't brought any.

"Have you got nothing to make yourself decent?"

Red shook the water out of his hair and cocked his head to each side to release the drops trapped in his ears. "You said we needed to talk."

"Aye. How did it go, then? Picking up the woman."

"She was seasick all the way from Fitzroy."

"Good, good. Was she frightened at all?"

87

"Angus, you would have been frightened."

"Good, good!" There was genuine glee in the Scot's voice, and he'd come as close to a smile as Red had ever seen.

"So? What next? I trust you just left her standing on the beach." There was something indecent in the delight Angus was taking in Rosie's suffering, and it disgusted Red.

"I took her up to Bernie's."

"You didn't carry her bags?"

"Some of the way, yes."

"Then you're a bloody fool, man!"

"She'd collapsed on the track, Angus. She could hardly put one foot in front of the other. She'd spent the best part of the previous two hours puking."

"Collapsed, had she? Very good. You probably did the best thing. You didn't stay there?"

"Not for long. Started her generator, showed her how to switch it off and where the lavatory was."

"I assume Bernie had left the place in a mess?"

"No. When I looked after Bernie, I looked after his place as well."

"Pity. How did she seem? Disappointed?"

"No, just tired and sick. She seems to have lots of spirit."

"Lots of spirit, eh? Well, we'll see about that. If anywhere can knock that out of her it's here. Provided you don't go soft on me. You understand what I'm saying?"

"Yeah."

"Now tell me, you didn't make any arrangements to see her today?"

"I said I'd show her how to work the stove."

"Heaven's sake, man! We have an agreement! Are you already hell-bent on becoming her slave? Has she sunk her claws into your soft, daft hide already?"

"No!" The anger that had been building all morning began to seethe and foment.

"Now don't you take that tone with me. I'll not put up with it. I thought we had an agreement. You've gone soft already, haven't you, you gormless fool?"

"No, I told you!"

"You have, man. Already she's got you running after her. 'Start my generator. Light my stove.' Next she'll have you digging her garden and sinking a new toilet. Help her now and you'll help her forever. I'm telling you, man. Do this! Do that! Fetch this! Mend that! There'll be no letup. There'll be no peace for either of us."

"All I said was I'd show her how to work the stove!"

"You'll not do any such thing!"

"I gave my word!"

"Then un-give it. Don't you see?" Angus sensed he'd pushed Red far enough and softened his voice. He didn't want to be the cause of one of Red's turns. "Any minute it's going to rain cats and dogs. Let her sit up there all alone, no television, no telephone, no heat and nowhere to go. She won't last long. Every time she wants a pee she'll have to go outside and get a soaking. She'll have no hot shower and no hot bath. No city woman is going to put up with that for long."

Red could see that Angus was right. He forced himself to breathe deeply, felt the ebb of his anger and frustrations.

"Okay. I'll do it your way."

"There'll be no taking her fish, either. Not fresh, not smoked. You'll give her nothing."

"Okay."

"Good. Then it's agreed." The Scot turned abruptly and strode back up the beach toward the track.

Red turned around to look for Archie. He could hear the first rain squall battering the leaves on the trees high up on the ridges. It wouldn't be long before it reached them. At least it would wash the salt out of his hair and off his body. He spotted Archie farther down the beach, about thirty yards out from shore. His tail was wagging furiously as he dog-paddled after small mullet. Red smiled. If there were no seagulls to chase, Archie chased fish. If he ever caught one it would be because the fish had collapsed laughing. Red shaped his lips to whistle him in but thought better of it. Archie was enjoying himself and not hurting anyone. Red wished he could say the same for himself.

The curtains Bernie had hung over his bedroom window so that he could sleep late worked just as well for Rosie. She slept until the rain squall began its frenetic tattoo on her iron roof. She opened her eyes and looked around her. The room was not unlike many of the bachs she'd weekended in, practical, even comfortable, but in no way cosy. There was a tired-looking tallboy and an empty wardrobe with its door half open. The linoleum on the floor was worn, and there was a tattered wool rug that might once have been cream-colored, covering what she suspected was a hole. But there was no doubting the place was clean. Hospital clean.

It didn't bother her that she was lying in the bed Bernie had died in, because she'd been brought up around hospitals. When somebody died you changed the sheets, not the bed. What did worry her was that she desperately needed a pee. She got up, unzipped her bags and rifled through them to find something warm to put on. She shivered in the cold and pulled her jeans and sweater on as fast as she could in preparation for the mad dash to the outhouse. The pounding on her roof swelled to a continuous roar. Thunder crackled and threatened to split her roof apart. She thought of the wet run up to the smelly toilet and considered squatting over the washbasin in the bathroom instead. According to a salesman she knew who stayed in country pubs, the old trick of peeing in the washbasin was an institution. You could do whatever you liked in them, he'd maintained, so long as you never actually washed in them. She dismissed the idea. This was her new home, not a country pub. And if she was going to make a go of things, the sooner she started doing things properly, the better.

She reached under the bed to find her shoes, and her hand touched something cold and smooth. And round. She pulled the chamber pot out from under the bed and looked at it with an overwhelming sense of relief. Of course the old bastard would have had a pot. Sick and probably lazy, there was no way the old codger would have crawled out of a warm bed on a cold, wet night to go up the hill for a pee. Down came the jeans. She couldn't help smiling. Excitement mixed with relief and she felt like a kid again. And it wasn't just the novelty of squatting over a potty, she was excited about her new life and the prospects of a new beginning. She looked for her tissues. Where had she seen them and were they in reach? She blessed Bernie's weakness and then realized she was thanking the wrong person. Red could have cleared out the pot along with Bernie's effects, but he hadn't. Instead he'd scrubbed it as he'd scrubbed everything else, and popped it back under the bed where he knew she'd find it. He amazed her. Both Captain Ladd and Col had been right about him. He was a decent bloke and he did have a heart of gold. It wasn't buried very deep, either, just hidden away behind a veneer of stupidity.

As she washed and cleaned her teeth she considered the problem of emptying her chamber pot. What would Bernie have done, she wondered? She went outside and stood in the shelter of the veranda, looking for a solution. Rainwater tumbled in a torrent where the gutters returned toward the downspout fixed to the wall of the house. Clearly the downspout was blocked with leaves and probably had been for some time. Blocked gutters seemed destined to haunt her wherever she went. She looked at the torrent and saw it had gouged a gully in the soil below and run off into the bush. She tipped the contents of the potty into the gully and let the rain wash it away. Problem solved. Bernie would have been proud of her.

The episode brought home how much her life would have to change if she was to make a go of it. Everything was different. Even a simple visit to the loo was an expedition, a trip to the grocer's an adventure currently beyond her capabilities. All along she'd imagined there would be some kind of a track through to Fitzroy. She'd pictured herself tramping through the bush, a cross between Heidi and an Outward Bounder, a rousing song on her lips and a rucksack filled with groceries on her back. The sun had shone in all her imaginings. Perhaps there was a track, but it seemed unlikely. From the moment she'd arrived in Fitzroy, the talk had been of a boat picking her up. If ensuring there was food to eat presented such a challenge, how would she manage with everything else? It was one thing to change lightbulbs, rewire plugs, change washers in taps and fix handles to cupboards, but she suspected the sort of attention the bach needed was work for tradesmen. She'd been many things, but never that.

She found the old Pye radio sitting on a water-stained veneer cabinet as she continued her inspection, and wondered what else had slipped her notice during Red's tour. The cabinet was stuffed with old papers and magazines, but she could see the corroded chrome fittings that had once supported glass shelves and mirrors at a time when it had been a cocktail cabinet and probably a very nice one. She switched on the radio and discovered it was tuned to the national station, 1YA. News, weather and corny music, yet probably good company for an old man. Even though the signal came through laced with static from the storm, it was also welcome company for a young city woman unaccustomed to solitude. The stack of papers bothered her. Why hadn't Red thrown them out? She was about to dismiss it as oversight when the penny dropped. At Wreck Bay, paper was precious.

She looked for matches, found a box with three in it on the shelf above the Shacklock, turned on the propane camp stove and made herself a cup of Nescafé. That was another thing. Col had given her milk powder, but there was a jug of milk already made up in the fridge. That man Red again. She couldn't help thinking about him as she sipped her coffee, not just as his neighbor but as a psychologist and an eminent psychiatrist's daughter. She'd seen his elsewhere look before. That dead-fish look of being in one place but living in another. As a social worker she'd counseled returned soldiers suffering from battle fatigue, shell shock, or lack of moral fiber, the diagnosis depending on the sympathies of the diagnostician. She started wondering if she could do anything to help him.

She decided to make breakfast and worry about Red and everything else later, but first she had to check out her supplies. So far, Col hadn't missed a trick. She'd needed a torch and found one, wanted coffee and found a jar. She was curious as to what other treasures were in store for her. She found blocks of butter and packets of Chesdale cheese. Chesdale cheese, for Christ's sake, the curse of every schoolkid's lunch box. Cans of peas, sweet corn and baked beans. Exactly what a man would pack. Four rolls of toilet paper, packets of flypaper and a soggy parcel wrapped in white butcher's paper. Whatever was in it had thawed. Lamb chops. A dozen of them. She wished she'd had the brains to sort through the box before going to bed. There was dinner for the next three nights, which was about as long as she figured the thawed meat would last. She found tea, flour, salt, sugar and rice. Rice? Did she look like the kind who made rice puddings?

Vinegar, cornstarch, hand soap, dish soap, tomato soup, tomato soup, tomato soup. Every tin of soup the same. Soy sauce. What the hell did she need soy sauce for? Honey, raisins, sultanas, dried apricots, prunes. Tins of ham, corned beef and one of Spam. Baker's yeast! With a recipe for baking bread on the packet. Yes! A bottle of ketchup. Spare batteries. A potato peeler and can opener. But no vegetables other than the canned corn and peas. Ah! But she had a vegetable garden. She had no idea that Col had been influenced by Red's require-ments.

She looked at the sorry assortment and wondered how she was going to survive the two-week trial before she went back to Auck-land to collect her things—or not—whatever the case might be. She helped herself to one of the eggs Red had stacked in a line across one of her kitchen shelves and fried it. Ray Conniff's chorus and orches-tra were displaced by Burt Clampert's golden trumpet playing "Oh My Papa." "A Mother as Lovely as You" followed. She'd caught the Sunday-morning request session. If they played "You Will Never Grow Old" she resolved to throw the frying pan at the radio. A girl could only stand so much. She would have made toast but first she had to make bread. To make bread she had to fire up the Shacklock, which brought her back to Red. Would he come or wouldn't he? That was the question.

She grew tired of the radio and switched it off. *Brass Band Parade* had begun, and silence was infinitely better than that. She made an-other cup of coffee and stared at her dirty plate. She figured she had two options. Hang around hoping Red would come, or start doing things for herself. The seeping cold left her no option. She decided to light a fire in the Shacklock and see what happened. See if she got hot water. If not, why not? She'd roll some dough and make bread so long as she didn't have to leave the dough standing for half the day. She went and examined the packet of yeast. Leave standing for a cou-ple of hours. No problem. It would take that long to get the oven up to temperature. And at least she'd have a chance to warm up. Fire on, bread baked, what next? Garden. Vegetables for dinner, whatever went well with lamb chops. Then what? The boat. Obviously one of the boats on the mooring went with the house and was hers. Which one? Whichever one was least looked after. Her day stretched ahead like a never-ending adventure.

The boat was a major priority because it was her lifeline, her communication with the outside world and her shopping cart. It might also help her catch the odd fish and take her away on picnics. She made up her mind to wander down to the beach, if and when the rain stopped, and learn how to start the motor and steer. But first she had to do something about the Shacklock. Inactivity had made her cold despite the hot coffee and the heavy pullover she wore. She started to put Jean's foul-weather gear back on and reeled back at the smell. The upside was that the rain would wash off some of her vomit.

She knew Bernie would've had a stack of dry wood somewhere, but where? By the back door or under the veranda. Because the back door was on the high side, she realized there'd be nothing to store wood under and headed straight for the veranda. The rain seemed to have been saving its strength for her to set foot outside and crackled like machine-gun fire on her waterproofs. She peered into the gloom beneath the house and saw stacks of wood neatly split and sawed to length and kindling alongside. It all seemed so very easy until she picked up the first piece of wood and a large black spider shot across her hand. She screamed. The spider was heading up her sleeve to what it foolishly imagined was safety when Rosie banged her arm against a foundation post in fright. It was the spider's misfortune to run between arm and post at the precise moment of impact. Rosie looked at her wrist to make sure the spider had gone, saw it fixed there, immobile as if feasting on her blood, and screamed once more. She danced backward out into the rain, shaking her wrist, screaming, panicking, wondering at what point she was going to die. The rain washed the spider off.

She stood shaking, a quivering wet mess, and tried to collect her wits. The spider didn't look anywhere near as big dead as it had alive. But big or otherwise, she didn't want a repeat performance. From then on, she whacked every piece of wood she picked up against the stack of firewood. Not once, but half a dozen times. Satisfied that any self-respecting spider would have got the heck out of there, she picked up another piece. And another. And another. She filled her arms with as much wood as she could carry and staggered back up the steps and inside. She unloaded the wood into the box the supplies had occupied and took off Jean's coat and hat.

Bloody hell, she wondered, was this how things would always be? Did every simple thing have to turn into a drama? She thought she'd make a pot of tea and sit down while she recovered her breath and her confidence. But no! She looked grimly at the Shacklock. First things first, and the next cup of tea or coffee would be brewed on the stove top. Henceforth, she decided, the propane camp stove was out of bounds except for emergencies. She stuffed paper and kindling into the Shacklock's firebox, unscrewed the vent as far as it could go, reached for the matches and stared dumbstruck at the last remaining match. She realized the vital omission from Col's supplies. She fought back a wave of despair as she realized she'd have to go begging to Red for something as basic as matches. Red? Hang on. A man who'd left a potty under the bed would also make sure there were matches. She began opening cupboards and drawers. Bingo! There in the drawer next to the stove, not just a box of matches but almost an entire packet. She could have kissed him. She struck a match and held the flame to the paper, laughed out loud when she saw how much her hand still shook.

"Oh, Norma," she said. "If only you could see me now."

Angus had decided the day was good only for writing. That, as far as he was concerned, was also the best kind of day. He had a steaming mug of tea by his side, a head bursting with words and ideas, Bonnie curled up on his lap, doing her power-mower impressions, and Red nailed to a promise. The story of the boy who fought the fearsome griffin and saved the village was Angus's fourth book. Only the second and third had been published. The publishers had returned his first manuscript with regret, but not without complimenting him on his ability and the freshness of his style. They'd loved the character of Hamish, but found the first half of the story too dark and depressing. "Bleak" was the word they used to describe it. What had stunned Angus was that they thought the story of the boy who grew up in grinding poverty in a mud-and-stone crofter's hut was fiction.

Once Hamish sailed away to the Summer Isles in an abandoned dinghy, the young lad sprouted wings on his heels. This was the Hamish the publishers loved, and they encouraged Angus to concentrate future books on his adventures. They now regarded him as one of their foremost children's authors and paid him advances. Angus's happiness knew no bounds. Hamish, his courageous young hero, was making a name for himself and attracting a following both in New Zealand and the United Kingdom. All he had to do was keep the dark side out of his books. Not the frightening and gory bits, because he suspected his young audience liked those bits best of all. He mixed the blood and guts with humor, and laced his stories with morality and principles. Hamish was a lad any parent would be proud to call his own, and Angus was very proud.

He worked all morning, his typewriter competing with the drumming of the rain on his roof. The words came easily and the story flowed. Sometimes the boy seemed to take on a life all his own and surprised Angus with his courage and intelligence. These were the times he liked best. When his brain thought and his hands typed and he just went along for the ride. He filled page after page until he felt he'd filled enough for the morning. He'd done well, and there was no point in wearing himself out. It took him a moment or two to realize that the rain had stopped. He pulled the kettle across the top of the Stanley, put it on the hottest burner and strolled out onto his veranda. The wind had dropped and the misty clouds were slowly dragging themselves free from the treetops. The air had the earthy freshness that he savored. When he closed his eyes he could believe he was in Scotland. The sound of rainwater running off in little gullies reminded him of the myriad little streams that ran down off Mount Conneville after every storm, carving a pathway through the peat. He inhaled deeply and stretched his back and arms. Bonnie threaded through his legs, butting and rubbing. He gazed up toward the lower ridges, wondering how the woman was coping. Badly, he hoped. He was slow to recognize the wisp of smoke wafting blue through the mist, but once he did he knew instantly his worst fears had been realized.

"The bloody fool!" he shouted out loud, causing Bonnie to leap away in fright. The madman had done it! He'd lit the woman's fire. He clenched his fists in anger and damned Red for the soft fool he was.

Rain brought Red no respite. There were always things to do when there was the will to work. Red had both will and need. He sat on his veranda, patiently winding the Japanese longlines he'd recovered onto electrician's spools salvaged from a building site in Okiwi. He could only admire the monofilament the Japanese used. It was both finer and stronger than other monofilaments, and he had already witnessed its effectiveness. As he wound, he snipped the hooks off and dropped them into tins. There were thousands, all of which he had to rinse in fresh water, dry and dip in diesel so that they wouldn't rust. It was tedious work, but Red could not bear to throw anything away. In time everything had a use. He decided to leave the fourth line intact. He'd soaked newspaper and made little wads that he pinched over the barbs of each hook so they wouldn't snag on each other. Red took pride in his thoroughness and worked head down without a break. There was merit in work, and it helped him forget his promise to Rosie. He only looked up when Archie leaped to his feet and barked. He blushed with shame. It had to be Rosie coming to see why he hadn't lit her fire. Up on the railway, his promise had been his word when his word was all he had to give.

"You!" The contemptuous tone identified his caller. He breathed a sigh of relief as Angus emerged from the scrub.

"More words?"

"More words indeed, you bloody fool!"

"What have I done now?"

"Don't you play smart with me!" Angus stood at the foot of the veranda stairs, bristling with anger, holding his gnarled manuka walking stick as if he intended to bend it over Red's head. "Don't you take me for a fool. I'll not put up with that from the likes of you!"

"Angus, there's no need to shout."

"Let me be the judge of that! Admit it! You lit her bloody fire!"

"She's got her fire going?"

"Don't you play all innocent with me!"

"Angus, come up here."

"There's no need for that. I don't encourage familiarity."

"Come here."

Angus glared at Red but saw that the madman would not be moved. "If I must, I suppose I must!" Grudgingly he slipped off his clay-choked gum boots and plastic mac and climbed the few steps up onto the veranda. He looked around suspiciously.

"What do you see, Angus?"

"You know very well what I see!"

"Good. Then you can see what I've been doing all morning since I came up from the bay."

"Aye . . ." Angus looked at the miles of coiled lines and the cans of fishhooks. "Perhaps I was a wee bit hasty. But she has a fire burning! I've seen the smoke!"

"Angus, anyone can light a fire. She was probably cold."

"You haven't been there? Haven't given her any of your snapper?"

"I haven't been anywhere except to the boat." Both men stared off into the bush in the direction of Bernie's bach, neither knowing where the conversation might head next.

"Ah well, I'm sorry for intruding. I apologize. I'll be gone, then."

"I'm about to make some tea."

"I'll not stay."

"Would you like a smoked snapper or two? I have surplus."

"Aye . . . if that's the case, I'll not let them go to waste. Both Bonnie and I are partial to the smoked fish, and I admit a fondness for the kedgeree. Don't go giving them away to that woman, mind!"

"Angus, we've agreed."

"Aye, aye, we've agreed!"

Nine

The windows were steamed up, and Rosie had stripped down to shorts and T-shirt. Both front and back door were wide open, yet sweat trickled from every pore. Through trial and error, she'd finally got the hang of the Shacklock. She'd burned almost all the firewood she'd brought in, an unsustainable rate of consumption, and in the process boiled the kettle, heated enough water for a hot bath and turned the bach into a sauna. The trouble was, the idea of a hot bath had been usurped by the need for a cold shower. But she'd mastered the beast and learned how to control the rate of burn and the oven and the stove-top temperatures. She'd also learned how to bake bread, not just one humble loaf but two, big, hearty, round country-style cobs. She thought of taking one around to Red as a thank-you for picking her up and cleaning up the shack but thought better of it. If she'd understood Col correctly, rule one was look after yourself first and only share your surplus. She had no surplus. Half of one loaf was for now, the rest she divided into quarters for freezing. With a bit of luck she wouldn't have to bake any more bread until she returned for good.

She cut herself off a thick slice, spread it generously with butter and a veneer of honey and wandered out onto the veranda. The air tasted like water from a mountain stream, a pleasure she'd discovered on a skiing holiday. The sun hadn't broken through, but the clouds were lifting and sucking up wisps of mist from the trees and scrub.

Fantails, white-eyes and goldfinches chirped and flitted in the tight weave of bushes, relishing the end of the wind and rain. The punga palms seemed poised to stretch their monkey tails, and the nikau palms glistened. The world glowed squeaky clean. The only thing missing was a hard-earned cuppa.

She left her slice of bread on the veranda rail, and wandered inside to put the kettle back over the heat. By the time she wandered back outside she'd been gone for less than a minute. She paused, puzzled. Her bread had disappeared. She went back indoors to see if she'd taken it inside with her. She hadn't. She wandered back outside, wondering if she was going mad.

"Okay, Red," she said, as she seized on the obvious solution. "You win. Give me my lunch back." Silence. "Red! A joke's a bloody joke! Even a childish joke!" Silence. "I'll fix another slice for you." No answer. "Stuff you. You enjoy it. I'll make myself another." She went back inside, buttered another slice and spread it with honey. She poured her tea, wandered back outside and looked around. "If you want a cup of tea to go with my lunch, you can damn well pour your own." She put her new slice of bread down on the rail to take a sip of tea and immediately discovered who'd come calling. It wasn't Red, but a brazen pair of dusky green-brown parrots. "Bloody hell!" she cried. Her tea splashed into her saucer as she grabbed her bread, narrowly beating the birds. "Thanks, Bernie," she said.

The birds, who'd kept Bernie company and benefited from his handouts, waited patiently for the new Bernie to show similar generosity. She broke off a piece of bread and gently reached forward to put it down on the rail. One of the kakas fluttered onto her wrist and ripped the offering from her fingers. The other turned its head to the side as if looking for its share.

"Bloody hell," said Rosie, her heart thumping. "How about a bit of respect for a lady?" She broke off another piece and this time held still. The remaining bird flew onto her wrist, settled and calmly ate the bread out of her hand. "You cute thing." The bird looked up at her doubtfully. She began to chuckle. The kaka ignored her, finished its meal and took wing. She sat back on the veranda chair and sipped her tea. It felt like her whole body was smiling. The sun peeped through the clouds, bathing the palms and bushes, trees and ferns in crystal light. She'd forgotten how good it felt to be really happy.

She finished her tea and began an unhurried tour of inspection. There was no doubt that the half drum at the bottom of the lavatory pit needed raising and emptying or a new hole dug. This was one problem no amount of toilet cleaner could fix. She wondered how the precious ladies with their obsession with skid marks would cope, and smiled. They belonged in another world, one she hoped she'd left behind forever. She had no idea how to raise the drum or dispose of its contents and concluded that the toilet was best moved to another location and the hole filled in. But that raised its own set of problems. Digging a new hole and resiting the toilet was a formidable job, one that was way beyond her limited abilities. One way or another, she had to get help.

Her next stop was the laundry, a parched weatherboard shed with a rusting iron roof. Given that she had a generator, she hoped to find a washing machine inside. Nothing fancy, but one of the old round Whiteways with a wringer on top. Instead she found a concrete sink presided over by a single cold tap with a partially perished black rubber hose attached. The hose was just long enough to reach the copper boiler. Rosie groaned. Against the wall was a cut-down oar that Bernie had obviously used as a paddle to stir his washing, and a washboard. When she made a list of things she needed, her Bendix washing machine would sit at the top of it.

The rest of the washhouse was given over to a tangle of fishing lines, fishing rods covered in cobwebs, Alvey side-cast reels, and tins of oily hooks. There were rotted flippers and a brass-ringed face mask that belonged in a museum. An array of sinkers sat on the horizontal braces of the timber frame, along with three fishing knives in leather scabbards. She withdrew one of the knives from its sheath and examined it. She expected it to be blunt and rusty but was instantly proved wrong. The blade gleamed blackly with its light coating of oil and appeared razor sharp. She could see where the edges had been worked on. Yes, Rosie thought to herself, if a man was going to look after anything, that's probably what he'd look after. If only he'd put the effort into the toilet or painting the weatherboards.

The garden was her next stop. Its soil was rock hard, and the rains had carved channels between the lines of vegetables. It desperately needed fertilizing and a good digging over. But the quantity and variety of vegetables delighted her. She picked off the few snails and lobbed them into the scrub and began plucking the weeds. Bernie had also loved his garden, and she thought she'd soon get it back in order. She noticed the absence of broccoli and mentally added it to her list. Rotting windfall tree tomatoes, peaches, plums and nectarines testified to the productivity of her fruit trees. She wished she'd come earlier, when they were in season.

She wandered over to the shed housing the generator. It was in similar condition to the washhouse. A coat of paint and it would scrub up well. Inside she found Bernie's tools. All bore the blackish sheen of oil. Dusty step and extension ladders rested on the rafters. There were also six four-gallon tins of diesel, two of which were full and one half full. She remembered the jerry can she'd left on the beach and decided to make that her next job for the day.

When she stood back and looked critically at the shack, she realized a lot of its apparent disrepair was cosmetic. The old man had obviously let the place go as he'd become increasingly unwell or uninterested, but had done a reasonable maintenance job up until then. There were rusting buckets and old cans leaning against the walls. Old tools that would never again perform their function. An old pit saw from the days proud kauri trees were milled for their timber, broken kerosene lamps, bullock yokes. A beautiful old weathered anchor, largely made from wood and braced with iron, and what looked like a flensing knife salvaged from the ruins of the whaling station. All the anchor and flensing knife needed were time and love to become showpieces. The same was true of the bach. In truth it would never inspire poets, but a little love and a coat of paint would go a long way. Overall there were few grounds for dismay. All she had to do was make a list of the help she needed and give it to Col on her way back to Auckland to collect her things. She'd worked in business long enough to know how to solve problems. She made them someone else's.

Rosie was feeling very pleased with herself. Her slow-combustion

Shacklock was now working as it was supposed to. Nice and slowly. She'd baked bread and it had turned out fine. She took all the credit for this, denying any to the author of the recipe she'd followed to the letter. And she had the pleasure of an evening soak in a hot bath to look forward to. She might have forgotten some basics like matches and a torch, but she'd remembered to pack other essentials like her bath crystals, oils and talc, things men wouldn't even think to bring. She smiled. Men look after their toys, she looked after herself.

She put her bathing suit on under her shorts and shirt, grabbed her beach towel and a lamb chop for bait. She chose the best of the fishing rods and the sturdiest of the fishing knives. The rod was already rigged with a two-hook trace and two-ounce sinker. She felt like singing, adding her voice to the chorus of the birds around her, and couldn't immediately put her finger on the reason for the sheer joy welling up inside her. It wasn't just the feeling of being on holiday, it was something much more potent, something that seemed to originate in her soul. Then she realized. It was the feeling of being in control. Yes! Stuff Red and Angus McLeod. She didn't need them. She didn't need anybody. She could do without them just as she could do without her flatmates, her brothers and their wives, her father and the judge who took away the keys to her Volkswagen.

She passed by the old pohutukawas, absorbed in her thoughts until she burst into the clearing that fronted the beach. The brilliance of the sun on sand and water dazzled her. She couldn't help herself. She ran onto the sand, whooping like a child on a Sunday outing. Why not? The beach was deserted but for her jerry can. She stripped off her shorts and shirt and ran down to the water's edge. The water lapped around her ankles, cold but not yet forbidding. She stared at the two marine-ply half-cabins and tried to guess which one was hers. Both were roughly the same size, painted white with faded storm covers caked in seagull droppings. There was no way of telling which one belonged to her and which belonged to Angus. One had a faded red hull, the other dark blue. She decided to check out the closest, the red one, to see if there was anything on it that might identify its owner.

She swam out with her knife, lamb chop and fishing rod held

high, pulled herself up onto the duckboard and began to untie the storm cover. She straightened the flip clips and lifted the canvas so that she could climb into the boat. She saw a hollow cylinder screwed into the transom that looked a likely place to stow her fishing rod and did so. She peeled the rest of the storm cover back as far as the windshield and took a good look around. Two seats, storage pockets down the side, plenty of deck room and a roomy dry-storage area up front. But no indication of who the owner might be. No kilts or sporrans hanging up to dry. No Celtic or Glasgow Rangers stickers. No evidence that a Scot had ever been near it. She decided to bait her line while she continued her investigations and let the fish hook themselves. She replaced the rod in the rod holder, feeling very pleased with herself. There she was on her first full day, checking out her boat and fishing. Norma would never have believed it. She spotted a small striped towel draped over the instrument panel to protect it from the sun beaming in through the windscreen and recognized the pattern as similar to the ones Bernie had left behind. There was the identification she needed. She cast her eye around the boat once more, this time with an owner's pride, unaware that three hundred feet above her, set back from the beach on the second ridge, ex-Inspector Angus McLeod was once more going ballistic.

Rosie lay back on the deck, out of what little breeze there was, and let the autumn sun dry and warm her. Lying on her back, she could also keep an eye on the tip of her rod, which, unfortunately for her, showed every sign of remaining equally as relaxed. She slipped her shoulder straps over her arms, rolled her swimsuit down to her waist and, like a lizard, let the afternoon sun soak into her. She found it harder and harder to keep her eyes open.

"You!"

She sat bolt upright.

"You, you ignorant woman!"

She jumped to her feet. There not twenty feet away was a tiny rowboat.

"What do you think you're doing on my boat?" Angus pulled hard on his oars and glanced over his shoulder to judge his direction and distance. He saw Rosie standing there, her mouth a perfect O, her hands up to her cheeks and her two breasts staring him straight in the eye. "Dear God, woman! Make yourself decent." He turned his head back to face the shore. "You're as bad as the madman."

Rosie pulled her top up as quickly as she could.

"Here. Grab the painter and tie me off." Angus threw her a rope, which she wrapped round and around the stern cleat. "That's not how it's done. Do you not know anything?"

Rosie began to recover from her initial surprise, aided by the Scot's belligerence. She hated his kind and resented the implication in his voice and manner that all women were useless and incompetent, except in their proper place, which was the kitchen, or flat on their back with their legs apart. She felt the familiar rush of anger she'd hoped to leave behind in Auckland. Her eyes blazed. She opened with all guns.

"Listen, mister. One, don't you ever speak to me like that again. Two, don't you ever call me woman. Three, if I decide to tie your painter or whatever it is you call it off like this, I'll tie it off like this. Don't you presume to tell me how to do things on my boat. What are you doing?"

Angus stowed his oars and climbed onto the duckboard. He stepped over the transom and into the boat. "Now you listen here, woman. One, I'll address you any way I like. If you don't like it you can leave. Two, I don't give a tinker's cuss how you do things on your boat, but this is not your boat. It's mine. And I'll thank you to leave it immediately."

"Your boat?"

"Aye. My boat."

"But it's got one of Bernie's towels over the instrument panel. There are others that match up at the house."

"And others that match at mine. Where do you think you are, woman? There are no department stores here. If you need towels you buy them from Fitzroy, and this is the only pattern Col carries."

"Oh." Rosie thought of the cans of tomato soup and had no trouble following the logic.

"If you wish I'll row you ashore."

"Thanks. But I don't accept rides with strangers." Just as she reached for the fishing rod to wind it in, it doubled over. "Ohhh . . . a fish!" She tried to wind, but the fish was stronger and whipped the handle of the reel painfully across her fingers.

"Don't you go bringing that thing on board my boat! I've just cleaned it."

Rosie rested the heel of her hand against the reel as she'd seen her brothers do on family fishing trips, and gradually applied pressure. The reel slowed and stopped.

"I'm warning you."

"Drop dead."

"Don't you talk to me like that!"

"Why not, you old fraud? That's how you talk to me. Now belt up for a second." Rosie smiled inwardly at the shock on the old Scot's face. Obviously he wasn't used to people standing up to him. Another paper-thin bully. She pumped and wound, pumped and wound. Fortunately the fish's first run had tired it and it began to wallow from side to side. As soon as it broke the surface, Rosie dipped the tip of the rod and lifted it aboard. A good-sized snapper, at least a two-mealer. Rosie wanted to scream with excitement. She'd caught fish before but this was the first she'd caught all by herself. She decided she had to be matter-of-fact, as if she caught fish all the time. She grabbed the towel off the instrument panel and wrapped it around the wriggling fish to protect her hands from its fins.

"What on earth are you doing, woman? Who gave you permission to use my towel?"

"What's your problem? I hear you've got half a dozen more like it at home."

Again Angus was struck speechless. Rosie wrestled with the fish, not knowing quite what to do. There'd always been someone to take the hook out for her. The snapper held its mouth wide open so she could see the hook stuck deep in its throat. She grabbed hold of the hook's shaft and wrenched. The fish snapped its jaws shut.

"Arghhh . . ." She cried out in pain as its teeth closed around her fingers. She dropped the fish. Blood splattered onto the deck and up the sides.

"Look at the mess you're making!"

"Shut up and pass me my knife." She cut the line and tried to remember what her brothers did next to stop fish wriggling. She recalled seeing a piece of wood in one of the side pockets, pointed at one end with a dowel peg through the middle, and thick and solid at the other. Just the thing, she figured, to stun fish. She reached into the side pocket, withdrew the stick and belted the snapper over the head. She surprised herself with the strength of the blow. The gob-stick Angus had made to extract hooks stuck in the throats of fish broke in two.

"Now look what you've done!"

"I'm sorry," said Rosie helplessly. "I didn't know what else to use."

"Go. Get off my boat before you destroy anything else. Dear God, look at the mess you've made, you ignorant woman."

Rosie's right hand was free and she used it to slap the Scot's face. One of her boyfriends had been a boxer and had shown her how to set her feet and put her shoulder into the blow. It had the effect of knocking Angus flying into the side of the boat, very nearly toppling him overboard. "I warned you, you old bastard, don't call me woman." She threw her rod and the fish, still wrapped in the towel, into the dinghy, stepped over the transom and untied the painter. "Enjoy your swim. Might remind you how to treat a lady."

Angus rubbed the side of his face, which had already flamed angry red, and wondered what in the hell he'd run into. He dragged himself to his feet and watched her row his dinghy ashore. Her slap, he noticed drily, was a good deal more accomplished than her rowing. She pulled the boat up onto the sand, turned her back on him and walked away. He watched her go. Aye, he thought, the madman had warned him that she had spirit. Well, he'd soon fix that. He'd make it his business to. "Arrgh!" The discarded chop bone cut into his bare left foot. He hopped onto his right leg and tripped backward onto the engine housing. "You infernal woman!" he growled, but not so loud that she might hear. There was blood on his foot, and it wasn't hers or the fish's.

Rosie picked up the jerry can and was momentarily staggered by its weight. How could she possibly carry it all the way up the hill? She picked up her bath towel, and an idea slowly dawned on her. She'd shifted flats often enough to have seen how movers went about their business. She knotted the two ends of her towel together to make a loop, stood the jerry can in the middle of the towel at one end of the loop, squatted down on her haunches, then slipped the other end of the loop over her head. She folded the towel over so that it made a pad against her forehead. With both hands reaching behind her, she steadied the jerry can against her back and stood up. Easy. She bent forward to make sure her load was secure, and picked up her fishing rod, her snapper and her clothes and began the journey back up the hill.

She'd almost reached the fork to her house when she saw Red and Archie coming down the trail toward her. He stepped aside to let her pass.

"Thanks for showing me how to use the Shacklock." She paused when she was directly alongside him.

"I see you managed."

"No thanks to you."

"I was busy, Rosie."

"I'm sure you were. It's all go around here."

"Nice fish."

"Why don't you come around for dinner one night?"

Red paused, uncertain how to deal with the invitation. He couldn't accept, because that would clearly breach his agreement with the Scotsman. He didn't want to be rude so said the only thing he could think of. "Thank you."

"I was talking to Archie," said Rosie.

Red winced. He felt no anger or need to respond. The Aussies in Burma had employed the same mocking humor, and he'd learned that the best way to handle it was to laugh along. He watched her walk away up the hill, struggling under the load of the diesel. He felt strangely pleased that she'd worked out how to carry it. The *romusha*—the Asian laborers the Japanese pressed into work gangs—carried bags filled with rocks the same way, with the canvas strap across their foreheads. He walked on down the trail, his mind reaching across time and distance to Burma, and the endless lines of weary men no better than beasts of burden slowly snaking up the hill. He stopped, stunned, as soon as he set foot on the beach. There in front of him was a naked Angus, wading out of the water with his clothes held head high. Wash day at Aungganaung Camp.

"What are you staring at, man?"

Red dragged his mind back to the present. "What happened?"

"I ordered the harridan off my boat and she had the effrontery to slap my face. I've a mind to charge her with assault."

Red guessed the scenario. "Well," he said at length, "at least we've learned something."

"And what might that be, Mr. Clever Dick?"

"Rosie now knows which boat is hers, and you don't have to worry about me giving her fish. She can catch her own."

"We'll see about that! The battle's just begun. I'll not have that woman here, I'm telling you."

Red left the naked Scotsman fuming on the beach. He swam out to his boat and hauled himself up over the gunwale. The tide was dropping, and soon the tuatuas would be easy pickings in the shallows of Whangapoua Beach. Red had a passion for the big clamlike shellfish, steamed over fish rice mixed through with finely chopped chilies and shallots. The Straits Malays and Japanese guards had taught him how to cook in the camp kitchens back in Singapore, had beaten competence into him. The tuatua were plentiful and needed to be because it was impossible for him to keep whistling as he gathered them. As many went straight down his throat as went into his bucket.

As he cast off and motored out of the bay he found himself thinking about the woman once more. She'd burst into their lives with the subtlety of an exploding shell and in the course of a single day had upset the order of things. She'd brought Angus to Red's door, an event so rare as to be almost unthinkable, and had turned the old Scot incandescent with rage. Red had passed her on the trail when he was unaccustomed to sharing the path with anyone or anything except Archie and occasionally Bernie. It was abundantly clear that there'd be no escaping her if she chose to stay, yet the prospect failed to alarm him to the extent that he expected it to. But concerns still nagged. The troubles of the night were still fresh in his mind, and the way she intruded unbidden and unwelcome into his thoughts. She created tension, and tension was an old and implacable enemy, waiting to swallow him up the instant he weakened. He had to acknowledge the fact. Nevertheless, he began to wonder if he could adjust to her as he had adjusted to the arrival of the Scot, always provided she kept her distance. It was early days, but he was tempted to give her a chance.

"Well, Archie, what do you make of her?"

Archie looked up into his master's face and wagged his tail furiously.

Rosie lay back in her bath hardly daring to breathe. The water was scaldingly hot, and her every little movement seemed to make it hotter. She let waves of bliss and contentment wash over her. She was under no illusions about the difficulties that lay ahead, the repairs she'd have to make and the task of moving her things over from Auckland. How, she wondered, would she ever get her Bendix Gyramatic up the hill? And her potter's wheel? She'd also need her Hoover Constellation vacuum cleaner if she brought her kelim rugs, and there was no way she was going to leave them behind. Neither would she leave her queen-size bed behind. It would occupy most of her bedroom but, she rationalized, that's what bedrooms were for. She let her mind wander over her decorating options as the hot water and bath salts soothed her tired muscles and made a woman once more of the pioneer. She was halfway through contemplating the removal of the Laminex countertops and the resanding of the kauri beneath, when she heard a knock at her door.

"What the hell?" she said, angrily. She couldn't believe it! There was always someone or something to spoil her bath. When she was a girl it was usually her brothers wanting to clean their teeth and brush up on their knowledge of anatomy. Then it was her flatmates with motives as transparent as her bathwater. Why did the whole world want to interrupt her one passion in life?

"Who is it?" she barked.

"It's Red. I've brought you some tuatuas." Angus hadn't said anything about not giving Rosie the clamlike tuatuas. "I'll leave them in a bucket by your door."

"That's very kind of you. What's the big occasion?"

"I've more than I need."

"Oh. Thanks anyway. I thought they might've been your way of saying sorry for not helping me with the Shacklock. You know, like flowers?" She listened for a response but there was none. Red had already gone. All she could hear were the lonely sounds she was becoming accustomed to. The murmur of wind in the trees up on the ridge, the rattle of her downspout, the scratch of tea tree on windowpane, and every so often the soulful, mourning cry of the mopoke owl. She couldn't help but wonder if this was really all the company she wanted for the rest of her life.

BOOK TWO

BOOK TWO

Ten

~~~~~~~~~~

A nother day. Red woke at first light as he always did, convinced as always that he should be dead and ashamed that he wasn't. The woman had gone, and he lapsed back into his routine, grateful for its comfort and predictability. He'd begun to set aside stores against the winter days when his garden lay fallow and the seas were too rough to put out. His fear of hunger, of failing in his commitment to survive always led him to overstock, yet on this occasion he exceeded even his usual caution. It never occurred to him to question why. He filled his freezer with fresh fish, smoked fish and tubs of oily fish stock. In the cool and dark of his shed, potatoes, onions, apples and kumara— sweet potatoes—were piled high on vegetable racks. His kitchen cupboards groaned under the weight of preserves; cotton bags of sun-dried carrots, peas, beans and corn; and the inevitable bags of Thai rice. Red was a man who could survive on a handful of rice a day, yet he'd put aside enough food to see him through a long Russian winter. In truth, he'd set aside more than enough food for two.

Once he'd completed his morning duties, Red put his noon rations in his canvas shoulder bag, grabbed his slashing tools and set off with Archie up the ridge toward Tataweka Hill to honor his commitment to the lieutenant commander. Rosie had come and gone, and he no longer expected to see her again. But she had not yet gone entirely from his mind.

·   ·   ·

Angus was as happy as he'd ever been. Every day the woman failed to reappear hardened his conviction that they'd seen the last of her. A full month had passed since Red had taken her back to Fitzroy, and there'd been no word from her since. He'd stopped panicking every time Red called by to give him surplus vegetables or fish, stopped fearing he'd bring news of her return. But the madman had held the line and kept to the bargain they'd made. The fool was obsessed by the need to give, yet it appeared the woman had not been a beneficiary. Angus took full credit for that. If Red had started running after her, giving her fish and fixing this and that, the creature would still be living up at Bernie's. But the woman was gone, and so was the fear of old hopes rekindled. Doubtless she'd renewed her acquaintance with the soft life of Auckland and come to her senses. Angus was convinced she'd not trouble them again with her presence.

Life slipped back into a familiar routine, and it was even possible to believe that the woman had never come. Once again he could accept that the boy who'd saved his village from the fierce griffin would be the only son he'd ever have, and he was content with that. As content as he could ever be.

He was considering a change of pace for his next story, moving the setting from Britain to New Zealand. He had an idea that involved having his young hero, Hamish, be the lone survivor of a shipwreck and wash ashore on an island not entirely unlike Great Barrier. He thought there might be two Maori tribes sharing the island, one friendly and the other warlike. Hamish would be the only *pakeha*— non-Maori—and, through a series of adventures in which he would demonstrate the superiority of Western civilization and the virtue of a Christian upbringing, bring peace between the two tribes, end cannibalism, convert them to the faith and have them unanimously appoint him their sole ruler. Angus thought he knew a lot about Maoris, though there wasn't a Maori in the country who'd agree with him.

Only one cloud darkened his horizon. Red had begun to hack a path westward along the ridge top toward the Tataweka trail, a bushwalkers' track which ran from Whangapoua Beach over the headland and up to the peak of Tataweka Hill. The madman claimed he was doing it so that he could spy on Japanese trawlers. Angus had tried to dissuade him on the grounds that if Red could get through to the bushwalkers' track, bushwalkers could also get through to Wreck Bay. What privacy would they have then? But the man had refused to listen. He'd taken upon himself the notion that he needed to spy on Japanese trawlers and refused to give an inch. Angus had damned Red for the fool he was and stormed off.

Angus wandered out onto his veranda and listened for the telltale slashing sound of Red's parang. The day had dawned still and lifeless, neither overcast nor clear, neither warm nor cool. If the early birds had bothered to rise they hadn't felt the urge to announce the fact. Down in the bay the water contrived to make a perfect mirror image of the hills above. Gulls sat on the surface like a flotilla of decoy ducks. It seemed as though nature was conserving its energies for the winter storms ahead. Angus didn't mind because they made his little haven seem all the more like Scotland. The winter storms reminded him of the Minch, the icy waters between his birthplace and the Summer Isles, lifeblood and all too often tomb of the men who fished for the herring, pollock and salmon trout. As a boy, Angus had once complained of the cold when the icy wind came in off the sea, howling and whistling through the cracks and crevices in the stone walls of their croft, bringing a dusting of snow and making little icicles on his blanket. His father had scorned him for his softness and told him to thank the Lord that he wasn't at sea.

In the garden below, Bonnie sniffed the remains of a feral cat that had come calling, and which had kept her inside until Angus had put a bullet into its head. Angus looked over the calm water and made his decision. The needs of the tomcat had been a sore reminder of his own. He had an urge as old as mankind itself. Ten miles down the east coast at Awana Bay there was a woman, a widow and fellow Scot, who ran a small farm. She had orange trees that locals claimed had been grown from the seeds of oranges thrown into the water when the *Wairarapa* went down off Miners Head. It had taken fifty years and a number of grafts for the trees to bear fruit, and since then there'd rarely been a time when the branches weren't heavy with oranges. They made the finest marmalade Angus had ever tasted. There was also a proud oak tree on the property, brought to Great Barrier by an early settler who wanted a reminder of home. Just looking at the tree brought joy to Angus's heart. In his mind the oak was a proper tree, broad and broad of leaf, pale green and vibrant, so unlike the New Zealand native trees. But the oak and the marmalade weren't sufficient in themselves to induce Angus to make the long trip. There was the widow, Mrs. Fiona Campbell from Aberdeen, whose husband had succumbed to cancer. She was the reason he went and stayed overnight. He counted his blessings as he bathed and dressed, left food and water for Bonnie and the door open so she could come and go. Rosie had gone, and his publishers had accepted another manuscript. Angus was a happy man as he strolled down to his boat, with a happy time ahead of him.

Up on the ridge, Red heard the half-cabin cough into life and watched as it putt-putted out of the bay and out of sight around Bernie's Head. He knew exactly where the Scot was headed and why. Both Angus and Fiona Campbell were as discreet as two people could be, and her farm was tucked away in a valley on its own, but Angus could not hide his boat, nor conceal his destination nor the duration of his stay. It didn't take long for someone to put two and two together and pass the word. Nobody minded that two lonely people occasionally took comfort in each other's arms. On the contrary, it gave folk something to talk about, and most speculation centered on whether the widow Campbell would one day get Angus to walk with her down the aisle. She was a warm and generous woman who enjoyed company and a good laugh. And she needed a man to help her run the farm. Everyone who knew her hoped she'd succeed. Everyone who knew Angus hoped for her sake that she wouldn't.

Red made a mental note to drop by and keep Bonnie company so that she wouldn't fret, and once more began to chop away at his path. The track didn't need to be anything fancy, just negotiable in the dark. He had an axe, bush saw and a parang, but worked mainly with the parang. That was another legacy of Burma. He'd never even seen a parang until they'd sent him up to work on the railway, and now he couldn't imagine ever being without one. He kept it razor sharp, and in his hand it was lethal. He always slashed diagonally, going with the grain never across it, so that he didn't rob the blade of its edge. The *romusha* had taught him that, too.

He wore his digger's hat, shorts and a football jersey for protection from the scrub, but the greatest luxury was his work boots. Like most of the men on the railway he'd suffered from "happy feet," and had taken meticulous care of his feet ever since, drying them carefully and disinfecting every cut and scratch. He'd seen men beaten senseless for failing to haul their day's quota of fill simply because their feet had let them down. The guards had made them carry extra the following day or face another beating. It was a prospect that had brought hard men to tears. Red had been one of them, but Archie had helped him out. He'd always been able to rely on Archie.

He found his thoughts trespassing into dangerous territory and increased his work rate. His parang flashed in the weak autumn light. Work kept the nightmares at bay. Work stopped him thinking. The constant westerlies had deformed and twisted the manuka and kanuka on even the lower ridges so that their heads leaned away to the lee, exposing their trunks and inviting execution. Red slashed relentlessly, hacking, chopping, clearing away, till his mind emptied and his shirt clung wetly to his body.

"*Yasume,* Archie," he called. Rest time. He eased his parang into its scabbard, which he'd fashioned out of two slats of wood bound tightly together with string. He dropped down below the lip of the ridge and found a rock to sit on that was sheltered from the wind and gave him a view over the ocean and the entrance to the bay. He opened his water bottle, poured a half inch into the plastic bowl he'd brought for the dog, then took a long pull on the bottle himself. He reached into his canvas work bag for the two buckwheat pancakes, both of which wore a thin Vegemite varnish. He gave one to Archie and ate the other. His eyes swept the horizon for any sign of foreign fishing boats but saw nothing. Even if he had, there was nothing he could do about it until they sent him his radio.

He looked for other things to occupy his mind and deny Rosie entry, but to no avail. She was never far away, waiting patiently for him to rest and drop his guard. There was no point in thinking about her.

She'd come and gone and that was all there was to it. Yet she'd made an impression on him. She'd done well in surviving her fortnight at Wreck Bay, despite receiving next to no help from him and none at all from Angus. She'd cleared away the rubbish around Bernie's shack, dragged it to a little tip out of sight and mind. She'd dug over her garden. Found some creosote and coated the outhouse and generator shed. She'd felled dead trees and sawed them up for firewood. In fact, when he'd checked Bernie's shack after she'd gone, he'd discovered that she'd replaced all the firewood she'd used. She'd caught fish to feed herself and hadn't once come begging or borrowing. But what had both frightened and impressed him was the fact that she'd made plans. Plans to fix the old shack up. Plans to make pottery. Plans to live at Wreck Bay, where no woman in her right mind would consider living. Red had had to concede that Rosie was the type who would have done well in Burma. So long as she kept to herself, she could do okay at Wreck Bay. But she'd gone and that was that.

When Rosie had told Red her plans on the run back around to Fitzroy, he'd believed everything she'd said. He'd believed her when she said she was coming back. She'd even named a date, one that had passed two weeks earlier. In the end she didn't have what it took. He wasn't sure whether he was relieved or disappointed, not so much for himself but for her. He shook his head to clear her from his thoughts. It was time to resume battle with the scrub. At least, her change of heart had made the Scotsman a happy man. Archie barked as he rose to his feet.

"What's up? Found a rabbit?"

But Archie wasn't sniffing the ground or pointing at any suspicious shapes in the underbrush. He was gazing straight out to sea. He barked again. Red turned, puzzled. He gazed out toward the horizon, scanned left then right. Nothing. Unless Archie had spotted a whale or submarine surfacing, there couldn't be anything out there or Red would have noticed it before. He looked down at Archie. He was still gazing out to sea. No! Not out to sea. Lower. Down at the bay. Red glanced down but was too late. All he could see was a broad wake rippling and expanding on the water beneath him. Whatever had made it had passed by out of sight behind the lower ridge. A boat, a

120

large one at that, had crept down the coast, hugging the shoreline, and sneaked into the bay.

His anger flared, sudden and violent. He grabbed his work bag and his tools and set off back down the trail. Archie raced on ahead of him. He dropped off his bag, axe and saw on his veranda steps but kept hold of his parang. He called Archie to heel. His parang rattled in its wooden scabbard as he ran down the track, crossing from side to side to avoid tripping on roots and tea-tree stumps. Foreign fishing boat or locals? It didn't matter. He didn't let anybody fish Wreck Bay, and he was prepared to enforce his embargo with all the means at his disposal. Perhaps it was a foreign boat coming in to net bait fish. Or a mainland crayfish boat. He would allow neither. And nor would he give the crew a chance to ransack his boat or Angus's cabin. Similar things had happened farther down the coast.

He heard an anchor chain, loud in the still air, and strained his ears to hear voices, trying to determine whether the intruders were foreigners or from the mainland. He heard commands but they were soon swallowed beneath the rumble of a straining diesel as the vessel backed off the chain to set the anchor. Just short of the beach he cut off the track into the bushes to work his way through to the sand. The trail entrance was obvious and that was where they'd be watching. He dropped to his hands and knees, knowing it was easier, quicker and quieter to crawl beneath the spread of the bushes and ferns than to force a path through them. His heart pounded from exertion and apprehension, and from memories of stealing out of camp to trade illegally with the Burmese for food. Archie crawled along behind him, tummy touching the ground, growling softly. Red felt the sand beneath his hands, drew his parang and raised his head to peer through the silver-fern screen above the edge of the dune. He recognized the boat immediately, collapsed back on his elbows and called Archie up alongside to take a look. He didn't know what to feel or how to react. It was the Barrier's lifeline, the scow *Rahiri,* and it had a punt-shaped barge tied alongside it. Red stood, finally, and walked out into the open and onto the beach. The little outboard-powered barge was perfect for bringing ashore a Bendix Gyramatic and a potter's wheel.

Red held his ground, but Archie raced down the beach to greet Rosie as the barge butted up against the shore. The dog ignored the burly men she'd brought with her to haul her things up the hill, and danced in circles around her, barking madly.

"Hello, Archie." She reached down and ruffled the dog's ears. She looked up at Red. "What a welcome. Almost every man and his dog's here."

"Hello, Rosie. I thought you weren't coming back."

"Thought or hoped?"

The four men Rosie had hired stood by grinning, waiting to see Red's reaction. They were all Barrier men and knew Red or at least knew of him. If he welcomed her there'd be a little more spice to feed into the bush telegraph.

"I'll give you a hand."

"Thank you, Red."

The men howled and whistled. Rosie was a good-looking lady, which, in their eyes, made Red a lucky man. It would never occur to them that it was possible to have a relationship with a woman other than the kind they fancied for themselves. Or that Red didn't want a relationship with any woman regardless of how good-looking she was. They could hardly wait to get back to their homes scattered down the west coast and spread the news. Rosie turned to them.

"Would you blokes get your minds back on the job? The skipper wants to get back to Fitzroy tonight, and I want all my stuff in my home."

The four men lifted their heads simultaneously to look at the challenge ahead of them. They'd known when they'd accepted the job that they'd have to earn their money, but the steepness of the hill and the narrowness of the trail still came as unpleasant confirmation. Two Maoris from Katherine Bay, with short, stocky arms and bodies like house bricks, slipped their canvas harness beneath the Bendix and over their shoulders.

"I'll go on ahead and clear the path."

"Thanks, Red. I'll come with you so I can show these blokes where to put things. Where's Angus?"

"He's gone down to Awana. Went this morning."

122

"Widow's lucky day?"

"You know about her?"

"Jean told me."

Red shook his head as he wondered if there was anybody on the Barrier who didn't know what everyone else was doing.

"How often does he go to see her?"

"Two, maybe three times a year."

"Drought-breakers, eh? What about you, Red?" She arched her head mischievously so that she looked right into his face.

"Me? I've never even met the woman."

The little barge punted backward and forward from ship to shore as the wind freshened and brought the threat of rain, hurried on by the anxious skipper at one end and an equally anxious Rosie at the other. Red volunteered to help carry her possessions up the hill so that the men could take turns to rest without the process grinding to a halt. He worked willingly and without guilt, because it was clear he and Angus had failed miserably in their efforts to dissuade Rosie from returning, and because it was the right thing to do. He set her potter's wheel down in the corner of her veranda, and promised to help secure it there later.

He returned to the beach and joined the others as they made a conga line up the hill, each man carrying half a dozen fireproof bricks for her kiln. He should have known better. It was a mistake, the sort of mistake he'd made before and was powerless to prevent recurring. He automatically fell into step with the man in front as he'd done a thousand times before in another country, in another time. He began to worry that they weren't going fast enough, overtook the man in front, then the next and the next, head down, urging them on, setting the example. New men had to know what was expected of them. There was a *speedo* on. Didn't they know? Hadn't they realized? "*Speedo! Speedo!*" he shouted. The men reacted, partly from surprise and partly because they didn't want to be shown up, totally unaware of the demons that had begun to emerge and drive Red on.

To a man treated as a beast of burden, there was little difference between carrying bricks and carrying ballast. Red's mind had instantly made the connection and begun to flash back to the chain of broken, weary men, of their despair every time the Japanese raised the quota they had to carry, of the beatings and punishments when men's spirits and bodies let them down. Anger, fear and desperation pushed him on to work harder, part of him trying to fight off the memories, part of him lost in them. He lapsed into the prisoner's fear-filled plod, eyes fixed on the trail immediately ahead of him, step after endless step, pushing his body to an effort that was beyond it, praying that the guards would find some other back to bend their bamboo rods across. Sweat ran from his body in rivers, his breath rasped, his eyes glazed. *"Speedo! Speedo!"* The men gave up trying to keep up with him. He became an automaton, a human packhorse spurred on by threat of torture and death.

Rosie caught the look of anguish on his face as he dumped his bricks and turned blindly back down the trail. Without hesitating, she dropped the suitcase she was carrying, grabbed him and dragged him by the hand up onto her veranda. She forced him to sit.

"Hell's bells, Red, what do you think you're doing?"

Sweat glazed his body, and he shrank back from her. He answered her in Japanese and tried to get back on his feet. She grabbed his shoulders and peered into his unfocused eyes. Captain Ladd had called Red's look the thousand-yard stare. He was wrong. It was more like a thousand miles. "Red, look at me!"

Red looked but all he saw was Archie and his namesake. Archie couldn't help him this time. He reached out to his friend one last time before the hot bullet tore through flesh and bone and death swallowed him up.

"Don't worry, miss." One of the Maoris was looking up at them. "Red goes funny sometimes. I seen him do that before, eh? At Port Fitzroy. He'll be okay."

"Thanks." She nodded to the Maori, who wandered off back down the trail. But things were clearly not okay. She tried to remember what her father did and what she'd been taught. She recalled how her father used to distract his patients to force them to abandon the world inside their heads. Once he'd stunned her by producing a pistol and waving it backward and forward in front of the eyes of a returned soldier who was lost in wartime nightmares. The man's eyes had immediately locked onto the pistol and followed it wherever it was waved. As the patient's ravings and tremors had begun to ease, her father had put the pistol down on the table and just moved his hand instead. The patient's eyes had flickered backward and forward, not missing a beat, as her father had begun talking to him. He'd told the patient to take deep breaths, and the ex-soldier had instantly obeyed. In minutes her father had calmed a man who'd seemed beyond reach and had brought him back, shaken but approaching normality. Rosie had been impressed. Typically, her father had dismissed it all as "pure theatrics and mumbo jumbo, the self-hypnosis of a feeble mind." His arrogance had appalled her. Rosie had wondered angrily just whose mind was feeble.

She picked up the parang and tried moving it in front of Red's face. He shrank away from her in fear. Wrong move. She put her hand in front of his eyes and moved it rapidly from side to side. His eyes focused and locked on. "It's rest time, Red. Rest time."

"*Yasume . . .*" he said feebly.

Yasume? Rosie hadn't a clue what *yasume* was but thought it worth a try. "Yes, Red, *yasume. Yasume. Yasume,* Red. *Yasume.*" She repeated the word over and over as her hand moved rapidly from side to side.

"*Yasume?*" Red shook his head and began to sit up. She stopped waving her hand in front of him.

"Jesus Christ, Red. Where have you been?" She looked anxiously into his eyes, put her arm around his shoulders and her hand on his forehead.

"Sorry, Arch."

"It's okay, Red, okay. I'll get you some water." She rose and went into her kitchen, her mind reeling. So Archie was not just a dog. What did that mean? Oh, Christ! Her return to Wreck Bay had begun better than she'd hoped. Perhaps her welcome hadn't been the warmest, but it hadn't been frosty, either. Red had accepted her, which was a vast improvement on her previous arrival. Now this. Christ! The man sure picked a good time to go off into orbit. When she took a glass of water back out to him he was gone, and Archie with him.

•   •   •

Rosie was tempted to drop everything and look for him. He needed help and she wanted to help, though it was moot whether she was responding to her training as a doctor and psychologist, or as a woman. In mitigation, she had little opportunity to consider her motives, because she had more urgent things to attend to. The men carting her things up the hill needed her to tell them where everything went, where to stack her gallon cans of paint, where to put the tea chests with her crockery, her pots and pans, her cleaning liquids. As she paused to make sense of some unidentified boxes she heard someone slashing scrub up high on the ridge. The man had his problems and his own peculiar way of dealing with them. She looked up toward the sound and felt an unfamiliar and disturbing emotion building inside her.

"You poor bastard," she said, barely audibly but with all her heart. Her eyes began to water, which was ridiculous. She didn't cry over men.

Gradually all of her prized possessions, her bed, her sofa and her precious plastic-wrapped kelims made it ashore and up the hill, along with lengths of new, copper guttering and downspouts. She thanked each of the men and gave them the money she'd promised, plus a bit extra as an inducement against the day she might need their services again. They refused her offer of coffee and biscuits, saying the skipper was anxious to get back to Port Fitzroy before the storm broke and settled in. It looked like settling in for days, they said. She waved farewell and turned her attention to the mess around her. The place was in turmoil. There were cartons and boxes everywhere, and strips of packing strewn all over the floor. But these were the things she'd longed for during her two-week trial, things that would transform her bach not just into her home, but into a little piece of heaven on earth. Her kettle and tea caddy were where she'd left them, and a relaxing cup of tea beckoned. It seemed the perfect starting point to the business of unpacking.

She made tea and walked back out onto her veranda to enjoy the last of the afternoon light. A tui called out in warning, but there was no sound from Red's parang. Instead she heard a far-off roaring, almost like heavy traffic or a distant train coming closer and closer, yet she knew it could be neither. She cocked her head in puzzlement. The roaring increased and suddenly accelerated toward her. Almost

126

too late she realized what was happening and raced for the door. The storm had arrived.

The rain slammed into the windows just as Rosie managed to close them. The wind drove in hard over the ridges, deflected upward, then bore down in gusts that shook her shack to its foundations. Tea trees whipped into the eaves and battered windowpanes. The temperature plummeted. Rosie wished she'd lit the Shacklock while she'd had the chance, but how could she have known? She didn't fancy going outside and crawling under the veranda for firewood, but what choice did she have? No firewood meant no heat and no hot water. No hot water meant no bath, and never had a bath been more deserved. Where, she wondered as she surveyed the mess of cartons, bags and boxes, had she packed her new foul-weather gear? She had no choice but to do things Red's way. She stripped off and dashed outside, down the veranda steps and into the teeth of the gale. Icy rain drenched her in seconds, but it didn't matter. She dipped under the house and grabbed an armful of firewood without giving spiders a second thought. The rain caught her again as she made the dash back inside. It flattened her hair against her scalp and ran in rivers down her body. She dropped the wood in a heap in front of the old stove and fell back shivering onto the floor. She hadn't run naked in the rain since the wild weekends of her student days, and here there was no one to frown or disapprove. It was her moment of liberation as she realized that henceforth she could do whatever she liked. She wanted to shout and scream and whoop for sheer joy, and would've if she hadn't been so cold. She grabbed a bath towel out of the airing cupboard and wrapped it around her, stuffed paper into the firebox and broke boxwood over her knee for kindling. Her shaking hand held a match to the paper, and immediately the flame radiated warmth back to her. She snuggled deeper into her towel and fed more splintered boxwood to the fire. Hot tea, warm towel, a fire and a house of her own. No more crappy jobs, lousy flats, or lost life going nowhere.

"Let 'er rip, Huey!" she shouted, and laughed as another gust slammed into her little home in response. "I'm back, you hear me? I'm back and back for good!" A thousand drummers beat a welcome on her roof.

Eleven

"Angus is not back."

Rosie looked up from chopping vegetables to the silhouette framed in the doorway, and smiled. She'd wondered how long it would take Red to find a reason to visit.

"You all right?"

"Yes. Why?"

Why? The absurdity of his response overwhelmed her. The day before he'd been a shivering, jabbering idiot, a man in as much need of help as any patient she'd ever attended.

"You did leave rather abruptly yesterday."

"Had work to do."

"Yes, I heard you." She looked at him doubtfully. "Come on in."

"No thanks, Rosie. We'll drip everywhere."

"Okay, I'll come out." She joined him on the veranda and gave him a quick once-over. He looked pretty much as she remembered him from her first visit, distant, almost vacant, with no sign of the previous day's troubles. "Nice look."

Red had a way of dressing she'd never encountered before. Plastic yellow foul-weather hat and a green-slicked, oilskin coat that fell to mid calf. Over a football jersey, shorts and rubber thongs.

"Angus is not back."

"So you said."

"I have to go look for him."

"Oh come on, Red. Maybe Angus and the widow have a lot to talk about." She smiled mischievously. "Or not, whatever the case may be."

"No. He never stays longer than one night. He wouldn't leave Bonnie."

"Have you been down to check on her?"

"Last evening and this morning."

"Well, there you go. Angus knows you'd look after her if he decided to stay over an extra night."

"No, Rosie. That would make Angus beholden to me. He'd never allow that."

"Beholden?"

"That's what Angus says. He says he'll not be beholden. . . ."

"I get the picture. What do you want me to do?"

"Feed Bonnie." He pulled a plastic bag out of his pocket. There were pieces of chopped-up fish in the bottom. "Could you go down this evening and keep her company for a while?"

"Okay, Red. Nice to know I can be useful around here." She watched for a reaction but the irony was lost on him. Red was set upon finding Angus and nothing would distract him. "Look after yourself, and don't go peeping through any bedroom windows. People might misinterpret your intentions. But if you do, take a camera." She smiled wickedly, but her attempt at humor also failed. Red's mind was focused on the fact that Angus was missing and was reluctant to acknowledge anything else. Rosie had seen similar single-mindedness before in people suffering from nervous breakdowns, and she knew enough not to delay him any longer. He was already beginning to fidget. She glanced out of the main windows, hoping that the rain had let up. The wind had settled to a steady fifteen to twenty knots, but the rain was constant. "Before you go, Red . . . I'm making a vegetable soup. Drop by when you get back."

Red stood awkwardly for a moment, not sure what the appropriate response should be. They'd done that in Burma, of course, kept soup for men who worked late filling their quota. It had precious little vegetable or anything else in it. They called it white death after the white melon added as filling. Lord knows what it filled, but it certainly didn't fill their stomachs.

"Red? Hello?"

"We'll see," he said. "First I have to find Angus." He turned away.

Rosie watched Red and Archie until they were swallowed by the scrub. She couldn't help wondering whether Angus would show the same concern for Red if the situation were reversed. She doubted it. She doubted it very much. Sooner or later someone had to bring the cantankerous bastard around and remind him that he was still a member of the human race and of the courtesies that entailed. She figured she might as well make a start by taking him some soup in a pot when she went to feed Bonnie. Sort of a peace offering. She went back inside as another gust of wind shook the house. The last place she wanted to be right then was out in an open boat. Maybe Angus felt the same way. Maybe he was waiting for the weather to ease. That's what any sane person would do. But then, as she had to remind herself, sanity was one criterion that didn't always apply on the Barrier.

Once he'd cleared the bay, Red hugged the shoreline to shelter from the wind. A curtain of rain cut his visibility to two hundred yards whichever way he looked. Archie stood on his hind legs, front paws on the bow deck, trying to pierce the gloom, relieved to be outside and off his mat. A light swell rolled in lethargically to meet waves diminished in the lee and flattened by the weight of the rain. Red rounded Waikaro Point and cut in close along Whangapoua Beach, certain that Angus would follow a similar route northward. The wind hit him broadside-on as he knew it would once he passed in front of the flats. Windblown sand mixed with rain attacked him almost horizontally. Archie ducked down into his favorite spot below the foredeck. The marshlands that stretched behind the beach reached halfway across to Katherine Bay, enabling the winds to bear down and gather momentum before they reached the sea. Even so, Red reasoned that Angus would have stayed in close and clear of the heavy chop out wide.

Red knew the weather wasn't bad enough to deter Angus from returning. Had it been a nor'easter, that would have been a different story. But Angus was canny with boats and read the sea and weather well. Something must have happened. Red turned his boat southeast and gained the protection of the southern headlands. Archie resumed his station as bow lookout, watching for the swirls that marked barely submerged rocks. Red moved in closer to the shore and away from the fluky gusts that occasionally whipped in over the cliff tops. He spotted a float bobbing in the water ahead. And another. And another. He cursed the fisherman who'd laid the crayfish traps, obviously a novice who couldn't read the weather, or one of the Tryphena mob who just didn't care. But whoever had laid the traps had been busy. There were dozens of them in Indian file, stretching down the coast, new ones bobbing into view as others slipped by. Red cursed again and moved farther out to sea. He was tempted to stop, haul in the traps and set their occupants free as he'd done many times before. No one had a right to set so many traps in such a small area. There was no way the crayfish could survive that sort of overfishing. He slowed momentarily, remembered what he'd set out to do and once more picked up speed. Bastards, he thought to himself, they were as bad as the Japs.

He passed inside Arid Island and prepared to meet the rough seas as he rounded the next headland for the run down toward Awana Bay and the widow's farm. Ahead of him a jagged line of rough water reached out from the point, forcing him wide to gain sea room. Spotting floats was hard enough in the calmer water and near impossible in the chop. Archie barked just as he swung the helm. Red turned to see where Archie was looking, in case the dog had spotted a float he'd missed. But the dog was looking inshore toward the point, where the exposed water met the calmer water. Moreover, he was wagging his tail.

Red brought the bow back around toward shore and peered into the driving rain. He saw it, lost it, saw it again, a dark, faintly red shape barely discernible against the shadows of the cliffs.

"Well done, Archie!" Red knew instantly what had happened. Angus had motored in close to get the protection of the cliff and fouled his prop on crayfish floats. He slowed so he could scour the water ahead of him. The last thing they needed was two immobilized boats.

"Ahoy, Angus!" The Scot's head appeared above the roof of the half-cabin.

"Aye, it's you. Thought you'd come." He coiled a rope to throw to Red so that he could raft up. Red swung astern, steadied, threw his bumpers over the side to protect his paint, and tied off. The two boats rocked and bumped disconcertingly in the chop.

"Been over to take a look?"

"Aye, but it's way too rough for me." He turned his hands over so that Red could see the cuts and bruises on the backs of them. "I used the bandages in the first-aid kit on my forehead." Red looked closely and saw a white strip peeking out below Angus's rain hat. "It'll not stay still one second, the propeller."

"I'll have a look."

"Aye. I'd be grateful if you would."

Red stripped off, stowed his clothes in the forward compartment, grabbed his knife, face mask and snorkel from the box beneath his seat, and dived overboard. For once there were no complaints from Angus about his nakedness. Red used the rudder to steady himself and took a good look at the damage. The trap line was coiled tightly around the prop shaft and prop, and the cork float had pulled tight, becoming wedged between the prop and rudder. One way or another he had to get a loose end he could work with to loosen the coils. He cut the trap free. With no weight tethering it, the stern leaped sharply on the chop and crashed back down on his head. He reeled back in pain, pushing himself away from the stern half stunned, his face mask knocked down around his mouth. The Scot had allowed barnacles to grow on the hull, and several of them had carved a path down Red's forehead. The water in front of him turned murky with his blood. He clawed his way to the surface, face stinging, head pounding. Another wave caught him and swept his naked body under the hull, where barnacles gouged and shredded the skin on his legs.

"Good Lord, man, are you all right?"

"Help me aboard."

With Angus's help, Red dragged himself up onto the duckboard and onto the deck of the half-cabin. He collapsed and lay there, waiting for the throbbing in his skull to subside. The rain mixed with the blood oozing from the cuts and formed red puddles on the deck.

"I did warn you."

"Yes, Angus, you warned me." Red caught his breath and thought through his next step. "I'm going to have to tow you to calmer waters before I dive again. If that doesn't work I'll tow you all the way home."

He climbed back aboard his boat and fixed Angus's bow line to his stern cleats. He waited until Angus had upped anchor, before engaging gear and motoring slowly into the lee. The throb of his diesel exacerbated the pounding in his head. He grimaced as he watched the half-cabin slew and pull to starboard, ever obedient to its jammed rudder. The trip back to Wreck Bay would take forever if he had to tow Angus all the way. Red shivered. It was colder in the rain than the sea. He made for the shelter of a little rocky bay, no more than an indentation in the cliff face, and dropped anchor.

"We'll try here," he shouted. The saltwater stung as he dived overboard, but there was nothing he could do but accept it. He was good at that. He'd lived with pain for months on end, the deep, penetrating pain of tropical ulcers and infections. His scratches were nothing in comparison. With his knife clamped firmly between his teeth and one hand braced on the rudder, he began to uncoil the rope around the prop. But it was slow going and even in the lee, the half-cabin still bucked and rolled. He grabbed his knife and chipped away at the thick cork float until he could cut it free and push it clear. Chips of cork and blood clouded the water and obscured his vision. He surfaced, dived, surfaced, dived. The muscles in his arms began to cramp up in the cold. But he persevered and endured until finally the rope pulled free. Angus helped him aboard.

"How is it?"

"Turn her over."

The motor coughed, twice, three times and kicked into life. Red clambered back on board his own boat and cast off Angus's bow line. His shivering had intensified as the cold reached through to his bones. He waited until Angus had engaged gear and moved smoothly away before putting his clothes back on. Gusts swept the bay, driving the rain into him, soaking his shirt and shorts as he dressed. He knew his oilskins would act as a windbreaker and hoped his body would heat the water trapped against his skin. His feet had turned white and arched with cramp. Archie came aft to see if he could help lick his master's wounds.

"Heel, Archie. Lie down!" Archie did as instructed, curled up around his master's frozen feet, sharing his body heat just as they shared everything else.

Bonnie took an immediate liking to Rosie. The cat followed her as she took an uninvited tour of Angus's shack. At some stage someone had splashed mustard yellow on cupboard doors, which gave the place a look of disrepair that was entirely undeserved. His fridge made hers look like an old-fashioned icebox, and his Stanley wood-stove was a perfect example of tradition colliding head-on with technology, rustic looking, but oozing efficiency. She tested his sofa and approved. Likewise his bed, though it was a little firmer than she was accustomed to. His table and chairs were sturdy and functional but not entirely without a rough charm. She smiled at the clumps of dried heather dangling from the kitchen beams. But what intrigued her were the desk, typewriter and the stack of double-spaced pages. She picked them up and began to read. She read until the gathering gloom strained her eyes, and Bonnie patted her lap, impatient for her dinner. Rosie was absorbed by what she read and intrigued that the dour old Scot was the unlikely author. Momentarily, she considered starting up his generator but thought better of it. Instead she put the manuscript back where she'd found it and wrote a short note saying that Bonnie had been fed and that the soup was for his dinner. As a final gesture of goodwill, she started a fire in the Stanley so that the bach would be warm and welcoming when he finally returned, and he'd have hot water for a shower.

She closed the door, locking Bonnie in with her bowl of fish pieces, and set off back down the trail. When she reached the fork where the track split, she hesitated. There was no reason for her to ignore the path leading up to her home but she did, and took the other, which dipped down to the beach.

Angus watched Red pass him, then followed in his wake. He envied the way the old lifeboat carved effortlessly through the swells and crushed the chop, wishing he'd been in it when he'd fouled the trap line. His old half-cabin wasn't a bad boat but, unlike Red's, it sat on top of the water and was skittish in a blow. He'd been tempted when Mrs. Campbell encouraged him to stay on until the weather had cleared, but he didn't want her getting designs on him. They had a comfortable arrangement that was best left as it was. He wondered if Bonnie had been fed. Surely Red would have fed her before he left. The man was mad and he was soft, but no one could accuse him of being thoughtless.

He rounded Bernie's Point into Wreck Bay unaware that his day, which had begun so badly, was also destined to end the same way. The solitary figure on the beach was obscured by rain and poor light, and occasionally Red's boat came between them. The truth was, he was of no mind to see anyone or anything other than the Bronlund and Anderson dinghy he'd left bobbing on his mooring. He held his course as Red reduced his revs and steered off to port to his own mooring. Angus eased the throttle back and disengaged gear. Even sore, weary and cold he couldn't resist the conceit of gliding up to his mooring without power and having his half-cabin slow to a halt just as it reached the buoy. He tied off, feeling a weariness that only a hot meal and a good night's sleep could dispel, worked his way to the stern, clipping his storm cover into place, climbed over the transom and into his dinghy. He stroked toward shore, his back to the beach, his mind dulled by cold and fatigue. The moment his dinghy bumped sand, he swung his feet over the side, his wet, heavy socks and gum boots combining with his tiredness to make them feel cast in lead. He paused for breath with his boots in the water and his bottom on the seat, gathering the strength to haul himself up.

"Need a hand?"

Angus spun around, barely comprehending. "You!"

"Yes. Aren't you going to welcome me back?"

"You!" His brain grappled with the enormity of the disaster.

"Yes, Angus. It's me. And yes, I'm back to stay."

Angus dragged himself to his feet and turned his back on her. "Red! Red! That infernal woman's come back!"

"He can't hear you and, besides, he knows. He helped carry my things up the hill."

135

"I'll bet he did! I'll bet he did! The gormless fool! Well, don't think you can involve me in any of your schemes. I'll not be pandering to the likes of you, let me tell you that! You don't belong here. Go away back to your cars and your televisions."

"Christ! What have you done to your hands?"

"None of your business, woman. Now out of my way!" Angus lifted the bow of his dinghy and began to drag it up the beach to the dunes.

"One thing before you go, you cantankerous old fraud. I've fed Bonnie and left you some soup."

"You've not been in my house?"

"Yes. That's if you live in the same place as your cat."

"You've been snooping! You've been snooping around my house!" Angus's fists were clenched in anger as if he were setting himself to strike her. "I'll not have you snooping around my house. I'll not have you on my property!"

Rosie reddened beneath her rain hat. "I've been in your house to feed Bonnie and leave soup. That's all. I'm not a snoop. What have you got that could possibly interest me?"

"Away with you! You couldn't help yourself. No woman could. And I'll know the truth the instant I walk inside."

"Then I've got nothing to worry about, have I."

"We'll see about that!" Angus flipped his dinghy over, hull up, and stormed off up the track.

"Enjoy your soup," she called after him and tried desperately to recall if she'd straightened the cover on the bed and the cushions on the sofa. She was pretty sure she'd put the manuscript down in the exact spot she'd found it but wasn't prepared to bet money on it. Ah . . . so what, she thought. How could she ruin a friendship when there was none and seemingly no prospect of one? She turned her attention to Red, straining to see him through the rain and gloom. He appeared to be fixing his storm cover into place.

"Hang on!" she shouted. She flipped Angus's dinghy back onto its keel, dragged it down to the water, hopped in and rowed to the mooring. Red had tied off the storm cover and sat with Archie on the stern.

"Thanks, Rosie." He lowered his stiff body gingerly into the boat. Archie followed. "Couldn't swim."

"What's the matter?"

"Cold."

"Never mind, angel pie. I've got just the thing for you. How would you like a bowl of soup served to you in a hot bath?" She gazed into the shadows beneath his ridiculous yellow hat, expecting some kind of acknowledgment, but he gave no response at all. She stopped rowing. Moody silences were one thing, but this was plainly ridiculous. "Is that a yes or a no, Red?"

"I'm cold, Rosie," he said. "So cold."

"Bloody hell!" Rosie gazed in horror at the bloody weals and scrapes on Red's forehead. She couldn't imagine what had happened to cause them, and Red wasn't up to talking. She started to strip him and discovered that in places his shirt was stuck to his body. The dark brown stains explained why. "What the hell have you done to yourself?"

Blood from the scrapes on his chest and stomach had oozed into the wet fabric and dried there, gluing his shirt to skin. Rosie took him by the hand and led him into the bathroom. She began to run water for his bath.

"There are two ways of doing this. You can soak your shirt off in the bath or you can let me try to sponge it off."

Red had begun to shiver violently and rock on his feet. She made the decision for him and dipped her sponge into the hot bathwater. She held it over each of the trouble spots and, as gently as she could, pulled his shirt away from his skin. She didn't know whether she was hurting him or not for he gave no sign. He felt cold to the touch, and his wounds stood out livid against his numbed skin.

"Now drop them."

Red took off his shorts, revealing a similar array of scratches and gouges on his shaking thighs.

"Saints on roller skates," Rosie muttered to herself. She lifted his penis up in her cupped hand and inspected it. Red flinched.

"Relax. I'm just making sure the important bits are still in working order." She breathed an exaggerated sigh of relief. "Now hop in

137

the bath, hero. I'll go towel down your mate and heat your soup."

"Thanks, Rosie." Barely a murmur, but Rosie heard and smiled.

Red lay in the bath as it slowly filled. His frozen flesh tingled agonizingly, and his scratches and scrapes shrieked as the water slowly deepened. He raised his knees to get as much of his body underwater as he could. Bit by bit the heat worked through muscle and sinew, and seeped into his bones. He stopped shaking. He'd forgotten what a pleasure a hot bath could be and savored the rediscovery. He closed his eyes and let his mind wander. It seized on his weariness and took him in directions he normally resisted. He'd met Yvonne in a bath, the angel in white who'd bathed and cared for him in Alexandra Hospital. His body had been worse for wear then, too. Ribs broken and skull fractured, injuries that had kept him away from the Western Desert, where his pals had gone on to fight the Germans, and caused him to be left behind in Singapore to greet the Japanese. For once he allowed the warm water to seduce him into opening long-closed doors. He could see her face, hear her voice, feel her gentle touch as she bathed him. See the white tiles with the bottle-green hospital insignia in their center, and hear the whump-whump-whump of the ceiling fan. The water hadn't been hot but tepid, not cold but cooler than the sweaty air in the ward. Red wasn't the first soldier to fall in love with his nurse, but that was yet to come. He recalled her kindness and her confidence, his awkwardness and shyness, a boy barely twenty, naked and vulnerable before a beautiful girl no older than himself.

"Sit up. C'mon, sit up!"

Red opened his eyes slowly. The bathroom had shrunk, and the tiles had disappeared along with the revolving fan in the ceiling.

"Your soup." Rosie had put the soup bowl inside another so that it wouldn't burn his hands as he held it. He took it from her. "Bon appétit!" she said, and left him to eat it in peace. If there was one thing Rosie understood, it was the sanctity of the bath.

Red dipped his spoon into liquid thick with lentils, beans, carrots and cabbage. He spotted a piece of meat that had separated from the ham bone and instinctively seized upon it. A blessing! He thought back to how the men used to give their soup a quick stir to see what lumps it had, if any. Sometimes a piece of sweet potato, radish, or worthless white melon, but sometimes the rare treasure of a piece of meat. It didn't matter that it was fish, buffalo, rat flesh, snake or dog. It was protein, and the recipient was grateful for it. The men were so starved for meat they invested it with mystical powers. There was iron in meat, and protein. Meat brought strength and endurance, replenished muscle. Meat meant survival. But the unaccustomed treat sometimes triggered diarrhea, and the meal and all its sustenance were often lost in sudden, foul rejection. Nevertheless the unfortunate stirred their soup and bitterly resented the lucky. They'd risk diarrhea. They'd risk a beating. Anything. All for a piece of meat.

"Time's up. Important bits are beginning to shrivel."

Red dragged himself back from his reveries and handed Rosie his empty bowl. When had he emptied it? How long had he lain there like a prostrate Buddha with his bowl cupped beggarlike in his fingers? His bathwater had cooled and lost its comfort.

"I'll help you get dry, then you can put this on." She held up her white terry-cloth bathrobe. "Then come and sit in front of the fire while I anoint you with antiseptic. By the way, Archie likes my soup."

"I like your soup, too."

"Good. Just don't fart like him."

Red laughed suddenly. The sound seemed to surprise him as much as her. Rosie had never seen him smile and never expected laughter. It ended as abruptly as it had begun, leaving both of them feeling awkward. She held the towel wide and he stepped into it. She gently patted him dry like a mother tending a small child, while Red just stood quietly accepting. He put on the dressing gown she gave him, unconcerned by how foolish it made him look. Rosie couldn't help wondering if Red was displaying past conditioning or trust. Was she becoming his friend or just his nurse? She led him into the main room where the chair sat waiting in front of the Shacklock. Archie lay curled up on a sugar sack to one side, watching, tail beating a rhythm on the floor.

"I'm going to clean all these scratches and scrapes properly and pare away some of the dead skin." She used tweezers to pick up a wad

139

of cotton, dipped it in a little dish of gentian violet antiseptic and began swabbing the deeper gouges. She picked up a small curette blade and scraped away dead skin.

"I could have done with some of this stuff in Burma."

His comment surprised her, but she didn't let on. "How did you wind up in Burma?" Rosie kept her voice as casual as she could.

"We were heading for Egypt. Our troopship ran into a typhoon up near the Solomons. Some of our equipment broke loose in the hold, and I was one of the lucky volunteers sent down to secure it."

"What happened?"

"We got smashed up. One bloke died, one had both his legs broken. I scored a fractured skull and broken ribs. They off-loaded us into a British naval launch in the straits off Singapore."

"Didn't they have any medical equipment in Singapore?" Rosie worked away, swabbing and scraping, taking advantage of his distraction.

"Yeah, they had plenty in Singapore." His voice trailed away. "Could've done with some at Thanbyuzayat."

Rosie saw the elsewhere look creep back into his eyes, settling like a ground mist. She encouraged him to continue. One time her father had got through to a patient diagnosed as catatonic and managed to get him talking. The man had talked nonstop for four days. "Go on."

"I helped out in the camp hospitals from time to time. The Japs thought I was a doctor or orderly of some sort. If they'd asked Archie where he was from first instead of me I would have copied him and said Eighth AIF. Instead I said the Alexandra Hospital. The camp hospitals weren't much by way of hospitals, just huts with more than their fair share of sick and dying."

The images that appeared in his mind furrowed his brow. These weren't pleasant memories borne on the soothing waters of his bath, of a nurse whom he'd come to love and who'd loved him in return. Instead he saw men rotting away with dysentery, cholera and putrefying ulcers. Saw his hands helping in the daily curettage, trying not to vomit with the stench. Saw the needle blackening in the flame before lancing boils. Saw pieces of clothing, threadbare and boiled, scouring infection from wounds. Heard men scream, scream, scream, plead for him to stop. He saw men no more than skeletons dehydrate in explosions of diarrhea and seeping sweat. Saw men apologizing with their eyes for the fact that their life was dribbling away down their legs and over their soiled sheets. Saw his hands scrubbing the shit off beds and off the floor of the typhus death house, scrubbing and scrubbing, cleaning and disinfecting so the stronger would have a chance. So the strong could survive.

"That'll do, Red. That'll do!" Rosie was shaking him. "That'll do, hero." Rosie held him by the shoulders as his eyes flickered and groped for recognition. Had she really thought it would be so easy? Soften him up with a hot bath, then open him up like a steamed tuatua? Red looked up at her steadily, reality slowly replacing the images in his mind.

"Welcome back, Red. Where did you go to? You keep disappearing on me."

"Sorry."

"Tea or coffee?"

"Tea," he said automatically. He looked down at his chest and stomach, blotched purple with antiseptic, and wondered when that had happened.

"A cup of tea before bed." As Rosie stirred the water in her teapot she casually undid the top buttons of her blouse. "A cup of tea before bed," she repeated, "and then, my good man, you are going to repay your nurse for her kindness."

Twelve

Mickey Finn likened himself to a boxer who had no defense, and only one punch in his kit, which he was rarely allowed to use. There were times when he honestly believed he was the most useless individual in the whole of New Zealand. He longed for the opportunity to prove otherwise, yet was wary when it seemed the chance had finally arrived.

"When did this come in?" Lieutenant Commander Mickey Finn asked cautiously. He'd thought the day had delivered more than its quota of surprises when he'd found a radio fresh from stores—though hardly fresh from its maker—sitting on his desk with a note earmarking it for the hermit on Great Barrier Island. But Gloria had another surprise for him.

"Eight o'clock this morning, sir. I took the call myself." Third Officer (PA) Gloria Wainscott ran her hands down the sides of her skirt as if checking the straightness of the seams. "Your man on Cape Brett. Couldn't sleep, got up to spend a penny and saw this heavenly vision appear out of nowhere." She was clearly excited and fought hard to contain it. "One moment nothing, next a foreign trawler lit up like a Christmas tree right outside his window, maybe three miles out. He put his binoculars on them and watched them haul their net in. A big catch, too, according to him. He reckons he watched for over an hour before the lights went out. Two and a half hours later, they lit up again just inside the Poor Knights Islands. They've got a nerve, sir, you've got to give them that."

"Did he get any idea of nationality?" Mickey was beginning to share his young assistant's excitement.

"No flags, but he says they could be Japanese. Could be anything. We'll just have to find out what's in the area."

"First get confirmation. I don't know that too many of our spotters are teetotalers, if you get my drift. Ring the local cop shop and see if they've got anything. Once we've got confirmation I'll try for air surveillance. Off you go."

Mickey Finn watched Gloria scurry away, her enthusiasm, loyalty and devotion beyond question. In her next life she'd make someone a wonderful puppy, but it was the disposition of her present life that often had him wondering. How did someone his age get someone her age interested? There were times he thought they came from different planets. He sat back in his chair and rubbed his eyes to try and clear his head for the job at hand.

He spread his charts out on his table. If the sighting was confirmed he was certain the incursion would not be a one-shot. It was too well thought through. No running lights, no lights at all until the catch was up to the stern ramp. That spoke of a well-drilled crew and clear intent. The question was, what pattern would the trawler skipper adopt? He'd had one good haul, so would he backtrack for a second run? Or would he go out wide and fish the depths before striking in close again? Random incursions would be impossible to anticipate and set traps for. Or was the skipper so arrogant that he thought he could run south, appearing and disappearing at will? If so, they stood a fair chance of catching him. Mickey wished he had more people strung out along the coast, but he'd never thought he'd need them. Too many people lived along the northeast coast for foreign boats to risk fishing in close where they could be easily spotted. But nobody had thought to try the lights-out trick before and that changed everything. The skipper's audacity made Mickey pause and draw a long, deep breath. It was early in the morning and it had only just dawned on Mickey that the lights-on-lights-off routine had been specially developed for that purpose. What also worried him was a sense of déjà vu.

"Action stations." Gloria almost danced into his office. She beamed

143

down at him with a catlike look of satisfaction, hazel eyes shining with excitement. The chase was on.

"Top tart! What have you got?"

Gloria winced. "Police at Russell have a report from three fishermen in a motorboat who claim they were nearly run down by a foreign trawler under way without lights. Two and a half miles out from Cape Brett and they never saw or heard a thing until one of the men picked up the bow wave less than one hundred yards from them. Apparently it was as dark as the inside of a cow. Their description, sir, not mine. They barely had time to cut their anchor rope and start their outboard."

"Nice of the police to phone and tell us."

"They rang the fisheries."

"They'd have been better off ringing my mum. Anything else?"

"Report from a woman in Kawakawa who saw a submarine surface and disappear near the Poor Knights Islands about five-thirty this morning. Came up in a blaze of light and disappeared. She's convinced it's the Russians. Several more reports of bright lights appearing and disappearing out at sea. I think we have confirmation."

"I don't suppose there's any chance of keeping any of this out of the papers?"

"No, sir. The Bay of Islands papers are already onto it. And I think you can count on the *Herald* or *Star* picking up the story."

"Thanks, Gloria."

"Some good news."

"Ahhh . . . I thought you were a bit smug. Let's have it."

"Well, we could request a search and photo reconnaisance by one of our Sunderlands. We'd probably get knocked back or delayed so long we might as well have been knocked back in the first place. On the other hand, if the commodore accepts our recommendation and we do get our Sunderland, overflying them would only show our hand. It would be like sending the skipper a telegram saying we're onto him."

"So?"

"One of the men in the motorboat is an Auckland businessman. And a pilot. He flew up there in his own Cessna. The police are trying to get hold of him for us. They say he's a bit of a character and will probably jump at the chance to help."

"Thank you, God!" Mickey put his hands together in mock prayer and cast his eyes heavenward. "When the pilot calls, put him through to me. And Gloria, good work." He smiled, she saluted. What hope did he have?

Mickey settled over his charts to try and work out the trawler's likely position. He didn't want the Cessna whizzing around in circles all over the place, warning off his quarry. A good arrest now could win the public over, put pressure on the politicians to support the fisheries protection squadron, and maybe secure the means by which they could do their jobs properly. The opportunity was God given, and he was determined not to let it slip away.

He tried to put himself in the position of the trawler skipper. Clearly the man wanted to play phantom, so logically he'd want to be as far from shore as possible by morning. Out of sight and out of mind. Mickey plotted a course for the Cessna beginning thirty miles south of the Poor Knights and thirty miles out to sea. It was important that the pilot flew low enough to get a decent photo, but even more important that he didn't deviate from his course. Mickey knew the bridge watch would follow the flight of the lightplane on their radar to see if it did anything suspicious. He'd have to make sure the pilot understood the nature of the game and didn't try any John Wayne stuff. He settled back to spend the morning on the phone.

The pilot rang from Russell, understood his instructions and the reason for them. He was ex-air force. Once he had the pilot onside, Mickey decided to alert his counterpart at Hobsonville Air Base. Afterward he called a contact at the National Airways Corporation with his usual request for pilots on scheduled flights in the area to report any sightings of foreign trawlers. The pilots were usually only too happy to oblige. Again he cautioned against them deviating from their flight path, a necessary precaution given that many of them had also flown combat missions in the Second World War and had retained their enthusiasm for engagement. He hadn't forgotten the occasion when an overly enthusiastic DC-3 pilot, on regular service from Tauranga to Auckland with a nearly full complement of passengers, had put his aircraft through a switchback dive to get a better look. Mickey made a final call to Captain Fred Ladd to ask him to keep an eye open around the gulf and Great Barrier. Then he kept his line free for a return call from the Cessna pilot.

While he waited, he prepared a report for his commanding officer and a request for information from the Japanese embassy in Wellington. It was time to update his files. He wanted the names of all the Japanese fishing vessels operating around New Zealand along with the names of their skippers. The embassy staff had made an art of procrastination. They were always obliging and always gave an excellent impression of cooperation, but by the time they responded the information was always a little old—"So sorry." Nevertheless it was useful. Mickey Finn was a firm believer in knowing his enemy and kept a dossier on every skipper who ventured into his territory. He studied their operational methods as best he could, determining who was law abiding, who wasn't, who was cautious and who was aggressive. Apart from anything else, it helped fill in the blank spaces in his reports and never failed to impress his superiors.

Was the skipper a new chum, he wondered, or one of his old adversaries? He opened his filing cabinet and rifled through for suspects. The lights-on-lights-off routine led him straight to the file on Shimojo Seiichi. The profile was spot on, but Shimojo was a longliner. Or had he been reassigned? Mickey winced when he recalled their abortive attempt to catch the *Aiko Maru* off the tip of Great Barrier. The man was a known poacher, but there was a vast difference between running dories without lights and an operational trawler. If not Shimojo, then who? Were other skippers adopting the same practice, was it a directive from Japan? Mickey could hardly imagine a more chilling prospect. He kept Shimojo's file in his pile of suspects on the sound principle that he was guilty until proven innocent.

The Japanese trawler backtracked north thirty miles offshore in search of mackerel. Though not in the class of snapper, the mackerel were still a valued catch, and the trawler had plenty of freezer space. The night's trawl had netted twenty tons of snapper, and there were

146

many more to be had. With no patrol boats within two hundred miles, another fruitful night beckoned. But a thief did not advertise his intentions, and as a natural precaution the trawler kept out of sight of land by day. Life aboard the *Shoto Maru* had settled into routine when the radar operator alerted the skipper to an incoming aircraft. It was approaching low and to starboard, less than half a mile away. Shimojo Seiichi immediately ordered the off-duty crew to the foredeck to wave to the passing aircraft. It was a friendly gesture calculated to obscure the trawler's identity, which was painted on the lower part of the superstructure. But there was nothing anyone could do to obscure the name painted on the stern. All eyes on both deck and bridge watched carefully to see if there was any deviation in the plane's course. It passed by without showing any apparent interest.

Captain Shimojo Seiichi dismissed the aircraft as nothing more than passing traffic. It gave him no cause to change his mind. When night fell he would again take his new command inshore and test the mettle of his crew.

Thirteen

Rosie woke at first light. She was tired, snug and happy as a kitten. Her bedroom was still dark and chilled by the morning air. Rain beat a soft and soporific rhythm on the iron roof. She had no reason at all to wake up or get out of bed. She reached across to put her arm around Red and snuggle into him for warmth but came up empty-handed. It took a moment to register on her sleepy mind that Red was no longer there. Realizing his side of the bed was still warm, she lifted her head from the pillow and forced her bleary eyes to focus. What she saw in the pale light by the window made her wonder if she was still dreaming. She watched spellbound as Red performed his silent, slow-motion ballet, balancing first on one leg and then the other while his arms and body writhed to an unheard melody. The sheer grace and fluidity of his movements, and the intensity with which he performed them, amazed her. She felt guilty for watching, an outsider intruding on something immensely private, but she could no more drag her eyes away than give up sex.

Her curiosity was aroused and other parts as well. He had his back to her and was never more than a silhouette against the awakening dawn, but she knew he was naked, and the wan light gave faint, teasing definition to those parts it touched upon. He was beautiful, like a beautiful animal. The ritual—whatever it was—was also exquisite and powerfully moving. Once again, Red managed to drag a tear from her eye. She wanted to reach out and grab her troubled neighbor and haul him back into her bed, where she'd engage him in ritualistic movements of her own, but she didn't dare move so much as an eyelid. So she watched and waited, unsure whether she wanted him to stop or go on forever. How many more surprises did this man have for her, she wondered?

Red slowly brought his movements to a halt and stood motionless, gazing out toward the spot in the ocean where he knew the cloud-shrouded sun would rise.

"Red, what were you doing?" Her voice sounded unnaturally loud even though she'd done little more than whisper.

"Exercising."

"Weird exercises. Aren't you cold?"

"No."

"What about all your scratches and scrapes?"

"They're nothing, Rosie."

"Says who? Your doctor orders you back to bed."

"No. You stay there. I'll make breakfast." He wandered out of the bedroom to the kitchen. Rosie watched him go in amazement. No man she'd ever slept with had ever refused her offer of a dawn-breaker. She didn't want to put too fine a point on it, but she believed that if lovemaking ever became an Olympic sport she'd place among the medals. Her performance certainly hadn't disappointed Red. She'd opened his eyes and introduced him to pleasures he'd probably never imagined. He'd been a clumsy, naïve lover, but one who was ever willing. She'd made love to him and resurrected the dead more times than she could count, and clearly more times than even he had thought possible. But there were moments when she got the feeling he was only acting under orders, responding to conditioning. His rejection of a repeat performance stunned her: Any other man would have ended up wearing her chamber pot around his head. But she had no anger for Red, only wonder. She didn't think he was diffident, merely different. Very different. She yawned and snuggled down under the blankets. That was another thing. No other man had ever offered to bring her breakfast in bed the morning after. Most of them had been grateful just to have survived.

As she awoke for the second time, the light filtered green and yellow through the curtains she was about to replace. Red the thought-ful, Red the truly amazing had pulled the curtains together again so that she could sleep in. That was worth ten points. That rated above not leaving the toilet seat up and mopping up the splashes on the floor tiles. She felt well pleased with herself. Only two nights on the island and Red had already shared her bed. It didn't matter that he'd not whispered endearments into her ear, or even whispered anything other than answers to direct questions. He'd shared her bed. He'd had a taste of something both good and available. And tradeable. She wondered how many nights of lovemaking it would take before she had enough leverage to convince him to sink a new pit for her toilet.

The thought of toilets reminded her of her own pressing need. This was no time to drag out Bernie's trusty old potty. She rose, pulled on her dressing gown, staggered to the bedroom door and out into the main room. The unpacked boxes had been stacked neatly against one wall. Her floors had been swept. The table set for breakfast. The woodbox in front of the Shacklock was full and freshly stacked. Red was washing the previous night's dishes, and a heady, unmistakably fishy, unbreakfasty smell pervaded everything. Another surprise.

"Good morning."

"Good morning, Rosie. Ready for breakfast?"

"Red, a wise man would not engage me in conversation until af-ter I've been to the toilet." She walked past him and out of the door. Good Lord! she wondered. What in God's name was he making? She ran through the drizzle to the outhouse, slammed the door behind her and sat shivering. She could understand the need for ventilation but could not forgive the icy drafts and infiltrating rain. How did men manage, she wondered, when the drafts caught them with their trousers down? Did it leave them with anything to hold onto? She began to formulate a theory on the correlation between cold drafts, frozen, shriveled penises and splashes on floor tiles as she made her way back inside. Then she smelled that fishy smell again and all other thoughts vanished. She made her way to the bathroom, washed her hands and face and finally decided against running a toothbrush around her mouth. Waste of time, she thought.

"Bed or table?"

"Table will do nicely."

"I found the rice and soy. I got the rest from home."

"Very clever of you. What is it?"

"Breakfast."

"Specifically, Red."

"Fish rice. Me and Archie always have it for breakfast."

"I suppose toast and Vegemite is out of the question?"

"No. Not if that's what you want."

"No, no . . . this will do nicely." She smiled and steeled her stomach against the impending assault. She dipped her fork doubtfully into the rice and raised it to her mouth. The touch of chilies and white pepper surprised her as did the unexpected oiliness, but not at all unpleasantly. Without thinking she dipped her fork in again. There was no doubt that it smelled fishier than it tasted, and it tasted strangely satisfying. "Mmmmm . . . this is good!" she said. That *really* surprised her. One that she'd said it and two that it was true.

"Protein and rice," said Red. "Muscles build and rejuvenate more readily during the first hour after sleep. That's why you need protein. Rice gives you energy."

"Red, I come from a family of doctors."

"Sorry."

"Your mother teach you to cook this?"

"No. The *romusha.*"

"Do you want to tell me who or what *romusha* are?"

"Asian laborers. The Japs used them as cheap labor. When they caught or bought fish this is what they cooked. When we got back to Singapore I had to work in the kitchen and vegetable gardens. They taught me."

"The war's over, Red. Don't you think it's strange eating coolie food?"

Red looked away. His shoulders hunched, and she guessed she'd touched on an issue he didn't want to face. She could only guess at the struggle within.

"I'll get the tea." He rose and walked over to the kitchen, his jaw tight, brow furrowed.

"Hey, it's no big deal, Red. Eat what you like. Perhaps if I'd known it was going to taste as good as this I would have taken to eating it sooner. Beats the hell out of cornflakes." She was wasting her words and she knew it. Part of him had never returned from Burma and perhaps never would. He'd learned to live with it, but Rosie was already beginning to believe she could make the living easier. The man needed help, and she was fast convincing herself that she was the one person able to provide it. "Thanks." She smiled as Red placed her cup in front of her. "What do I do with the rest of my breakfast? Save some for Archie?"

"Archie's had his."

"I'll save it for the chooks."

"I've fed them."

"You have been busy."

"Sorry."

"No, don't apologize." Rosie wondered if this was the right time to ask the question that had been gnawing at her since Red's flashback on the first day. "Archie was your mate in Burma, right?"

"Yes."

"Saved your life, I suppose?"

"Yes."

"So you named your dog after him. Jesus, Red, you have a strange way of saying thanks."

Red looked at her and suddenly laughed, not robustly but shrilly, almost childishly, as if it was something he shouldn't be doing. He rocked backward and forward on his chair. Rosie began to laugh with him, not knowing why, not caring, either. Laughter was good therapy. If it helped drag some of the ghosts raging inside him out into the light, then he could only benefit. She hoped.

"A *romusha* gave one of the Aussies a pet monkey," Red began. His face was flushed, and he seemed impatient to tell the story. "He was devoted to the thing. He named it Tao because it was the spitting image of one of the guards we called Monkey Man but whose real name was Tao. One day the guards gave him a stick and ordered him to beat his pet monkey to death. They did that sort of thing a lot. They liked to watch suffering. Enjoyed it. They told him if he refused they'd beat him to death instead. So with the camp looking on, he clubbed his little mate to a pulp. The guards laughed at him because he was crying as he did it. I went up to him afterward to offer my sympathies. He just pushed me away. 'Joke's on them, mate,' he said. 'I pretended I was killing Monkey Man.'" Red began laughing again, but his laughter sounded forced and desperate. Rosie could see that he wanted—needed—her to laugh along with him, but she couldn't find a vestige of laughter in her. The story appalled her. The men had made a joke of the killing and created a little fantasy because they couldn't cope with the reality. Red still couldn't. She rose and put her arms around him, clung onto him as his laughter degenerated into choking sobs. They hadn't prepared her for this at university.

"It's over, Red," she soothed, knowing damn well it wasn't.

Red left the moment the breakfast dishes were washed and put away. There were few of them, but Rosie was beginning to understand that Red couldn't leave things untidy or out of place. He didn't kiss her good-bye, comment on their lovemaking or make any statements of attachment. It was as if nothing at all had occurred. There'd be no roses, no cards, no tender notes or poetry from this man. Rosie watched him head off down the track toward the beach, doubtless to scrub off any blood that might have splashed over his boat's paint, and collapsed back into her veranda chair, drained and exhausted. The man was an emotional minefield! She realized she could waste the day worrying about him, or put him out of her mind and get on with the work that needed doing. The unpacking, the rusted-out gutters, the broken downspouts, the pungent outhouse, the tired garden, the unmade kiln, the idle potter's wheel, and everywhere the bare and parched timbers screaming for a lick of paint or creosote.

"God damn you, Red," she said aloud. "I've got enough problems without taking on yours!" She began to understand why Red and Angus cherished their solitude and clung to it. Why they'd tried to convince her to go back to Auckland and stay there. There was a lot to be said for giving up people and all their problems and just looking after number one, for running away from the world. Rosie was not unintelligent nor insensitive and could see the parallels between

Red, Angus and herself. All three of them were fugitives. All the same, it seemed a hard call to run away from each other as well.

The splattering of rain on the edge of her veranda made her look up at the gutters. The man in the shop had told her exactly what she had to do to repair them and had made it sound so easy. She'd had every intention of doing the job herself. But what had sounded easy in the shop was now a totally different matter. The man in the shop hadn't been perched on a ladder twenty feet up in the air with a fifteen-foot length of gutter waving in the breeze. She needed help but also knew she couldn't ask for it. At Wreck Bay help was given at the discretion of the giver. Somehow she'd have to get Angus or Red to offer, and of the two, Red was by far the most likely candidate. Perhaps she could barter services, but what could she offer him in exchange? What did any man want? She smiled to herself but without her usual confidence. What had seemed fair trade in the afterglow of lovemaking had been devalued by Red's passionless departure. She realized she was on her own once more and couldn't count on further boating mishaps to deliver Red into her clutches. Would he call by of his own accord, she wondered, not to give her surplus or ask favors, but simply for her company? They'd made love, but had they made friends?

The wind picked up and forced her back indoors. There was no joy in sitting and thinking when she could be doing something useful. Bath, dress, unpack, put away. Day three of her new life began to resolve in a list of domestic chores. Perhaps later she could also have a go at connecting up the Bendix so she could do a load of washing—not that there appeared any chance of it drying. Jobs for the hands, she thought as she turned on the hot tap over her bathtub, and a couple for the mind. She decided to surprise her father and write to him about Red. Maybe he'd condescend to throw her a few scraps of advice on possible therapies. She thought she'd also write to Norma and ask her to make inquiries about a certain Scottish ex-policeman who wrote children's stories with a boy hero called Hamish. Information was wealth, even in the wastelands of Wreck Bay. She lay back in the luxury of her bath to plot and make plans, as certain as anyone could be that she would not be interrupted. But she was, not immediately, though certainly before the water had reached the temperature where there was no point in remaining.

"Hello! Anybody home?"

"Aye, there is," she said, irritated enough to mimic him. "And I'll have you know you've come at a very inconvenient time. I'm in the bath."

"I apologize. We normally bathe earlier around here."

"Do we now?"

"Aye, we do. Would you prefer me to leave?"

"No, I'm coming. Make yourself at home." She dragged herself reluctantly from the bath, wrapped a towel around her body and slipped on her dressing gown. "What can I do for you?" She looked Angus up and down in disbelief. Red dressed badly, but Angus surpassed him. His khaki shorts showed through his plastic mac, which he wore buttoned right up to the neck over something red and tartan. Black gum boots completed the picture. She wanted to smile but remembered their last encounter on the beach and decided against appearing too friendly. Besides, the bastard had interrupted her bath.

"I've come to thank you for the soup and for lighting the fire. I needed the soup and a hot bath to warm myself through. I thought I should tell you that."

"Thank you. You've made my day." She smiled sweetly.

"I've also come to give you back your saucepan."

"Along with your gratitude?" Rosie could see that he was wary and uncertain but thought she'd press her luck nevertheless.

"Aye."

"I don't suppose your gratitude extends to returning favors?"

"Depends."

"I need a hand to repair the gutters."

"My gratitude does not extend to repairing gutters." His arrogance and chauvinism returned in a flash. He seized on her inadequacy and actually began to gloat. "I told you before. I'll not be your lackey." He made no attempt to conceal the glee in his voice. "You don't belong here. It's not an easy life, and I'll not waste mine making it easier for you. If you can't cope you should leave now. That's all I've got to say."

"That's a pity, Angus," said Rosie sweetly. "You have such a lovely voice."

"What's that? Aye. It's been said before." The anxiety and suspicion returned.

"Pity you waste it by talking through your arse."

Angus's eyes widened, and his mouth groped for words like a stranded goldfish gulping for oxygen. None came and he spun on his heel and stormed off back down the track. Rosie watched him go, saw the bushes shake as he bumped into them in his anger. She hoped the leaves dumped buckets of rainwater onto him. She speculated idly who was in most need of help, Angus or Red? Or herself? Between her ambitions and reality lay the realization that there were some jobs that she simply couldn't do by herself. Left entirely to her own resources she would not be able to cope. It hurt her to admit it. But the grim truth stared her in the face. She hadn't even settled in and already she'd sent both her neighbors packing. Either things changed, or her days at Wreck Bay were numbered.

Fourteen

Mickey Finn would probably have advanced further in the ranks of the Royal New Zealand Navy but for his unfortunate tendency to speak the truth. He saw stupidity all around him, heard the same pathetic excuses for not taking appropriate action when opportunities presented and found it hard to suppress his anger. He tried hard enough to button his lip, but he couldn't stop seeing what he saw, hearing what he heard and feeling what he felt. Whenever he was engaged in any operation he was continually on the lookout for the leg which would reach out to trip him. He never knew where it would come from. Political interference, interservice bickering, budget constraints or simple mechanical breakdown. More things went wrong than ever went right. If the foreign trawlers ever realized how completely they had the navy by the balls, they'd run riot. Mickey worked hard to prolong their ignorance. The phantom trawler provided a rare opportunity to strike a telling blow for his side, but that only had the effect of putting him more on his guard. How, he wondered, would the bastards get him this time?

By midafternoon, he figured he'd earned the right to a beer. Queen's Regulations, however, disagreed, and there were few ways more certain to shorten a career than being caught drinking on duty. The pilot's film had arrived and gone off for processing, hopefully by someone who knew what he was doing and not some fresh-faced rating straight out of school. Negatives had been blurred or lost before. The big question was, did the pilot get a good enough shot to identify the trawler? The game was on, he was sure of it, but he had no idea what plays would be involved. He likened it to the opening gambit in a game of chess played against an opponent he did not know but who knew all about him. He felt the first intimations of a thrill as old as time—the thrill of the hunt, the chase and the capture. He only wished he knew who he was up against.

While he waited for the photos, he organized a ride on the patrol boat *Shearwater,* which had undergone repairs and was scheduled for a shakedown cruise around the Hauraki Gulf and Great Barrier Island. He'd explained his needs, and the *Shearwater*'s commanding officer had seen no reason why they couldn't anchor awhile in Wreck Bay to drop off a radio and explain operating procedures to a volunteer coast watcher. After all, as the young lieutenant had smugly agreed, coast watchers had an illustrious history of service to the navy. Besides, he'd also heard about the giant packhorse crayfish and thought it might be opportune to send a couple of divers down to check the effect of the navy's new antifoul on the indigenous aquatic species.

"Your happy snaps, sir."

He turned at the sound of Gloria's voice. She'd kept her face and voice deadpan, allowing no hint of what the photos showed.

"Well, go on for Christ's sake! Are they any good?"

"I did say they were happy snaps, sir."

"You beauty!"

Gloria winced.

"Well? Show them to me!" He held his hand out for the prints, but Gloria refused to give them to him.

"Sir, I am a third officer in the Royal New Zealand Navy."

"Yes, Third, you are." Mickey tried to sound contrite. Almost succeeded. "Now give me the prints."

"Couldn't you simply say 'Well done,' sir?"

"Yes, Third Officer Wainscott, I could. I definitely could. Well done. Now give me the prints!" He reached up and snatched the photos from her hand. The top print had been greatly enlarged and had grain the size of gull's eggs, but the name on the ship's stern, though indistinct and blurred, was still legible. Prior agreements were instantly forgotten.

"You beauty!" he shouted. "Gloria, you bloody beauty!"

His eyes swung instantly to the chart he'd pinned on his wall. What would the Jap bastard do next, he wondered? He felt sure he'd sneak inshore again after nightfall, but which way would he trawl? A cautious man would run north, a bold man south. But if the man was cautious he probably wouldn't have risked trawling so close in the first place, nor drilled his crew to work in the dark. That showed clear intent. So it had to be south. But if he was both bold and smart, he'd probably head north. "Goddamn!" said Mickey under his breath. It was like trying to guess which direction a seagull would fly off in after it had stolen his sandwich.

He realized he could do nothing with any degree of confidence until the phantom made enough raids to establish a pattern. But would the skipper hang around long enough for the navy to creak into gear? Probably not. Once again he'd have to rely on intuition and guesswork, act on the basis of one more sighting and put his balls on the line for everyone to take a swing at. He hoped he'd get through the exercise with them still attached. He'd hardly begun the long and speculative business of examining options, of making decisions based on next to no information, when fate stuck a leg out to trip him.

"Sir?" Gloria the bright and beautiful had reappeared. "A message for you, sir." She handed Mickey the message and left immediately. That should have warned him.

Mickey skimmed through the note and slammed it down on his desk. "Buggeration!" he screamed. Under cover of darkness, a Taiwanese fishing boat had slipped in close to the northern shore of Bank's Peninsula, off the mideast coast of the South Island, and set nets. A local fisherman had chanced upon them and sent out an urgent call for help. A school of rare and protected Hector's dolphins was swimming among the nets, probably attracted by the trapped fish. According to the fisherman, some had already become entangled and drowned. A patrol boat had been diverted to assist the locals in an attempt to herd the dolphins away from the danger zone. That had left Mickey with the job of identifying and locating the culprit. It was a distraction he didn't need, but he had no choice.

He picked up the phone and rang his counterpart at the Ohakea Air Force Base with a request for aerial surveillance. The squadron commander was happy to oblige. Secretly, Mickey wished they'd send a fully armed Canberra bomber to blow the offender out of the water, and doubtless his counterpart would also have preferred to resolve the matter that way. The fact was, there wasn't a New Zealander who didn't have a soft spot for Hector's dolphins. They occurred nowhere else in the world, had the black-and-white markings of killer whales, but with almost childishly joyful expressions on their faces. They were the pygmies of the dolphin world, rarely bigger as adults than the newborn calves of bottlenose dolphins. It was impossible to watch these miniature clowns of the sea and not share their joy. Naturally they were a protected species, and it was Mickey's job to protect them from the foreign fishermen.

Ideally he would have liked the nets left in place to trap the invaders when they came to collect them. But the risk of snaring more dolphins excluded that option. He had to accept that the offenders had got away and were safe until their next incursion. He was aware of two Taiwanese boats operating outside the limit off Bank's Peninsula, and each would provide an alibi for the other. To add to the difficulties in apportioning blame, there were also a Japanese trawler and a Russian trawler operating nearby. There was a chance that the impounded nets would reveal the identity of the offender, but many of the foreign ships had long since realized the foolishness of marking nets in such a way that they could be traced back to their owner.

As far as Mickey was concerned, the incursion could only split his focus and divide his resources. He could accomplish nothing. But public opinion would demand action, and action would have to be seen to be taken. The navy was getting very good at doing things like that. Mickey reckoned PR was the only naval department that worked to its full potential. Nevertheless, the incursion meant work for him, and it was work best got out of the way so that he could concentrate on his phantom. He attacked his file and began to prepare a background report on the two Taiwanese boats and their captains to give to the commodore, who in turn would prepare a statement for the Minister of Marine, or whoever else put his hand up to be spokesman. The routine was all too familiar. A protest note would be sent to the Taiwanese government, which officially at least, would be contrite. A patrol boat would be stationed off the peninsula for a couple of days, the air force would fly a few more patrols, accompanied by the odd reporter to take photos and reassure the public that something was being done.

Mickey sighed. The charts on his desk and wall demanded attention he was unable to give. His throat was dry, and the old cloud of despondency had returned to hover above him. The search for the *Shoto Maru* had stalled before it had really begun. He'd earned a beer, needed a beer, but would have to make do with Gloria's poisonously strong Nescafé. She had many talents, he reflected, but coffee making did not number among them.

Shimojo Seiichi read the latest intelligence reports and assessed the risks. Snapper were seasonal, and the season was in its death throes. The rest of the Japanese trawler fleet had already moved south to the winter fishing grounds, chasing mackerel and hoki. There were still snapper to the south, and logic suggested that was where he should fish. But there were risks. The navy would almost certainly be aware of their presence, but what could they do about it?

He'd just been informed that a patrol boat had left its station off the west coast of Taranaki Province and was heading north to round the tip of the North Island and make its way down the east coast to its home base at Devonport. This coincided with reports of activity around the patrol boat *Shearwater*, suggesting that it was being readied to put to sea. If the two patrol boats were swapping places, the *Shoto Maru* ran the risk of being caught in a pincer movement. The patrol boats were a threat but not one he had to face within twenty-four hours. Only the Sunderlands posed an immediate danger, but they were ineffective at night and rarely used. The skipper made his decision. Trouble, if there was to be any, would not come until the third or fourth night, when the navy would have begun to realize what he was up to. But what could they do? How could they find him? The new moon and overcast hid him except when he had to use his lights. And soon he'd slip into the cover of the rain that was drenching the Hauraki Gulf and Great Barrier Island. Then he'd be as good as invisible, lights on or off.

Lieutenant Commander Mickey Finn arrived at the naval base HMNZS *Philomel* half an hour early, despite his late night, and sincerely wished that he hadn't. Unlike the foreign fishing fleet, his department did not work around the clock and had only a skeleton staff at weekends. He was on call if an emergency arose, but breaches of territorial waters hardly rated as an emergency unless they were by an invading fleet. There'd been little likelihood of that since 1945. Even as he'd parked his Triumph Herald convertible, he'd heard the phone ringing in his office. It seemed as though half of the population of North Auckland had stayed up all night to catch a glimpse of the intruder and were now determined to let the navy in on their secret. Once he'd established that the *Shoto Maru* had fished in as close as two miles and as far south as Bream Head, he took the phone off the hook. If anyone had a problem with that, their complaints would go to the PR department, which wasn't understaffed or sleep deprived.

During the first lull in calls, he penned two more requests to the Japanese embassy and a draft press release. He'd spent the night formulating a plan, but it wasn't without significant flaws. Its biggest problem was that it required the cooperation of Commodore Auckland, unless he could think of a way to convince his immediate superior to act on his own initiative, something Staff Officer Operations, Lieutenant Commander Philip Scriven, had successfully resisted doing for the entire duration of his career. Mickey was not hopeful. Superior officers tended not to be enthusiastic about allowing the navy to be portrayed as incompetent, a suspicion they normally went to great lengths to allay. But Mickey was concerned that the *Shoto Maru* might be in touch with their agents in Auckland, and he needed to conceal the extent of his knowledge. Again, under normal circumstances, the navy usually tried to make it appear they knew more than they actually did. Mickey tried to imagine how Lieutenant Commander Scriven would react to a reversal in tactics and thought about tearing up his press release and tossing it in the bin. But on the dubious basis that the navy was always most likely to do what was least expected, he made the walk down the corridor to the corner office instead.

Lieutenant Commander Scriven's guardian was absent from her post behind her desk, where she did a pretty good job of preventing access to her boss. She was a petite but pneumatic brunette with a fiery temperament who could type like a tornado, make instant coffee taste percolated and who, it was widely rumored, allowed her boss to slip his submarine into her pen. Mickey knocked discreetly and stuck his head through the doorway.

"Ahhh . . . Mickey, come in, come in."

"Thank you. Morning, Phil." It grated with Mickey that Lieutenant Commander Scriven held seniority over him, but he had to accept that the dapper little man in front of him had qualities he lacked, which in the navy's eyes made him better equipped for the job. He was diplomatic, politically aware and a stickler for protocol, attributes that Mickey had never troubled himself to acquire. He also looked impressive on television and had the sort of rich voice people respected. They believed him when he assured them that the navy "would take strong action," even though Lieutenant Commander Scriven hadn't the slightest idea just what that might entail.

"Sit down, sit down. Time I had a chat with you."

Mickey sat, groaning inwardly. He'd been the recipient of Phil Scriven's little fireside chats before. He couldn't imagine what he'd want to talk to him about this time. He decided to take the initiative, something he at least was capable of doing. "Phil, I've come to talk to you about this latest incursion by the *Shoto Maru* and how we should handle it."

"Yes, yes. But I got in first." Lieutenant Commander Scriven settled back in his chair and tried to look fatherly. "Been a complaint, you know. Nothing official, of course. Strictly off the record."

"A complaint?" Mickey recognized the tone, Phil's self-styled quiet voice-of-authority, and went on his guard. "Yes, from . . . let me see now . . ." He rummaged through some papers on his desk, found the one he was looking for, held it at arm's length and pre-

163

tended to read from it. "From Third Officer Wainscott, your personal assistant."

"Gloria?"

"Yes . . . that appears to be her name. Seems you've been overly familiar with her."

"Overly familiar, sir?" Mickey was stunned. Here was this jumped-up squirt, who everybody knew was knocking off his secretary, accusing him of being overly familiar with Gloria. Gloria, the untouchable and uncommonly stitched-up. Meanwhile the Japanese fleet was fishing so close inshore they were practically chipping oysters off the rocks. How the hell did this man decide his priorities?

"Yes, apparently you ignore her salutes and address her in a manner which she regards as altogether too informal."

"She said that?"

"She objects to being called 'gorgeous, darling, sweetheart'—that sort of thing."

"Phil, is this a formal reprimand?"

"Oh, good God no! No, strictly off the record, she insisted upon that. Didn't want to involve the commodore. Asked me if I'd have a word with you, man to man, as it were. She's obviously fond of you."

"Man to man?" Mickey bit his tongue. It was bad enough having to defer to Philip Scriven without having to cop the pompous little bastard's advice.

"Better she complains to me, Mickey, than to her father?"

"Her father? What's her father got to do with it, for Christ's sake?"

"Quite a good deal, actually. Commander Wainscott is attached to the Chief of Naval Staff, Director of Plans, actually."

Mickey felt the floor sink away beneath him. "Commander Wainscott? Gloria is Commander Wainscott's daughter?"

"I think it's Queen's Regulations from now on, Mickey, don't you? Either that or take her out and give her a darn good boffing. That'll do the trick. Bring her into line."

"Is that a practice you recommend, Phil?"

"That'll do, Lieutenant Commander!" The man-to-man protocol had clearly ended. "Now, you mentioned some other business?"

"The *Shoto Maru* made another inshore trawl last night. From

Cape Brett to Bream Head. Same routine. Lights out during the trawl, lights on when they haul the catch aboard. It's a deliberate tactic on their part and well rehearsed. If our information is correct, they made four trawls before heading back outside territorial waters. They've got their turn-around time down to around twenty-five minutes, so we're not dealing with a bunch of lucky amateurs. These guys are serious, and they're going to try again. When they do that, we stand a chance of catching them."

"You have a plan?"

"Yes, I do. I'm convinced the *Shoto Maru* is heading south. We've got the *Shearwater* ready to go to sea. I know it needs a shakedown, but I'm not asking for it to go much farther than twenty or thirty miles north of Great Barrier. The *Cormorant* must be close to rounding North Cape and heading for home. If we can get them to run at full speed, there's a fair chance that the *Shoto Maru* could become meat in our sandwich."

"How will you know where the trawler is? Do you need aerial surveillance?"

"No, that'll tip our hand."

"Then I ask again, how will you find your trawler?"

"Listen to the phones ringing, Phil. Everyone between Russell and Whangarei has been on the phone to us. They'll find our ship for us. But we need to keep our phones manned twenty-four hours a day."

"Easier said than done."

"Gloria and I will manage." He caught the little man's look. "Sorry, Third Officer Wainscott, Daughter of the Commander, Friend of the Powerful. Plus I don't expect to have any difficulties in finding volunteers. This is what we're here for, isn't it? That's why we joined the navy. It's a rare opportunity to go on the offensive and get some results."

"Mmmm . . . not sure that everybody will be quite as pleased as you if we're successful."

"I need the *Shearwater* on standby, but on no account is she to put to sea. I believe the *Shoto Maru* is in contact with their agents in Auckland. If the *Shearwater* makes any move whatsoever, we may just as well send the skipper of the *Shoto Maru* a telegram advising him of our intentions."

"Point taken."

Mickey took a deep breath. He'd poured the foundations, paved the way, now it was time to test his handiwork under load. "On the same basis, I believe we should be rather circumspect in what we tell the press. They're already chasing a statement. The Ministry of Marine is chasing us, too. I've prepared a draft release in which we do little more than acknowledge what they already know. We should give no indication that we are aware of the name of the intruder or its nationality. Or whether we regard it as the action of one trawler or more. We should simply acknowledge that we are aware of the incursions and are investigating."

"Show me." Lieutenant Commander Scriven scanned the brief release. "Heavens above, Mickey, you're not serious! You've built the cross, provided the nails and now you want me to go for a fitting. Are you out of your mind? Yesterday we had a Taiwanese trawler steal in right under our noses and drown our pet dolphins. That did not make us look particularly clever. Now you want me to prove that we're positively incompetent."

"Yes, Phil."

"This is outrageous, Mickey."

"And in two or three days or less, it could prove to be pure genius. Phil, if we name the trawler they'll know they're under surveillance. I've already blundered by sending a request off to the Japanese embassy for crew details. I covered my mistake this morning by sending off similar requests relating to two other trawlers. Hopefully that's muddied the water. But if we go full frontal with everything we know, then we tip our hand, and the skipper of the *Shoto Maru* will laugh in our faces."

"All right, Mickey, I'll take this up to the old man. But if you foul up you can forget all about boffing Third Officer Wainscott. You can forget about boffing anyone ever again, because vital parts will be missing. You understand me?"

"Yes, sir! Thank you, sir!" Mickey stood, flashed his best smile and bent his elbow.

"Mickey?"

"Sir?"

"Was that supposed to be a salute?"

"What was wrong with it?"

"Get Third Officer Wainscott to show you how before you try another. And Mickey . . . please try and reflect the dignity of your rank. We have the junior ratings to think about, too, you know." Philip Scriven watched Mickey leave his office and glanced back down at the press release. He added a couple of lines, high sounding and utterly meaningless, but which could provide cover if he was forced back on the defensive. But the power of obfuscation was not unlimited, and Phil Scriven wasn't foolish enough to believe that it was. He could improve the presentation of the apple, but that didn't alter the fact that the core was rotten.

He sighed and leaned back in his captain's chair, which his wife had bought at an auction and given to him as a Christmas present. Only decent Christmas present he'd ever had from her. He speculated on which was likely to cause him the most aggravation. The press release with its implied incompetence? Or the apprehension of the *Shoto Maru?* He just hoped there weren't any delicate trade negotiations in progress to bring the politicians down upon them.

"Third Officer Wainscott!"

"Sir!"

"Battle stations! Get these orders to the *Cormorant* and *Shearwater* back to Staff Officer Operations. Stay there until he signs them and then take them personally over to Signals."

"Sir!"

"I've got a feeling the *Shoto Maru* is going to drive on south toward the Barrier. See if you can get a call through to that weirdo over at Wreck Bay. It's a long shot, but leave a message anyway. Finally, see if you can get Lieutenant Moffat of the *Shearwater* to drop by for a chat."

"Yes, sir!"

"One more thing, my extremely capable third officer. If you're going to complain about my conduct, make your complaint official. I'd rather be kicked out of the service than endure another of fearless

167

Phil's friendly chats. Okay?" He looked up at her sharply and saw her sudden embarrassment.

"Yes, sir."

"Round up some volunteers to help us man the phones."

"Yes, sir!"

"And organize us some food. See if you can get the cafe across the road to keep their kitchen open and send us over a dozen or so hamburgers around midnight. Tell them it's their patriotic duty."

"Yes, sir!"

"Now hop it."

"Sir!"

Mickey watched her go. He'd never seen her looking so vibrant. She glowed with excitement. Soon the word would go around and the whole base would buzz. Gloria would have no trouble finding volunteers and probably have to beat them off. He was feeling pretty excited himself, partly at the prospect of action but also partly because of Phil Scriven's advice. Perhaps she did need a good boffing. Well, if she didn't, he did. There were parts of him that hadn't stood at attention for too long.

He turned his attention back to the *Shoto Maru*, placed an eraser on the chart to represent the trawler, and two paper clips farther out to sea to represent the patrol boats, and tried to think through all the possibilities. His spirits sank. There was simply too much water and too few resources. All he could do was set a trap and hope that the *Shoto Maru* had the extraordinary misfortune of sailing into it. He didn't need to look out the window to know that the rain still hadn't let up. The met report had the bank of clouds stretching all the way back across the Tasman to Australia. What chance would his informal army of coast watchers have as the trawler moved south? Dear God! He ran his fingers wearily through his hair. All he needed was one sighting, one little old lady with a flask of coffee, good eyesight and the desire to become a national hero so they'd know where the trawler was and where it was heading. Then he could unleash the patrol boats with at least a modicum of confidence. Circumstances were hardly in their favor, but Mickey had been in the navy long enough to know they were as good as they ever got.

Fifteen

〜〜〜〜〜

*R*osie *awoke early. Her bedroom was still dark, but enough light showed around the edges of her new curtains to indicate that dawn had occurred* somewhere beyond the endless canopy of clouds. She curled deeper into her blankets, dreading the moment when she'd have to get up and leave her warm bed for the cold and damp of morning. It was the kind of seeping cold that bypassed flesh and skin and went straight for the bones, the kind that only activity could ward off. Further sleep was a lost possibility, besides which her bladder had begun to complain. Still she hesitated, reluctant to set warm foot upon cold floor. What on earth was there to get up for, she wondered? There was no place she had to be and no one to tell her what to do. Not so very long ago, this had been her idea of heaven. But the gray days were endless and changeless, the rain ceaseless, and the monotony of a nine-to-five job seemed infinitely more appealing in comparison. At least she met people, heard happy voices other than the blather on the radio. Apart from routine chores, hours spent trying to achieve what a trip to the corner store could accomplish in five minutes, her only work was the work she made for herself. Still, this was the life she'd chosen. She wished she'd given it a longer trial before she'd shipped over all her worldly possessions. She was on the verge of feeling sorry for herself when she realized the trap she was falling into. She couldn't blame her father for her predicament, or her flatmates, Red, Angus or the weather. Wreck Bay was her choice.

Her decision. Her rude, raised finger to a world that had failed her.

"Love thy neighbor," said the Bible, but copy them seemed more appropriate. Red and Angus had what it took to survive at Wreck Bay and had learned the method. Rise early, exercise, start the day positively, do what had to be done to survive. They lived life the way it was meant to be—simple, uncomplicated and elemental.

She whipped aside her blankets and leaped to her feet and tried to remember what she used to do in gym classes. Visions of leaping rows of schoolgirls flooded her mind, hands clapping overhead, legs flying apart and together again, never in time and not always willingly. It seemed the perfect way to start. She jumped. But gone was the grace, the rhythm and timing. Instead she felt like a rheumatic spastic with a bladder problem. She reached for the potty under her bed. No! She grabbed her dressing gown, which she'd draped over the end of the bed to keep her feet warm during the night, and headed for the outhouse. She climbed into her gum boots at the door, picked up her umbrella and ran.

She sat shivering on the loo, refusing to accept that the cold was anything other than normal, part and parcel of her new life, neither encouraging nor discouraging and not worthy of notice. From habit she turned to flush the toilet, forgetting there was no toilet to flush, nothing beneath her for six feet and nothing that she ever wanted to know about beneath that. Her mind inevitably returned to the problem of re-siting. She'd make sure the lavatory at the new site had a removable drum that she—or preferably some coerced neighbor—could haul up and dispose of into a distant pit. She again sensed the onset of frustration and the futility of what she was attempting to do. The wind snatched the outhouse door from her hand as she opened it and pulled it hard on its hinges. She was fortunate that they didn't buckle. It took both hands to push the door closed with the wind driving the rain hard into her face and soaking her dressing gown. There was no point in opening her umbrella for the run back to the house.

She stripped off her sodden dressing gown and began to stoke up the Shacklock. How many times did she have to make the same mistake before she learned the lesson? Wear her raincoat to the toilet when it rained, not her dressing gown. It was such an obvious thing to do. She slumped under the weight of her own stupidity, cold, wet and ill-equipped for the life she'd chosen. She heard a tearing noise behind her and spun around, listening, searching, seeking the cause. The wind gusted once more, and she heard the scrape and bang loud and clear enough to identify the source. The rusted guttering had given way and was dragging over the veranda roof. And something else. A glistening on the wall beneath, and a dark, spreading shadow. The rain had backed up under the iron and was running down the inside wall onto the old cabinet in which Bernie had stored his newspapers. At least now she knew how it had become water stained. She raced to move her radio away and stood looking on helplessly at the spreading stain.

"Norma!" she shouted. "Norma!" She needed help. She needed a little moral support, someone to take the reins for a day or two so she could take stock and give her new life some momentum. But it wasn't Norma she needed, it was Red. If Red would give her just one day she could cope. That's all she needed, a man for a day. She'd willingly trade the pleasures of the nights if only she could have a man for a day.

Rosie retreated to the one place she knew where she could bring her crumbling dreams back together. She stripped off her nightie and climbed into the bath before it was even half full. She sat there, bottom half scalding and top half shivering, arms clasped tightly across her breasts hugging herself for warmth. The tide inched deeper with agonizing slowness. Old pipes, low water pressure, hard washers. Too bad. She raised her knees and gradually eased her body beneath the surface. The water from the hot tap was beginning to lose its sting as she knew it would, but there'd be enough for a good long soak and a good long think. It didn't matter that she hadn't turned the generator on so that her bathroom was as dark as the rest of the house. She closed her eyes. It was a fact that negative thoughts dissolved in hot water, along with despair and self-pity. She lay back in womblike serenity and let her blessings come to her, unforced and unhurried, to be remembered, cherished and counted. No family, no focus groups, no farting flatmates, no presiding over an empty life going nowhere.

She slipped into pleasant reveries, imagining how idyllic life at

Wreck Bay could be once she'd got organized. She pictured herself at her potter's wheel, the wet clay glistening in the sun, surrounded by all manner of birds feeding on the veranda rail. It wasn't such an impossible dream. She saw herself slipping into a regime of health and activity, rising with the morning sun, exercising, tending her vegetable garden, gathering flowers. She saw herself catching fish each morning off the rocks or from her boat. She saw her little cottage, freshly painted and gleaming whitely amid the lush greens of ferns, pungas and tea trees. She saw the manner and pattern of her survival. But she also saw the model she was imitating, the inspiration for her dreams. His red hair and beard, his dedication to survival and his lost-boy ways. She saw his silhouette as he exercised at her window before the rising sun, felt his warmth as they snuggled together in bed, tasted again the fish rice breakfast. A smile spread across her face. He was weird, but there was sound method in his madness. Red would be her model, her inspiration and source of determination. But resolve needs more than an example to follow, it needs a focal point for the many obstacles it must overcome. She needed something to fight against. Something to cut the insurmountable down to manageable pieces and sharpen the edges of her determination. Something tangible and an easy target for her anger. Angus McLeod, she decided, would do nicely. Everybody should have someone to loathe, and Angus had gone out of his way to apply for the role.

But both love and hatred need fuel to sustain them, and Rosie sensed that it would be some days before she set eyes on either of her neighbors again. They were solitary men and set in their ways, resenting each other's presence as surely as they resented hers. Oh, Red would tolerate her, even be kind and generous toward her, so long as she was careful not to intrude too far upon his routine. They weren't a community but three individuals with lives that occasionally trespassed on one another's. It wouldn't be easy to coerce Red into helping her, but not impossible. He'd had a taste of what she had to give, and every man she'd ever slept with had come back eager for seconds. Red, she convinced herself, just needed more time. Until then, she just had to cope. What was it Col Chadwick had told her right at the very beginning? Don't ask either man for favors but accept them when offered. She thought about that as her bathwater cooled. Col hadn't said anything about building up a bank of favors or a sense of obligation. Surely a stream of unexpected, unasked for favors might merit a favor in return?

Rosie dragged herself out of the bath, dried and began to exercise naked in front of the Shacklock. That seemed the approved method at Wreck Bay. Unused muscles stretched and strained in unfamiliar attitudes, yet Rosie found an intense sense of satisfaction and accomplishment in the ache of their awakening, and in her rebuttal of the cold. She dressed and decided to bake bread after breakfast. To bake more than she needed so that she had surplus to give away. Jesus performed a miracle with a few loaves of bread. Perhaps she could, too. How many loaves of bread would it take, she wondered, to replace rusted gutters?

Red was confused, and that fact alone was sufficient to concern him. Confusion affected the focus of his mind, and he'd already suffered enough from that. Survival lay in single-mindedness, in concentrating on the job at hand. Confusion led to distraction, and distraction led to despair. Rosie was his problem. He liked her well enough, but she tricked him into talking, and conversation only opened doors he'd closed long ago. Doors that were best left closed. She frightened him the way the psychiatrists had frightened him, stumbling and bumbling around inside his head, digging up things no human being should ever be made to remember, flippant in their reasoning, ignorant of their torture. What was the point? It only brought pain and changed nothing. Yet Rosie had a kindness and vulnerability, where the doctors hid behind a cold, impenetrable wall, a wall of knowledge and training, fortified by the certainty of their rightness. But Red knew that ignorance was the cement that really held the bricks together. What they didn't know and the help they couldn't give far exceeded their capacity to heal. That was the real purpose of the wall—to conceal their ineffectiveness from their patients. Their arrogance was born of the fear that their patients would discover the unpalatable truth that, in the final analysis, all their knowledge, training and experience amounted to nothing. Nothing! Rosie didn't have a wall. She listened, felt and tried to help. A bit like Archie, but Archie had had an advantage. Archie had been there. He'd understood the suffering, the desperation to survive, the loneliness of dying and the purposelessness of death. Archie had understood the terrifying, shredding power of fear, the scream as sharp as the snapping of a twig at the very instant when reason parted company with brain. Archie had understood the slide toward insanity, the gut-wrenching fear of beatings and the dread of being made the plaything of sadistic guards. How could a psychiatrist understand? How could anyone ever understand?

Red made his way down the track toward the shore, alien looking in his rubber, war surplus frogman's suit, his bare toes clawing into the slippery clay for purchase. The clay also reminded him of Rosie. She'd need some for her pottery, and he speculated on the best source. It worried him that she kept intruding on his thoughts. He didn't dare contemplate the implications of the night they'd spent together, he dutifully doing what was expected of him, what was required. But what did it mean? How many nights could they lie bound together before their lives would become inextricably entwined, and she a demanding, questioning, constant presence? He no longer objected to the fact that she'd come to Wreck Bay—he'd long got over that—but she had to keep her distance as Angus did. He wondered if it was in the nature of women to do so. He suspected it wasn't. It worried him that things would change and he wouldn't be prepared when they did.

He gathered up his crayfish pots from their storage place among the ferns behind the sand dune and carried them out onto the jetty. Archie loped along the beach, investigating patches of seaweed, sniffing, searching, looking for anything that might have changed since the day before. Red checked the zip on his wet suit and stepped off the jetty into the water. The rain that had infiltrated beneath the rubber had not prepared him for the cold of the seawater. It snapped his breath, and he shuddered. There were some men who pissed themselves before stepping into the water so they wouldn't feel the cold as much, but he wasn't one of them. He struck out vigorously for his boat, generating body heat to warm the water trapped against his skin and provide the insulation he needed. He hauled himself aboard and whistled for Archie. He needn't have. The dog was already racing back to the jetty.

Once he'd loaded his traps and Archie had taken his position on the bow, Red motored out of the bay, hugging the shore northward toward Aiguilles Island. He needed to go to sea to absorb himself in the work of the crayfisherman, to study the run of the currents, the variation in tides, the pattern of the waves and where best to set his traps, all jobs that would leave him no time to think. The clouds hung low, and the drizzle was unrelenting. Red knew where the rocks were but looked hard for them all the same, each sighting confirming his knowledge and seamanship. He liked to fish in close, where the professionals from Leigh and the Whangaparoa Peninsula didn't dare, particularly on days when everything was a uniform gray and the water as impenetrable to the eye as potato soup.

He found the gullies and gutters he was looking for and set his traps, judging the wash of the light swells, hands working quickly and knowingly. All too soon the job was done, and he was no better off than he'd been before he'd set out. He needed work to occupy his mind and repel the intruder. He needed work to give him a rest from Rosie. He nudged back out to sea toward Aiguilles Island, a gray, brooding presence upon a gray sea, weathered, worn and crumbling, home to gannets and headstone to Bernie's last resting place. The bow swung north almost of its own volition, as if the boat had decided how Red should occupy his mind. Archie barked and was answered immediately by twin coughs, one hard on the heels of the other, from either side of the bow. Two smiling faces propelled by eight feet of muscle. Porpoises looking for a playmate, a bow wave to ride, an audience for their antics. Red smiled back. They'd leave him soon enough, once he'd cleared the lee of Aiguilles Island and caught the wind and chop. In the meantime, he could enjoy their company.

But the waves surged lethargically, unable to muster the force needed to foam their peaks, and the porpoises held their station. The rain angled in steeper as the wind eased, gravity now its motivator, seeming for all the world as if it, too, were infected by the gloom and depression of the day. Red wondered if he'd be able to find his markers through the murk. He lined up with the tip of Aiguilles Island and held the compass bearing Bernie had given him. Archie raced from side to side, keeping tabs on their companions, anxious whenever one disappeared from sight. Already the forbidding cliffs of Miners Head were all but lost, only the angry frothing at their feet hinting at their presence. Red motored on, relying on judgment and instinct to find his destination. His Cummins diesel changed pitch as he slowed to watch the swells, looking for a little extra height and steepness on the face. The porpoises adjusted their game to the pace of the boat, no longer riding the bow wave but swooping beneath the hull as if the whole point of their existence was to surprise Archie by reappearing where he least expected them. Red cut the motor. He made his way forward and shackled up his reef anchor. He waited until the boat had glided to a halt before tossing it overboard and paying out the line. If his instincts were correct, they'd hook up on Bernie's rise, if not, his anchor would dangle uselessly in the void. He felt a bounce, a pull on the rope and payed out more line before tying off. The bow pulled sharply to port as the anchor bit. Red reached into the forward compartment for his fins and face mask.

The porpoises came up to investigate the moment he dropped into their realm. Yet another diversion. Their day was turning out better than they'd ever imagined. They followed Red as he swam down the anchor rope, angling in for a good look at the ungainly creature, amused by his presumption. Red kicked with his practiced, unhurried action, conserving the air in his lungs as he plunged deeper. At around sixty feet he paused and peered at the landscape beneath him. The water was clear but the light levels too low for definition. Nevertheless he saw what he'd come to see, and it was much as Bernie had said it would be. Silted up and almost hidden by weeds, metal gleamed dully among the brightly colored sponges and urchins. Nature had begun the job of covering and burying the thousands of army shells that had been dumped there, but it was patient work and far from complete. Curiosity satisfied, he set off back up the anchor rope, blowing bubbles to entertain his companions. As he burst to the surface he heard his urgent gasp for breath reprised twice. One of the porpoises brushed his leg to thank him for the game or entice him to do an encore. He hauled himself aboard, wishing he had bait fish to give them for their company. But all he could offer were a few more revolutions from the diesel and a more energetic bow wave.

He turned south, heading not for home but for his crayfish traps. The crays were plentiful when you knew where to look, and half a dozen would do him nicely. If he left the traps down any longer he'd only end up putting unneeded crays back, and he couldn't see the point in distressing them unnecessarily. He didn't need the money because he was still living off the windfall from the snapper caught in the Jap longlines three months earlier. The porpoises peeled off to look for another distraction as he passed into the lee of Aiguilles Island. Up on the bow, Archie gave up searching for his friends and ducked under the deck for shelter. Red thought back over the morning, pleased to have salvaged something from the day and delighted to have confirmed the existence of the rise. On the right days it would be a magical place to dive and to fish, a marine garden known only to himself. He saw the rise as Bernie's bequest to him, as fine a gift as he could ever receive, never considering for an instant the fact that it also included several tons of military ordnance. Nor did it occur to him that one day he'd draw upon the munitions, when, once again, he'd take up arms against the Japanese.

His first trap yielded three crays, the second three more and the third just one, but it was by far the largest. One for Angus, one for Rosie and one to share with Archie. The rest would be cooked and frozen, or boiled up with their shells to make stock. As he picked a flat-topped swell to make his exit from the gutter, he began to feel uneasy that Rosie would misinterpret the motive for his gift. Would she understand that he was merely sharing his surplus or read more into it? Would she see it as evidence of a growing friendship? He didn't want that. He wanted things to stay as they were. Coexistence at a distance. He didn't want to feel drawn to her, to wonder where she was and what she was doing and how she was managing. He didn't want to think about her when he climbed into his bed at night and arose from it at first light. He didn't want to think about her at all. Most of all, he didn't want her to think about him. He didn't want the complication. All he wanted to do was the one thing his life had trained him to do—survive.

As he climbed the trail around the ancient pohutukawas to Angus's bach, he was still wondering whether he should give Rosie a crayfish at all. But how could he give one to Angus and not to Rosie? They were both in his group whether he liked it or not, and in Burma where they'd grouped together to help each other survive, it was unthinkable to share with some and not with all. He called Archie to heel and paused at the edge of Angus's garden, two half-drowned creatures, shivering and saturated by sea and rain.

"Hello!" He didn't have to wait long.

"God's sake, man! What do you think this is? Piccadilly Circus?" The Scot appeared at his doorway, red faced and indignant. "What is it this time? Get on with it and leave. I didn't come here to be interrupted every five minutes."

"I've come to give you a cray, that's all."

"Aye. And that woman just wanted to give me some bread. What do you think I am? Have you two decided I'm senile and need mollycoddling? Or is this just part of a campaign to annoy me into leaving? You may well succeed, let me tell you."

"Rosie brought you some bread?"

"Aye, and don't you play all innocence with me, laddie. I'll not put up with it. The two of you are in bed together, and don't think I don't know it."

Red stood lost for words. The two of them in bed together? Why would Rosie tell Angus that? He felt mortified and caught and had difficulty hiding his shame.

"What's the matter with you? Afraid to admit it, are you?"

"No. We did spend a night in bed together."

"Speak up, man! What are you talking about? Make yourself clear."

"I'm talking about what you're talking about."

"What I'm talking about? I'm just saying you're in league with that woman, for what purpose beyond interrupting and tormenting me every hour of the day I can't imagine. What are you saying?"

Red realized his error and indiscretion. He turned away to stare at the ground, hoping to find some inspiration in the mud and puddles. He found none and glanced up guiltily at the Scot.

"Are you saying she's already trapped you in her bed, you soft fool?" Angus asked the question quietly, incredulously, fearing the truth.

Red nodded.

"Then there's no saving you, man! You'll be the downfall of us both! Lord give me strength and save me from the blunderings of fools!"

"I had nothing to do with the bread," Red said miserably. "I just caught some crays. Here, take one and I'll be on my way."

"One minute. You'll not leave here without some gherkins. I'll not be indebted to you or any man. Or woman! Bring the jars back, mind, and their caps." He disappeared indoors while Red plucked a reluctant cray from his sugar sack. Every leg and feeler seemed snagged in the weave. But Red prevailed, and the cray snapped its tail in anger and indignity. Angus reappeared with two large jars. "Slice one onto your bread with whatever you're having for dinner. Doubtless that harridan's left a loaf for you, too."

Red climbed up onto the veranda and made the exchange. "I'll see you later."

"Aye. And if you've an ounce of brain left inside your head you'll give that woman a wide berth. She'll use you as her own personal handyman until you've no life left of your own. She's nothing but trouble, man, I'm telling you. For God's sake, keep your trousers on or we'll never get rid of her!"

Red turned and made his way back down the trail to where it forked up the hill toward his place and Rosie's, feeling cold, miserable and, worst of all, riddled with uncertainty.

Angus watched Red's retreat and nearly sobbed with despair. He hadn't considered for a moment that the woman would take either of them into her bed, certainly not so soon, and certainly not the madman. Part of him wanted desperately to deny the truth, the part bruised, beaten and humiliated by the women who had rejected his advances, and those others who'd refused his offers of money. But the truth sat there, naked and undeniable. She'd taken the madman into her bed when it could have been him! The chance of making the boy child he'd longed for had beckoned, and he'd spurned it. His pride

179

and fear of rejection had pushed Rosie away from him, lost him any hope he might have had. He wondered desperately whether it was too late to make amends, to make his peace with her. What if he was less rude to her? What if he helped repair her gutters? What if he befriended her? Would she not also take him into her bed? What woman wouldn't prefer him to the madman?

The flapping of the crayfish in his hand dragged him back to reality. A half-filled page sat in his typewriter, stopped in midsentence. But Angus knew there'd be no more writing while possibilities nagged and jealousy and self-disgust ate away at his heart. Dare he try once more? Could he endure another rejection? Had he already gone too far? He screwed his eyes tight in anguish and tried to deny the forces that urged him to her. It was just not meant to be! His fate, like the crayfish's, was already decided and he was just deluding himself. He put water on to boil. "Damn you!" he shouted. "Damn you!" Why had the woman come to tease and torment him and try to make him believe things could be otherwise?

Rosie had cleaned the metal parts of the old anchor with Brasso and steel wool and begun oiling the woodwork. By no stretch of the imagination was this her most pressing task, but it was one that offered the most satisfaction. The hard, weathered timber gleamed softly in her hands. She was so involved in her task and in trying to imagine the anchor's history, Archie's warning barks startled her. Red? She rose to meet him and almost laughed out loud when she saw him in his rubber diving suit with the sugar sack over his shoulder. But then the implications of the sack dawned on her, and she had a sinking feeling that her scheme to build up a debt of gratitude had faltered before it had begun.

"Afternoon, Red," she called, sounding far more optimistic than she felt. "Now I know why you wander around naked. Whatever you wear makes you look ridiculous."

"Afternoon, Rosie. Angus said you've dropped off some bread for me. I've brought you a crayfish in return."

"How very thoughtful of you," said Rosie. She loved crayfish, but given the choice, would have swapped it gladly for two hours with a good plumber. She gingerly grabbed hold of the crayfish's feelers as Red handed it to her, live and kicking. "What the hell am I supposed to do now?"

"Boil it. I've got to keep moving, Rosie, or I'd show you. I've got to get Archie dry and warm. We're both frozen. See you."

"I've hot water for a bath. Come in and show me afterward."

"No thanks, Rosie. I'll manage."

"I know you will, Red. But will I?" Her crayfish held at arm's length, Rosie watched him head back the way he'd come, knowing that she was wasting her breath. It was too much to expect the lure of her bath to work twice, especially when the lure of the bed would almost certainly follow. If that was what he wanted, he would have been back sooner. Nevertheless his quick refusal disturbed her. Had she scared him off? She'd done that to men before, but was it for the same reason? She went inside wondering where to turn next.

Red had come, briefly raised her hopes and dashed them just as quickly. Her attempt to build a bank of debts had failed. Angus had handed her abuse and a jar of gherkins in return for her loaf. Red had also negated her gift with one of his own. Where did that leave her? Back at square one with a leaky roof, a smelly loo and no immediate remedy in sight. But she wasn't beaten, not by a long shot. She didn't know what she'd try next, but she'd think of something. In the meantime, she'd boil her crayfish for dinner and learn how to do that in the process. As much as she loved crays, she preferred them brought to her Mornay or thermidor, or warm in a salad and with a glass of wine. Well, at least dinner was taken care of. Warm crayfish with Heinz mayonnaise, fresh garden salad with sliced gherkins sprinkled through it and freshly baked bread thickly buttered. Probably exactly what her neighbors would prepare for themselves. Red to share with Archie. Angus to share with Bonnie. And herself to share with her leaking roof. She allowed the morning's depression to sneak back up on her momentarily, unaware that a possible solution to her problems had already announced itself. It had tapped on her consciousness, rhythmically and insistently, but she was deaf to its call. For that matter, so were her neighbors. Red, quite unwittingly, was solving her problems for her.

Sixteen

One thousand miles south of Auckland, the captain of the Taiwanese trawler Yu Shan *was cursing the gods, the spirits of his ancestors and* the pox-ridden son of a Japanese whore who'd dropped a container overboard from his ship. The container had settled, its bulk underwater and invisible to both eye and radar. But one corner was sufficiently buoyant to surface occasionally in the trough of a wave. It was that corner which had bent the *Yu Shan's* propeller shaft and rudder. The captain cursed again. He was a superstitious man and believed that bad joss always struck in threes, and what had happened only confirmed his beliefs. First, he'd lost three nets he could ill afford to lose. Second, he'd hit the container in his very next incursion into territorial waters. Now he had to face the prospect of a storm building in the Southern Ocean. He had no choice but to make for port as quickly as he could, and the only port nearby was Lyttelton, within a few miles of where he'd left his nets. The captain of their sister trawler had offered him a tow, but there was no point in both vessels risking impoundment. He had no doubt that representatives of the Royal New Zealand Navy would be waiting for him. Besides, if the wind picked up there was a strong chance he'd have to radio for assistance. He cursed the gods again and wondered which of his enemies had brought this misfortune upon him.

Mickey Finn looked down at the chart on top of his desk with a growing sense of resignation. Lieutenant Moffat, the commander of the *Shearwater*, had been briefed and was ready to put to sea as soon as darkness had fallen. His instructions were to take up position ten nautical miles north of Aiguilles Island. The *Cormorant* had radioed in its position thirty miles due east of Whangarei, eighty miles to the north, and was steaming south, awaiting further orders. Between them lay the fishing grounds in which Mickey Finn hoped the *Shoto Maru* would make its last trawl in New Zealand waters. At least, its last trawl for a while. A clean capture within the three-mile limit— never mind the twelve-mile limit—and the severity of the breaches of international agreements and laws could result in the *Shoto Maru* being tied up in Auckland for some time.

The trouble was the two paper clips representing the patrol boats were in position, but in position for what? More erasers, tops from ballpoint pens, and three pieces of P.K. gum fresh from the packet represented possible grounds that the *Shoto Maru* could choose to trawl. It didn't matter where he placed his paper clips, he was never in position to cover more than two options, and even then with only an outside chance of actually making an arrest.

Yet the excitement around the base was electric. Even Gloria's coffee had improved. As he'd expected, there'd been no shortage of volunteers to man the phones, run messages or just keep the coffee coming. Others asked if they could just hang around and watch and feel part of the action. Mickey sighed and pushed back in his chair. So many people set up for disappointment. He wondered if there'd ever been a group of people anywhere more hungry for success, for the chance to strike a blow and do something that mattered, that changed things. That was why young people joined up and senior officers stayed on.

Even the met people had been infected and were sending him weather updates on the hour, even though they indicated little change. At least he now knew that the northern edge of the rainstorm lay on the thirty-sixth parallel just south of the Mokohinau Islands, Great Barrier Island's distant northern neighbors, and was tending more toward the south than north. A glance out his window confirmed the report. As hard as he looked he couldn't see the outline of the destroyer he knew was moored little over two hundred yards directly in front of him. If the *Shoto Maru* ran south of the

Mokes, it could fish wherever it liked and they'd never even know it had been there.

The thought stopped him in his tracks. The Hauraki Gulf, playground of Auckland's sailors and fishermen, spawning grounds and snapper nursery, gaped open on the chart in front of him, bounded on one side by the east coast beaches, at its base by the Thames Estuary, and on its eastern boundary by the Coromandel Peninsula and Great Barrier Island. A wave of apprehension washed over him, turning to acid in his stomach. Who was he up against? How brave was he? He'd never really considered that any skipper would be rash enough to attempt a trawl through the gulf, but what was there to stop him? Mickey's heart began to pound in his chest. What would he do if he were the skipper? The rain cover was heaven sent, and good catches guaranteed. Sure, the fish would be small and undersized, but the Japanese often preferred them that way. The *Shoto Maru*'s gaping nets would wreak havoc. But would the skipper be crazy enough to attempt it? Why not? Where was the risk? The Sunderlands were grounded, and Mickey's spotters would be useless. He mentally ran through his list of suspects, paused on the name Shimojo Seiichi, but again dismissed him as a longliner. He moved one of the erasers into the gulf and stared at it. Once inside, the trawler would have three escape routes. One east of Little Barrier, the gulf's lofty guardian, one west and one through Colville Channel, which separated Great Barrier from the Coromandel Peninsula. His excitement blossomed as he realized the potential for trapping the *Shoto Maru,* provided he could get the *Cormorant* far enough south in time.

He ran his hand through his hair and stared at the scenario in front of him. It was madness, insanity and a magnificent stroke of genius. But if he targeted the gulf and the *Shoto Maru* was spotted fishing its favored grounds up north, he'd be defenseless when the operation was postmortemed. Targeting the gulf meant ignoring all other options, which no one would ever regard as sound naval procedure. He looked around at the drab walls of his office, the ancient, fly-specked print of the *Achilles,* at the remains of a poisonous cup of coffee, and wondered what he really had to lose.

"Gloria!" he bellowed. "Sorry! PA Wainscott!" Mickey heard laughter from the adjoining offices. Everyone knew where Gloria stood on the issue of correct naval procedures. But for once Mickey was in no mood to join in the humor.

"Sir!"

"Change of orders! I think the *Shoto Maru* will use the rain as cover and do a raid on the gulf."

"On the *gulf?*"

Mickey closed his eyes. If that was Gloria's reaction what would Phil Scriven's be?

"Get hold of Lieutenant Moffat on the *Cormorant*. I want him to run full speed down to the Mokes and wait there for further instructions."

"Sir, the *Cormorant* has advised that they're low on fuel. Would three-quarter speed be adequate?"

Mickey looked at Gloria and slowly digested her report. Why hadn't he been told? Why hadn't he worked it out for himself? Why would he expect a returning vessel to have full fuel tanks, especially after running the previous hundred miles at two-thirds speed or better? "Three quarters or marginally less would be fine, Gloria. Thank you for bringing the fuel situation to my attention. Now be a good little naval officer and find out precisely how much fuel the *Cormorant* has left—so that I can make my plans with some degree of confidence! Move!"

The laughter in the corridor stopped abruptly. Mickey turned his attention to his charts. He'd made his decision on the basis of no information and had nothing to back it up other than intuition. Ordering the *Cormorant* south hadn't hurt. He still had time to change his mind. He needed to think. Time to think things through. Make plans and contingencies. Dear God, he wondered once more, who was he up against? He looked up to find Gloria standing in front of his desk.

"Yes? What is it? Have you done what I asked?"

"Sir . . . Lieutenant Commander Scriven wants to see you in his office."

Mickey sensed something was wrong and looked at her closely. She'd turned pale, and her shoulders were bowed. "For God's sake, Gloria, what now?"

"He's called the operation off."

"What?!"

"Apparently aircrew from Ohakea have spotted a Taiwanese trawler inside territorial waters off Bank's Peninsula."

"So?"

"That's all he asked me to tell you, sir. And to ask you to report to his office immediately."

"Shit! Gloria, tell no one. The show's not over, not by a long shot." He took off down the corridor to the corner office, pushed past Miss Office Boff 1966, and charged into Philip Scriven's office.

"I see you got my message, Mickey." Lieutenant Commander Scriven was calmness itself. His affected disinterest was a ploy he frequently used on subordinates, one, to remind them who was boss and, two, because it made it seem as if he was in control. "Take a look at this." He handed Mickey a telexed message. "And sit down. Seems one of the Taiwanese fishing boats is straying right into our hands. With luck it'll be the one that left the nets behind that drowned those poor Hector's dolphins. If the markings on the nets still on board match up, we'll prosecute. The public's calling out for vengeance, Mickey, and this is our chance to give it to them. I want you to direct the operation."

"Jesus, Phil!"

"Mickey, don't shout. I have perfect hearing."

"What about the *Shoto Maru?*"

"Well, we'll just have to hold a watching brief."

"No way!"

"Steady, Mickey."

"Sorry, Phil, but what I mean is this." Mickey thought quickly, trying to translate his suspicions into terms that Phil Scriven could understand and sympathize with. "The *Shoto Maru* has the greatest potential to embarrass us and discredit the fisheries squadron." Mickey could see that he suddenly had Scriven's full attention.

"This had better be good, Mickey." Philip Scriven gave Mickey what he imagined was his look of steel. Mickey had seen it before and, laughable as it was, knew better than to ignore it.

"I've been doing a lot of thinking about where our friend is likely

186

to show. I suspect it'll be where we'd least like him to, where he can do irreparable damage to the navy's reputation."

"And pray where might that be?"

"On our doorstep, Phil. I think the blighter is going to use the rain and poor visibility to run a trawl through the gulf."

"What?!"

Mickey knew he had him. "Why would a skipper trawl where he would be visible and possibly expected, when he could trawl where he would be invisible and not expected at all? And be assured of a good catch!"

"I hope you're wrong, Mickey." The arrest of a Taiwanese trawler off the South Island would do nothing to ease the fury of Auckland's half-million residents if they ever found out.

"I hope I'm right. I've asked for the *Cormorant* to be moved south to the Mokes and wait there. I'm now debating whether to hold the *Shearwater* off Katherine Bay on Great Barrier, or farther south to cut off the Colville Channel."

"Sit down, Mickey, sit down. Coffee!" he yelled, all pretext of calm abandoned now that his career prospects were under threat. "Two cups. Now! Righto, Mickey, let's look at each of our problems in turn and work out what to do. Let's start with the Taiwanese boat."

"If you insist."

"As Staff Officer Operations, I do! Now, latest reports put the *Yu Shan*—that's the intruder involved—about ten miles east of Lyttelton and apparently heading for it. I say apparently because they're wandering about a bit like a drunk on Friday night, probably having trouble with their steering. They're down to about three knots, but they're not fishing."

"Clearly they've got problems. They've hit something or broken something."

"Even I can work that out, Mickey. Because they're not fishing there's no point in photographing them; after all, they're allowed inside territorial waters if they're making for port, which this one appears to be. However, they could just be heading into calmer waters to effect repairs before heading back out to sea again, in which case we lose them and the chance to link them with the dolphins."

"What's the weather forecast for the area?"

"Winds fifteen knots gusting to twenty-five, seas moderate to rough on six-foot swells, and quite a severe storm building in the Southern Ocean to the west. All in all, good reasons to come inshore to effect repairs."

"How close is our nearest patrol boat?"

"We'd just sent it back up to Kaikoura. Reports of a tuna boat fishing the drop-off in close. We've recalled it to the peninsula, of course."

"Let me see if I've got this right. We have a disabled Taiwanese trawler heading toward Lyttelton, heavy seas and a storm imminent, and a patrol boat, say, twelve hours away—probably less—which the *Yu Shan* would know was in the vicinity. We also know there happen to be two Taiwanese trawlers working off Bank's Peninsula. It occurs to me that if the *Yu Shan*'s problems were capable of being remedied at sea, the sister ship would have offered assistance and they would have headed farther south, away from prying eyes and patrol boats. With me?"

"Mickey, you can be irritating at times."

"Now can we discuss the *Shoto Maru?*"

"Not so fast. You're absolutely convinced the *Yu Shan*'s heading for port?"

"No other explanation. How far off is that storm?"

"I would imagine it'll reach them by the early hours of the morning."

"Then stand by for a request for assistance. Five pounds says we'll get a call before midnight, probably before nine tonight. The smartest thing we can do is alert the Lyttelton Port Authority to get a tug standing by. No point putting our lads through the mill for the sake of a bunch of ratbag Chinese poachers. In fact, I'd send the tug out now with instructions to offer assistance. That same five pounds says it won't be refused."

"I tend to agree with you, Mickey. Perhaps our bird is being handed to us on a plate. Well, I think we've put that one to bed. All we have to do is arrange a reception committee, which hardly requires your considerable skills."

"Indeed."

"I think I'll handle this one myself."

"Thank you, Phil. Now about the *Shoto Maru?*"

"Just do it, Mickey. I'll attend to the *Yu Shan*. Just keep me informed." Philip Scriven began to relax and congratulate himself on his skill in handling the situation. First he'd get the kudos for the arrest of the *Yu Shan* and then for the apprehension of the *Shoto Maru*. No politician would dare come thundering down on his head for arresting a Japanese trawler fishing in the Hauraki Gulf. On the contrary, he'd probably take a step nearer to the promotion he wanted—as an advisor to Chief of Naval Staff. He began to plan his schedule. A day of press conferences and media interviews followed by a quick flight to Christchurch to be there when a positive connection was made between the *Yu Shan*'s nets and the killer nets that had drowned the dolphins. All front-page stuff. Provided he could keep the commodore out of it.

Gloria was waiting for Mickey as he strolled casually back to his office. He made a point of whistling his favorite song, "Sea of Love," certain that he wouldn't swap his life for the prime minister's. Grinning faces poked out of offices. Gloria stood with her most admiring, marry-me-tomorrow look on her face. Mickey enjoyed it all, enjoyed it all a whole lot.

"No questions, Wainscott, just your unbridled admiration. We're back in business, Gloria of the beautiful brown eyes, and we are going to spend a long and exciting night together."

"They're hazel."

"What?"

"My eyes are hazel."

Mickey watched color once more invade Gloria's cheeks. She was blushing like a schoolgirl. And smiling. So there was hope. Yes, perhaps she did need a good boffing. Perhaps for once Lieutenant Commander Scriven had got something right.

At five-thirty, under cover of darkness and a blinding rain squall, the patrol boat *Shearwater* cast off and motored out toward the Rangitoto Channel. Forty-five miles to the north, the *Shoto Maru* penetrated

New Zealand territorial waters eight miles southeast of the Moko-hinau Islands, a thief in the night, running without lights and with visibility cut to less than five hundred yards. The pouring rain made the chances of detection virtually negligible. Shimojo Seiichi ordered speed reduced to six knots and posted lookouts on either side of the bridge to watch for lights from any small craft that might have slipped beneath his radar, not that any were expected so far from land in such atrocious conditions. His radar operator reported a clear screen, but the rainstorm had brought interference, which cut his effective oper-ating range to less than five miles. The only compensation was that it also blinded the navy's radar if they were out there looking for him. The skipper picked up the intercom microphone. The time had come to light up and deploy the nets. Almost immediately Shimojo felt the boat shudder, seem to pull up, then surge forward as the otter boards—which kept the sides of the net apart—turned side-on be-fore straightening. They were on the navy's doorstep and about to beard the lion in his den.

There was still the remote chance of being spotted by a small craft that might be equipped with radio. He assumed his radar operator would be smart enough to alternate between mid and short range but gave no specific instruction to that effect.

It was precisely the sort of mistake Mickey Finn was praying for.

"Weather's worsening, sir. Lieutenant Moffat reports the *Shearwater*'s visibility down to less than four hundred yards."

"Thank you, Third." Mickey looked up grimly. He'd been won-dering morosely if God was Japanese. He'd ordered the *Shearwater* to head straight for the Colville Channel and to stand off Port Jackson, using the gulf islands as cover along the way. They were down to playing radar games and for once had a level playing field. He picked up his mug of coffee. The good news was that it was percolated. Lieu-tenant Commander Scriven had seen fit to contribute his percolator if not his actual presence. The bad news was that coffee grounds had escaped and made every mouthful gritty. But even if they hadn't, the coffee probably wouldn't have improved his mood. They'd managed to tee up a small army of coast watchers on the off chance that the rain lifted. Instead it had intensified. Mickey guessed they'd all be making plans for bed and an early night, and wondered if he shouldn't be doing likewise.

The *Cormorant* was speeding southward, using the Mokes as a radar screen on the assumption that the *Shoto Maru* had already penetrated the gulf. Their only hope of locating the *Shoto Maru* was by radar, but to do so they had to close to within five miles of their quarry. Then it would be a case of who saw whom first. Just to make their job even more difficult, they had to catch the *Shoto Maru* by surprise and in the act. If the Japs had time to recover their net they could claim they were only taking shelter. Then the navy would have the burden of proving that they'd been fishing. If they could get a boarding party onto the *Shoto Maru* to search the holds for live fish, they'd be home and hosed. But the chances of the *Shoto Maru* accepting a boarding party at night and in a storm were nonexistent unless they had solid grounds. The Japanese would respectfully suggest they wait until morning, then work overtime processing the fish so that it would be packaged, frozen and stored before the boarding party set foot on board.

Mickey took another swig from his mug. There was more bad news. His coffee had grown cold. The reality was the *Shoto Maru* could have gone anywhere. Back up north or out to sea, trawling the deep water. Or it could already be in the gulf out of radar range. All he could do was wait. And pray. For a sighting. A snagged net. A hot coffee with no grounds. A decent hamburger. And for a hot and breathy, triumphant Third Officer Wainscott, offering her body as tribute to the victorious.

By ten o'clock, most of the hangers-on had given up the search as a lost cause. The excitement that had caused the volunteers to raise their hands had evaporated and left in its place a sullenness and resentment toward the hangers-on for leaving, and toward Mickey for not allowing them to leave, too. The rain smashed against their windows, and whoever had offered to cross the road and pick up the hamburgers had found a place to hide. The phone had rung four times to report sightings from the Bay of Islands down to Whangamata, a hundred miles south of Cape Colville. None of the sightings had been confirmed. Nobody held out much hope when the phone rang once more.

"Lieutenant Commander Finn." Mickey automatically assumed it was Philip Scriven checking in.

"Signals, sir. Good news."

"Yeah?" The excitement in Mickey's voice caused ears to prick up and heads to appear around the doorjamb.

"Message from the lighthouse keeper on the Mokohinaus. Some hardy soul has just run out there in a supply boat."

"Yeah?" Mickey's heart began to race. The long shot was coming in. The one-in-a-million chance of a sighting.

"Apparently he was minding his business about ten miles south-west of the Mokes when a trawler running without lights lit up less than half a mile away from him."

"You beauty!"

"He cut his own running lights and watched. He's sure it was a Jap and they were deploying their net."

"When was this?"

"Around eighteen hundred hours, sir."

"Jesus Christ! Why didn't he tell us sooner?"

"Out of range of his radio. Too much static. He couldn't reach us until he'd anchored up in the lee beneath the lighthouse. Then he had to row ashore to use the lighthouse keeper's transmitter. All takes time. But the man's no fool. He's given us a bearing. The trawler was heading southwest on a course that would take it west of Little Barrier, sir."

"Who am I talking to?"

"Able Radioman John Press, sir."

"Listen, John. You talked to the man. How much credence do you give him?"

"Like I said, sir, the man's no fool. He turned off his running lights to avoid detection. He took a bearing. He rowed ashore in conditions that could not have been very pleasant to make sure we got the message. I'd say he was a good seaman and very much on the level. Do I believe him? Yes, sir, I do."

"Owe you a beer, Sparks." He rang off. "Action stations! Gloria, get hold of the *Cormorant*. Tell them we have a positive sighting of the target . . . let's see, where would the trawler be now? . . . five miles west of Little Barrier and heading south at between four and five knots. Plot the likely position of the target and tell them to approach at full speed, using Little Barrier Island as a radar shield. Got it?"

"Sir!"

"Then, get going!" For a moment he thought she was going to kiss him. West of Little Barrier and heading south. Whoever the skipper of the *Shoto Maru* was, the man had balls like pumpkins. Mickey moved his eraser into position and tried to predict the trawler's likely course. How greedy were they? Would they hit and run or, having got in there and found the conditions to their liking, go for all they could get? He felt a tremor of excitement. He didn't see Pumpkin Balls as the hit-and-run type. It had to be the Colville Channel. One broad sweep, then out through the channel before dawn and away south. It seemed so logical that Mickey wondered why he hadn't thought of it sooner. The *Shoto Maru* was heading south to the winter grounds, taking what it could along the way.

He thought about ordering the *Shearwater* to make full speed to cover the channel, then hesitated. There was no guarantee that the *Shoto Maru* would still be fishing when it reached there. That would depend on how wide an arc they fished, whether they were catching fish and how late they arrived there. He could do everything right and still end up with no evidence to make an arrest. Mickey groaned. He had to catch them at it, which meant he had to catch them actually fishing. But would they be where he wanted them to be in three hours' time? And how could he get a patrol boat within five miles of them?

"Gloria! Contact the *Shearwater* and tell them to hold their present position until the *Cormorant* is within five miles of Little Barrier, then make full speed toward the intercept point." He moved his eraser and paper clips into position on his chart. The odds had shortened but nowhere near enough. If the *Shoto Maru* deviated at all from its projected course, the *Cormorant* had little chance of finding her, and even if it did, his patrol boats could still come up empty-handed.

He couldn't count on the crew of the *Shoto Maru* taking twenty minutes to retrieve the net. The gulf waters were too shallow and the crew too well drilled. Five miles gave them time to get their catch safely on board and below decks, or to take the low-risk option and dump it. His only chance lay in catching them unawares. In the patrol boats' favor, they had a low profile that could be missed in the steep chop and interference. They also had the element of surprise. The Japanese skipper wouldn't be expecting them, and wouldn't be looking over his shoulder. If the *Cormorant* ran up behind them in their wake, and if the *Shoto Maru*'s radar operator was less than vigilant, there was an outside chance they might just catch the Japs with their trousers down.

Seventeen

Lieutenant Brian Littlemore was twenty-nine years old and the Cormorant was his first command. Like every young officer, he dreamed of the opportunities that could fast-track him through the ranks. The *Shoto Maru* offered him precisely the sort of opportunity he was looking for. An heroic arrest in appalling weather, unshakable grounds for conviction, justifiable public outrage—and plenty of publicity for the arresting officer. Provided he beat the *Shearwater* to the prize. He ran in close to the eastern shore of Little Barrier, taking advantage of the wind shadow and calmer seas to coax a few extra knots out of his boat. White water flew up from the bow and slammed into the bridge, a clear warning that they were rounding Little Barrier and running straight into the teeth of the westerly. The hull shuddered and the engine strained. Lieutenant Littlemore had no choice but to ease back to two-thirds speed. He consoled himself with the thought that the *Shearwater* would be doing things just as tough. He took his mark as he rounded East Cape and began his search in earnest. Five miles west-southwest, then due south with fingers crossed if no contact was made. Lieutenant Littlemore allowed himself a smile. It was hardly normal regulation naval search procedure, but Mickey Finn was hardly regulation navy, and certainly not normal. He regarded him as yesterday's hero, a relic from the war, full of passion and hatred of the enemy, with an ill-concealed disrespect for the navy's softly-softly approach to poachers. But he was a navy man's man, and relentless when he was on the trail of a poacher. There was nobody Lieutenant Littlemore would have preferred to have orchestrating the search, and he followed Mickey's instructions to the letter. Twenty miles to the south, the *Shearwater* was charging northward ten miles out from shore, equally hell-bent on glory and with the advantage of full tanks. But if Mickey Finn's best guess was right and if he stuck to the plan, Lieutenant Littlemore knew the *Shoto Maru* was his.

Down below him, his radar operator was twiddling with the settings, trying desperately to make some sense out of the noise and interference on his screen, searching for a contact. Effective range hovered around four and a half miles, and nothing he did afforded much improvement. Lieutenant Littlemore had no doubt that the *Shoto Maru* would spot them first if they ever got close enough, because its radar scanners were not only more powerful but positioned higher than his own and able to see farther. But he knew the weather would be limiting them, too, and a lot would depend on the human factor—the diligence of the Japanese radar operator.

"Coffee, sir."

Lieutenant Littlemore hadn't noticed his cox'n ghost up alongside him in the dark. "Thank you, Cox'n, you must be psychic."

"One mile to go, sir, before we turn south."

"One mile."

"Yes, sir. Then it's scrotum scrunch time."

Mickey had given up staring at the phone in his office. He couldn't will it to ring any more than he'd been able to will Gloria into his arms. He stared at her instead and considered his tactics. He'd been taught that people's resistance was at its lowest in the early hours of the morning, and he tried to decide whether or not to put the theory to test. Once again his mouth anticipated his brain.

"Something I've been meaning to ask you."

"Sir?"

Mickey looked up into her face, giving her his full and undivided attention. There wasn't the slightest hint of weariness about her, in fact he couldn't recall seeing her quite so alert and eager before. So much for theories. She met his gaze, expectantly, her big hazel eyes as round as saucers and as innocent as a schoolgirl's. He felt himself go weak at the knees and all his carefully marshaled words scramble into a heap inside his brain. Forty-three years old and a war veteran and he was still nervous about asking a young lady to have dinner with him. Not that dinner was the ultimate aim of the engagement. Should he or shouldn't he? The temptation was certainly there along with the opportunity. Time to make contact of the personal kind.

"Gloria . . ." he began and was suddenly relieved when the phone rang. "Excuse me. Lieutenant Commander Finn."

"Signals, sir. *Cormorant* reports a contact. Made and lost at the very limit of their range. Dead ahead and heading south. Approximately five miles. Almost spot on the predicted position."

"Bingo." Mickey spoke softly into the phone, suppressing his excitement for the sake of his audience. He gave Gloria a triumphant wink. "What speed is the *Cormorant* making?"

"Down to ten knots, sir. Weather dead abeam."

"Notify the *Shearwater*. We're coming down. I want to hear this ball by bloody ball." He stood up. Gloria still hadn't moved. She just gazed at him in awe and admiration. He threw his massive arms around her and hugged her. She responded with a strength he never suspected she possessed. "Right on the nail, Gloria. Right on the bloody nail. We've got them stone motherless cold with their noses in the trough. This is why we joined the navy. This is why you and I are going to have dinner together tomorrow night and celebrate."

"Whatever you say, sir."

"You got it! Now go. Round up the team."

The *Shoto Maru*'s winches whined as they struggled under the load. The ship pitched and rolled, treading water at half trawl speed as it hauled in the heavily laden net. The rear lights burst into life, lighting up the deck and the sea for a hundred yards all around. The otter boards inched toward the stern, were gathered in and coupled into sheaths. The water reflected pink. The pink of blood and thousands upon thousands of juvenile snapper. The net began its crawl up the stern ramp, creeping when Shimojo wanted it to rush. The deck crew glanced around nervously at the halo of light surrounding the stern, but the powerful arcs were unable to penetrate more than two or three hundred yards through the rain. The skipper watched approvingly as the crew connected the gantry cables to the lifting loops. A rope was already in position to split the load. The hours of training were paying dividends when it mattered most. Everything was under control, until the intercom blared.

"Captain! Contact two miles astern!"

Shimojo stared at the speaker, stunned speechless. Two miles! How had another vessel managed to come so close without detection? He was even less prepared when the intercom blared a second time.

"Captain! Second contact five miles southeast!"

The crew hesitated, awaiting instructions. The port chute was open and gaping hungrily.

"Continue!" barked Shimojo.

The codend lifted off the deck and swung toward the port chute, tore open, releasing the catch into the hold below. Shimojo looked on grimly. He checked his watch. They had time—just enough time—to stow fish and nets and clear the rear deck, but no reason to deny a request to board. They were caught red-handed unless . . . unless . . . His eyes hardened. Just as his crewmen opened the starboard chutes to accept the second half of the catch, he ordered a hard turn to starboard and full power. The bows lifted under the sudden thrust of the engines, heeled over sharply as the full force of wind and wave caught them broadside. The load of fish that had been slowly swinging from the port to the starboard chute accelerated. He heard the scream above the sound of the wind and knew his maneuver had succeeded. The second officer ran toward him with confirmation. Shimojo cut speed to four knots and turned back into the wind.

"Continue!" he ordered. "Discharge the catch!"

Lieutenant Littlemore peered intently into the murk, trying to spot the trawler in front of him. The contact had given no indication that it was aware of his presence and appeared to be maintaining trawl speed as best he could tell. He wished he could crank a few more

198

knots out of his boat, but the conditions made that impossible. Hopefully they had the *Shoto Maru* with its nets still in the water.

"Heading southwest, sir. Trawl speed."

"Good man." Why hadn't the trawler reacted? No matter how sleepy or incompetent their radar operator was, the *Cormorant* had to be showing up on their screen like a Christmas tree. The same with the *Shearwater*. In the end, he didn't care. All the evidence pointed to the fact that they had the *Shoto Maru* on toast. A dead duck waiting to be snapped up by the hounds.

"Cox'n!" he bellowed.

"Sir." The reply came soft but clear, without a hint of irony. The coxswain hadn't moved and was standing right alongside him.

"Sorry. Get a camera and stand by."

"Aye-aye, sir."

"Christ! Look! Dead ahead! Get that camera!" Lieutenant Littlemore could hardly believe his eyes. The rain ahead had begun to glow. He strained to catch detail in the hot spot at the center, but a wave crashed over the starboard bow, sending a solid wall of water onto his windscreen. But there was no doubting what he was seeing. The trawler had its stern lights on. It was still working. They'd caught the Japs red-handed. "Hurry, Cox'n!" But the words had barely left his lips when the boat disappeared, swallowed up into the night.

Mickey stared at the speakers in the communications room. Against all the odds they'd done it! Caught the Jap trawler cold with their hands in the till. He hardly dared breathe as Lieutenant Littlemore repeated his request.

"*Shoto Maru, Shoto Maru.* This is HMNZS *Cormorant* two hundred yards off your port bow. You are in breach of sovereign waters. Please hove to. You are ordered to stop, now! Over." Everyone was staring at the speakers, nobody breathing. Nothing. The Japanese were ignoring the *Cormorant*. Mickey pictured the patrol boat's spotlight playing on the trawler's bridge and wondered how anybody could possibly ignore it.

"They're goners," he pronounced. He listened as Lieutenant Littlemore again repeated his request. Almost leaped with joy when the Japanese voice responded, was instantly glad he hadn't.

"This is *Shoto Maru* 375. We request assistance. Repeat, we request assistance. Over."

"Request assistance?!" Mickey stared at the speaker in disbelief.

"Give me Lieutenant Littlemore!" Mickey brushed aside the radio operator.

"Littlemore, do you read me? Over."

"Come in, Lieutenant Commander. Over."

"Brian, for God's sake what's going on? They had their stern lights on. They were fishing. You caught them red-handed. What's happening on the rear deck? Over."

"Nothing, sir. The rear deck is deserted. Over."

"Christ!" Mickey put his head in his hands. "But you did see them fishing?"

"No, sir."

"Navigation lights?"

"On when we drew alongside."

Mickey groaned. What were the Japanese up to? He'd pulled off the impossible. He'd found them, caught them! They were fishing. "Brian, ask them what grounds they have for their request, and get a boarding party over immediately to check out the process line. Their request has given you grounds to board them. Christ! You don't need grounds! You have enough reason to send an army of occupation aboard. Go ahead. We'll listen in. Over."

The communications room sat silent, numbed, all eyes on the speakers. The exchange was labored, the voice hesitant, the English barely understandable, but its message was clear. It told them they'd lost. Their plan had been perfect, the execution faultless, yet they'd lost. Mickey stared down at the floor, aware that everyone was watching him, waiting for him to pull a miracle out of the hat. But there were no miracles left. The captain of the *Shoto Maru* had used up the last of them.

"You have to admire the bastard," Mickey said at last. "We had him, but he still beat us. Right now you can bet he has every man on board topping, tailing and packing fish, and there's not a bloody thing we can do about it."

He turned and left the communications room, dragging himself leaden-footed back to his office. The trawler's skipper had found the only way out of his predicament. But how had he managed to get someone to break his back for him at such a convenient time? What kind of man volunteered to fall down a fish chute? It was beautiful. What was the *Shoto Maru* doing in New Zealand waters? Coming into port on a mercy mission. Why were they traveling at trawl speed? To prevent further harm to the injured seaman. Why wouldn't they accept a boarding party? No point unless the *Cormorant* could provide them with a doctor, which it couldn't. Heaving to served no purpose. There was no choice but to let the *Shoto Maru* make its own time into port, which would be governed by the number of fish they needed to process. The skipper could take all the time in the world and crawl into port with a comet tail of seagulls eagerly gobbling up the waste from the processing line. Traitorous seagulls devouring the evidence. Mickey made up his mind to meet the *Shoto Maru* when it berthed at Marsden Wharf, even though he knew all the fish they'd hauled out of the gulf would be packed and frozen as solid as rocks. He wanted to meet the man who had beaten him

In the meantime, he had a report to write and a draft press release to prepare. TWO PATROL BOATS IN MERCY DASH TO RESCUE INJURED SEAMAN. Naval PR would love it, but anybody with any kind of a brain would realize that the *Shoto Maru* was almost certainly the boat that had been stealing fish right along the northeast coast and wonder why the navy was being so nice to them. After Lieutenant Commander Scriven's performance with the media, they'd also probably wonder why the navy was so stupid. Mickey swallowed a mouthful of coffee. It was stone cold but it didn't matter. It wasn't any colder than his career prospects.

Eighteen

~~~~~~~~~

Rosie awoke early, made an oilskinned dash to the loo, then, true to her new resolutions, began to exercise. Her muscles were stiff from the exertions of the preceding days but gradually warmed to the task. She began to realize what her more physical friends had been trying to tell her all her life. Her exercises made her feel alive and vital, unbelievably righteous and even buoyant. She'd had a number of men friends who'd exercised with weights, and divided their time equally between their apparatus and their mirror. Rosie had thought they were motivated by narcissism even though they talked grandly about the sense of well-being lifting weights gave them. Rosie didn't care about muscle definition or tone. She exercised to survive.

Crisp, slightly burned toast spread with Vegemite and accompanied by a cup of tea constituted breakfast. She planned her day as she nibbled at her toast. There were many things she could do, in fact, needed to do. For a start she had to get her boat working and learn how to operate it, against the day when she needed to take it around to Fitzroy. She was down to four small cans of diesel. She could do without butter, or meat, and had enough essential foodstuffs to get by, provided the occasional fish obliged her by hooking up on her line. The one thing she couldn't do without was power, and she couldn't have power without fuel for the generator. The boat was definitely a priority.

But so, too, was the toilet. She reasoned that if she only dug a little every day she'd dig a new pit soon enough. It was the perfect job for newly aroused muscles. She figured she could move the outhouse the same way. Dismantle it bit by bit, then put it back together again over the new pit. It all seemed so simple to a mind that had yet to wake up to the realities of foundations, verticals, levels and right angles. It didn't matter. In her heart, Rosie knew nothing was ever as simple as it seemed, but in the afterglow of her exercises, refused to entertain any negative thoughts. The longer she sat contemplating her next bold step, the more determined she became to strike a blow that would proclaim her permanence. In the strange logic of the moment it occurred to her to tackle the most dangerous but ultimately most satisfying job first. She decided to get rid of her greatest irritation. The scrape of torn guttering on her veranda roof had mocked and ridiculed her for not being man enough to fix it. There was her challenge, and her potential for triumph as proud and glorious as any flag atop any mountain. It was time to climb her Everest and stake her claim to Wreck Bay.

She washed her breakfast dishes, dressed in old clothes and overalls and wandered outside onto her veranda. The rain had eased to an exhausted drizzle. It was still cold, but there was no wind to cut through the fabric and chill her. She decided to spare her new oilskins and stepped out into the yard to examine her gutters and downspout. It amazed her the way things always rusted out first in the most inaccessible and inconvenient places. The hillside had been dug away to accommodate the western end of her bach and fell away sharply at the eastern end where the gutters had rotted. Even if she'd been able to find secure footing, Bernie's old extension ladder had no hope of reaching up to the corner. She had no choice but to crawl out over the roof. That presented its own problems. The roof sloped north and south from a central ridge, steep enough to indicate that Bernie had once taken pride in his workmanship. It glistened wetly and looked as slippery as all hell.

Rosie was no genius with rope but had endured enough knotted shoelaces as a schoolgirl to believe that a good granny could do most jobs. She threw two loops around the chimney stack, which poked up through the ridge in the uphill half of the roof. It would have

203

suited her better if it had been in the other half, but she still figured it could save her from catastrophe. She pulled the rope as tight as she could and tied it off with a triple granny. She looped the other end around her waist and tied it off also. Her ambition was limited. All she wanted to do was take a close look at the gutters and examine her options. Temporary repairs would suffice. With the rope attached, there was no way she could tip over the high side if the worst came to the worst. Nor would she hit the ground if she slipped and tumbled over the veranda. She judged that the rope would pull her up well short.

Confident that she wasn't about to kill herself, she gently eased herself across the ridge, then, with her head uppermost and belly flat to the corrugated-iron sheets, inched slowly down the slope. The roof had looked high from the ground, but somewhere along the way the height appeared to have doubled. She felt the first intimations that she might have made a terrible mistake. But her resolve held firm, and she had the consolation of knowing that once she reached the edge, she could put a hand or leg on the veranda roof to steady herself. When she reached the edge of the roof, she twisted onto her back, and began to inch forward on her bottom. The paint was old and flaking in places, but at least its worn and oxidized surface afforded some grip. She sighed with relief when her feet finally touched the roof of the veranda below. She wriggled into a secure position and sat up to examine the guttering. It had sprung loose from its supports and bent backward. But she quickly saw that if the two supports could be bent back into shape and the guttering refitted, it would do temporarily, provided she could also refit the downspout.

The downspout was in a sorrier state, with rust holes the size of a penny, but Rosie believed water preferred to fall vertically rather than sideways. Provided she could drag the pipe backward so that it ran pretty well straight up and down, she thought she could live with that as well, at least for the time being. The more she looked, the more confident she felt. She didn't need a drill, screws or nails to do the repairs, just a good length of wire. There were two old nail holes where the corrugated-iron sheet overhung the eaves that she could run wire through to support both gutters and downspout. The two holes couldn't have been better placed if she'd made them herself. Things were definitely looking up. She began to feel it was her lucky day.

Bonnie crouched in the corner of the sofa, staring at Angus eating his breakfast, and wondered why things had changed. When she'd gone to wake Angus, he'd thrown her off the bed. When she'd done her usual trick of weaving in and out of his legs while he prepared her breakfast, he'd yelled at her and pushed her away with his foot. He hadn't talked to her, hadn't played with her and was doing a very good job of ignoring her. Cats don't like that, and Bonnie didn't like that one bit.

Angus poured more salt on his porridge and tried to resolve the issue that had kept him tossing and turning all night. He still didn't know what to do about the woman. Had he been given one last chance? Or was he better off sticking to his original plan in the hope that she'd pack up and leave? His porridge had the consistency of glue, the way he liked it, so that it would stick to his ribs. But he had to be careful it didn't drip and stick to his shirt. Angus had decided to take his boat around to Fitzroy for fuel and supplies. For some reason he'd put on his best shirt for the occasion.

The more he thought about it, the more obvious it seemed that Rosie was precisely the woman he'd been looking for. She was the kind that liked men, and she didn't appear to be particularly discerning about who she gave her favors to, not if Red was any example. She had strong hips, ideal for carrying his child. She was also intelligent—he had to concede that—but he wondered if she had any other gifts with which to endow his offspring. He wished he knew her better but decided in the end it wouldn't matter. He expected his own stock to prevail in his son. He sighed and shook his head. It was too easy to get carried away by hopes and dreams and ignore the hurdles. There was a lot of ground to cover first; he had to befriend her, and more importantly, she had to befriend him and ultimately become indebted to him. She needed help, and he would provide it, and along the way weasel into her affections until the debt had grown to equal the one service he required of her.

He realized he'd have to tread carefully because any overt change in his attitude could put her on guard. He also had Red to consider, and their agreement. If Red saw him helping her, he would interpret that as a green light to run after her and attend to her every whim. That would spoil everything. Rosie wouldn't need him and that would be an end to his scheme. Another bitter defeat. More humiliation. He scraped the remains of his porridge off the bottom of the bowl and sat staring out through the window. The wind had died and the rain had eased, but there was no telling how long the lull would last. He knew he should leave early for Fitzroy and take advantage of the conditions while they lasted, but he couldn't drag himself up off his chair. For all his planning, scheming and wishful thinking, he still wasn't certain which path to follow.

Angus found Red sitting on his veranda, repairing the net he used to catch bait fish in the bay. It was the sort of job Angus also liked doing because it reminded him of the herring fishermen back in his home on the Minch. It was a skill he'd learned as a boy, and he looked critically at Red's handiwork as they exchanged greetings, making sure the repairs to the mesh were regular and uniform in size.

"I'm going around to Fitzroy," he said. "Do you have your list ready?"

"I'll get it." Red rose immediately.

"I'm not in such a hurry that you can't finish that repair first."

"Would you like to take over?"

"Aye, I would. Have you been to see the woman, since the crayfish?"

"Rosie? No cause."

"Ah, that's for the best."

"I'll get my list."

Angus looked around nervously and impatiently. There was no closeness between Rosie and the madman, which augured well. But he was still uncertain about pressing ahead with his plan. He wove the line through the torn mesh, fingers relishing the skill.

"You going to get Rosie's?"

Red was standing in front of him with his grocery list. Angus hadn't heard him return.

206

"Do you think I should?"

"She needs fuel."

"Well, if I must I suppose I must." He shrugged his shoulders in resignation, not just for Red's benefit but in acceptance. "I'll be away, then." When he reached the fork to Rosie's he paused briefly before taking the plunge. He picked up his step. Fortune never favored the fainthearted, nor women the weak. Angus had generated a sense of purpose to mask his real intent as he broke into the clearing in front of Rosie's bach. He looked up automatically. What he saw stopped him dead in his tracks.

"Dear God!"

"Help!" said Rosie unnecessarily.

Rosie had slipped off her Everest and hung, as helpless as a side of beef, midway between the veranda roof and the ground. There was no wall for her to brace her feet against so that she could haul herself back up. Nor did she have the strength to climb the rope. She'd been falling headfirst when the rope had pulled her up. The shock had winded her and left her dangling upside down, a livid welt around her hips. It had taken all her energy to pull herself upright. The rope had ridden up under her arms, dragging her shirt and sweater with it and leaving her midriff exposed beneath her overalls. Her shirt and sweater cushioned the chafing from the rope, but she could do nothing about the cold. At one point she'd considered trying to untie the knots but gave up the idea when she realized she would have landed on her veranda steps. She couldn't see how two broken legs would improve her situation.

"Dear God! Are you all right, woman?"

"I'll feel a whole lot better when you get me down." Angus had found her just when she'd thought she might be left hanging there for days. She could've kissed him.

"Do you have a stepladder?"

"Not one that's big enough."

"Well, I can't help you myself."

"What do you mean?" Rosie began to panic. Surely the old bastard wasn't going to leave her there? That would be carrying a grudge too far.

"I'll have to fetch Red." Angus tried to think of something encouraging to say. "Just hang on."

"Please hurry!" said Rosie. "Please!" She gritted her teeth and hung on. Her arms and body ached more than she'd ever thought possible. The welt around her hips stung like she'd been branded. Angus had found her but she couldn't help thinking what a ridiculous and pathetic spectacle she must have presented. An imposter in overalls. The seconds dragged, and the minutes marked their passage in pain. How long before she heard Archie's bark? How long before Red rushed to her rescue? Tears began to well in her eyes and trickle down her cheeks. That was okay. For once, she felt entitled.

When Archie burst into the clearing she thought her ordeal was over, but it wasn't, not quite. Red positioned his stepladder at the foot of the veranda steps and then had to climb up onto the roof to maneuver her toward it before he could begin to lower her. He seemed to take forever. Angus stood as far up the ladder as he dared, guiding her feet, then finally putting his arm around her waist and helping her down. Her legs buckled and refused to support her weight, and she would have fallen if Angus hadn't held her.

"Are you all right, woman?"

"Better than I was, thanks to you."

"Aye." He stood there, holding on to her, not knowing what to do next, wondering if this was the beginning of his plan. Here was a heaven-sent opportunity to break the ice, to be her hero, but the sudden intimacy unnerved him. Red climbed down from the roof and solved his dilemma.

"You okay, Rosie?" he said.

"Had better days."

Angus let Red take Rosie off him, lift her up gently and carry her indoors. He watched them go and wondered why he hadn't thought to do that. He hopped from one foot to the other in frustration and self-recrimination. He decided to follow them inside.

"My hero," he heard Rosie say. Watched as she blew Red a kiss. "How am I ever going to repay you?" How was she ever going to repay him!

"I played my part, too, you know," he said.

Rosie smiled at him. "Yes, you certainly did, Angus. I guess I owe you a kiss, too, a big one at that."

"Aye, you do."

Red lowered Rosie gently onto the sofa, stacked cushions around her and went into the bedroom for a blanket.

"I'd have been in serious trouble if you hadn't come around."

"Aye." Angus looked down at his feet and back up at her. He had no talent for small talk, never had. "What made you do such a damn fool thing?" He meant it kindly, but it didn't quite come out the way he intended.

Rosie bridled. "Someone had to fix the gutters, Angus, and there was a marked shortage of volunteers." She glanced up at Red as he tucked a blanket around her.

"Aye. I'll not deny that what you did took courage, but it was also foolhardy."

"Perhaps, but also necessary."

"Couldn't you at least have waited until the roof was dry?"

"Rainwater was flowing down the inside wall."

"Even so you had no right going up there on your own."

"I had every right and no alternative!" said Rosie, losing patience and snapping. She couldn't be bothered with Angus's criticism. She was too weary and too sore. "At least the downspout's connected up and the gutters back in place."

"Aye, but you could have got yourself killed doing it."

"Okay Angus, you saved my life. I'm grateful! God knows I'm grateful. You're right, I'm a weak and foolish woman. There! I've said it! What more do you want?"

"That's not what I meant."

"That's exactly what you meant. You don't want me here." Tears began to well in her eyes once more, and this time there was no rain to disguise them. "I know that. You know that. Red knows that. Now leave me alone!"

Angus turned away confused, unable to grasp exactly where he'd gone wrong. Why did women have to be so difficult? Why couldn't she see he meant well? He turned back to her for one last try.

"I'm going to Fitzroy. I came around to see if you needed anything. Fuel, perhaps?"

"I wondered what brought you."

"I came for your list."

"Well, thanks but no thanks. I don't want to put you to any more trouble on my behalf."

"Don't be stubborn, woman! It's the way things are done here." Angus closed his eyes. It was all slipping away, slipping inexorably away . . .

"Angus is right, Rosie."

"Butt out, Red," cut in Rosie. "Who rang your bell? Stay out of this!"

"I'll be off, then," said Angus stiffly. "I can see I'm not welcome."

"Get another drum of diesel," said Red. "And some chops."

"What the hell." Rosie thought of her diminished reserves of diesel and relented. "If this is the way things are done, who am I to argue? Get me pen and paper, Red, and I'll make my list."

"Don't go to any trouble on my behalf," said Angus.

Rosie laughed and looked at the dour old Scot in astonishment. "By Christ, Angus," she said, "that almost qualified as a joke."

Angus made his way down to his boat, congratulating himself on his wit. Things had got off to a poor start, but he'd managed to save the day. She owed him for his part in rescuing her and for fetching her fuel and groceries. It was a fair beginning, a fair deposit on the favor he'd one day ask. He was halfway across Katherine Bay before he stopped congratulating himself and realized his tactical blunder. He'd left Rosie in the arms of his rival. He'd left her with Red to reap the rewards of her gratitude.

"Damn woman!" he screamed. It had all been for nothing. Nothing! All his hopes and his dreams. Gone. He was a foolish old man who should've known better. He cursed again. The gulls screeched in scorn, and he had no doubt that their ridicule was aimed at him.

BOOK THREE

Nineteen

Another month passed. Rosie made her way back up to her bach after her morning jog along the beach. Red had waved to her from his boat, and that was all the company she expected to have that day. She was acknowledged, accepted and largely ignored. The unseasonal warm weather had brought with it an injection of hope and confidence. The downspout and gutters rattled in the wind but did their job. Her wall was slowly drying. The days were surprisingly mild, and though the temperatures plummeted overnight, her Shacklock kept the bach warm and cosy. She regretted her decision to spend the day scraping and painting. Three sides of her home now glistened with a fresh coat of paint, but the fourth was a rude reminder that the job was not yet finished, and the reason she hadn't gone fishing.

She'd used her injuries shamelessly to keep Red in attendance and twice enticed him back into her bed. In the intimate hours of early morning she'd made him promise to help her get her boat going. Even then she sensed his reluctance, but he stood by his word. He'd changed the oil and water and lent her a battery while hers had recharged. "A plodder," was how he'd described her boat, and that suited Rosie perfectly. She wasn't yet game enough to take it around to Port Fitzroy, but she was having a ball running it out to the close-in fishing reefs.

Her favorite spot was the pinnacles off Bernie's Head, where she went at sunset. The pinnacles were the remains of an island that had simply eroded away, leaving five vertical tombstones of rock to mark its passing. The terns, cormorants and gannets that jostled for room on the peaks were Rosie's audience while she fished, and entertainment when they scrambled for her leftover bait and fish guts. She never came home without a good catch of snapper, trumpeter or tarakihi, and was rapidly becoming addicted to the sport. Her one disappointment was that Red still kept his distance.

Rosie had taken him into her bed, but it was clear that it gave her no bargaining power. He never asked to stay the night, she asked him. They'd given each other company and affection, and the measures were equal. There was no debt to call upon. The toilet sat resolutely immobile, and every visit was punishment. Weeds grew between the lengths of new guttering.

"Why won't you help me do the things I can't do?" she'd asked him bluntly one morning as he made breakfast. He'd squirmed so much that Rosie wished she'd never asked.

"Can't, Rosie," he'd said finally. "It's not that I don't want to, I just can't."

"Why not?"

"Got other work, Rosie. Other work to do." The anguish in his voice had warned Rosie to back off. Once again she'd glimpsed the symptoms her patients used to display. The fixation with routine. The inability to cope with more than one thing at a time. The unwillingness to change plans.

"What other work?" she'd asked.

"Got to cut a track up to Tataweka." He'd turned away and stirred his fish rice.

"Okay. And afterward?"

"Dunno! I dunno."

Rosie had let the matter drop.

The unpainted side of the bach faced southeast, where the hill fell away and left just a narrow strip for her to seat her ladder. On Red's suggestion, she'd hunted through the generator shed and found the means by which Bernie had managed before her. It had come as a relief to realize that she didn't have to reinvent the wheel every time a job needed doing. Bernie had managed, and the tools that had enabled him to manage were usually in the shed. She drove heavy wooden pegs into the ground about eight feet away from either side of the ladder and ran ropes from the pegs to a rung two-thirds of the way up to secure it. Wedges, another discovery, kept the ladder level and stable. She stepped back and admired her handiwork, enjoying her new skills and usefulness, but aware that the final quarter of the wall, where the guttering hung suspended from wires, would remain unpainted until she found a safe way to get to it, or someone to do it for her. It was simply beyond her confidence and competence to perch on the very tip of her ladder or hang over the roof. Nevertheless, another day of achievement beckoned, after which she'd soak her tired muscles in a healing bath before sitting down to a healthy meal of steamed tarakihi and vegetables over rice à la Red O'Hara.

She couldn't help noticing that her body was changing. Parts that sagged had either toned up or disappeared. She'd lost weight and found muscles she never knew she possessed. She'd never felt so healthy and full of energy in all her life. Regrettably her breasts had also adapted to the new regime by losing some of their fullness, but she consoled herself with the knowledge that there was no one around to care. She doubted that Red would notice if she woke up one day as flat as the wall she was scraping. She could hear him high up on the ridge above her, taking his parang to the scrub. She smiled. She found it hard to think of Red and not smile. She liked having a man in her bed and wanted him there more often. She was good in that department, and sleeping alone seemed to her a waste of her God-given talent. Red was kind, strong, sensitive and undemanding. He was everything she wanted and more. It was the more that was the problem, and she wished her father would hurry up and answer her letter. The man needed help, and it was unfair that he had to fight his battles alone.

As she sanded the weatherboards she couldn't help but see the back of her hands, one braced against the wall while the other rubbed. They were no longer the soft hands of a doctor or office worker, but two indispensable tools. They'd become chafed, callused and wrinkled, work worn and weathered by sun and wind. In a per-

215

verse way, she was proud of them. They were no longer hands that wrote reports, but working hands that baited hooks, hauled in hard-fighting fish and filleted them. They were the hands of a survivor.

She worked her way down from the eaves to the cement-block foundations and prepared to shift her ladder, but her thirst got the better of her. She washed her hands in the laundry and stripped off her overalls. They were so masculine and functional, simply pulling them on made her feel competent. She threw a couple of sticks of hakea into the Shacklock and opened the vent, then collapsed on a chair on her veranda while she waited for her kettle to boil. The cicadas had gone with summer, and the bees had vacated her neck of the woods for others with blossom. There was nothing to interrupt the silence of the bush except the occasional birdcall and the distant, lonely, chip-chop-chip of Red's parang. She knew what he was doing—cutting a trail through to the top of Tataweka Hill so that he could watch for Japanese trawlers—but had no idea why he would want to. Her mistake was to dismiss it as another of Red's eccentricities, another hangover from the war. She put her head back and closed her eyes, as happy as a lizard on a hot rock.

Whoop, whoop, whoop!

The sound made her leap bolt upright. High on the hill, Red had stopped chopping. She wasn't imagining things. The terrible noise, wherever it had come from, was real.

Whoop, whoop, whoop!

It took her a moment before she remembered where she'd heard the sound before. In war movies. Her head swam with images of submarines diving, charging destroyers, sailors rushing to action stations. For reasons she couldn't begin to imagine, the navy had come calling. She forgot about her tea and set off down the trail, checked, remembered that she was only wearing bikini bottoms and a ragged T-shirt in which her breasts flapped around like snapper in a sack. Hardly proper attire to greet the navy although, given her current state of near celibacy and the reputation of sailors in port, she thought it might actually send an appropriate message. Nevertheless she raced back to her bach to change. She took her kettle off the heat as she passed by, and opened drawers of clothing. She settled on white shorts and a halter top that showed off her new slim-line waist and made the most of what remained of her breasts. She tried to run a comb through her hair, but it jammed in the paint dust.

"Oh, shit!" She looked in the mirror and saw that the dust had turned her dark, Spanish hair prematurely gray. She had no choice but to try to sluice some of it off. Better she look a mermaid than a painted lady, she thought savagely. She gave herself one last check in the mirror, shook her head in despair at what she saw and set off.

Red hadn't recommenced chopping, so she figured he was also heading for the beach. She'd puttered around, changing and washing, but she still thought she could beat him. She had no idea why this should be important, but it was. Perhaps because she was so unaccustomed to living alone, she wanted first call on any fresh faces that showed up. She discounted Angus, deciding he'd be content to stand on his veranda and shake his fist at the intruders. Nevertheless she ran as fast as the track would allow, dodging the stumps and roots and the dried-up puddles where the clay was still damp and treacherous. She slowed and composed herself before calmly strolling onto the beach. The patrol boat was standing off in the deeper water, its crew lowering a tender. Red and Archie were waiting patiently on the beach in front of her.

"I assume they're ours," she said.

"They're bringing my radio." His voice was flat. Cold.

"I would have given you mine if you'd asked."

"Not that kind of radio, Rosie. He promised me a radio so I could report on the Jap trawlers."

"He? Who is he? Father Christmas?"

"Lieutenant Commander Finn."

"First name's not Huckleberry, is it?"

"No, it's Mickey."

"That'll do, that'll do." Rosie couldn't help smiling. She turned to look at Red to share the joke but could see immediately that the elsewhere look had crept back into his eyes. And something she hadn't seen before. A hardness. His face was set, grim and stony, and the lines that wrinkled on the few occasions he smiled revealed their true origins. She wondered if she'd finally glimpsed what it was that

217

held his body and soul together against the ghosts that inhabited him. She took his hand in hers and squeezed hard. He neither resisted nor reacted. She wanted to give him a reassuring hug, but the hardness in his face dissuaded her. Rosie kept her eyes on the tender, the rating at the helm, the other standing at the bow and the officer sitting nonchalantly between. She was suddenly aware of the fact that she was holding Red's hand and let go. The helmsman cut the engine, and the tender ran up onto the sand.

"Morning, Red. Morning, Archie. Sorry for the intrusion."

"Morning, sir."

Sir? Rosie looked around at Red as if expecting him to have suddenly acquired a uniform.

"And good morning to you, madam." Mickey held out his hand toward her. "I'm Lieutenant Commander Michael Finn and—?"

"And everyone calls you Mickey."

"Ahhhh. Yes. And you are . . . ?"

"Rosie," cut in Red. "She's my neighbor."

"Pleased to meet you, Rosie." Mickey looked inquiringly at Red as if he'd been withholding vital information.

"I'm pleased to meet you, too, Mickey," said Rosie. "We don't get many visitors here. Do your friends have names, or are they too insignificant?"

Mickey turned to the two grinning ratings. "This one's Gary and that one's Gavin. It's naval policy to put men with similar-sounding names together to cause maximum confusion."

Rosie shook hands with them both. "Nice to see you, boys." She gave them her best smile, something for them to fantasize about during the long nights on watch. Something for her to fantasize about on the long nights when Red kept his distance.

"Did you bring my radio?" said Red.

"Yep, and your glasses." Mickey dragged himself away from Rosie and back to the reason for his visit. He hadn't expected much of a welcome and hadn't got one. It was clear Red was determined to keep strictly to business, and not keep them a second longer than was absolutely necessary. "I suppose I'd better start showing you how to use it. Is there somewhere we can go?"

"There certainly is." Rosie smiled engagingly.

Mickey was sure Red wouldn't allow him to go any farther than the long grass bordering the beach. He seized on the prospect of a better alternative. "Where do you suggest?"

"My place. I'll make lunch while you show Red how to play with his new toy." She smiled sweetly. "Gary and Gavin can carry the radio and batteries. I'm sure I can find ways of amusing them while you and Red do what you have to do."

"Thank you. Red, do you have any objections?"

Red had, but nonetheless shook his head as if he hadn't. The two ratings looked at Rosie, their mouths open as each speculated on the type of amusement Rosie had in mind. Not surprisingly, worn gutters did not feature in any of their frantic speculations.

Red led the way up the track, wondering how something so simple had suddenly become so complicated. He'd thought that the lieutenant commander would just hand over the radio, show him which knobs to turn, give him a frequency, a call sign and sched, then sail off into the sunset. Instead, here he was escorting him up to Rosie's bach with two grinning ratings in tow. It wasn't right. It wasn't what they'd agreed. They'd barely made it to the old pohutukawas where the track split when Angus stepped out onto the trail in front of them.

"That'll do! You've come far enough. Be gone the lot of you, or I'll be forced to defend my property." He waved his rifle menacingly. "Go on! Be gone! You've no right to be here!"

The column stopped dead in its tracks. Mickey turned to Red for inspiration. Rosie started laughing.

"Lieutenant Commander Mickey Finn," she began, "please meet ex-Inspector Angus McLeod." Neither man took a step toward the other. "Angus is the director and organizer of our social club."

"That's enough! I've told you before. I'll not be mocked by the likes of you!"

"Then listen carefully, Angus. One, this is crown land we're standing on. These men have every right to be here. Two, they've brought Red a radio so he can report on foreign trawlers in the area. Three, if Red doesn't do this for them, they're going to set up a permanent

219

watch on Tataweka Hill. Would you like that? A permanent naval presence in our backyard?"

"Is this true?" Angus turned to Red for confirmation.

"Use your eyes, Angus!" Rosie didn't trust Red to continue her little fiction. "Would the navy send a lieutenant commander if they weren't serious?"

Angus lowered his rifle. "Aye, I suppose you've got a point. Let me see the radio."

Gary held up the radio so Angus could see it.

"I've seen the likes before. I accept your need for a lookout, but there's no cause for you to proceed any farther. I used similar equipment in the war. I'll teach Red how to use it. You can all go. You're not needed. Just give me the frequencies on the way down to the beach."

"I've invited everyone to lunch, and they've accepted. So stand aside, you old fart, or I'll start telling stories. Stories, Angus, about little boys and fearsome griffins. Are we on the same frequency?"

"God damn you, woman!" Angus's eyes flared wide in anger.

Rosie pushed past him, and the rest followed. Mickey rolled his eyes. The two ratings were trotting after Rosie like dogs after a bitch on heat. What the hell was she doing here, he wondered, a beautiful woman with two madmen for company? "Does Angus normally greet visitors with a rifle?"

"Angus doesn't normally greet visitors." Rosie laughed again. "I don't know why, but for some reason we tend not to get many."

"The rifle is for shooting feral cats," cut in Red matter-of-factly. "Lee Enfield .303. The safety catch was on."

"Relieved to hear it." Mickey sighed, wondering how to approach Red in light of Angus's revelation. "Red, do you think you could encourage Angus to assist in spotting trawlers? There'll be times when you'll be out fishing or around at Fitzroy when he could cover for you. What do you think?"

"If you say so."

"Good." Mickey decided to leave things at that. He'd planted the seed and knew Red was incapable of not following up on his suggestion. Besides, the trail was steeper and longer than he'd expected. He was fast running out of breath and what little he had left he didn't want to use up talking. He heard a bird call high above them on Tataweka Hill and glanced up to see what all the lines on the survey maps had been trying to tell him. Tataweka hadn't looked quite so dominating on the map nor from sea level. As the track opened up into the clearing in front of Rosie's bach, he stopped to take a longer, more critical look. He closed his eyes, pictured his maps and looked once more. "God Almighty," he murmured.

"Pretty, isn't it?"

"More than that, Rosie." Excitement crept into his voice. "That hill overlooks the entire entrance to the gulf. Red, how far north can you see?"

"Way past the Mokes."

"And south?"

"Only southeast past Arid Island."

"Doesn't matter. I've got a man on the hill at Mercury Bay to cover your blind spot."

"I'll take you up there. I'm cutting a path through to the Tataweka trail."

"Not necessary," said Mickey hastily. He'd done all the hill climbing he was capable of. "Maybe you can show Gary and Gavin."

"I'll put the kettle on while you set up your gear." Rosie turned and gave the two ratings her best smile. "Come with me, boys, I'm going to take you to heights you never imagined."

Rosie sat in a shallow bath and did her best to make herself presentable. The two young ratings had clipped her new guttering into place and splashed paint on the parts of the wall she couldn't reach. She'd rewarded them with a lunch of curried eggs and rice, after which they'd set off up Tataweka with Red. Mickey dozed in the sun on her veranda with his feet up on the rail. She washed her hair under the tap, threw on some eau de cologne, shorts and a shirt knotted at the front. All in all, she had every reason to feel pleased with herself. Her gutters were finally fixed permanently, and the covert looks from the two ratings were proof she still had what it took. Mickey also fascinated her. When he'd wandered out onto the veranda and rocked back in his chair, she'd suddenly realized how long it had been since a man had relaxed in her company. What's more, she was thoroughly relaxed with him, despite the fact that he wore a uniform and was a senior officer in the armed forces.

Ever since her student days, when she'd marched to ban the bomb and war in general, she'd always distrusted anyone in uniform. Yet Mickey contradicted all her preconceptions. He was a big, cuddly bear, charming and disarmingly offhand, not disrespectful toward his uniform, but he didn't exactly dignify it, either. She decided to join him on the veranda. His eyes were closed, and he hadn't moved. He didn't bother opening his eyes when she spoke to him.

"Hope you don't mind my taking advantage of your men."

"Not at all. It's the job of the armed forces to serve."

Rosie smiled. That was precisely the sort of response she'd expected, flippant and lightly facetious. She couldn't help liking him. "I can handle most things, but there are some jobs I can't do."

"I think you're doing brilliantly." He turned to look Rosie in the eye. "Anyone who can make it out here has my unqualified admiration."

Rosie blushed. "If the gutter had broken anywhere else I think I could have managed."

"Rosie, relax. You don't have to apologize. Gary and Gavin are good lads, they were happy to help out." Mickey looked at her quizzically. "It sounds like a really bad line, but what's a nice girl like you doing in a place like this? Why aren't you married to a disgustingly rich, embarrassingly handsome man who is devoted to you and your two-point-two children?"

Rosie laughed. "Tried that, but it didn't appeal."

"Can't think why not."

"I come from a family of doctors and overachievers. My brothers captained the first fifteen and first eleven, graduated with high honors, became doctors and each married a brainless beauty with flawless complexion, long legs and conversation that centered on the *Woman's Weekly.* I was expected to marry a doctor, too, and I did. He was handsome, talented and bound for riches, and if I'm totally honest, he was a genuinely nice guy. One day he expected me to have his child and I saw myself turning into the same sort of silly, vacuous woman that my brothers married. I looked at where my life was heading and decided I wanted out. Look where it got me."

"Abandoned and penniless," said Mickey.

"Not exactly penniless. My grandfather provided for me in his will by setting up a trust fund that earns just about enough to get by on, and I do have some money of my own in the bank."

"So just abandoned?"

"Like Orphan Annie," said Rosie. She really enjoyed the banter. That was something else she missed. "What about you?"

"Also abandoned." Mickey closed his eyes as if the subject was both boring and tiring. "Married during the war, came home to a wife who'd fallen in love with a U.S. Marine lieutenant. She now has three kids and lives in Fort Lauderdale. She left me the dog, but it got run over."

"Maybe we should team up," said Rosie. "We could always get another dog."

"Too far to go to work," said Mickey. "Besides, I can't mend gutters."

"Pity," said Rosie. "Can you move toilets?"

"Far too hard."

"I suppose it would be pushing it a bit to ask Gary and Gavin to do it?"

Mickey smiled. "Yes, I think that would be pushing it. That's a big job, and I think they're planning on diving for some crayfish. Why don't you get Red or Angus to help?"

"Angus doesn't want me here."

"And Red?"

"He doesn't object. But his life wouldn't change if I left."

"He's madder than I thought. Why don't you hire someone to move the toilet for you?"

"Who?"

"I assume one of those boats in the bay is yours."

"Yeah, but I'm not yet confident enough to take it around to Fitzroy. I don't want to sink like the *Wairarapa.*"

"Then why don't you walk?"

"How?"

"Well, if Red's cut a path through to the Tataweka trail, all you'd have to do is turn down the trail to the road. It goes all the way through to Fitzroy. Take you three hours at the most."

Rosie looked at Mickey in absolute astonishment. Trail? Road? How many days had she heard Red chopping away at the scrub above her, not realizing for an instant that he was providing the means of her salvation? Her original vision of herself tramping the hills as a latter-day Heidi sprung back into her mind. Yes! All things were now possible. She had a supply route and access to workmen. Her permanence was guaranteed. Her joy boiled over and descended on Mickey.

"My God!" she cried, threw her arms around him and kissed him full on his lips. She lifted her head and screamed with joy and triumph, an action that drew Mickey's head hard against her breasts. All her problems were solved. Gone! It was only when she felt Mickey struggle that she realized what she was doing. She pulled back so that he could breathe, but her breasts were still mere inches from his face.

"I'm sorry, but you can't imagine what this means to me!"

"Did I object?"

"You've saved my life, do you know that?"

"God knows you've taken years off mine." Mickey smiled, embarrassed, still caught up in the feel of her lips and the crush of her breasts, intimacies he'd always imagined with Gloria and never expected again from anyone else. Rosie took his hand and pulled him gently up out of his chair, eyes locked onto his like radar. Mickey had seen that look before, a long time before, but hadn't the slightest doubt what it meant. Systems reactivated and long-dormant parts stirred. Rosie led him indoors, and even though Mickey had never set foot in her home before, he knew exactly where they were headed.

Angus stood at the end of the track where it opened onto Rosie's plot, mouth agape and speechless. Like Mickey, he had absolutely no doubt what Rosie had in mind. He'd come up to offer his expertise with the radio. After due consideration and much muttering, he'd de-

224

cided his best interests lay in helping the navy rather than having more neighbors. He'd intended to offer himself as a backup for Red—well, not so much his backup as his controller. He saw himself as the organizer and decision maker, and Red as the willing pair of legs. With Red under his guidance, he was certain that they could satisfy the navy's requirements. That had been his intention until he'd seen Rosie hijack the officer and drag him off to her lair. He was stunned and outraged, but more than anything, stung by this further proof of his failure. It could have been him. Should have been him! He'd been given his chance but hadn't been smart enough to take it.

"Damn you!" he said aloud and in anguish. "Damn you and your scheming ways!" Everything she did only served to confirm his worst fears. She was destined to torment him, to tempt and tease him to the point of madness. Yet he believed she was precisely the kind of woman he'd spent his life searching for. He stumbled blindly down the trail, overwhelmed by bitterness and resentment, yet still searching for reason not to give up hope. What if he changed his ways, apologized, offered to help? What if, what if, what if? His mind reeled with options fanciful and fleeting, owing more to desperation than reason. He had to do something or leave, because it was a situation he could not bear to live with. But what could he do?

Twenty

*R*osie didn't rush to hike over the hills to Fitzroy. Red still hadn't quite *finished the track, and there was no need. She had enough diesel and* food to get by. Besides, the colder weather had taken some of the sting out of visiting the toilet. It was enough for her to know that a solution was at hand whenever she was ready. She'd busied herself by preparing her garden for spring planting, and enjoying the things she treasured. She decided to take advantage of a brief dry spell to give her kelim rugs a long-overdue beating, dragged them out onto her veranda and draped them over the rail. It was the kind of work Rosie relished, the kind she'd rarely found time for back in the rat race in Auckland. She'd already cleaned up the old anchor, revarnished its woodwork and given it pride of place in her living room. She'd done the same with the bullock yoke, and together they gave Rosie a sense of permanence, a feeling of belonging and of being part of the island's history. The bach no longer bore any trace of Bernie's previous occupancy and had become her home, saturated in her taste and character. She was debating whether to wash her rugs when Angus appeared at the top of the track. Rosie believed her months at Wreck Bay had prepared her for anything, but nothing had prepared her for the Angus that marched up to the foot of her steps with half a dozen pink roses in his hand.

"Morning, Angus," she said. "Are they for me or are you lost?"

"Good morning, Rosie. How are you?"

"Fine. And you?"

"Oh, I'm fine."

"Are you lost?"

"No . . ."

"Then I assume the roses are for me."

"Aye, they are. Winter blooms. I grow them in a little sheltered sun trap. They think it's spring."

"They can think what they like. They're beautiful. Come on up."

"Thank you."

Rosie took the roses from Angus. "May I ask what the occasion is?"

"I'm not a young man, Rosie, and I am rather set in my ways. I concede my rudeness has been unwarranted, and I've come to apologize."

"You've what?!"

"You heard me. And I mean it, mind."

"Angus, I'm overwhelmed. Sit down, sit down! I'll go find a vase for these and put the kettle on."

Angus sat. He hadn't a clue what to say next. "I see you're managing," he called out. "New paint and gutters. It does you credit. It's not an easy life out here."

"I rather suspect you wouldn't have it any other way," said Rosie. She placed a tray of cake and biscuits on the table. "Am I right?"

"Aye, possibly."

"I'll get the tea, and while we drink it you can tell me why."

Once again Angus wondered if his visit was a terrible mistake. He'd barely said hello and already she wanted him to tell his life story. He gritted his teeth and decided to tell her a bit in the hope that she'd tell him a bit about herself. It never hurt to know the background of the woman who was potentially the mother of his child.

Rosie brought the tea out and sat down. "I'm all ears," she said.

"Have you heard of a place called Achiltibuie?"

"No."

"Have you heard of Ullapool?"

"No."

"Few people have. Ullapool is about as far as you can go on the northwest coast of Scotland. Achiltibuie is a little bit farther, a little

227

fishing village loved by summer visitors. If they ever came in winter they'd never come back. My father was a crofter. We had a few sheep and a garden and did a bit of fishing in summer. There were seven of us, three boys and two girls, and two others that didn't make it past their first year. There is more food in my house now for one person than there ever was in the croft for seven. There was no radio nor cinemas. I remember sitting around a fire in the evenings when I was a lad, listening to tales my uncle told of faraway lands. He was chief engineer on the *Dumbarton* and encouraged me to follow in his footsteps. From the day I was born I was always destined to leave Achiltibuie. I had no choice in the matter. Achiltibuie is no different to many villages in Scotland and casts off its surplus. There was no work nor the prospect of any, and families could not afford to carry passengers. I knew I'd be forced to leave once I was old enough.

"My uncle paid for me to go to England when I was ten years old, to relatives in Barrow, up in the north. I worked hard to become an engineer, but other boys had a gift I lacked, and they were the ones who got the jobs. In the end I joined the Lancashire constabulary. One day I read about New Zealand, and it rekindled dreams of the fair country in the southern oceans my uncle used to talk about, the wee bit of Scotland transplanted to the other end of the earth. There was nothing holding me in Barrow so I sold everything I owned and bought my passage. You've seen my face on television, so you know the rest."

"Who could forget those eyebrows?"

"Are you mocking me?"

"Not at all. I think they give you character." Rosie laughed. "But tell me something, if things were so dire and so hard as a child, why do you still hanker for the life?"

"Aye, there's no denying it was hard, but it was also good. Man pitted against nature. None of the silliness or shallowness of these times. Now, is there more tea in that pot? It's your turn to tell me about yourself."

"What about your writing?"

"I don't discuss my writing!"

"Okay, calm down. What can I tell you about myself? Not a lot. I'm a child of privilege born into a family of doctors. I was educated

228

to be a doctor, became a doctor, even married a doctor. One day I ceased being a doctor and a wife and lived happily ever after."

"You're a doctor?"

"Yes, Angus. Didn't Red tell you?" Rosie was stunned by Angus's sudden intensity. His face had lit up into an almost beatific smile.

"A doctor? Of medicine?"

"Yes. I really wanted to be a witch doctor, but no one was offering the course."

"A doctor! That changes everything."

"Changes what? What are you talking about?"

"Of course your father was a doctor! I'd forgotten. Red told me about Bernie's letter, so I knew he was a doctor. Red never told me you were a doctor."

"Would you have been nice to me if you'd known?"

"Aye, I would've."

"You would've mended my gutters, shifted my toilet, fixed my boat?"

"Aye, I would've helped."

"But you wouldn't have helped a market researcher, a reporter or a fruit picker?"

Angus began to realize the dangerous ground he'd trespassed upon. "I'm not saying I wouldn't have helped."

"You're not saying you wouldn't have, but the fact is you didn't."

"No . . . I didn't, there's no denying it." He stared unhappily at his plate. "I did apologize, you know."

Rosie softened but wasn't ready to forgive. "Yes, you did, and for your sake it's best I don't forget it. Oh my, is that the time? Thank you for the roses and the chat."

Angus rose instantly to his feet. "Thank you for the tea. I'll not keep you from your work. Is there, perhaps, something I could help you with?"

"Thank you, Angus, but I think I'll manage."

"Well, the offer stands. I enjoyed your company."

"People have always complimented me on my bedside manner."

"Aye, well, I'll be away. You're welcome to drop by my house anytime."

"I can hardly wait."

"Aye, I'll be off, then."

"See you later."

"Aye."

Rosie watched Angus walk off down the track, wondering whether boiling the Scot in oil would be too merciful.

Angus left Rosie scarcely able to contain his joy. Rosie was a doctor! From a family of doctors! He saw her as ideal breeding stock and couldn't help speculating on the wonderful gifts she could pass on to his son. His joy was not diminished by the recognition that he still had a long way to go before he could present her with his proposition. But he'd broken the ice and established a basis for friendship. He'd made the offer of help and believed it was only a matter of time before she took him up on it. Then he could begin to build the debt of gratitude.

"There is hope," he told himself, and the realization sent a thrill through his body. There was still hope after all.

Two days passed before Rosie saw Angus again. She'd begun to make a chocolate cake when she realized the omission from her last order. She'd run out of cocoa. There was no point in going around to Red's, because he'd gone fishing, and their relationship hadn't reached the stage where she could help herself to his supplies in his absence. Rosie could've changed her mind and made a sponge, but she had a craving for chocolate. There'd been nights when she and Norma had eaten an entire Cadbury's Family Block between them and fought over the crumbs. Her craving left her no choice but to pull on a jersey and boots and head off down the hill to make a house call. She wondered how Angus would react to the breach of protocol when she came begging cup in hand.

As she turned up the path by the pohutukawas she began to have second thoughts. She wasn't sure she wanted to face Angus as a pathetic woman on the scrounge. But her heart was set on making a chocolate cake, and in that instant she realized there was no limit to how low she would stoop to get what she wanted. She entered the

230

clearing below his bach. The sound of his typewriter carried clearly to her. Oh well, she thought, in for a penny . . .

"Hello, Angus!"

The typing stopped. She waited until his lean frame filled the doorway. She was determined to get the first word in and set the agenda.

"It's Dr. Trethewey. I need some cocoa for medical research."

"It's you, Rosie. Come on up, come on up. I was just about to put the kettle on. You've time for tea?"

"I dare say my research can wait." Rosie laughed and climbed the steps up onto his veranda. She was both puzzled and pleased by Angus's reaction. He'd changed and done a full about-face, but for the life of her she couldn't think why. She decided to press the advantage while she still had it. "I need a whole cup of cocoa, but don't leave yourself short whatever you do. I'll replace it when I get my next order."

"Don't worry, I've plenty. Sit down, sit down! Aye, it's nice to see you, Rosie."

"Give me all you can spare," said Rosie. Angus made no move to take her cup.

"Bonnie will look after you while I put the kettle on and get your cocoa."

Rosie was totally bemused and determined not to relax until she had the cup of cocoa firmly in her possession. Angus had the same idiot smile on his face that had appeared when he discovered she was a doctor, and that worried her. There was something sickeningly syrupy about him, and she knew Angus well enough to know he never did anything without a good reason. Bonnie jumped up on her lap and arched her back to be stroked.

"What's going on, Bonnie? He's not growing marijuana out back, is he? Not getting into the sauce more than is good for him? Come on, you can tell me, I'm a doctor." But Bonnie was too blissed out on the new, soft, padded lap and wafts of Rosie's bath oil and perfumed talc to respond. "You're as stupid as he is," said Rosie.

"Tea and cocoa. You may as well take the whole packet. I have a spare."

"That's very kind of you. I'll get you another."

"Now, what kind of research is it you have in mind, exactly?"

"I want to know how much chocolate cake I can eat in a hot bath before the steam makes it go soggy."

Angus laughed nervously. "No, seriously."

"I am serious."

"You eat chocolate cake in the bath?"

"I'm about to."

"Well, I never."

"If you like I'll save you a piece."

"Aye, that would be nice. I'll not eat it in the bath, mind."

"Angus, don't you ever get the urge to live a little?"

"If that's living I'll happily stay the way I am. Now, is there anything else you need? Some sugar, perhaps?"

"No, I have everything I need, thank you."

"Good, good. And the work? How is the work going?"

"Fine. I'm waiting for a wet day to strip my counters and table back to kauri and varnish them."

"There'll be plenty of them before winter's out. Anything else?"

"I'm thinking of getting a couple of men in to move the toilet and dig a new cesspit."

"What?"

"When Red finishes the trail up to Tataweka, I'm going to walk through to Fitzroy and hire a work crew."

"You'll do no such thing! I'll not stand for it!" Angus slammed his cup down on the table. His eyebrows danced and bristled. "I'll not have this place crawling with strangers! Have you lost your senses, woman?"

"Welcome back, Angus." Rosie tucked the packet of cocoa under her jersey and stood. If there was going to be a fight she wanted to make sure her cocoa didn't fall casualty.

"I'll not have strangers here! Do you hear me?"

"Hard not to. Now you listen to me. You cope your way and I'll cope mine. The toilet needs moving, and I need men to help me. End of story."

"I'll speak to Red. He'll not allow it either."

"It's not your business or Red's. Good day!"

"Not so fast, not so fast. I'm sorry Rosie, I'm sorry for shouting." Angus slumped forward with his head in his hands. "Dear God, I didn't mean to upset you. I just don't want strangers here. We'll do the job for you. Red and I will move your toilet and dig a new pit. Will that satisfy you?"

"Both you and Red had your chance. From now on I do things my way. You both value your independence, and I value mine. I'll not be beholden to either of you. Good day!" Rosie left, clutching the packet of cocoa as tightly as she could, trying not to smile until she was out of sight.

Angus watched Rosie disappear behind the tea tree in utter desolation. Somehow he'd done it again, pushed her away from him. "Damn you!" he said although he knew he only had himself to blame. A packet of cocoa did not amount to a debt of gratitude, and Rosie had denied him the opportunity of ever building one up. It wasn't just Rosie who disappeared behind the tea tree but the last flickering and spluttering of a dying dream.

He made no attempt to detain Rosie or engage her in conversation when she brought the wedge of chocolate cake she'd promised him. He'd intended to feed it to the birds for fear that it would stick in his throat and choke him. But the cake was freshly baked and thick with chocolate icing. He weakened and put the kettle on instead. As he sat out on his veranda, he watched Red motor back to his mooring and begin to swim ashore with his fish box. It was a sight he was accustomed to, and he could almost predict every move Red made. He was unprepared when another naked figure dashed into the water and swam out to greet him. Red disappeared behind the trees as he brought the fish box ashore, then reappeared when he rejoined Rosie. Late winter and the two of them were frolicking about in the shallows like children. Angus suddenly felt very old.

The rain came the following morning and settled in for five days. The leaden, sluggish clouds matched Angus's depression. When Red brought him fish he declined to answer his call and pretended he was out. He didn't want to see or speak to anyone. He tried to immerse himself in his writing, but few thoughts came and those that did failed to sparkle. When he tried reading he soon wearied of his books and spent his days either gazing through his rain-hazed windows or into the flames of his Stanley. He could not recall a time when he'd been more unhappy.

The sixth day dawned dry but cold and no more full of promise than those preceding it. Angus sat at his typewriter more in hope than belief that anything worthwhile would happen. Hamish awaited resurrection on the half-filled sheet of paper, and Angus was acutely aware of his obligation to the boy. He backtracked half a dozen pages, rereading them to see if he could pick up the mood and flow. Under pressure the human mind is capable of extraordinary leaps of logic, and Angus was about to become a beneficiary. Somewhere along the way an idea began to form that had nothing to do with the story he was reading. He stopped dead in his tracks, mouth agape, eyes unseeing, stunned by the force of the idea.

Rosie took advantage of the break in the weather to do a wash. Her Bendix gurgled contentedly in the laundry, and her clothesline waited to be dressed. After five days cooped up indoors she was desperate to get out. There was nothing like a bit of a blow to bring the fish on the bite, and she'd acquired a taste for the pink pigfish that had moved in on the reefs by the pinnacles. She was pegging the first load to the clothesline when Angus called out to her.

"Rosie, may I speak with you?"

"Oh my God!"

"Is that a yes or a no?"

"It's a yes, Angus. Come up by all means. Has someone died?"

Angus squirmed with embarrassment. He wore freshly pressed shirt and trousers, a jacket and shoes. His hair was slicked down and his beard newly shaven. He brought more roses. "I need to speak to you."

"Is that all?"

"Don't mock me, Rosie."

"I'm sorry. We'll have to sit out here because the varnish on the table is still wet. It's the weather."

"Aye."

"Tea or coffee?"

"Tea, if it's no trouble."

Rosie took the roses inside with her and shifted the kettle over to the stove top. She glanced cautiously back outside. Angus looked ludicrous and made her feel uncomfortable. This wasn't the Angus she'd come to know and loathe, in fact, he reminded her of a beaten puppy, trying to insinuate its way back into its owner's affections after a smelly indiscretion. He wanted something, and she dreaded to think what. She looked at the slicked hair and slid unwillingly toward a sickening conclusion. But if he'd come to put the hard word on her, why hadn't he picked a more appropriate time? Midmorning had never struck her as particularly conducive to romance. The kettle whistled start of play. She made the tea and took the tray outside. If he started in on small talk, she decided, she'd be rude. He hadn't tarted himself up to talk about the weather.

"Thank you, Rosie." Angus shifted uncomfortably on the wooden seat, cleared his throat and took a deep breath. "Rosie," he began, "you know I write books, so I expect nothing that I am about to say will come as a surprise." He looked away from her as if unwilling to meet her eyes. "I want a son, Rosie. All my life I've wanted a son to raise and instruct in the ways of the world. Are you with me?"

Rosie was and for once was lost for a reply. She'd been propositioned many times before but never so bluntly. She waited aghast, expecting at any moment to be asked to take him into her bed and become his baby factory. Why else was he all dressed up? "Go on," she said weakly.

"That's where I thought you could be of service."

Be of service! Rosie gritted her teeth.

"I know I got off to a bad start, and things between us haven't been perhaps as they should have been. It could be different, you know. Things aren't always as they might appear, you follow?"

"Angus, you're stalling."

"Rosie, you're not making it any easier for me."

"You've never made it any easier for me!"

"Well, what the devil did you expect, woman!" Angus looked away and bit his lip. "I'm sorry, Rosie, I apologize for that. I can't help it. I've no way with women." He squirmed with embarrassment.

235

Rosie let the silence hang. Hanging seemed an appropriate sentiment.

"I've never wanted to marry, you understand. Besides, I'm not sure any woman would want to have me. But I've always wanted a child. I came here to get away from women like you, Rosie. Women who . . . who are . . . accommodating . . . but don't necessarily wish to be tied down to any man."

He looked up to see her reaction. It took all of Rosie's self-control for there to be none. She decided to contain her rage until the man had said his piece. Then she planned to accommodate him with a right cross.

"Oh, I've had women friends," he continued, "but none who would agree to give me a child. I was laughed at and scorned, and at times I even resorted to offering money. I suffered humiliation after humiliation until finally I'd had enough. I escaped, I came here. Then you had to come on the scene."

Rosie tensed as she waited for the punch line, flexed and bunched her fists under the table. The old Scot had felt her anger before. She was amazed that he'd stick his chin out so far again.

"I couldn't face another revival of my hopes and another disappointment. I'd made my compromise, you follow? I'd invented a son of my own in my writing, and there are times, Rosie, when Hamish is as real to me as any child of flesh and blood."

Rosie unclenched her fists. His sales pitch had begun to sound dangerously like confession time. It was her turn to feel uncomfortable.

"It was a compromise, you understand, but one I was prepared to accept and live with. When you left after your first visit, I must confess I was glad to see the back of you. When you returned and announced you were staying, I realized I would have to live with the torment of your presence every single day for the rest of my life. Oh, I could run away, find another Wreck Bay in which to hide, but in my heart I know there is no hiding. Wherever I go there'll always be another you, another Rosie, another reminder of what might have been."

His pain reached out to her and touched her. She waited for the next revelation, bewildered and dumbfounded. Bewildered by his story. Dumbfounded by what she was sure he was going to ask of her.

"I know you have lain with Red and the lieutenant commander."

Lain with! Dear God! Next would come the begatting! It didn't occur to her to ask how he'd found out about Mickey Finn. All that concerned her was the terrifying direction the conversation was heading.

"So?" she asked weakly.

"So I have to ask, Rosie, though it's not easy for me as you well know. But I have to ask for my peace of mind, you follow?" He gazed at her intently, his tension clearly evident in the play of his twitching eyebrows.

"Ask what, Angus?"

"Don't tease me, Rosie!"

"Ask what, Angus!"

She watched as he fought to recover his composure and salvage his dignity. He pumped himself up and straightened his back. If he'd been wearing a tie he would have tightened the knot. Anyone watching would have thought he was about to propose, but Rosie was certain it was an altogether different proposition he had in mind.

"I have to ask," he said, "whether you're prepared to consider having a child?"

Rosie stared at him blankly. The worst had happened as she knew it would, but she still had no idea how to respond. Her choices appalled her. On one hand he'd invited her to shatter his hopes one last time, and on the other he was asking her to submit to becoming the incubator of his child. Neither option held any joy, but the latter was clearly beyond contemplation. Angus seemed to shrink while he waited for her response. What had it taken for him to ask the question? What would it take for her to respond?

"Angus," she began tentatively, "you have totally misread me. You have no understanding of the person I am. Under any other circumstances I would be deeply offended, and the color of both of your eyes would now match Louis Armstrong's. Do you follow me?"

"Rosie, I—"

"I have some sympathy for you, Angus, and respect for your motives if not your manner. But know this. One, I choose who I sleep with. Two, if I elect to have a child, it will be my child, and regardless of what else you think of me, I am not the sort to give away my own flesh and blood!"

"Rosie—"

"Hear me out! So, Angus, in the unlikely event that we ever had a child we would have to share it, and that implies some kind of common understanding, an agreement as to how the child would be raised."

"Rosie, you don't—"

She gave him a look that would have silenced a jackhammer. "Angus, we'd never agree to anything. We'd fight over every single thing. Would that be fair? A child deserves parents who are loving, not constantly at war. Your proposal is ludicrous!"

"Rosie, for God's sake, woman! Shut up and listen!"

"No, you listen!"

"Shut up, woman!" The Scot leaped to his feet, his voice shaking not with rage but with anguish. "I'm not asking you to have my child."

"What?" For the umpteenth time Rosie was dumbfounded. Dumbfounded and utterly confused.

"I'm not asking you to have my child." His voice had softened away to a whisper and trembled with emotion. He slumped back into his chair. "I can be a foolish man, Rosie, but I am not a fool. I'm not so foolish that I would expect you to have my child. Oh, I admit the idea did cross my mind, but it had the good sense not to linger there." He smiled thinly, and it was Rosie's turn to feel acutely embarrassed.

"I'm sorry, Angus. I misunderstood."

"Ahhh . . . away with you. It's me. I apologize for my clumsiness. I didn't make myself clear."

"Enlighten me, Angus."

"Well, if you were to have a child, and if you were not married, I was wondering if perhaps you could put the past behind you and allow me time with the child."

"Allow you time?"

"Would it harm the boy to have more than one father?"

"Go on."

"Rosie, all I'm asking is that if you were to have a child you'd allow me to read to him, sit him on my knee and tell him stories, take him fishing with me, perhaps teach him history and about nature . . ."

"What you're asking is to share his childhood."

Angus hesitated, thought for a moment as if faced with a revelation. "Yes, Rosie, that's what I'm asking."

"You wouldn't try to change the way I'd choose to bring him up—assuming it's a boy—nor interfere with the beliefs of his father, assuming he's around?"

"No, Rosie. I'd not interfere. I swear it."

"You understand the consequences if you did?"

"Aye . . ."

Rosie stared at him, her mind still reeling from her initial misunderstanding. Gradually she gathered her wits and with them came inspiration.

"I can't speak for the father . . ." she began, "whoever he might be. But in principle I have no objection to what you propose."

"Rosie . . ."

"Except there is no place for a second father. One is generally considered adequate, two, surplus to requirements." She watched his jaw sag, waited, then delivered her gift. "However, there is always room in a child's life for a grandfather."

"Grandfather!" His eyes lit up like the lights on a Christmas tree. He grabbed the concept instantly, drew it to him and embraced it. "Grandfather!" he repeated, savoring the sound of the word and all its implications. "Rosie, you're a marvel!"

"But not yet a mother. And on current levels of activity, not overly likely to become one."

"I'll have a word with Red."

"You'll do no such thing!" Rosie burst out laughing. "Angus, before we go any further there are some things you'll have to get straight. I won't put up with any sideline encouragement. I haven't even decided if I want a child, and I don't want a cheering squad urging me on."

"Could I just say I'd prefer the father were the naval officer rather than the madman?"

"No, you may not! That's precisely what I mean. Angus, any further discussion is purely academic. If I ever decide to have a child, I will choose the father."

"So you might have a child?"

"I haven't ruled out the possibility, as remote as it may be."

"Oh, Rosie, you've made me happier than you can ever imagine. I don't deserve your kindness, I concede I've done nothing to earn it. But if I can't be a father, I rejoice at the prospect of being a grandfather. Perhaps I'm even more suited to the part. Aye! A grandfather!" He picked up his cup of tea and sipped noisily. He reached for a shortbread, snapped it in two and pushed half in his mouth.

"You can undo the top button of your shirt now, Angus. You look like a chicken with a rubber band around its neck."

Angus laughed and did as she suggested. "There is one other small matter I'd like to discuss with you."

"And what is that?" Rosie tried to sound pleasant and maintain the mood, but inwardly braced for the Scotsman's next assault.

"It's about the workmen you're thinking of bringing here. I'd really prefer you didn't."

"You've left me no choice, Angus."

"Don't bring them here, Rosie. I couldn't tolerate that. I came here to get away from the crowds, not to invite them in. Surely you can accept that? I don't want my privacy invaded."

"Tell me something new."

"We—Red and I—have been remiss in the past, I freely admit it, and you have every reason to punish us. All I can say is we want to make amends for earlier indiscretions. Please allow us to move your toilet. We'll do it if you'll just give us the chance."

"Maybe."

"Who would you rather have do the jobs you can't? Strangers from the other side, or Red and me?"

"Depends who's cheapest."

"You'll not find cheaper than free, woman. We'll ask no consideration, only that you don't abuse our services."

240

"I thought I'd bring my guys over next week," Rosie lied. "When can you start?"

"I'll speak to Red." The Scot sighed and helped himself to another cup of tea. He didn't relish the interruption to his writing, but sacrifices had to be made. "We'll start next week since that's convenient with you."

"I need the lavatory moved and a new pit dug and a triangle and beam I can slot in over the top to winch the drum up. And I need help to rebuild the chookhouse. Searching for the eggs every morning is becoming rather tedious."

"Aye," said Angus heavily. "And if there's anything else, speak up now. We'll need to know what we're letting ourselves in for."

"I'll make a list." Rosie smiled sweetly. Why not? She had an overland route to Katherine Bay and Fitzroy. And now she had a labor force on hand to help her. She had everything she needed to survive and could turn to her potting, her fishing and her garden, and to living the kind of life she'd fantasized about. She'd secured her foothold in paradise and, in the glow of her victory, didn't immediately dismiss the Scotsman's fond hopes out of hand. The odd thing was for the first time in her life she could picture herself with a child and not see it as a squealing, puking, nappy-filling jailer.

"There is one more matter," said Angus. "I'm taking the boat around to Fitzroy. Is there something I can get you?"

"No, but there are some things I could get for myself."

Angus grimaced. He'd given the woman an inch and she'd taken a yard, much as he'd feared she would. When had it ever been different? "Be on the beach in half an hour," he said sourly.

Jean and Col Chadwick greeted Rosie like a long-lost daughter and immediately invited the two of them to stay for lunch. Rosie's immediate acceptance caused Angus to bridle, though he knew better than to protest. There was no mail for Angus or Red and none expected, but Rosie had a letter from Mickey waiting for her, and a large manila envelope from her father. She decided to leave both unopened until she'd returned to Wreck Bay. She'd had enough surprises for one day.

Twenty-one

W hen Angus had arrived wrapped like a Christmas toffee, with a bunch of roses and a request for his shopping list, Red's plans for the day collapsed. He looked around in desperation for something that would drain him physically and dull his mind so that the nightmares, still fresh and lurking on the edge of his consciousness, would fade and seep away in the sweat of toil.

Red had battled through a bad night, one of the worst, and it had caught him by surprise. Over the years at Wreck Bay the nightmares had diminished in both severity and frequency. He'd even begun to entertain the possibility that one day he might be free of them. He could find no reason for the sudden attack other than the disruption to his routine. He'd spent the dark hours in a twilight world, reliving the forced march from the seventy-five-kilo camp to the one-oh-five, raggle-taggle remnants of an army, weakened from overwork, sickness, malnutrition, and infections that ate away at their bodies like rust in soft steel. He'd tossed and turned, bathing himself in sweat and drenching his sheets in the process, reliving what he tried so hard to forget. They'd willed their legs onward, one step after another, knowing that to fall was to give in and that to give in was to die. Yet no matter how hard they'd pushed themselves, the camp at Aungganaung had remained as far away and unattainable as it had at the commencement of their journey. He'd relived the despair, the tears of frustration and exhaustion, death never more than one faltering step away.

Dawn had come as a merciful release, and he'd risen trembling and weak to begin his exercises. Years of practice brought him the calm he needed. He'd slipped into the long, thin, even breaths of diaphragm breathing and the gentle rhythmic exercises of ch'i kung; separating clouds by wheeling arms, rowing the boat in the center of the lake, scooping the sea while looking at the sky. He repeated the exercises until a meditational calm had soothed and stilled his mind, and he could feel energy radiating outward to his extremities, relaxing and reinvigorating his muscles. He varied his movements to those of t'ai chi ch'uan—the grand ultimate fist—the slow, balletic martial arts movements that he'd first seen practiced from his hospital window in Singapore. Years later, a Chinese medical student in Auckland had explained the meaning and reason behind the strange behavior he'd witnessed and introduced him to a teacher. Red had presented the teacher with a gift of money in a red envelope as tradition demanded and the medical student had advised. He hadn't skimped on the gift, because the little red envelope had also carried inside it his last hopes.

Western medicine had failed him, and he'd turned to the East for salvation. His generosity had been repaid many times over as the t'ai chi and ch'i kung helped him where drugs, psychotherapy and electroconvulsive therapy had only hastened his descent into madness. His teacher had made no attempt to understand or treat him but had simply taught him the ancient ways of balancing the opposing forces of yin and yang, of controlling mind and body. The unpredictable, irrational, explosive outbursts of temper and tears had begun to ease. He'd found peace within himself, albeit fragile and in need of supplement. That supplement he found in work.

After breakfast he'd scrubbed floors and countertops and washed windows. He'd searched his vegetable patch for weeds and snails. He'd washed his sheets and spare clothing, wrung them vigorously and hung them out to dry. Then he'd begun a desperate search for work. After he'd showered, he set off with two four-gallon tins to fetch diesel up from the jetty, pausing briefly on the way to renew acquaintance with his kauri tree and feel its resilience. He'd checked his boat while he was at the beach, but it was spotless, started first time and he knew without looking that the engine needed neither oil nor water. It was still early as he'd climbed back up the hill. He'd searched for more work but found little heart for what there was. He'd emptied the latrine bucket the day before and there was neither need nor room for more firewood. He thought about cutting back more scrub, cleaning the leaves out of his gutters, splashing more creosote onto his weatherboards. Many jobs beckoned but none appealed. The trip around to Fitzroy seemed to offer the diversion he was seeking, but Angus had put a quick end to that.

He decided to take his binoculars and radio and climb Tataweka Hill. Perhaps there'd be a foreign trawler on the horizon to give him a reason to call the lieutenant commander. He packed food and water for himself and Archie. He called his dog to heel as he hoisted his pack over his shoulders. It felt satisfyingly heavy with the radio, batteries, binoculars and lunch. But its weight triggered memories, more reminders of the skeletal battalions clawing their way up to the one-oh-five, through mud and driving rain, carrying their worldly possessions until sheer exhaustion forced them to abandon precious items one by one. A thin but treasured blanket, saturated and leaden. A book, sodden but no less invaluable. Chess pieces, lovingly carved from scavenged material and irreplaceable. Red strode off up the track he'd hewn, almost in panic, feet pounding into the hard, gray earth, trying with each step to leave the memories behind. Tataweka was a stiff climb and a hot one in the lee of the westerlies with no protection from the morning sun, but it needed to be Mount Everest.

He heard the putt-putt of Angus's diesel and paused to watch his boat nose out of the bay. He saw that Rosie was with him. He pulled the binoculars out of his backpack to make sure. Why was Angus taking Rosie to Fitzroy? Why had he dressed up for the occasion? He watched until the little boat was lost behind a headland, then turned his binoculars seaward to the dark sawtooth of the horizon. Not too bad now, he thought to himself, but still bumpy. He wondered whether Rosie would be as sick in the Scotsman's boat as she'd been in his. He looked again at the horizon. Probably not. He heaved his pack back onto his shoulders and continued his forced march up the hill, until effort at last displaced old memories.

Once on the lookout he began a systematic sweep northward to the Mokohinau Islands, before swinging eastward in sectors until he faced southeast and could see no farther. The binoculars told him nothing that his naked eyes hadn't already ascertained. There was no traffic out to sea. No trawlers, no cargo ships, no pleasure craft. He turned westward and scanned the gulf. Two local trawlers were working in tandem south of Little Barrier, using the power of both vessels to drag a net that was large by their standards, but still no more than a third the size of those routinely deployed by the Japanese. The two boats battled the westerly wind, their inefficiency a crude form of conservation. As he watched, Red felt an impending sense of loss. Soon the Japanese longliners would head back north from the winter grounds, plundering the snapper heavy with roe as they migrated to spawn in the gulf. The stupidity of the Japanese infuriated him. Didn't they know what happened to farmers who sold all their seed and kept none to sow?

He turned his binoculars on the usual gulf traffic to practice focusing and identification. He briefly held on a Greek liner that had barely cleared Rangitoto Channel on its long journey back to Europe. Even through the haze of distance he could make out the blue cross on the funnels and quickly identified it as the *Ellinis*. It had passed by two months earlier, while he'd been fishing off Aiguilles Island, crammed with eager young faces heading for a working holiday in England. He'd waved and been rewarded with a forest of waving arms and a friendly blast from the ship's horn. He recalled the loneliness he'd felt as a young-man-turned-soldier on his way to war, clinging to the rail as he watched the land that was his home and everything he knew slip away behind him. He'd had a lump in his throat then, and when a mellow Polynesian voice had begun singing "Now Is the Hour," the thought had occurred that he might be saying good-bye forever. Silence had descended over the throng of soldiers until the young Maori had finished. It had been a while before anyone had trusted himself to speak, aware that not all of them would be coming home, and that those who did might be vastly different from those who'd left. Red had come back different. The man had returned, but the boy had been lost forever in the jungles of Burma.

He picked up movement beneath him. It was Angus's boat, pounding across the entrance to Katherine Bay. He trained the glasses on it and saw Rosie sitting sidesaddle on the transom. Probably fishing. That was something else that amazed him. Rosie had taken to fishing like Archie to his breakfast. She couldn't get enough of it, but at least she released the fish she didn't need. He whistled for Archie, who'd taken off to investigate the whereabouts of the rabbit that had just left a pile of warm pellets on the trail, and ducked down below the lookout to shelter from the wind. He cut a thick slice of bread, carved off some pieces of cheese and tomato and folded the slice over them. He wondered why Rosie had gone around to Fitzroy instead of just giving Angus a list. Why had the old Scot taken her when he'd sworn never to lift a finger to help? Why was he dressed up? Nothing made sense.

He began to feel vaguely uncomfortable. Rosie troubled him, but he could sense she was becoming part of his life, an adjustment to his routine. Her little bach was a credit to her, and he liked going there. Liked it when she asked him to stay the night. Liked listening to her, liked it less when she listened to him. But he didn't like the idea of Rosie and Angus becoming friends, yet wasn't sure why. Where would that leave him? What did becoming friends entail? Would she take Angus into her bed as she'd taken him? The thought troubled him so much that he was hardly aware that Archie had answered his call and was patiently waiting for his drink.

"Sorry, mate," he said, filled the dog's bowl and, even though he limited Archie to two meals a day with only water in between, decided to give him the rind off the cheese. He made himself another sandwich and took a long pull from the canteen. Even damp from the tea towel the bread was hard to swallow. He broke off a piece for Archie. "Eat up, mate, then back to work." The Japanese had been very specific about that. No work, no food, and it didn't matter how sick a man was. It was left to his comrades to share what little they had, little gifts of half-cooked, half-rotten rice and a share in whatever meat and vegetables they'd been able to scrounge or buy from the local Burmese. Archie had scrounged for duck eggs and fed them to him when he'd gone down with the dog's disease. The shakes had been so bad he couldn't even hold on to his mess kit.

"No work, no *mishi*," the camp commander had decreed. *"Speedo! Speedo!* All mens must work! Sick must starve until die or go back to work."

Each spoonful to a sick man deprived his exhausted comrades and made their burden that much more intolerable. But they gave willingly, the bond of mateship broken only by death. Who was his mate now besides Archie? Was Rosie? He wanted to share with her as they'd shared in the camps, help her as they'd helped each other, laugh as they'd laughed. But it was hard, so very, very hard to get that feeling back. The passion, the intensity, the total reliance upon each other. Beatings, starvation, disease and death were the hammers and anvils that had forged their mateship. He wanted desperately to get the feeling back. The bad times, the good times and the times they'd done nothing but wait. The camps had taken all he had to give, and repatriation had taken his reason to give. He was alone, isolated, the only New Zealand soldier to work on the railway. The sole New Zealand survivor.

With nothing better to do, but needing to be active, he swung the radio onto his back and climbed up to the lookout. He wasn't scheduled to call, nor did he have anything to report, and even as he began to transmit his call sign, had no idea what he was going to say. His signal was picked up immediately by Devonport and, to his surprise, he was asked to stand by for a return transmission. Apparently the lieutenant commander had left a standing instruction to be informed if Red radioed in. He didn't have long to wait.

"Hello, Red? Mickey here. I don't know whether Rosie has picked up my letter yet, but I'm coming by the day after tomorrow. Routine patrol, and I've hitched a ride. They still haven't forgiven me for the fiasco with the *Shoto Maru,* and I think they're happy to have me out of the place occasionally. You got that? Over."

Red acknowledged.

"One more thing, Red, talking of the *Shoto Maru.* Time to get on our toes. I don't know whether I told you, but the air force is switching over from Sunderlands to Orions. Some of their blokes just did a familiarization flight in an Orion down the east coast to Wellington, and guess who crossed their path heading north? Only our old friend Shimojo Seiichi and the *Shoto Maru.* My guess is that he'll start working the Bay of Plenty, then head north with the snapper. That would be the logical thing to do. But knowing Shimojo, he might run wide out of sight and out of mind, then do a night run straight through Colville. Whatever, it's getting close to action stations. So keep your eyes peeled. I'll talk to you more the day after tomorrow. Meanwhile, let Rosie know my movements. Okay? Over."

Red stared at the radio, hurt and bewildered. Why was the lieutenant commander sending messages to Rosie and not him? Why did she need to know Mickey's movements? She wasn't the one reporting on trawlers. He grabbed his backpack and set off down the hill, wondering what he'd done wrong until another possibility occurred to him. Maybe the lieutenant commander was Rosie's friend as well.

Rosie staggered up the hill under the weight of her supplies. She had a bag over each shoulder, one filled with six bottles of wine courtesy of the Last Gasp's newly acquired liquor license, and held a large carton crammed full of groceries in her arms. She'd considered dividing the load and leaving both bags on the beach for a second trip, but had decided instead to put her faith in her newfound muscle tone and fitness. It had been a mistake, and she was paying for it. Her arms and back ached so badly she'd twice had to stop to readjust the position of her loads. Red-faced and dripping sweat, she staggered into the clearing at the foot of her section and dumped her bags and the box onto the ground. She collapsed alongside them with a heartfelt groan, and rolled lifelessly onto her back.

"Rosie! Are you all right?"

Red? What was Red doing at her place, she wondered? A wet nose touched her cheek, a wet tongue washed it. Archie.

"Rosie?"

She heard his feet pounding across the grass toward her. She thought it was nice to come home tired and find someone who cared.

"Relax, Red. I'm not dying."

"Can I help?"

"Sure. Carry me to my castle and pour me into a bath. Be generous with the bath salts and bubbles."

"Rosie . . . ?"

"Be a sweetie and just carry my bags and the box." She dragged herself up to a sitting position and watched Red effortlessly pick up the heavy box and bags. Then it struck her. Red was naked but for his shorts, and his body was streaked with mud and sweat. "Red, what are you doing here?"

"Fencing." He walked away from her toward the veranda.

She looked around and saw the partly built fence enclosing her garden, turning it into a high-security prison for wayward vegetables. Why? The question should not have been what he was doing, but why he was doing it. She'd known Red long enough already to realize he only answered questions in the most literal way. She hauled herself wearily to her feet, ruffled Archie's ears and followed Red up to the veranda. He stood at the doorway waiting for her, too muddy to enter. She'd left the place clean, but now it was spotless. Swept, mopped, scrubbed, shined. Red's trademark. She fought to suppress her sudden anger, then indignation that Red didn't think she kept her home clean enough.

"I'm not Bernie, Red. You don't have to clean house for me."

"Sorry, Rosie."

"That's okay, Red. You meant well. But don't do it again."

"Sorry." Red stood at her door like a scolded schoolboy.

"Now why were you fencing my garden?"

"It needed fencing. Gardens have to be fenced, Rosie."

Rosie listened patiently. "That's not the answer, Red. The question is, why were you working on my garden and not your garden? Do you think I can't fence my own garden myself?"

"I thought you'd be pleased."

"That's all? You did it because you thought I'd be pleased?"

"I've fastened your potting wheel to the veranda deck, too."

"Anything else I should know?"

"I emptied your latrine bucket."

"Did you, now?"

Red's shoulders sagged and his head dropped. "I need to work, Rosie. You know that." Red was squirming with embarrassment at his admission. Archie's ears had flattened, and his tail lay still.

Rosie closed her eyes and silently counted to ten. She cursed her-

249

self for being so slow and insensitive. Red needed to work, his self-administered therapy demanded it. She opened her eyes to find Red watching her, his expression a combination of guilt and anxiety. "I'm sorry, Red. I know you have to work, and I'm grateful that you chose to expend so much energy on my behalf. Thank you. Particularly for bolting down my potting wheel."

"That's okay, Rosie." His face had brightened. If he'd had a tail he would have wagged it.

"Tell me something. Why didn't you bring your need to work around sooner, when my gutters were broken? Why didn't you come and help me relocate the outhouse?"

Red's face flushed. "I had to cut the trail, Rosie."

"Couldn't the trail have waited a couple of days? I had rain pouring down my wall."

Red's face creased in frustration, and he turned away from her. "I had to cut the trail!"

"Hey, Red! It's no big deal. I was just curious, that's all." She decided her shirt needed a wash anyway and threw her arms around him. His body was as rigid as a corpse. "Anyway, Angus has offered his and your services next week to relocate my lav. So no problem."

"You don't understand, Rosie."

"Then help me understand."

"It's not always a question of choice, Rosie. I had to cut the trail."

"It's okay."

"I think I'd better go." He pulled himself free of her arms.

"Yeah, you go. Go home and shower while I take a bath. Then come back for dinner. I've bought us a leg of lamb, which I'm going to roast with potatoes and kumara and all the trimmings. I need a rest from fish. I've asked Angus to come as well."

"Angus?"

"Yes, Angus. You remember him? A Scotsman, tall, bushy eyebrows and knobbly knees. Fetchingly rude."

Red looked down at his feet.

"What's the matter now?"

"Why did he offer to dig a new pit for your lavatory?"

"Because he didn't want me bringing workmen in from Katherine Bay or Fitzroy. He doesn't want strangers tiptoeing through his turnips."

"Are you going to ask him to stay?"

"Stay?"

"The night?"

"No! No way!"

"Can I stay, then?"

Rosie rocked back on her heels in surprise. Nothing had happened for months and then the floodgates had opened. He was asking if he could sleep with her. From both a personal and professional point of view the breakthrough was staggering. It took a moment for her to digest what had happened, then a slow comprehending smile slowly spread across her face. She reached up and kissed him again. "Just you try to get away. Now go."

"Okay, Rosie." Red turned, propped and spun back to face her. "Oh, one other thing. I spoke to the lieutenant commander on the radio. He asked me to tell you that he's coming over the day after tomorrow."

"Mickey's coming?"

"Yeah. Why did he send the message to you, Rosie?"

Rosie did her best to look innocent. She shrugged noncommittally. "Maybe he thinks I'm the only one who'd make him feel welcome. Now hop it." She watched Red head off down to the track and went inside to begin unpacking, her mind whirling. Incredible as it seemed, Red was showing every sign of being jealous. She laughed. About bloody time he showed some feeling! She wandered into her bathroom to begin running her bath. She opened the cupboard for her bath salts and was confronted by her diaphragm and tube of jelly, sitting on the shelf right in front of her eyes. She stared at them, aware of their significance and the consequences of the decision that faced her. If she was going to make Angus a grandfather, the next three days were the perfect time to begin trying. The grandfather had put his hand up, but had the mother?

Angus sat at the table, doing his best to feel miserable despite the tantalizing aromas that assaulted him. He studiously ignored Red and

251

Rosie and made no attempt at conversation. He'd seen enough of Rosie, more of her in one day than in all the preceding months. Obligation had brought him to her dinner table, nothing else. Someone had to make sure Red stayed and did his duty as a man, and Angus had unilaterally taken the responsibility upon himself.

"Can not that mangy creature wait outside where he belongs?" He glared at Archie curled up on the mat by the Shacklock.

"Archie and Red always share, Angus, you know that. Red's enjoying the smell of roast lamb just like you are, and Archie's entitled to enjoy it, too. Look at his nose. He's sucking in more air than my Hoover."

"There's a place for beasts, and it's not indoors."

"I'll pass that on to Bonnie. Now make yourself useful and open this."

Angus reluctantly took the bottle of Dalwood Burgundy and the corkscrew she handed him.

"Besides," she added, "it's raining outside. Who would send a dog out on a night like this?"

As if on cue a gust of wind whipped around the eaves and roared off through the treetops. Spring held sway during the days, but at night winter still lingered. Inside the bach, in the thick, smoky warmth generated by the old Shacklock, the occupants were reduced to shirtsleeves. This was the sort of night Angus had never imagined possible. The three of them together, sitting around a dinner table, the woman cackling about like a smug mother hen. He was determined not to enjoy a second of it. But the thickly sliced roast lamb, crisp on the outside and pink in the middle, the roast potatoes and kumara, and the thick, dark, heady gravy invoked pleasant memories of meals long past and sorely missed. His tummy rumbled, and he found it hard to be stern in the face of such temptation.

"Here's to you, Rosie," he said gruffly, raising his glass. "I thank you for this splendid meal here before us, and for inviting us to share it with you. A rare pleasure and one best kept that way." He turned to Red. "Raise your glass, man, in a toast to the lady."

"I don't drink."

"What? Don't be a fool, man!"

"Hold on, Angus, I'll handle this. Red, have you always been a teetotaler?"

"No."

"Did you stop drinking before or after the war?"

"After."

"Because of your medication?"

"Yes."

"Red, you're not on medication now. It's safe to have an occasional drink. Angus and I will see to it that you drink no more than your share. Okay?"

"If you say so, Rosie."

"Then raise your glass, man. To Rosie!"

"To Rosie."

"To me," Rosie added mischievously. "Queen of Wreck Bay."

Rosie had not expected scintillating dinner-party conversation, but neither had she expected to be left to eat in silence. Clearly, it had been a long time since either man had sat down to roast lamb. They focused on the food before them and switched off to everything else. Yet she felt overwhelmingly happy, found the way both men wolfed down their meals and helped themselves to seconds intensely satisfying. Instincts she never knew she possessed began to surface. Perhaps she really was ready for motherhood.

Angus reluctantly laid down his knife and fork and toyed with his glass. He wasn't normally a wine drinker, but it had gone well enough with the lamb.

"I'll start the dishes."

"Sit down, Red, the dishes aren't going anywhere."

Red stood. "They should be rinsed, Rosie."

"I know, but they can wait awhile. Sit down and have another glass of wine while your dinner settles."

A gust of wind hurdled the ridge and came hurtling down the valley, slamming into the bach, shaking it to its foundations and rattling the windows.

"Glad I'm in here and not out there," said Rosie.

"Aye, but it's time I was heading out there." Angus turned to Rosie and gave what he imagined was a subtle wink. "If Red's so keen to attend to the dishes, you'll not need me. I'll be getting back to Bonnie."

"At least stay until the wine's finished."

"No thank you, Rosie. I'll leave that to the two of you to finish. You know what they say about the effects of good wine upon the humor of man." He threw Rosie another wink.

"No, Angus, I don't."

"Ah well, it's perhaps best not said." A rogue gust of wind drove the rain hard into the windows. Momentarily it reminded him of the wild storms that used to rage across the Minch. "Would you listen to that! Pity all fishermen at sea."

"No!"

Angus spun around in time to see Red's chair crash to the floor. The madman stood, fists clenched, eyes aflame.

"Red! Calm down!" Rosie jumped to her feet and tried to pull Red down into her chair. But Red could have been a statue welded to the floor.

"Good Lord! What's the matter with you, man?"

"It's okay, Red, it's okay." Rosie imploring.

"Man's mad. I told you!"

"Keep out of this, Angus. Red, what's the problem? Tell me."

"I won't pity them!" Red slowly relaxed and let Rosie guide him onto her chair.

"What are you going on with, man?"

"The Japanese fishermen. The trawlers, the longliners. Shimojo Seiichi. The *Shoto Maru*. The bastards, they're coming back here."

"Oh?"

"Mickey told me. On the radio."

Angus turned to Rosie. "He spoke to the lieutenant commander?"

"Yes, apparently Mickey's coming here day after tomorrow."

"Is he, now?" The old man's eyes narrowed as he perceived the more attractive option. It called for a change in tactics. "The day after tomorrow?" The Scot's face lit up in delight as possible consequences registered. With Lieutenant Commander Finn due there was no need for Red to stay the night. Indeed, it would be far better from Angus's point of view if the madman *didn't* stay the night. He glanced furtively at Rosie and saw her watching him warningly. But he ignored her. Too many opportunities had slipped by to allow another to pass. "Well, Red, we mustn't keep this good woman up. I'll help you with the dishes, then walk with you down the path."

Red stood immediately; the opportunity to lose himself in work and attend to the dirty dishes was too good to pass up.

"Sit!"

Red sat, dropped like a shot duck. Rosie glowered at Angus.

"You haven't been listening, Angus," she said in a voice loaded with menace. "I decide when I do my dishes. I've told you that before. I also told you I wouldn't put up with any interference. I told you what the consequences of that would be. There is no role for you. Do you understand? No role. You can take this as a warning. Your last. Now don't let us keep you from your bed."

Angus rose, beaten but unbowed. "I meant well, Rosie. I only want what's best for you."

"For whom?"

"You know what I mean."

"I know exactly what you mean."

"Then don't be a sentimental fool, woman! It's not yourself you should be thinking of but the—"

"Angus! That'll do!"

"Aye . . . well I'll be off, then. I thank you for the meal and pray you come to your senses." He appeared to relent and softened his voice. "Before I go, do you think Red could give me some of the scrapings from the plates? For Bonnie. Be a treat for her."

"Of course." Rosie dropped her guard. The man was incorrigible. Red took a plain saucer from the cupboard, one he recognized as a leftover from Bernie's days, and scraped gravy-rich pieces of meat and roast potato onto it.

"Let me give you a hand." Angus leaned in close to Red. He cast a quick glance back at Rosie. She was still seated at the table, her back to them, wineglass in hand. He spoke softly, directly into Red's ear. "This Shimojo fishes at night, I understand. Do you not think it wise to run up to Tataweka and keep an eye out for him? Just in case."

"He's still too far south. Besides, he wouldn't dare come in close on a night like this."

"Aye, suppose you're right." Angus's shoulders sagged. He'd done all he could. If Red was going to be the father, then that was that. But he would have preferred a better, saner bloodline and, more importantly, an absentee father like the lieutenant commander so that he, Angus, could be the only man in the boy's life. De facto grandfather and father. He walked over to the door and pulled on his long plastic mac. He began buttoning it, working his way up to the very top. With the lieutenant commander coming, he was still in with a fifty-fifty chance. "I'll be away, then. Good night to you both."

"Good night, Angus," said Rosie menacingly. "Don't get your hopes up."

Angus slammed the door behind him, and another volley of wind-driven rain drumrolled against the windows.

Rosie turned to Red, who was patiently stacking dishes as he filled the sink with hot water. "Red, can't the dishes wait till morning just once? It's been a long day, and I need some sleep."

"In the camps we used to keep a drum of boiling water to dip our mess kits in the moment we'd finished eating. It was the flies. They're what spread the diseases."

"Okay, okay, Red, you win." Rosie could see instantly where the conversation would lead him. Back to his never-never land. She took his hand. She didn't want him going anywhere, not on such an important night. "You're right. It's better we do them now."

"Why didn't you let Angus help if you're so tired?"

"Long story."

Red waited for Rosie to elaborate but soon realized she had no intention of doing so. "Leave them to me, Rosie. You go on to bed. I promise I won't wake you."

"That, my friend, is the problem." She sighed and picked up a tea towel.

Twenty-two

"**B**astard's up to his tricks again." Mickey Finn put down the phone as Gloria brought him in a cup of dishwater coffee. But it was hot, wet and sweet, a condition in which he hoped one day to find his young assistant.

"Shimojo?"

"Yep. That was the Ministry of Marine. Bay of Plenty fishermen report a phantom trawler, appearing and disappearing through the night. Ring a bell with you? It already has with the newspapers. I've had a call from a reporter from the *Herald*."

"Have you informed Lieutenant Commander Scriven, sir?"

"Gloria . . . sorry, Third Officer Wainscott, I don't think either he or the Commodore want to hear Shimojo's name mentioned again."

"What are you going to do?"

"I'm going to nail the bastard, that's what I'm going to do. Don't know how, don't know when. In the meantime let's do the usual. See if we can get an aircraft up, dawn flight preferably, and try to nab him inside territorial waters. Failing that, let's at least let him know we're watching. We might save the lives of a few fish that way. Be a good girl and call the air base for me. Oh, and book a table at the Gourmet."

"For how many?"

"Two. Just you and me." Mickey watched for her reaction. She took her time.

257

"I can't make it tonight. How about tomorrow?"

"Ahhhh . . ." It was his turn to come under scrutiny. There was an edge to her voice that suggested the rumor mill had been at work. Gloria knew damn well that the following night was out of the question because of his visit to Great Barrier. She'd helped organize it. There'd been no hiding the smile on his face nor the spring in his step as he'd made his way back to the patrol boat with the two junior ratings after the first visit. Doubtless they'd guessed and blabbed. "How about the night after that?" he ventured tentatively.

"We'll see." She turned, tight lipped, and left his office.

Mickey slammed his fist down onto his desktop. Typical bloody woman! She showed no sign of wanting him until someone else did. But what could he do? Rosie before dinner, Gloria for dessert? Would he ever get that lucky? He shook his head. If the two incidents with Shimojo Seiichi had taught him anything it was that he was not a naturally lucky person. He leaned back in his chair and began to contemplate possible ways of trapping the *Shoto Maru*. He realized the phantom trawler was becoming something of an obsession with him and was aware of the dangers. Shimojo Seiichi was not the only foreign skipper to raid New Zealand's inshore waters. They all did whenever opportunity presented, but only Shimojo made it his principal modus operandi. Was it sheer nerve, or greed? Mickey couldn't guess. He was accustomed to longliners fishing in close, but this was the first occasion he'd had a trawler specifically target snapper. Shimojo's success would only encourage others, and that would be disastrous for the species. Mickey found it easy to justify his obsession with the *Shoto Maru* but also realized the downside. Other poachers could slip beneath his guard while his eyes were fixed on Shimojo. He couldn't allow that, either.

He'd had some success and regained some of the esteem he'd lost. He'd been instrumental in intercepting Japanese dories on two separate occasions, both groups working within a mile or two of Ninety Mile Beach. They'd been escorted back to their mother ships, and both mother ships had been recalled to Japan. The commodore had sent a curt note of congratulations, more notable for its brevity than its enthusiasm. Mickey had also hidden a patrol boat behind Kapiti

Island, near Wellington, to catch a Russian squid trawler. That gained him more credibility, but he still bore the burden of being the man who let the *Shoto Maru,* the famous phantom trawler, slip through his grasp. He was lost deep in thought when Gloria returned.

"No aircraft."

"What?"

"No aircraft. They're in the middle of changing over. The Sunderlands are being decommissioned, and they're rotating crews for familiarization flights on the Orions."

Mickey groaned.

"Apparently they were expecting to have three aircraft by now, but they've only taken delivery of two. The balance is due, hopefully, in the first half of next year."

"How long will this process of familiarization go on?"

"I don't know, sir, but I gathered it will take some time."

"Jesus wept! Any chance that they could organize their flight paths so that they familiarized themselves over encroaching foreign trawlers?"

"I asked them that, sir, but they're reluctant to send crews out on missions until they're fully trained and experienced."

"I suppose I'd better have a word with them. See if I have more luck, not that I'd ever be so foolish that I'd back my charm against yours." He smiled. A peace offering.

"Is that all, sir?" She was still giving him her impression of an Easter Island statue.

"Yes, Gloria. It is."

Shimojo's incursions forced Mickey to change his plans. Lieutenant Commander Scriven insisted that the *Cormorant* head south immediately to sit on the *Shoto Maru* and prevent any further incidents. Mickey argued vehemently, but the Staff Officer Operations was adamant that he would not allow the *Shoto Maru* to cause them further embarrassment. In the end, seniority won over reason, and Mickey lost his transport back to base from Wreck Bay. On an impulse, he rang Captain Ladd and discovered he had a pickup booked at Fitzroy late in the afternoon. He asked him if, in a gesture of goodwill toward the navy, he would mind picking him up from Wreck Bay at the same time. Captain Ladd laughed and agreed immediately. Apparently he'd heard the rumors, too.

The *Cormorant*'s tender dropped him on the beach just on eleven in the morning. Mickey was surprised to see that Red's boat was absent from its mooring and that a reception committee of two awaited him. What surprised him even more was that the Scotsman seemed pleased to see him.

"Welcome, man, it's a pleasure to have you here!"

"Thank you, Angus." The old recluse shook his hand as if reluctant to let go and fixed him with an ingratiating smile that almost turned Mickey's stomach. If he'd brought Angus a case of single malt, he doubted the old fraud would have been more delighted.

"Hello, Rosie."

"Hello, sailor." She kissed him lightly on the cheek. "Thanks for the card and the flowers."

Mickey froze momentarily, but the twinkle in her eyes gave her away.

"Would a letter do?" He proffered it. "We called in at Fitzroy on the way over."

"I'll not keep you," Angus interjected. "I just came down to extend a welcome and I've done that. Might I also ask if you'd mind dropping by my place on your way back down to the beach? There are some questions concerning the radio, you understand."

"Can't I deal with them now?"

"Noooo . . . There's plenty of time. Like I say, I'll not keep you."

Mickey watched the Scotsman head off back to the track, his stride more sprightly and his back straighter than he'd remembered. He turned to Rosie. "What's going on? What's brought the change of heart?"

Rosie shrugged. "You tell me. You know better than I what goes on inside a man's head."

"Beats me, Rosie."

"Maybe he hopes you'll rescue me from all this." She gestured toward the deserted hillsides. "If you do, you'll make my best friend, Norma, eternally grateful. She's finally written, so she must be missing me."

"Maybe," Mickey said doubtfully, but with waning interest. "Where's Red?"

"Gone fishing. The snapper are coming back, and he went off early this morning to set his longlines. He needs to catch fish to pay for his diesel and the occasional bargeload of rice. He's gone south to Coromandel, so I'm not expecting him back until sometime tomorrow. Come on. Unless you plan to go skinny dipping with me, let's start up the track."

"Bloody hell, Rosie," he said, recalling her naked in bed and picturing her wet and naked in the shallows. "You sure give a man a helluva choice."

Shimojo Seiichi had blundered. He'd left the winter grounds too early and struggled to make catches that justified his decision to move north. The snapper had begun to gather, but only in small schools that tended to congregate around reefs beyond the reach of his nets. The night raids produced disappointing results as the *Shoto Maru* was forced to duck and dive around snags. He needed to find a way to boost the tonnage and instinctively fell back upon his most recent experience. He was over longliner grounds and knew that one dory working its way in among the reefs would not just make a valuable contribution but make the night's fishing respectable. The tactic involved considerable risk. All he had to fish from was the ship's lifeboat. Shimojo was typical of Japanese skippers who believed in fortune favoring the brave, but he also knew it had a habit of turning and biting the foolhardy.

Later that day, the *Shoto Maru* rendezvoused with one of the company's tuna boats out wide, borrowed two spare longlines to cut and adapt for bottom fishing, then began practicing lowering and retrieving the lifeboat at trawl speed. At first the crew mistook the nature of the exercise, believing they were practicing emergency drills. Nobody thought for a second that their skipper would deliberately flout maritime law and company regulations, or compromise their safety by using their lifeboat for anything other than its intended purpose.

Mickey made his way back down toward the Scotsman's house, feeling simultaneously sixty years old and twenty years old, elated but exhausted. Rosie had recharged his spirit and his ego as she'd drained him physically. All he wanted to do was fall asleep on the beach until the amphibian arrived. But he had to keep his word, do his duty and call in on the Scotsman. He thought of Rosie lying brazenly naked on top of the sheets as he'd left. She'd be asleep by now, and why not? If ever a girl deserved a rest, she did. He turned right at the old pohutukawa as directed and kept going until he reached the clearing.

"Are you there, Angus?"

A head appeared almost immediately at the side window. Moments later the Scot was at his doorway to greet him.

"Come along, come along, man," he urged. "Take a seat."

Mickey collapsed into a chair on the veranda, where he could still catch the last of the afternoon sun before it dipped behind the ridge. He sat heavily, his thighs unwilling to support the weight of his body after their earlier exertions. He looked around him, noting the heather and the pohutukawas preparing to bloom. He tried to identify some of the larger trees, but botany wasn't one of his strong points. As far as he was concerned, the bush was to be admired and left to get on with it. He sat up as Angus plonked a bottle of Glenfiddich whisky and two glasses down on the table alongside him. Without asking, the Scotsman poured a double in each glass. Mickey looked around for water or ice, saw there was none and knew better than to ask. Angus was clearly a Scotsman's Scot.

"What's this?" he asked, trying to make polite conversation. "Are we celebrating something?"

"Aye, you could say that." There was a mischievous look in the Scot's eye that Mickey neither liked nor understood. "Here's to your continuing good health."

"And to yours."

The two men raised their glasses to each other and took a sip.

"Will we be seeing you back here again soon?"

"No saying, really. Depends on circumstances."

"I see. But you could come back if need be?"

"Maybe. Now, you want to talk to me about the radio."

"Well . . . not exactly."

"Then what exactly do you want to talk to me about, Angus?"

For all his scheming, Angus struggled to find the right words. How could he explain to the officer that he wanted him to sire Rosie's child? How could he explain his desire to be not just grandfather but also father to a child he'd never been able to have himself? How could he explain his preference for an absentee father rather than one who lived practically on his doorstep? "It's complicated," he said.

"Then let me help uncomplicate it."

"I don't know if I should tell you this, because you'll probably think it's none of my business."

"Go on." Mickey wished the Scot would do exactly the opposite. The sun and the whisky had sapped the last of his energy.

"Tell me, what's your opinion of Red?"

"Red?" The Scot's question caught him off guard. Why the hell would the old bastard want to know his opinion of Red? He wrestled lethargically with his dulled brain, trying to find suitable words. "I think he had a hard time in the war, but he seems to be coping. He handles the radio well enough, and I'm sure he'll be a diligent lookout and a valuable asset."

"Aye, I can guarantee you he'll be that. But that's not what I'm talking about. What do you think of him as a man?"

"I don't think I know him well enough to make that sort of judgment."

"Do you think he's stable?"

"Not entirely."

"Do you think he'd make a good father?"

"How the hell would I know? Why the hell should I care?"

"Think, man, it's important!"

Mickey forced his eyes open and looked at Angus. The urgency in the old Scot's voice demanded his attention. "I dunno. He seems to goof off a bit, go absent without leave, if you know what I mean. Given the state of his mind I'd have to say I have my doubts."

"That's the whole point." Angus moved in for the kill. He couldn't see how the lieutenant commander could possibly resist having Rosie all to himself and giving her the child she wanted, thereby saving her and future generations from the madman. He took his time and measured his words carefully. "Tell me, what do you think of Rosie?"

"None of your business."

"Humor me. I'm not intending to pry. You can keep your comments as broad as you wish. For a start, do you like her?"

"Of course I like her."

"Do you find her attractive?"

"What man wouldn't?"

"Do you think she'd make a good mother?"

"I think she'd make a wonderful mother, but for God's sake man, what are you driving at?"

"Rosie wants to have a child. She wants you to be the father."

"What?"

"Aye . . . I thought that would make you sit up. The beautiful Rosie has chosen you." Angus smiled, pleased with himself. Now he just had to steer the lieutenant commander around the problem of Red's presence and insist that Mickey stake first claim on her.

"Are you serious?" Mickey gazed at Angus, eyes bulging open, his voice barely above a whisper.

"Aye. I thought you'd like to know."

"Bloody hell!" Mickey exploded from his chair. This was not the reaction the Scot had anticipated.

"Aye," continued Angus, suddenly uncertain. "I thought you should know so that we can take the appropriate measures."

"Oh dear God. Sweet Jesus!" Mickey reached across and grabbed Angus's hand and pumped it vigorously. "Thanks, mate. But Christ! Why didn't you warn me this morning? Why did you wait till after I'd dipped my wick?"

Angus stood stunned, speechless and dismayed beyond measure as the lieutenant commander galloped back down the trail, alternately cursing and thanking him profusely.

Rosie hadn't fallen asleep the instant Mickey had left her. Instead she'd picked up Norma's letter and read it. Norma wasn't much of a letter writer and never picked up her pen without good reason. Rosie had read and reread the letter until the news had sunk in. Norma was getting married. She'd fallen pregnant and decided to take the plunge. Rosie had put the letter down feeling unaccountably miffed.

Twenty-three

Mickey arrived at his office in a foul mood after another sleepless night spent tossing and turning, wondering whether his little swimmers had hit the target. As much as he liked Rosie, he didn't want to be bound to her in any way, nor did he want the responsibility of a bastard child. What would Gloria think of that? If no other good had come from Angus's revelation, Mickey had at least been forced to acknowledge his feelings toward his young assistant. He wanted more from her than just her body. He wanted all of her. Forever. Her love, her respect, her companionship. And the fear he'd felt as the Scot had dropped his bombshell was the fear of losing her. He'd damned Rosie a thousand times every creeping hour as he'd lain awake, yet he still found it hard to accept that she'd deliberately set out to trap him. She just wasn't like that. She was too straightforward and honest. But something was up, something that had turned the cantankerous old Scot into a fawning fool who wanted to be his best mate. Something was definitely going on but he was at a loss to know what. Mickey felt used, abused and confused. If Rosie wanted to have a kid that was all right by him. But she should have made him aware of her decision and given him the choice of volunteering or declining to be the father, in which case he would have declined. Even if she'd only wanted him as a sperm donor, the child would still be his and have rights to the love and affection and care of his biological father. Mickey would not turn away from his own flesh and blood. He real-

265

ized he'd have to stay in touch with Rosie, find out if what the Scotsman had said was true, whether she was pregnant and if he was the culprit. He slumped at his desk and put his head in his hands.

"Damn the woman!" he said in a heartfelt but barely audible whisper.

"Morning, sir."

He looked up to see Gloria with his morning coffee. She couldn't have heard, couldn't have. But if she had, that would just be his luck.

"You look awful."

"You look wonderful."

"Is there anything I can do for you?"

Mickey held her eyes momentarily, then turned away. Dear God. Was there anything she could do for him? He felt mortally ashamed and stupid in the face of her innocence. Nobody had the right to look so fresh, youthful and radiant, so adorable and utterly irresistible. He wanted to sweep her up in his arms and propose to her. Without looking, he held his hand up toward her, willing her to take it, to take his hand and hold it. He waited, not daring to turn around. Then, mercifully, he felt her hand take hold of his, and hope welled up. Then he felt two fingers searching for his pulse.

"Are you all right, sir?"

Mickey couldn't help smiling. She was so naïve. What on earth had he been thinking of? He turned around and saw the concern in her face. "Yes, thank you, nurse. Just keep taking my pulse and stop when you've counted to three million."

"Sir?"

"At ease, Third. Was there any other reason you came to see me?"

"Yes, sir. The *Cormorant* has been ordered south to baby-sit the *Shoto Maru* as Lieutenant Commander Scriven requested. We also have reports of a dory fishing in close, which doesn't make sense with anything we know about. The local fishermen say it isn't them, and we have no reports of a longliner in the area."

"Big round filing cabinet, Gloria. Anything else?"

"Lieutenant Commander Scriven wants to see you."

"Any idea why?"

"I understand there's a large Japanese trawler just outside the twelve mile on the west coast, obviously after snapper. Lieutenant Commander Scriven is concerned that we may have another phantom."

"Another *Shoto Maru,*" Mickey corrected.

"Yes, sir."

"Is he in yet?"

"Yes, sir."

"Ah. In which case, I'd better run along." Mickey pushed his coffee aside untouched. If Phil the Pill wanted to see him, the least he could do is offer him a decent cup of percolated. He rose from his chair.

"Sir . . . ?"

"Yes, Gloria?"

"About dinner tonight, sir."

"Yes?" Mickey had forgotten about his hopeful invitation. Given the state of his mind, he would have preferred she'd forgotten as well. All he wanted was to go home, open a tin of something, watch television in bed and, hopefully, pass away in his sleep.

"Do you still want me to make the booking?"

"Beg your pardon?"

"Dinner for two. At the Gourmet restaurant."

"Absolutely."

"Very good, sir." She pivoted smartly and left him gaping open-mouthed.

Mickey wandered down the corridor toward Phil Scriven's office, wondering why women always got the better of him. Why they always refused when he was desperate for them to accept, and accepted when he was desperate for them to refuse. How did they know? He wondered if women were born with an innate sense of how to keep a man off balance, or whether it was a skill they acquired. He smiled ingratiatingly at Phil Scriven's secretary. He'd heard a rating describe her as a life-support system for a pair of tits and saw no reason to take issue. He knocked on the door.

"You wish to see me?"

"Ah . . . Mickey, come in, come in. Help yourself to coffee. It's freshly brewed."

Mickey poured, stirred, closed his eyes as he sipped. The aroma was heavenly, the taste divine and the caffeine exactly what his body was crying out for. The day was beginning to look up. Perhaps he'd be able to stay awake right through dinner and even be charming and witty. He pulled a chair over and sat down opposite his superior. Lieutenant Commander Scriven had the overconfident look on his face that immediately warned Mickey that he'd reached a decision. Mickey's spirits sagged. Philip Scriven was one of those people who should never make decisions, especially on their own.

"We have a latent incursion."

"A *latent* incursion?"

"You know the sort of thing, identifying a problem before it actually occurs."

"What exactly is the problem we haven't got?" Mickey's sarcasm was wasted, as he knew it would be.

"Jap trawler by the name of *Tsushima Maru* has moved into the west-coast snapper grounds. Two-and-a-half-thousand tonner at least. The *Egret* spotted her on the way down to the grounds off Taranaki. Think we may have another of these slippery fly-by-nights, another midnight phantom. There's no point in it being there unless the skipper intends to trawl in close. I've moved the *Shearwater* south to shadow her, see what she's up to."

"Good thinking."

"Yes, I think so."

"How long is the *Shearwater* going to shadow the *Tsushima Maru?*"

"As long as it takes for the *Tsushima Maru* to get the message."

"What if it's a decoy?"

"What?"

"There are two longliners working farther north. Who's watching them? And who's watching the two longliners on the east coast while the *Cormorant* baby-sits the *Shoto Maru?*"

"I take your point. But a two-and-a-half-thousand-ton trawler can take more fish in a night than a longliner can in a week."

"That's true. Except when the fish are scattered in close and around reefs, which is where they normally are this time of the year. The fact is we don't have the resources to assign a patrol boat to

268

every foreign fishing boat, and the problem is it won't take long for those boats without escorts to realize they have a totally free hand."

"You're forgetting the aircraft."

"There are no aircraft to forget. Until the air force has the Orions on stream they'll be no help to us. It won't take the foreign boats long to work out there are no eyes in the sky waiting to nail them."

"Well dammit, Mickey, we can't just let them come here and steal our fish willy-nilly."

"No, Phil, we can't. Particularly when they're stealing them right in front of the eyes of the press."

"Then we only have one option. We'll just have to set up a routine of patrols like before, and have our boats constantly on the move up and down the coast."

"Won't work, Phil. Hasn't in the past and won't in the future. The only way to stop them is to catch them. Getting caught costs them money, and that's the only thing they understand. If you mount patrols, they'll just watch our boats safely out of radar range and move inshore. But plant the fear of ambush in the skipper's head and it's an entirely different story. Look, we've just made two arrests. Make two more and the bastards will be too wary to come in. We've got to lure them in where we can trap them. Get them overconfident and then strike. Two more and we'll have them on the run, forever looking over their shoulders. We've got to give them something to worry about."

"Like you did with the *Shoto Maru*."

"The *Shoto Maru*'s escape was a fluke. We had them cold, Phil, and you know it. Those sort of things only happen once every hundred years."

"Every hundred years, eh? And how do you explain that boat you let get away off Great Barrier? Another hundred-year fluke? I'm sorry, Mickey, but I can't agree with you. I'm not prepared to have the Ministry of Marine around my neck again, plus every newspaper in the country, all because you want to play Errol Flynn. I can't afford another botched operation. I see no alternative to patrols. Prevention is always more effective than apprehension." Phil Scriven paused to review and admire his last sentence. It had a nice ring to it. He mentally shortened it. Prevention, not apprehension. Yes. It would make a nice heading for a report. It was also a damned fine encapsulation of his strategy.

Mickey sighed. They were heading down a familiar road. They'd argue for the duration of another two cups of coffee until Phil pulled seniority. At least the coffee was good. It would help him make it through the day and, hopefully, see him through the night as well.

The *Cormorant* patrolled the twelve-mile line directly inshore of the *Shoto Maru*. The trawler worked around the clock, while the crew of the *Cormorant* grew increasingly irritable with each other and more hostile toward Naval Command. The morning of the fourth day brought relief from the tedium. The *Cormorant* was ordered to return to Devonport before resuming patrol duties farther north.

As soon as the patrol boat disengaged, Shimojo Seiichi began planning his next nighttime incursion. As Mickey had predicted, the weakness in Lieutenant Commander Scriven's strategy was about to be exploited. And exploited to the full.

It took a few days for reports of the *Shoto Maru*'s resumption of illegal fishing to filter through to Mickey, and by then it was too late. The *Tsushima Maru* had withdrawn from its position on the west coast and motored back south to the grounds off Taranaki. Its departure had caused Lieutenant Commander Scriven to pronounce his strategy a total success, and he was deaf to all intelligence to the contrary. Reports began to come in from fishing grounds all around New Zealand as the foreign fishing fleets woke up to the fact that the navy had returned to its old, predictable strategy. The captains simply behaved themselves when a patrol boat came near, then returned to their poaching the moment it moved on. The radio waves buzzed with updates of the positions of the patrol boats and their headings. The foreign crews could hardly believe their luck.

Occasionally, in foul weather, a patrol boat would surprise a dory within the twelve-mile zone but, under instruction, did little more than escort them back out to sea, warn them and wait to ensure they heeded the warning. Prevention, not apprehension was the name of the game, and the game plan could have been devised by the wool marketers. Lieutenant Commander Scriven saw the lack of arrests as proof of the success of his prevention strategy. Not for the first time, Mickey thought about resigning his commission.

Instead he collected and collated every report from his network of spotters, from local fishermen, from aircraft pilots and passing shipping. He collected every report from every fishing ground. He thought of leaking the information to the press, but incursions and howls of protest had become so commonplace over the years that they no longer made news. Arrests and retribution were all that made news, and Mickey had none to give them. He decided to write a report of his own, not for the Staff Officer Operations, but to go directly to the commodore. Mickey thought he could come up with a snappy title, too. "Arrest Is Best," he wrote. Not a bad line to exit a career on.

Gloria remained the only light in his life, but his progress there remained steady rather than spectacular. He had not yet bedded her and hadn't pressed his claim. She had old-fashioned notions, and he was inhibited by a shadow reaching across the gulf from Great Barrier Island. When Red had called in to report on the activities of a longliner along Great Barrier's east coast, he'd resisted the temptation to ask about Rosie or even ask Red if he could get her to telephone him. What would he say to her? Besides, there was another reason why he was loath to contact Rosie, which he was ashamed to admit. He couldn't help feeling that he was better off not knowing, better off if he never heard another word from Wreck Bay for the remainder of his life. But then there'd always be the fear that one day there'd be a knock on his door and he'd find a smaller, younger version of himself standing there, holding out his hand and saying "Daddy." Sooner or later he'd have to face Rosie and find out the truth. It wasn't a day he looked forward to with any relish.

Twenty-four

"Tell me about the one-oh-five."

"Don't do it, Rosie."

"It's not doing you any good keeping it inside, Red."

"Please, Rosie, you don't know what you're doing. You don't understand."

"I understand all right, Red, and I want to understand more. You know you need help. I know you need help and what's more I'm the only person who can give it." Red would not meet her eye. His elbows rested on the dining table, and he stared stubbornly at the wall. The dinner plates had been cleared away to make room for the manila envelope Rosie's father had sent her and its contents. "No one else cares about you like I do, Red. You've never had anyone treat you before who cared about you. I know, Red, because it's all here in your file. My father was supposed to oversee all the psychiatric patients in the Auckland area and take responsibility for their welfare. But he never even met you. He never took the trouble. He read your case card and doubtless commented on your treatment, but you were left in the hands of others who obviously didn't care any more than he did."

"You've no right to read my file."

"I have every right. I'm your doctor. You're my patient."

"Says who?"

"I do. And I've got your file, so that rather tends to prove my case,

272

doesn't it? All I'm asking, Red, is that you give me a chance. Is that too much? Look, my father sent a note along with your file. He's reviewed your case, and according to him you should now be little more than a gibbering idiot. The fact that you're not he attributes to his therapies finally bearing results. But we know otherwise, don't we? You've developed your own therapies, and they work better than any the doctors gave you."

"That's right, Rosie. That's my point."

"And that's mine, Red! You've done a terrific job on yourself, one you have every right to feel proud of. You've beaten the system and beaten the doctors. You've done a terrific job, but the job's not finished. You know it isn't! I know it isn't. All I'm suggesting is that we work together with what you know works and we'll see if we can find what else works. Imagine it, Red. Imagine what it would be like to be free of the demons, to be free of fear, to look back over the past, accept it for what it was but no longer live in its shadow. Isn't that something worth fighting for? Isn't it worth giving me a chance?" She crouched down in front of Red so that he couldn't avoid looking at her. "Look at me, Red."

"You don't understand, Rosie." He turned his head slightly so that his eyes could meet hers. "You can never understand. You weren't there. No one can ever understand who wasn't there."

"Then take me there, Red, so I can understand. What happened at the one-oh-five? What happened to Archie?"

"No, Rosie, no!" He swiveled in his chair, away from her, and buried his head in his hands. "Don't make me do this, Rosie." He wasn't asking her, he was begging.

"All right, Red. All right." She put her arm around his shoulders. "I'll do a deal with you. I'll drop the one-oh-five for now if you tell me what happened to Yvonne?" She waited for a response. "What's it to be, Red? Is it a deal?" She reached for the half-empty bottle of burgundy and filled both glasses. "Well?"

"She died." Red stayed turned away, head hidden in his hands.

"How?"

"The Japs killed her."

"Why?"

273

"Because she tried to stop them killing her patients."

"Did you see them kill her?"

"Yes."

"How?"

"Through the window in the ward door."

"Did you try to stop them?"

"Yes."

"Why didn't you?"

"They wouldn't let me."

"Who?"

"Archie and Steve."

"Tell me what happened."

Silence.

"Look at me, Red. Take your head out of your hands and tell me what happened." She pulled at his arm and it came away easily. He raised his head slowly, as if every inch cost him unbearable pain. Tears rolled from eyes that didn't blink and saw things happening in another time.

"Ah, Jesus, Red!" Rosie realized she'd lost him and could do nothing but wait until he came back. She wondered whether she was right to meddle, whether Red wouldn't be better off if she just left him alone.

"Have a sip of wine, Red, and tell me what you saw. You hear me?"

The tears had stopped, but he still stared blank eyed at the table. She waited, neither patiently nor anxiously, but with a sense of resignation. Progress, if there was to be any, would be slow in coming. Her thoughts drifted back to the record of his treatment. It seemed to have been administered on a suck-it-and-see principle, all reactive according to his mood swings, with no long-term strategy in mind. She was stunned to read that he was once considered too violent and unpredictable to mix with other patients.

"They were old men. Bedridden. I wrote letters for them and brought them bottles and bed pans. I liked to help."

Rosie snapped her attention back to Red. His eyes didn't lift from the table, and his voice sounded distant and remote, as emotionally laden as a weather forecast. She reached for her glass of wine and took a long sip.

"The Japs ordered them out of their beds and onto their feet, then began to scream and wave their rifles around. The poor old blokes couldn't do anything. Some of them tried to swing their legs over the side of the bed, but it didn't get them very far. Those blokes couldn't have stood for the national anthem. They couldn't have stood if their arses were on fire. They should've been evacuated first, poor bastards."

"What were you doing at the doorway?"

"Someone ran past the ward yelling that the Japs had arrived and were shooting. I was worried about Yvonne. I knew she was on duty and where she'd be. I wanted to help if there was any trouble."

"Go on."

Red's voice faltered, and the muscles in his face began to twitch and tremble as his mind tried to find ways to protect itself from the horror of his memories. His expressions ran through endless permutations of emotions—anger, hatred, fear, revenge, bravado—but as hard as he tried, none locked in. He'd been hurt and bewildered then and was clearly still vulnerable. Rosie's heart went out to him.

"Just as I reached Yvonne's ward some Aussie soldiers came running toward me. They were pulling their uniforms on over their pajamas and bandages. The Japs had already started to rampage through the wards. I wanted to go in, but the Aussies grabbed me and held on. The Japs had their bayonets fixed and had begun prodding the patients to get them to stand up. Yvonne was screaming at the Japs. She ran between one of her patients and a Jap sergeant. She pushed his rifle away as he was about to give the old bloke some hurry-up. He slapped her, and she fell to the ground. She seemed stunned for a second, then got up and pushed the *gunso*'s rifle away again. Everything stopped. Soldiers and patients, they all stopped to see what would happen. The *gunso* screamed at her to stand aside. He held the bayonet at her chest. At first she refused to move, then she backed off toward the old bloke in bed, still staying between him and the Jap sergeant. Her face had turned deathly white, and I could see she was scared out of her wits. The *gunso* ordered her to stand aside, but she still stood her ground. I must have called out, because she turned her head toward the door. She saw me and I think that gave her hope. She started to smile. She thought I was coming to help. But the bastard just bayoneted her. He rammed his bayonet right through her. For no reason. No reason at all! Her mouth opened to scream but no sound came. She turned back to me, begging me to help. The *gunso* pulled his bloody bayonet out and stabbed her again. I started to shout, but one of the Aussies put his hand over my mouth. They pinned my arms behind my back and dragged me away as she slumped to the floor, still looking for me, still waiting for me to come to my rescue." His eyes looked up at Rosie's, pleading for absolution.

"The Aussies did the right thing." Rosie was now on familiar territory. She kept her voice matter-of-fact. "They were a lot smarter than you, Red. What do you think would have happened if you'd burst into the ward?"

"I might have been able to do something."

"What?"

"I don't know!"

"What were you wearing?"

"My uniform."

"So a uniformed soldier bursts into a ward full of armed Japanese soldiers to rescue the lady in distress. What do you think the Japanese soldiers would have done, Red?"

"I might have been able to do something, Rosie."

"Answer the question!"

"You don't understand!"

"Bullshit, Red! I understand perfectly. Answer the question. What do you think the Japanese would have done?"

"I dunno . . ."

"Well, I do. They would have shot you dead before you'd gone more than a few paces. How would that have helped Yvonne? Instead of having one incredibly brave dead nurse, we'd have one incredibly stupid dead soldier as well. How would that have helped Yvonne?"

"At least I would have done something!" Temper now.

"You would have done nothing, achieved nothing. Yvonne would still have been killed."

"I would have helped, Rosie! Yvonne wouldn't have died disappointed in me!"

"You would prefer that she died knowing she'd caused your

276

death? Do you think Yvonne would have died happier knowing she'd killed you?"

Silence.

"Answer me, Red."

"No, but . . ."

"Then put down your cross, Red, you've carried it long enough. You did nothing wrong. You did nothing because there was nothing you could do. And there's another point you should bear in mind. Yvonne made her own decision. She had a choice. She could have backed down. She chose not to. What she did was a wonderful, magnificent, courageous act of defiance, but it was also futile. It was her choice, not yours. She did what she felt she had to do. Once she'd made that decision her fate was sealed, and there was nothing you or anyone else could have done to change things."

"She wouldn't have died alone, Rosie. Nobody should be left to die alone."

"You're right, Red, absolutely right. Nobody should be left to die alone if it can be prevented. But sometimes it can't be. But I don't believe Yvonne died alone."

"What do you mean?"

"Isn't it obvious, Red? Who was she looking at when she died? She was looking at the face of the man who loved her and who was desperate to help her. Do you think she didn't see the soldiers trying to drag you away? Do you think she didn't see the hand over your mouth to stop you calling out? Do you think she didn't find comfort in your being there? Come on, Red! Yvonne was an intelligent and perceptive woman. In her last moments on this earth, every single detail of the man she loved would have been etched into her brain. You were there, Red, reaching out to her, giving her the comfort of your love. You say she looked to you for help. I say she looked helpless. Put yourself in her position. She saw the agony you were going through and was powerless to help you. She was a nurse, Red, and your lover. She'd already demonstrated her selflessness by standing up for her patients. It was her nature to put others before herself. Hasn't it ever occurred to you that she'd do the same for you—especially for you?" Rosie paused while Red absorbed her words. Clearly, he'd never thought to consider the events from Yvonne's point of view. He'd been overwhelmed by loss, despair and guilt and had never looked beyond. Rosie let the minutes tick by as Red relived the terrible moment from another perspective. But a point of view built up over years isn't changed in minutes, and Rosie was well aware of the hours and hours of work ahead of her. But they'd made a start. She decided to move on and try to get him talking again. "You were lovers, weren't you, Red?"

"Yes."

"How on earth did you manage that?" Rosie smiled coquettishly. "I imagine it would have been hard to be alone in a ward with thirty other patients."

"Hospitals are full of beds, Rosie."

She laughed. "Was Yvonne your first?"

"First I ever cared about."

"Had there been many others?"

"No."

"Were you engaged?"

"Sort of; we talked about getting married after the war."

"She must have been a wonderful girl."

"She was."

"Do you ever just sit and think of the good times you had together and the special things about her that you really liked?"

"I try not to think about her."

"Well, it's time you did. If you really loved her, you owe it to her memory. Let her come to you, Red."

"I'm not sure . . ."

"Trust me. Let her come to you and give her a warm welcome when she does. Have there been many other women since?"

"No. No one. No one except you, Rosie."

"You're kidding!" Rosie was stunned. It had never occurred to her that he'd gone without sex for more than twenty years. She was hard pressed to know what shocked her more—his story or his admission of chastity.

"It's not easy, Rosie. The war changed everything. Nothing means as much as it did." Red squirmed, embarrassed, as he tried to find

278

words to express his thoughts. "Feelings aren't the same. They don't seem to mean as much. Sometimes they don't mean anything."

"That's a common enough sentiment among people who've endured the sort of horrors you went through. It must have been absolutely appalling. But you have to adjust. And the people who adjust best are those who make a conscious effort to let the past go."

"It's not easy, Rosie."

"I'm sure it isn't. But your mind can be your ally if only you let it. It has a wonderful capacity to heal. You've got to let your mind do its job now. You've got to allow it back on your side to deal with all of your terrible memories. I can help you do that."

"You don't understand, Rosie. You're making the mistake they all make."

"For God's sake, Red! What is there to understand? You lived day to day, lucky to survive until the next. Starvation, deprivation, disease were your bedmates, the things you lived with every second of every day. Death, torture and endless drudgery. Slave labor under impossible conditions. People survived and wrote books about it. They've made films about it. We've all read the books and seen the films. It was disgusting, degrading and unforgivable. It was the worst, most horrifying experience anyone could undergo. What is there to understand?"

"You weren't there, Rosie! You can never understand!" Red kicked his chair back and stood shouting, every muscle in his body tensed, veins sticking out and throbbing, fists clenching.

"Damn you, Red, I do understand!" Rosie had had enough. It was time to stand up to him. Time for him to face up to his responsibilities to himself. She stood, kicking her chair so that it also crashed backward onto the floor. "I do understand! Get that through your thick skull. Now, sit down!"

"No!" His shoulders shook. His whole body trembled from the upheavals within. "You don't understand. No one understands. No one can understand!"

"Understand what, Red? Understand what?"

"Can't you see? It was the best time of my life! It was the best time of my life!"

Archie leaped up from his place by the side of the Shacklock to

279

join Red as he stumbled sobbing toward the door, overcome by the shame of his confession, by finally putting into words and admitting the terrible truth. Rosie stood stunned, then ran after him, grabbed him as he tried to wrench open the door.

"Don't you run from me, Red O'Hara! Don't you run from me!" She threw her arms around him and clung tightly to him. "Jesus Christ, look at the pair of us!" Tears rolled down her cheeks and soaked his shirt. "Don't you run from me, Red." She felt the tension seep away out of his body. Archie slunk over to his place by the Shacklock and sat down, watching, worrying. "Forgive me, Red, you were right. I don't understand. I'm sorry. I'm really sorry."

"You don't understand, Rosie. You can't begin to understand."

"I can if you help me."

"No, Rosie! Leave it. Leave me be!"

"Balls to you, Red O'Hara." Rosie pushed herself away and glowered at him through red-rimmed eyes. "We're not quitting. Look at you. You say it's hard to feel things anymore. Hard to love, hard to hate, hard to feel! But how are you feeling now, Red, how are you feeling now? You look like someone who's feeling things just fine. Something's working. So hug me, you selfish bastard. I feel pain, too, you know."

Twenty-five

~~~~~~~~~~

I t was Angus who spotted the lights from the tuna boat. Bonnie had woken
him by leaping onto his bedroom windowsill and pawing at the glass, as if
trying to trap the bobbing lights in her paws. He watched as the boat
slowly worked its way out to sea, laying parallel longlines at one-mile
intervals. He'd watched for an hour until he'd lost sight of the boat
behind Bernie's Head. He checked his watch.

He rose at dawn, fed Bonnie while he had his tea and toast, then
set off to alert Red so that he could pass the information on to
Mickey. When Archie failed to bark, Angus began to suspect that Red
had spent the night at Rosie's, working on the production of his
grandchild, a suspicion confirmed when his calls went unanswered.
Angus turned back toward Rosie's, wishing the lieutenant commander were sharing her bed instead. Still, if it had to be Red, it had
to be, and he believed he could always take Red aside and impress
upon him his unsuitability as a parent. Convince the man that it
would be in the child's best interests to hand over all fatherly duties to
him. Anyone with a brain at all could see the wisdom in that. He
paused at the clearing and called. He didn't want to approach too
close until he was sure he wouldn't catch them in compromising circumstances. Red appeared on the veranda almost immediately. He
was naked.

"Put some clothes on. I need to talk."

Red disappeared back inside to put shorts on. Angus sat at the veranda table and waited for Red to reappear.

"What do you need to talk about?"

"Did you see the Japanese boat last night?"

"No. Where?" Red's manner hardened instantly.

"Laying lines out from Whangapoua Beach. It worked north past Bernie's Head. It was five o'clock when I lost sight of it."

"Bastards! Angus, could you radio Mickey? I'm going after the lines."

"Aye, I suppose so."

"What's up?" Rosie emerged wearing her dressing gown. She held her hand up to her forehead to shield her eyes from the morning sun.

"Good morning, Rosie."

"Morning. What's going on?"

"Jap longliner. Angus spotted it last night. He's going to advise the navy. I'm going after their lines."

"Can I come?"

"Sure," said Red.

"No," said Angus.

The two men looked at each other. Finally Angus spoke.

"A nor'easter's blowing. It's the morning calm now, but it'll build up before too long. If you've had your breakfast you'll not be hanging on to it."

"He's right, Rosie."

"Well, if I'm sick, I'm sick. They're also my fish they're stealing."

"Aye, but a woman in your condition . . ."

"What condition, Angus?" Rosie's eyes blazed.

"Ahh . . . well . . ." Angus gazed around hopelessly looking for inspiration. "Your seasick condition. It'll get awful rough out there."

"It can get awful rough around here, too, Angus. Red, you go and get the radio." She waited until Red had gone indoors before turning on the Scot. "Get one thing through your head. I am a doctor. I know how not to make babies. And at the moment that is my preferred option. Understand?" Red reappeared with the radio before Angus had a chance to answer. "Red, you go on ahead. I'll make a flask of tea and sandwiches and meet you on the beach."

•   •   •

The sun was well clear of the top of Bernie's Head as Red and Rosie motored out of the bay, with Archie on the foredeck warning the gulls to keep clear. The wind was steady rather than strong, but had sufficient force to whip the spray up over the bow. Red steered due east on the assumption that the longliners would have worked northeast into the wind. Waves lined up in rows that stretched back to the horizon, steepled until their tops became too heavy, tumbled lazily forward and foamed down the face.

"Try and keep dry," Red counseled. "The wind's mild enough but you'll feel it if you get wet."

Rosie snuggled up as close as she could behind him, tucked her head down and held on like a pillion passenger on a motorbike. The old lifeboat seemed made for the conditions, riding through the swells and pushing aside the chop. But the odd wave still caught them and sent a shudder through the planking. She learned to pick the waves that would fling a shower of spray over the bow, catch the wind and hurtle bulletlike toward her. Like riding a horse, she thought.

"Oh Christ!"

She heard the anguish in Red's voice and looked up.

"Bastards! Bloody Jap bastards!"

"What's the matter?" Rosie tried to see over his shoulder but saw nothing unusual.

"The birds."

She looked over to her right and saw shearwaters, petrels, terns and gannets wheeling and diving. "What about them?"

"The bastards have laid surface lines! The birds are after the bait on the hooks." His hands began to shake, and his breath came in short, rapid gasps.

"Red! What's the matter? What's wrong?" The last thing she needed was Red to go AWOL on her four miles out to sea.

His eyes searched for the buoy that marked the head of the longline and the beginning of their long, sad, day's work. Work! Yes, that was what he needed. Already he could see a line of desperate birds flapping on the surface, pointing like a finger toward the marker. It took him a moment or two to spot the buoy in the chop. Then he steered to a point twenty feet to windward and slipped the engine out of gear so that the breeze would blow him back onto it.

"Rosie, look through the tackle box for one of the big red spools and put it on this mount."

She opened the box and had no trouble finding the right spool. Everything was in its own compartment, stored as neatly as silver cutlery in its drawer.

"Grab hold of the line and start winding it onto the spool, but watch out for the hooks." Red grabbed the buoy and sliced through the weighted line that held the longline in position. Their rate of drift made him glad Rosie had come with him, but he had no doubt she'd regret her decision by day's end. Rosie grabbed the line and began to wind. She wound as fast as she could, feet braced against the side of the boat, shoulders hunched over the spool. "Not too fast, not too fast! Don't wear yourself out."

"Ha!" Rosie smiled. Men never lost an opportunity to put a woman down. She couldn't see how winding the longline on the spool could possibly wear her out. It wasn't as if she was battling its weight. Red stood hauling the line in hand over hand, leaving her to reel in the slack. Where was the effort in that? Birds wheeled and swooped over her head, shouting abuse at them for interrupting their breakfast. It wasn't until she lifted her head from winding and saw Red reach over and pull up the first shearwater that she understood why he was upset.

"Is it all right?"

"Drowned." He wrenched the hook from the bird's beak and tossed the lifeless body back into the water. "Keep the tension on the line. Okay? Now keep winding!"

A lot of the hooks were still baited as Rosie wound the line in. She tried to push the baits over the rim of the spool so that they couldn't get in the way of the line. But there were too many, and she soon ran out of room. "Red! What do I do now?"

"Think you could feed the line into that fish box? Put it between your legs."

Rosie did as she was told. She pulled the slack line in arm over arm, picking the gaps between hooks, relieved at the change in action. It surprised her how quickly winding had tired her arm. She gave a small cheer as Red freed the first of the survivors and it flapped away to rest and recover from its wounds. But the dead birds far outnumbered the living. Most pathetic of all were the small terns, which had quickly succumbed. If Red had sympathy for them he never showed it. He ripped the hooks free and raced after the next, hoping each time that the bird was still alive. One by one he brought the birds in until the line stretched free ahead of them. Suddenly three black petrels dropped like missiles onto the baits, grabbing their free meal while they could. Rosie screamed at them, trying to scare them off, but they took no notice. All three were hooked.

"Hurry!"

Red was working as hard as he could, hands practiced, mind blank to everything but the next trapped bird. But he couldn't pull the line in faster than the boat drifted. Rosie almost cried out in frustration. The three petrels thrashed the water in desperation. She waved a free hand as other petrels swooped around their stricken comrades. Red hauled the first of the petrels aboard, freed and released it. Rosie held the heavy line taut. The remaining two birds were clearly weakening. Red reached over and plucked the second bird out of the water. It was hooked through the wing and attacked Red's hands viciously, clacking in pain and outrage. He ignored the pecks, but the flapping made it difficult to release the hook. He grabbed his knife and cut the line by the hook's eyelet and released the terrified bird. Its wing clipped Rosie across the face as it made good its escape. Red reached over and grabbed the third bird. It was almost dead from exhaustion. He unhooked it and handed it to Rosie.

"Hold this. I'll bring in the line. Black petrels normally feed on squid at night. Their bad luck the Japs used squid for bait."

Rosie swapped jobs gratefully. Her back and arms had begun to ache from the endless repetition. She settled the frightened bird in her lap, fingers around its breast and wings, thumbs vertical up the back of its neck where its beak couldn't reach. Excluding the kakas, which Bernie had hand-fed until they were as tame as any bird in a cage, the black petrel was the first wild bird Rosie had ever held. She found the experience intensely moving. She wanted to take it home, to mother it and nurse it back to health. She slowly and gently eased

285

a finger free so that she could stroke its neck. The bird was beautiful. It wasn't jet black all over as she'd first thought. Some of the feathers were edged with silver like fine filigree.

"You beautiful little thing," she whispered soothingly.

The petrel sensed the lessening of her grip, whipped its head around and clamped its beak around her finger. Rosie yelped and instinctively let go. The petrel took flight instantly, swore at her a couple of times, then settled on the water at what it judged to be a safe distance. Rosie shook her finger and laughed ruefully. She turned to Red. "Not exactly grateful, are they?"

"Why should they be? Birds didn't invent hooks, Rosie. Take over the line. We have to work faster." He engaged gear and motored along the length of the line while Rosie pulled it in. Her arms pumped, and though Red kept the weight off the line, they soon tired and felt as though they'd drop off.

"Dear God! How much more is there?"

"Dunno."

"What do you mean you dunno?"

"Could be five miles long, could be fifteen. Blokes from Tryphena have found Jap longlines as long as thirty miles. My guess is this close in they're likely to be short."

"This is short?"

"Another couple of miles will probably see the end of it."

Rosie's jaw dropped at the daunting prospect. No wonder Red had told her to take it easy at the start. "Red? How many lines did Angus say there were?"

"The boat made four runs."

"Bloody hell. Want to swap jobs? Swap back if we come across more birds?"

"Sure. But do you want to catch your first fish on longline?"

"What do you mean?"

"Feel the line."

Rosie did, and sure enough she could feel something wriggling. She forgot her weariness in her eagerness to get to the source of the struggle. Red reached over the side and lifted an exhausted kingfish into the boat. He unhooked it and dropped it into a fish box.

"Now take over the helm."

Rosie dragged herself to her feet. Every muscle in her back groaned. She took the wheel in her hands and fixed her eyes on a spot fifty yards away and parallel to the longline. She noticed Red had taken up all the slack and eased the throttle forward. Red settled into a rhythm, standing upright, feet wide apart. She had never imagined anyone could retrieve line so quickly. His body swayed with the sea, but his action never faltered. He was like a machine, a well-oiled, well-programmed machine. But, of course, it wasn't just work for Red but therapy. She began to wonder if she'd get any further if she questioned him while he was working. No one else had tried it. The more she thought about it, the more optimistic she became.

"Red, what was all that about before?"

"What was what about?"

"When you first spotted the birds. I thought I was going to lose you again."

"I get angry, Rosie."

"And what else?"

"You know."

"Yeah, I know. But I find it hard to reconcile your reaction with your comment last night."

"Don't start, Rosie, not now. Not out here."

"Why not? It's the perfect time. We're going to be working out here all day, Red. I bet nobody has ever talked to you about the Japanese while you were working. I bet nobody's ever asked you about the camp at the one-oh-five."

"Leave it, Rosie!"

"Just talk to me, Red. There's no bullshit out here. Just you and me and a bunch of birds. I know why your years as a prisoner of war were the worst in your life, how about you tell me why they were the best."

"Rosie . . . for God's sake!"

"Keep pulling that line in. You don't have to look at me to talk to me. Keep working. There's work to be done. There are three more lines. More birds to save. Now, what was so bloody good about the camps?"

287

Red kept the line coming in, hand over hand, oblivious to everything except the job he had to do. And Rosie's question. He thought back to Burma, to the skeletons in rags who'd helped him survive and whom he, in turn, had helped survive. To Archie and Steve, Bluey, Dougie, Hacker, Dustie and Stubbie, and all the men who'd shared the horror and the daily fight for survival. Names and faces scrolled through his mind, unchanged, unaged. Would they feel the same, he wondered? Would the other survivors feel as he did? Red envied his comrades in the camps, the Aussies who shook his hand and punched his arm as they climbed aboard the trucks and began their journey back to their homes in Australia. He envied them because they had each other to talk to, to reach out to, to remember together, to forget together and get drunk together. But he had no one. He'd only been their guest, a misplaced New Zealander temporarily hitched to the Aussies for lack of an alternative, adopted by Archie and Steve so that he wouldn't be alone. But he was alone now, had been alone from the instant he'd set foot back in New Zealand. The friendship, the mateship, the glue that bound them together body and soul, all beyond his reach. He'd never believed anyone could feel so alone. There was no one to talk to, no one to share with, no one to understand. No mates. No other survivors.

"Fish coming up."

He unhooked a string of kahawai and threw them in a fish box to keep for bait and fish cakes. They'd tried to make fish cakes in Burma. One of the boys had managed to buy half a dozen small fish from a villager and they'd mashed them up to make fish cakes so that everyone in their group could share. They'd used up three valuable duck eggs and dipped into their hoard of rice flour. A Dutch prisoner had given them some dried chilies, and they'd scavenged some native herbs. The patties had broken apart in the pan, and the fish had been hard to find, but nobody had complained. The fish cakes had been a luxury, a prize, a treasure and, more than that, an act of defiance toward their captors. They'd refused to starve and proclaimed their defiance with each precious mouthful. They'd survived another day and would survive the next. And the next! Red could remember the taste as clearly as the faces of his mates, as clearly as their voices, as distinctively as the rattle of the bamboo slats they slept on, each man playing his own peculiar, percussive tune as he turned in his sleep. He wondered if his old comrades remembered the fish cakes as vividly as he did. He wondered if it was possible to forget.

"Buoy ahead."

Red looked up automatically and saw it bobbing in the waves. He reached the last of the hooks and took a wrap on the line. "Put her in neutral," he called.

Rosie slipped the boat out of gear and let it glide toward the buoy. Red used the line to hold the boat on course, grabbed his knife and cut the buoy free of its weights.

"Look for birds, Rosie."

Rosie handed over the helm and scanned the horizon back in the direction they'd come. She hoped to see nothing, but there was no mistaking the whirling, plunging swarm of black dots.

"Hurry, Red!" She ducked for cover as a wave top hurdled the bow.

A school of tuna had hooked up on the second line and drowned. Red cut them free. There was no point in keeping them. He had no ice to stop the flesh from spoiling. Other than that, the second line was a repeat of the first. The birds simply didn't learn. They spent all day every day scavenging for food, covering hundreds of miles in the process, and simply couldn't resist easy pickings. Rosie finally threw up, sickened by the rocking of the boat and by the senseless slaughter. But seasickness could not excuse her from work. Once Red had released the last of a flock of birds, she relieved him on the line, standing like he had, feet apart, back straight, arms working like pistons. She heard Red curse and guessed there were more trapped birds ahead. Momentarily she felt glad because it meant that Red would take over the line again and give her back and arms another chance to recover.

"Gannets."

Red shifted into neutral and swapped places with Rosie. She shielded her eyes against the sun so that she could see them. Some were fighting the dead weight of the line, others had already given in, their golden heads flopping uselessly in the waves. It seemed so unfair and unjust. She wanted to help free them but didn't know how. The double barb on the Japanese hooks made Red's work all the more difficult. She winced as a struggling bird ripped the point of a hook across the back of Red's hand, gouging a furrow as it went. He seemed not to notice and ignored the injury until the bird was free. Then he reached his hand over the side and let the sea wash it.

"Rosie, pass me the bottle of meths. In the cupboard under the helm."

Rosie threw him the bottle, guessing immediately why he wanted it. She winced once more as he unscrewed the cap and poured the raw spirit straight into the wound. She decided then that she'd let Red handle all the birds. He released the last of the flock and yelled at her to haul in the slack. His stamina seemed limitless.

"Talk to me, Red."

"Not now, Rosie."

"I just want to know one thing. Tell me and I'll get off your back. What was so good about the camps?"

"There was nothing good about the camps. Nothing. Nothing!"

"So how come you enjoyed it?"

Red seemed to ignore her. His arms swung backward and forward, hauling in the longline with metronomic precision. Beads of sweat and spray dotted his forehead, ran down his face and dripped from the point of his nose and chin.

"I never said I enjoyed it, Rosie."

"Okay, okay . . . then what made you say it was the best time of your life? What made you say that?"

Red stared at the water in front of him as his arms pumped. "I can't explain. It's just that after the war there was nothing. Just emptiness. It was like I'd survived, but when the war ended they took away my reason for surviving. I didn't know where I fitted anymore. In the camps everything was so clear. Every waking moment was dedicated to survival. Then they brought me home and just let me get on with it. But what was I supposed to get on with, Rosie?" He cut more tuna free from the line.

"A normal life, Red. Job, wife, children, football on Saturdays, the pub after work."

"That wasn't normal to me! The camps were normal! The beatings were normal! Starving was normal! Dysentery, beriberi, malaria—"

"That'll do, Red!"

He began to haul in the line like a man possessed, so quickly that Rosie was forced to increase throttle to keep up. But that wasn't what concerned her. She could see his body begin to shake.

"Just one last question, Red, and then I promise, no more questions today. But slow down. We've got two more lines to pull in, and I can't do it by myself." She waited until Red's breathing slowed and deepened and his work rate slackened. She eased back on the throttle to match his pace. "What's the one thing you miss about the camps, Red? What's the one thing you miss most?"

"Belonging."

"Belonging?" Rosie thought she'd misheard.

"I miss belonging. I belonged in the camps."

"What do you mean?"

"I belonged to a group, Rosie. We survived for each other and because of each other. We made each other laugh when we had no reason to laugh. We lived our lives more intensely than you can ever imagine. We belonged to each other, Rosie, and I miss them. Every day of my life I miss them! I miss Archie! I miss them all!"

Rosie knew she'd pushed too hard, gone too far. There was nothing she could do but try to hold the helm steady. She began to digest the implications of what he'd said while Red hauled furiously on the line. She didn't try to slow him down. It was doubtful he'd have heard her, doubtful he was even aware of her anymore. Red had gone back to Burma. To his mates. To the hell that had reshaped them all and still held him prisoner.

They labored throughout the morning and well into the afternoon, working automatically, speaking only when the work made it necessary. The farther they went out to sea, the more dead birds they found. There were no survivors at all on the fourth line, but the effort of pulling in the miles of line had dulled Rosie's brain to the point where conversation was out of the question. Red had added another half-dozen kingfish to their catch, and a few yellowfin tuna, which he kept for bait.

The journey back to Wreck Bay was easier with the wind behind them and a following sea. Even so, Rosie crouched behind Red and snuggled into him, arms around his waist. She was numb with cold and weariness. Time and again she found herself rocking off into troubled sleep. There was no joy for her in thinking about the number of birds they'd saved, just despair at the needless slaughter. She wondered how the Japanese felt when they pulled in their tuna lines and found birds instead of fish impaled on the hooks. Didn't they care? Maybe she was beginning to understand Red in more ways than she'd intended, understand what drove him to protect the waters around Wreck Bay, what fueled his hatred. After all, it was her patch of water, too. She'd be damned if she'd let the Japs destroy it.

The change in engine note aroused her from her stupor. She opened her eyes, relieved to find she was back inside Wreck Bay. The half-cabins were leaping about on their moorings as if the water were boiling hot. She knew she should get the mooring rope for Red but lacked the will to move. Her hands and arms seemed set in concrete, her eyes swollen and the skin on her face sandblasted and stretched drum tight. She hadn't worn a hat, sunglasses or sun cream and was paying the penalty. All she could think of was a hot bath and bed. She didn't care if she didn't eat; all she wanted to do was sleep and the longer the better. She heard the creak of oarlocks, saw Angus rowing out to meet them and was overcome with relief.

"How was it?" Angus threw his painter around the stern cleat and tied off.

"Bad, Angus. They killed hundreds of birds."

"Aye." He turned to Rosie critically. "And what about you?"

"Had better days. Could you get me ashore and call a cab?"

"I did warn you."

"You should have come with us and helped."

"It's as well I didn't. It seems all I've done all day is talk on the radio."

"They sending a patrol boat?"

"Sorry, Red, they've none nearby to send. Mickey's hoping to do something by the end of the week. There are no boats and no planes available. He asked us to do what we can."

"Do what we can?!" Rosie's voice was unexpectedly shrill. It

292

seemed to surprise her as much as the two men. "Angus, what the hell does he think we've been doing?"

"I'm going back out tonight." Red spoke quietly but with finality. "The Japs will come back for their lines and set others. Better I go alone. Angus, can you keep watch while I get some sleep? Call me as soon as you see anything."

"Aye, I suppose it's my duty and I'll not shirk it."

"Red! You've got to be joking."

"You get some rest, Rosie. This is only the beginning. We have to stop them now or they'll fish here all summer. We'll need you on other nights."

Rosie lacked the strength to argue. "Help me into the dinghy, Angus. Take me home. You can come back for wonder boy later."

"There's one other small matter," said Angus. "Mickey asked me to tell you that your old friend is on our doorstep—Shimojo Seiichi. Mickey insists you keep clear and leave Shimojo to him. You hear me, Red?"

Red closed his eyes. He tried to imagine the damage a two-and-a-half-thousand-ton trawler would do. He tried to imagine the three-hundred-foot-wide net scouring the tuatua and scallop beds, stripping them, ripping through the seagrass and destroying the sea bottom. He pictured the thousands upon thousands of snapper in roe snatched away before they had a chance to spawn. There was no choice, no choice at all. He turned to face Angus, jaw set, eyes cold. "Tell Mickey to get stuffed."

Twenty-six

Mickey flattered himself that he was an astute tactician and liked to believe that others in the navy shared his opinion. Many did, but no one ever considered him anything other than naïve in the tactics of office politics. He'd tied the noose and was preparing to stick his head through it when Gloria had intervened. She'd read his report, flatly refused to type it and suggested an alternative course of action. Gloria didn't come on strong very often, but when she did he'd learned she was worth listening to. He'd agreed to her plan, though not without misgivings. But any doubts had vanished the instant Gloria's father had opened the door to him.

He'd convinced himself he'd find an older version of Lieutenant Commander Scriven, someone whose tactical sense hadn't advanced since Nelson's day. He'd glumly resigned himself to an afternoon of being indulged, patronized and bored to his back teeth, becoming increasingly depressed as Gloria's father became increasingly vocal on the wisdoms found in his bottle of port.

Commander John Cunningham Wainscott had proved the antithesis of his expectations. Though tall and patrician he was anything but patrician in attitude. He'd welcomed Mickey with a warmth that seemed genuine and put him at ease with a casual, unaffected charm. He had the knack intelligent people have of listening and giving the impression that every word they hear is valued. Mickey had warmed to him immediately. Besides, the commander wore a cardigan, and

Mickey was a cardigan man himself. He loved them when the elbows had stretched and they hung as shapeless as potato sacks and, obviously, so did the commander. It was precisely the sort of cardigan wives hate to see their husbands wearing when their daughter brings home the man in her life, particularly when that man is in the same business, of junior status and comes bearing a problem.

Mickey launched into a review of Phil Scriven's prevention not apprehension strategy, then presented his ambush theory. He tried to be fair minded and acknowledge the pros and cons of each, but despite his best efforts the pros of the current strategy as he presented them were tissue thin. The commander listened attentively without interruption, nodding as Mickey made his points.

"I see," said the commander at length. "I'm inclined to agree with your theories on ambush though not necessarily for the same reasons. The truth is, there is no real will in government for a campaign of arrests. The desired end result is as few incursions and arrests as possible. Do you follow me? If your ambush strategy is successful, then one should logically lead to the other. That would suit the Ministry of Marine and our primary producers who sell to Japan. The question is, do we have sufficient resources to sustain a viable threat of ambush?"

"No. But we have resources to introduce sufficient doubt to make the skippers of foreign vessels think twice. The fact is, after our attempt to trap the *Shoto Maru* in the gulf—I'm sure Gloria would have brought you up to speed on that—the number of incursions fell away dramatically. They picked up again until we caught the Japanese dories red-handed off Ninety Mile Beach. The incursions dropped off again immediately after. But now that we're patrolling the coast as predictably as the guardsmen outside Buckingham Palace, it's no holds barred."

"It would have to be an ongoing tactic, then?"

"Of course, but it needn't involve so many arrests that trade relations become strained or the government embarrassed."

"Explain."

"The ambushes themselves would not be our greatest weapon but the ongoing fear of an ambush. Sure, we'd have to strike hard at the commencement of our campaign to let them know we mean business. Beyond that, there would still be occasions for apprehension. But the real point of the exercise is to maintain the element of surprise. For example, have patrol boats suddenly pop onto their radar screens when they least expect it. Use the Orions to catch them by surprise and blow their hats off with their prop wash. It wouldn't matter whether the Japanese were within the twelve-mile limit or not. The trick is to let them know we know where they are, but leave them uncertain about where we are. Make them think twice about encroaching."

"How do you propose to do this?"

"The east coast is full of islands and promontories. We can use them as radar shields. If the Orions tell us a trawler is heading in a certain direction, we can anticipate them and dispatch a patrol boat to a suitable hiding place before they have a chance to pick it up on their radar. Then we sit and wait. Hopefully, the Japanese will wake up to our tactics fairly quickly. They always have in the past. The trick is to keep them guessing as to who has been targeted. Right now they have two demersal longliners, a pelagic longliner and a trawler operating between Coromandel and the Bay of Plenty. The question they'll be asking themselves is where will the patrol boat pop up? We'll have not one but four boat skippers looking over their shoulders, hesitating to risk encroachment. Repeat that around our coastline and we have an effective force. We'll never completely eliminate poaching but we can significantly impact on the frequency."

"You mount a persuasive argument. Let me think about it a little longer and I'll see what I can do. In the meantime keep your report in your pocket."

"Thank you, sir." Mickey smiled, chastened.

"By the way, that business with the *Shoto Maru*. It was an excellent piece of intelligence work on your part, and your planning was first-rate. It deserved to succeed. The tragedy is, we don't always get what we deserve."

"Thank you. The real tragedy is that the *Shoto Maru*'s back to its old tricks. If Shimojo starts making record hauls, you can expect all the other trawlers to follow his lead. One way or another the captain of the *Shoto Maru* is going to get what he deserves, even if I have to swim out and plant a bomb on board. Which incidentally, is about all I can do at the present."

"Where is the *Shoto Maru* now?"

"Just south of Colville Channel."

"Is there nothing we can do?"

"Well, not entirely, commander. I have two coast watchers armed with a radio on the northern tip of Great Barrier. One is an ex-police inspector turned recluse. The other is Red O'Hara, a veteran of the Burma railway with more hang-ups than a wardrobe. But he has a determination to protect what he regards as his patch of ocean. However, I'm not sure there's much he can do to frighten off a two-and-a-half-thousand-ton trawler."

"I can't promise miracles, but I'll get on to it."

"I'd appreciate that, sir. Red worries me. If the *Shoto Maru* decides to raid his patch, he's not going to sit idly by and watch them. He'll take the law into his own hands. God only knows where that might lead."

"Dinner."

Gloria stood at the door of the commander's study, looking as pretty as he'd ever seen her. She wore her "I told you so" smile, which Mickey had to concede was entirely justified.

Twenty-seven

The skipper of the tuna boat cursed silently. He watched the beam of his spotlight sweep back and forth over the choppy water but knew they were wasting their time. Someone had taken the line closest to shore and stolen their catch. He hoped that was the only one they'd taken and slowly worked to seaward in search of the others. There was no longer any doubt in his mind that the warm currents that attracted bait fish had swung inshore and carried the tuna with them. His instruments showed a four-degree rise in water temperature. He was tempted to lay a new line but decided against it until he'd discovered the fate of the others. He cursed again. No patrol boats for miles, yet he couldn't follow the schools in and fish. Perhaps the rumors were right. Perhaps the waters were protected by *kami*.

Shimojo ran northward beyond the twelve-mile limit, not even bothering to put his net in the water. The nights had been fruitful as he'd swept up the snapper in close. Yet the hauls had still disappointed. The numbers suggested the main school was elsewhere, and he'd set out to find it. As night fell, he ordered the *Shoto Maru* to change course and begin a long, sweeping trawl that would take them in an arc across Great Barrier's southeastern beaches before swinging wide around Arid Island. If they failed to find fish in quantity, the course gave them the option of trawling past Whangapoua Beach and Wreck Bay to Aiguilles Island. Somewhere along their path he was certain they'd find their fish.

He waited until nightfall before dispatching his lifeboat to fish the reefs along the shoreline west of Arid Island, where the risk of snags put trawling out of the question. Once the lifeboat had been safely lowered he ordered lights-out. Clouds that had been building during the day hid the new moon and many of the stars. The thief in Shimojo welcomed the darkness even though it made navigation difficult for the crew in the lifeboat. They were under strict instructions to use their lights sparingly so as not to attract attention. Even though reports placed the nearest patrol boat more than one hundred miles to the south, Shimojo was still cautious. He had nearly been caught napping once before fishing Barrier waters.

Twenty-eight

"Speedo! Speedo! Nogoodenah! Nogoodenah!" *The lieutenant's voice could barely be heard above the incessant drumming of the mon-*soon rains on the jungle canopy, but the thin, ragged, bone-weary battalion had no difficulty hearing the whack of his bamboo rod as it connected with some poor sod's back. They knew the feeling well—the explosion of pain, the bruising, the angry welts—had lived with it day in day out for what seemed like eternity. They heard the victim cry out. Expected him to cry out. Bravery was wasted, only infuriated their captors and invited more punishment.

Red did his best to keep up with Archie, to support his end of the *banga,* the bamboo litter they used to haul rocks and soil up to the rail line, but he could feel his body giving in. It always gave in, no matter how many times he reclimbed the hill, no matter how hard he dug his bleeding toes into the mud, no matter how hard he tried to keep his feet moving. His body always gave in, always failed him. And he always failed Archie.

"Hang on, Red, hang on. You can do it. Nearly there. Nearly there." Archie, soaked, exhausted. Eyes haunted and desperate. But mouth still smiling. Archie, smiling and encouraging. Don't give in. Don't give in. And Red didn't give in, refused to give in, willed his legs to keep moving, but it wasn't enough. Three feet from the lip of the embankment his bowels emptied, his legs buckled and he fell. The *banga* poles slipped from his shoulders, spilling its precious load.

Archie grabbing his arm, trying to drag him up but no longer having the strength. Someone screaming at them, the Jap lieutenant, the BBA—Big Bash Artist—bigger than his fellows and named for his brutality. Archie pleading "Get up! Get up. For Chrissake!" And he did try. He tried with everything he had, digging his fingers into the mud, trying to claw his way up on hands and knees, shitting and slipping and crying. Crying in helplessness and frustration, because his malnourished body no longer obeyed. Crying because he was letting his mate down. Saying sorry. "Sorry, mate, sorry." Over and over. So sorry. Then the bamboo crashing down on his head and his back. A rain of blows, skin rupturing, blood flowing and the Big Bash Artist screaming abuse. Then lying, dying, crying while Archie pleaded, while Archie pleaded for his life and bore his punishment.

"Daijobu desu ka?" Archie asking if it was all right for other prisoners to help him up and refill the *banga*. Archie placating. *"Daijobu desu ka!"* The BBA agreeing and clubbing them as they did so. And his mates dragging him, empty and floppy, light and lifeless like a sugar sack of Ping-Pong balls, up onto the embankment, holding him up as they refilled the *banga* and put the poles under his arms instead of over his shoulders, taking his load and dragging him, staggering along the embankment. Mates. Heroes. Everyday heroes. Ignoring the BBA's screams and the blows from his bamboo. Helping a mate who needed help, and all he had to do was hold on. Hold on! And he tried desperately to hold on as he always tried. Trying to hold on. Trying to change history. But it didn't matter how hard he tried. It didn't matter. He was doomed.

"Speedo! Speedo! Nogoodenah!" Not good enough. Not good enough. An accusation. An indictment. And perhaps even his epitaph.

Allied ships had command of the sea and allied planes command of the air. The Japanese needed their railway. They needed it finished and they were behind target. A *speedo* was on all along the railway, but especially from the one-oh-five, through Three Pagodas Pass, Songkurai and down into Thailand. The one-oh-five was behind target, Archie and Red were behind quota, and the lieutenant was looking to make an example. All Red had to do was hang on and they'd make it up. Hang on. Stay on his feet. Rest. Get back his strength. They'd make it up. Hang on. Hang on! But he fainted, collapsed his *banga* and took another two with him when he fell. He came around when a Japanese boot thudded into his ribs, when a bamboo stave split around his head. The BBA was screaming. Calling to the little man with the long rifle, kicking, beating, shouting, ordering the guard to shoot him.

For the millionth time, Red saw the barrel rise and point toward him. For the millionth time he reached out to Archie, to his mate, to say good-bye, to say thanks, to hold his hand as the bullet split his skull and ended his war, to hold his hand so he wouldn't die alone. Red reaching, reaching, knowing his time had come and accepting it. The BBA turning his back on them and heading down the embankment. And the little man with the long rifle, Private Akihiro Ohira, pivoting suddenly. Shooting Archie instead.

"Namu-saku," he said and laughed. Namesake. Pointing first to Red then to himself. Red, too stunned to speak, Red, stricken with horror. "You, Ohira! Me, Ohira! Namu-saku." A word Red had taught him to say. A little joke with a simple man who was also their captor but not always cruel. And Ohira had laughed again. Best of friends in a matter of life and death. The example was made. It really didn't matter who died.

Red shot bolt upright, lathered in sweat. There was banging. Someone was calling his name, calling his name. That wasn't how it happened! That wasn't how it happened! Stunned men blaming him and not blaming him, fighting to come to terms with their loss. Not Archie! It wasn't possible! Archie was the strong one. Archie was the one they relied on. But they were shouting his name. Someone was shouting his name. And Archie was barking. He dragged himself off his bed, locked in a twilight between dreams and reality, and staggered to his door.

"They're back, man. Same place. Off Arid."

Red opened the screen door, not comprehending.

"Good grief, man, are you all right?" Angus held his torch up to Red's face. Saw the sweat and tears and abject despair.

Red turned away from the light, stumbled back into the room and slumped into a chair.

"You're not well, man. I'll make you a cup of tea." Angus flashed his torch around the room, knowing the generator would be off, looking for a propane lamp, or at least some candles. He found the lamp where he expected it to be, in the middle of the table. He lit the wick. The flickering white light did nothing to improve Red's appearance. Angus had no wish to intrude upon Red's domain, held it as sacrosanct as his own, but the madman was in trouble. The policeman in Angus came to the fore. "Dear God, man, will you not tell me what's happened?"

"Nothing, Angus. A bad dream."

Angus was unconvinced. The man looked like he'd seen a ghost. "I'll put the kettle on."

Red needed his ch'i kung, to begin the exercises that could calm him and help him gather his wits, but was loath to begin with the Scot looking on. He sat upright and began to concentrate on drawing in long, thin breaths deep down past his diaphragm to the core of his stomach, to the sea of chi. He concentrated hard to center his mind and stop his thoughts racing away down treacherous paths. He exhaled long and slow, with barely enough force to cause a candle flame to flicker.

"Here's your tea. Drink up. It'll do no harm to allow the Japs their mischief this one night. Mickey can't expect us to chase them away twenty-four hours a day, seven days a week."

"I'm going after them."

"You'll do no such thing! You're in no fit state. I'll not allow it!"

Red sighed. The nightmares always drained him, robbed him of his strength and will, leaving him feeling empty and barely able to muster the energy to think. But he could work through it. He could work through his exhaustion, and the fact was he had work to do. "I'll be fine. I'll finish the tea and get ready."

"Don't be a bloody fool, man. I'll not let you go and that's all there is to it. I'm not leaving here until you're back tucked up in bed."

Bed, the playground of his nightmares, that was the last place Red wanted to be. "Just keep an eye out for me, Angus. Come looking if I'm not back by eight."

"Aye . . . aye . . ." Angus acquiesced. "I guessed there'd be no stopping you. I let you sleep as long as I could. They're well out to sea now." He paused and looked searchingly at Red. "They're not worth it, man. No matter what they did to you, they're not worth it."

Red smiled grimly. "I heard a story in Burma. A Jap soldier got caught in a current while he was crossing a river. He had all his gear on and couldn't swim. One of the Aussies, a bloke from Melbourne, dived in and rescued him. You know what? The Jap officers came by and formally thanked him. They gave him a reward, some coins in the local currency. When the soldier tallied it all up, it amounted to less than an Aussie sixpence. Of course his mates blew up over their meanness. But the digger just laughed it off. 'Sixpence is fair enough,' he said. 'That's all the little bastard was worth.' "

Angus laughed. "Fair point. I'd not give you sixpenneth for the whole lot of them. But there's my point. Does it really matter if we let them get away with it for just one night? What can one boat do?"

"It matters, Angus. They've got to learn that they can't fish here. Ever. They can't take our fish and kill our seabirds whenever they please. We have to be as vigilant as they are ruthless."

"Aye, well you're your own man."

"Angus, could you do me a favor?"

The old Scot was immediately on guard. "Depends."

"Could you lend me your .303?"

"My rifle?! Now what in God's name do you want that for?" His instinct was to refuse, but he saw an opportunity. It wouldn't harm to have Red in his debt, not if Red turned out to be the father. It might make him more open to persuasion.

"Think of it as a sleeping pill, Angus. If I put a few shots over their heads they'll stop coming in at night. That way I'll get some sleep."

"Don't you go starting a shooting war, now. The rifle is licensed to me. I don't want to be answering questions about dead Japanese fishermen."

"You'll let me have it?"

"Aye. The policeman in me says it's wrong, but if you think it'll help I can't refuse you."

"Good man. Give me a moment and I'll walk down with you. I'll just get some warm clothes."

"Aye," said Angus distastefully. "Any clothes would be an improvement."

The crew of the *Shoto Maru*'s lifeboat searched for a shape blacker than its surroundings, a land mass that would tell them where they were. Reluctantly the helmsman turned on his powerful spotlight and scanned left and right. The beam picked up the surf pounding in on Arid Island. He knew he should kill the light then and there but held it steady while he estimated both position and distance. Their task was perilous enough without making it any harder. Satisfied at last, he turned the light off and carefully motored in to shore.

Red searched the sea for a sign of a light and found none. He was mystified. He and Angus had clearly seen a spotlight, which meant that the tuna boat was laying new lines. If so, where was it? Archie stood with his front feet propped up on the foredeck, peering intently into the night. Overhead in a break in the clouds, stars twinkled steely bright, and way behind him Red could see the faint glow from the lamp Angus had left burning by his window to give him a reference point. The light helped, but Red could have managed without it. He knew the water well, knew exactly how close he could go in to Arid Island and where every reef and outcrop were. He ran up close to Arid's northern shore, waiting until the island's bulk began to block out the stars hanging low in the southern sky and he could pick out the faint halo of surf, then turned and followed the contours of the headland until the stars reappeared. Once clear he began to zigzag out to sea in search of the longlines.

His intention was to use the lines to lead him to the tuna boat. It puzzled him that he couldn't see its lights. Either they'd hooded them or worked so far out to sea that they were no longer visible. But how could a tuna boat lay lines so quickly? He completed his third port tack and made another right-angle turn to starboard. He couldn't understand why he hadn't run across any longlines. Perhaps they'd done the right thing this time and weighted them down to keep them below the surface and out of reach of birds. He decided to risk using his torch. He flashed it toward Arid, but he'd already motored beyond the

305

torch's range. He was tempted to turn back and search for the marker buoy but was reluctant to give up his pursuit. He wanted to find the tuna boat and send a few rounds from Angus's Lee Enfield whistling around the crew's ears. Whistling and whispering an urgent message. *Go away! Don't come back!* He knew that he'd find the lines as soon as the dawn sky began to lighten, but by then he'd probably be too late to prevent some birds from being hooked. At least the weighted lines would prevent a wholesale massacre. So he continued to crisscross, hoping to spot the buoy that marked the tail of the first longline or, better still, the head of the second. He still hoped it would lead him to the Japs. Up forward, Archie had lost interest. His eyes and ears told him there was nothing to see. He'd grown tired of waiting for Red to realize the obvious.

Around the five-mile mark, Red was prepared to concede defeat. Maybe the light they'd seen had come from a local boat, not the tuna boat. Maybe the Japanese had worked northeast and not due east. He decided to head back to Arid Island and spend the rest of the night at anchor in the shelter of Homestead Cove. Despite its off-putting name, Arid Island had a lush green top, a freshwater dam, cows and sheep, and even an airstrip. And it was a hospitable home to the family that farmed it. But instead of heading straight for the cove, Red repeated his zigzag pattern, using his torch intermittently but more frequently. He'd covered just on two miles when Archie shot to his feet and barked. Instinctively Red switched off his torch.

"What is it, Archie?"

The dog wasn't propped up on the foredeck but had his front paws on the gunwale, while he stared due south. Red heard him growl, low and in warning. But in warning of what? If Archie had spotted a buoy, why would he growl? No, there had to be someone or something out there. Red peered hard into the blackness, but the torch had taken the edge off his night vision. Perhaps Archie had heard a whale blow or a pod of porpoises, but he'd heard them plenty of times before and knew better than to growl. Perhaps they'd attracted a shark. Red stared intently at Archie, trying to judge the angle of his head so he could work out what his mate was looking at. Archie wasn't looking at the water but across the water. Red felt his blood run cold. Perhaps the Japs were playing his game. Perhaps they'd cut their lights and were stalking him while he stalked them. Perhaps they were angry about the loss of their lines and wanted revenge. Archie barked again. And again. Insistently.

"What is it, Archie? What is it?"

The dog ignored him. He kept staring south, and his gaze never wavered. Red pulled the throttle back and slipped the gearshift into neutral. "Hush, Archie!" The dog reluctantly obeyed. Red cupped his ears and faced due south. If he couldn't see what was out there, perhaps he could hear it. But the wind was pushing whatever sound there was away from him. He stared into the darkness. At last he saw movement. A star disappeared and then another. And another. He watched as stars were swallowed up into blackness, one by one. Something large, a ship, was headed directly toward them. He looked for a flickering bow wave to give him some indication of speed, saw none and surmised that the ship—or whatever it was—was traveling at low speed. At trawl speed! An unlit boat close in at trawl speed! In a flash Red knew exactly what he was looking at. He pointed his torch directly at the trawler and began to wave it. He couldn't stop them but thought he might be able to divert them, and having turned them, escort them out to sea. They wouldn't know who he was. They couldn't be sure he wasn't the navy or a fisheries boat. Natural caution would force them to turn out to sea. He waved the torch back and forth as vigorously as he could.

Twenty-nine

The blip Shimojo had observed on their radar screen had at last revealed itself by a waving light. Clearly it wasn't another of the lieutenant commander's traps, nor did it flash the signal that would indicate that it was the *Shoto Maru*'s lifeboat. Beneath him his net recorders reported a dense stream of fish flowing past. He instructed the helmsman to hold course and sent a man forward with a torch to investigate.

Red watched the dark, forbidding shape close in on him. It gave no indication of turning, no indication of even having seen him. But he knew that was impossible. He saw a light appear on the bow. Someone was shining a powerful torch at him. He turned off his torch instantly and reached for his rifle. Soon the bow would hide the bridge. He didn't have much time. He sighted along the barrel as best he could, aiming for the top third of the superstructure, as near to the middle as he could judge, and squeezed the trigger. The sudden explosion was deafening and the kick monstrous. Without doubt his shot had gone wide. He reloaded, sighted and fired again, this time with the rifle butt braced securely against his shoulder. Better. He reloaded and fired again. And again. The light had disappeared from the bow after his first shot, but still the trawler held its course. In fury he reloaded and fired, reloaded and fired, reloaded and fired. The noise, the tension! So like the executions of the would-be escapees at Thanbyuzayat. Brave soldiers shot for doing their duty, refusing blindfolds and hurling abuse at their executioners with their last breath. Good men. Young men. Mates. The rest of them had been forced to look on helplessly, to observe and absorb the lesson. To watch their battered and humiliated comrades gunned down. Red began to shake and lose concentration. He forced himself to lower the rifle, fought for control. When he steadied and looked back up at the trawler he immediately saw the danger his lapse had put him in. The bridge was completely lost behind the trawler's massive bows, which towered above him. He slammed the gearshift and throttle forward. But the old displacement hull was never designed for fast starts. The trawler bore down on him relentlessly, the flickering bow wave not twenty feet away. Archie snarled and barked and snapped at the shape looming above them. Red knew and so did Archie. They were in serious trouble.

"Turn, you bastard! Turn!"

Red realized there was little he could do to avoid a collision. He threw the wheel hard left and turned his boat toward the trawler to avoid being cut in two by the point of the bow. Instead the flare of the big ship's bow crashed down onto the gunwale just forward of where he was standing. It threatened to push his boat down and crush it beneath the hull. But Red was saved by the trawler's wash. It picked his boat up as if it weighed no more than an empty bottle and tossed it aside. It rolled violently from port to starboard, stood momentarily frozen on its gunwale, propeller out of the water and racing, before tumbling back upright. Red knew he was gone, fought desperately to hang on, but succeeded only in wrenching back the throttle. He tried to bring his free arm up to protect his head, to break his fall, but had no more control over his limbs than a rag doll. He hurtled forward, his head crashing sickeningly into one of his boat's ribs.

Thirty

The stars were in full retreat as the lifeboat crew hauled in the last of their longlines. Their weariness and the number of fish slowed them in their task. The helmsman glanced anxiously toward the east, expecting the sun to break free of the ocean at any moment. The indigo veil lifted, and the sky became translucent. Already the *Shoto Maru* would have run north to safety beyond the twelve-mile mark, leaving them with a long, uncomfortable run home. The winch strained under the weight, the line sang and crackled as it wound around the drum. His two companions were unhooking the snapper as quickly as they could. The lifeboat's deck was covered in boxes of fish, some of the snapper still flapping and protesting when the men finished hauling the last line in. As soon as the weights were aboard the helmsman engaged gear and pushed the throttle hard forward. The two crewmen came aft where it was dryer, sat and took a well-deserved rest. The sky was brightening by the minute, increasing their vulnerability. The sun's rays struck the upper slopes of Arid Island, painting the high pastures vivid emerald. Slowly the island came to life as the color seeped down toward the cliffs. The sun popped free of the horizon, dazzling them with its intensity. The helmsman didn't detect the movement immediately, but in response to a shout from one of his crew.

The man was pointing directly into the sun. The helmsman squinted through his fingers as he'd done one time before when his nightmares had come hurtling in at him. He gasped. The foam-white

310

boat was blocking his way, and somewhere inside it the devil was howling at them, its unearthly cries carried on the wind. He swung the lifeboat left. This time he didn't have the luxury of the lighter, faster dories to make his escape. The Red Devil rose up above the sides of the boat in front of him. The awful, blood-red specter raised an accusing arm and pointed at them, damning them, cursing them, howling retribution. In terror the helmsman tore his eyes away, thumped the throttle hard against its stops, and prayed that whatever power they had would suffice.

Archie was barking once more, and someone was calling his name.

"Red! Red!"

He wondered dully how long he'd been unconscious this time. His head swam, and he had trouble with his focus. His boat rolled sluggishly, gears engaged but motor silent, having run out of fuel after describing endless circles on the ocean. He tried to drag himself up to peer over the gunwale to see who was calling his name, but the moment he raised his head dizziness overwhelmed him. He forced his eyes open. Archie was standing on the forward deck, barking, wagging his tail.

"Red! Red!"

He could hear a motor putt-putting toward him. Diesel. Another boat. He wondered if this one would also run away from him. He remembered trying to stand, trying to wave and falling. Archie howling, standing over him and howling as he slipped back into dreamless sleep.

"He's there! I can see him, I can see him!" Red heard the triumph and then the despair. "Oh God, Angus, there's blood everywhere!"

Blood? Of course. The stickiness, the sickly-sweet smell. He wondered idly whose it was, knew it was his, but it didn't matter anyway. He felt a bump on the side of the boat. Heard a noise. Archie whining. A wave of tiredness swept over him, taking him with it, carrying him blissfully away.

"Red! Red! Can you hear me?"

He felt himself being pulled back against the undertow, nodded so that the voice would stop and he could continue to drift away.

"He's alive!" Rosie reached down and gently turned his head toward her. He opened his eyes, saw Rosie, tried to smile. "Red! Look at me, Red. Red!" Her face was right up close to his, staring into his eyes. But they were too heavy to keep open. She was shouting at him, calling his name, but her voice kept fading away until he could hear it no more. It had been a long time since he'd known such peace.

Thirty-one

*S*himojo turned south once he'd cleared the twelve-mile zone, narrowing the distance between the Shoto Maru *and its lifeboat. The morning* was beginning to warm up despite the gathering nor'easter. Even though the processing line was already working at full capacity, he resolved to repeat their trawl the moment night fell. His instincts had proved right and he'd located the main school of snapper. But he was also aware that the school would probably move north and on into the gulf within two or three days. His refrigeration space was almost exhausted, and he was due to rendezvous with the transporter the following day to off-load. If he didn't return that night, there was a risk he'd miss two nights. No one could say where the snapper would be by then.

He watched the lifeboat bludgeon its way through the rising seas toward them. He gave his helmsman a heading that took them farther east so that the trawler could provide shelter for the lifeboat as they took it aboard. Given the conditions, a wise man would have brought the trawler to a halt, but they were in midtrawl and catching fish. He put his binoculars on the lifeboat as it motored past preparatory to turning and coming in alongside. He could clearly make out fish boxes piled high with snapper. The *Shoto Maru* rolled and wallowed as it took the swells on its beam, seeming to pause as the weight of the net checked its progress, then surging forward as the propeller bit once more. Overhead seagulls battled the wind, burning off energy as fast as they replenished it, diving, wheeling, jockeying for the process-ing-line waste, spectators to a drama only just beginning.

The trawler yawed and rolled alarmingly as the lifeboat drew alongside. Even in the lee the waves were chopping up deceptively, standing high and pointed like pyramids, then falling away to noth-ing. They lifted and dropped the lifeboat with bone-jarring sudden-ness. At no stage had the lifeboat been recovered in such rough seas. The davit cables hung ready and were eagerly seized and secured.

The lifeboat jerked violently as the *Shoto Maru* rolled away, snatching it from the water. Its crew braced themselves for the in-evitable crash back into the water as the trawler tilted back toward them. The lifeboat seemed to hover weightless, then dropped like a stone. The cables bellied out with slack. Once again the cables snapped tight and wrenched them free of the sea. Again the lifeboat hung weightless as the trawler steadied before reversing its roll. Then down it fell, tipping on landing as it slid into the trough between the steep chop. Timbers cracked, seawater gushed in over the gunwales, but eventually the lifeboat steadied and settled. The damage had been done, but the trawler's crew was slow to realize it. The seawater dou-bled the weight within the overloaded lifeboat and exceeded the ca-pacity of the winches to haul it aboard. At first there was just a jerk like something slipping. The clutch on the forward winch slipped. The seawater followed gravity, heading irresistibly toward the lowest point and compounding the problem. The forward cables slipped, jammed, snapped. The bow dropped like a stone, hurling the hapless lifeboat crew to the deck. Two crewmen from the trawler shimmied down the cables to take control of the stricken lifeboat.

Shimojo watched grimly as the new men motored away from the trawler, working the bilge pumps and bailing furiously. He had no choice but to run to calmer waters behind Arid Island before at-tempting to recover the lifeboat. And what then? What of his injured seamen? What of the school of snapper he'd worked so hard to find?

"What?!" Mickey Finn couldn't help himself. He noticed both Glo-ria and the radio operator wince and rub their ears. He made a men-tal note not to get so excited.

"That's what I've been trying to tell you, man! The scoundrels who tried to ram Red. They're coming back! They're just off Arid now."

"Are they fishing, Angus?"

"How the hell would I know? It's no bloody picnic out there, let me tell you."

"What speed is the *Shoto Maru* making?"

"Ahhh . . . I can't tell you that. They're some way off, you understand. Not one boat, two. The trawler and their dory."

"Trawler and dory?"

"Aye, you heard correctly. What do you think they're doing if they're not fishing? Sightseeing? Do you think they'd risk arrest just to take in the scenery? Perhaps they left some lines out."

Mickey tried hard to absorb everything Angus was telling him, but not a lot made sense. Why would a trawler use a dory? Why would they risk fishing inshore in broad daylight? What on earth was Shimojo up to? Mickey couldn't guess, but if there was any truth in what Angus was saying, they stood a good chance of nabbing the *Shoto Maru* in territorial waters in possession of freshly caught fish or, unlikely as it seemed, with fishing equipment in use.

"Right, Angus, we'll get onto it straight away. Now, is there anything else we can do for Red?"

"Aye. If you can spare an amphibian and an armed detail you just might be able to force him to go to hospital. Rosie says he needs his skull and ribs x-rayed. She's stitched up his face, but it's swollen something terrible. And you can't see his ribs, either, for swelling. But it's the concussion Rosie's really worried about. How about the pharmaceuticals she asked for?"

"On the ferry to Fitzroy."

"I suppose that's something. I'll call back if there's anything else Rosie needs. Now do something about that trawler."

"Go take care of Red and leave the rest to us." Mickey passed the microphone to the radio operator to sign off. He turned to Gloria. "Come with me, Third. I want a word with you before you go see the MO." Mickey set off back to his office with Gloria in hot pursuit. He briefly examined his options. What could he do with no patrol boats in reserve and none in the area? What could he do with an air

315

force that wouldn't come out to play? The last thing he wanted was to ask Gloria's father for more help. It would show weakness on his part, an inability to cope, and it would torpedo whatever relationship he had left with Lieutenant Commander Scriven. There had to be another way. "Close the door behind you!" He didn't intend to snap at Gloria, but that's the way it came out. She didn't seem to mind. She loved the tension and being in on the action.

"I'm sure Daddy wouldn't mind if I called him on your behalf."

Mickey closed his eyes and gritted his teeth. Dear God, it was Daddy now. "I'm sure you mean Commander Wainscott."

Gloria blanched. "I'm sorry, I—"

Mickey waved aside her apology. At least she'd eliminated one option. Mickey could just about accept the possibility of contacting Commander Wainscott if that was the only way to get a plane, but there was no way he could ring Daddy. His colleagues would never let him forget it. "If in trouble, if in doubt, phone Daddy to help you out." He could imagine the legend scrawled on the back of toilet cubicle doors. Almost hear the sniggers. And then he'd have a volcanic Phil Scriven to deal with. But that still left him with the problem. Justice demanded retribution for what had happened to Red. He had the opportunity if only he could find the means. He looked to Gloria for inspiration. Dear God, he thought to himself, she's sulking. God save me from sulking women!

"If you don't want me to call the commander, you could see if Captain Ladd's amphibian is available."

"What did you say?"

"You heard, *sir.*"

"Gloria, you are a bloody genius! Well don't just stand there, get Fred on the phone! Now!" He sat back thinking as she grabbed his phone and began dialing. That was one of the great things about Gloria. He could take her from hero to zero and back again in seconds, and she never bore grudges. Next question. Would the air force let him have one of their photographers? He began to plan their approach, using Mount Hobson as a radar shield before swooping down over the Japanese and catching them red-handed, before they had time to get their nets in and before they could obscure the name of the boat.

"I've got Captain Ladd on the line."

"Freddie? Can you drop everything to help us nail a Jap trawler? You can? Good man!" As he began to fill in the details, Gloria rose in response to a knock on his door. There was a message from Signals. Gloria read it quickly and tugged on Mickey's sleeve.

"What is it? Hang on Freddie, there's a signal come in. Oh, sweet Jesus! Fred, I'll have to call you back." Mickey slumped over his desk. "The bastard! The bastard! The bastard!"

In his hand was another request for assistance from the *Shoto Maru*.

Rosie had lost count of the number of times her patients had fallen in love with her. Sometimes they were old men already married for what seemed to her a millennium, sometimes lonely, frightened returned soldiers, sometimes even other women. She was well aware of the phenomenon and felt neither flattered nor offended, smiled and joked and gently deflected their attentions. But sometimes the phenomenon worked in reverse, and Rosie suspected she'd fallen victim to it herself. Perhaps it was the overwhelming relief she'd felt at finding Red alive when she'd feared she'd lost him. Perhaps it was the way he'd surrendered to her care, his absolute trust and dependence on her, his hurt-puppy vulnerability. Perhaps she was just admitting to feelings that had been developing over months. Rosie tried hard to find a beginning, but couldn't. She only knew what was, and that she wanted to share the rest of her life with the confused and broken man asleep on her bed. She felt simultaneously foolish and weepy, anxious and elated, and more worried than she cared to admit.

Red hadn't complained except when she'd told him she was going to evacuate him to hospital in Auckland. She'd felt his anguish when he'd begged her not to, and reluctantly she'd bowed to his wishes. Medically she knew it was the wrong decision. The crack on the head he'd gotten concerned her. There was a chance his skull was fractured, his brain hemorrhaging and building up fatal pressures she had no means to alleviate. Yet she couldn't send him away. She'd had one stroke of good fortune. Red's blood had splashed everywhere in his boat, and he'd desperately needed a transfusion. All ex-servicemen know their blood group, and Angus had been outraged to find that the same type of blood flowed in the madman's veins as in his own. He'd reluctantly rolled his sleeve up when Rosie had explained the situation, sat, sipped his tea and railed at the perversity of nature.

"Maybe a pint of my blood will bring some sense to the man," he'd said.

Rosie had taken more than two and wondered how lacking in sense that left the Scot. Foolish enough to climb the ridges an hour later to contact Mickey and complain about light-headedness afterward. Red moved his arm in his sleep, groaned softly but did not wake up. Rosie wondered at the effect of the blankets she'd covered him with on his cracked and broken ribs. There were few things more painful, but at least the splinters hadn't punctured anything vital as far as she could tell. She stroked his hair and deeply regretted her foolishness with Mickey, couldn't imagine what had possessed her. The injuries to Red had clarified things. Right then, there were only two things she wanted from life—her flawed hero back on his feet and father to her child.

Angus decided it was not weakness on his part to rest on his bed awhile. He'd rescued Red, helped carry him up from the beach to the woman's, climbed the ridges twice and given up more of his blood than he cared to think about. He settled back against his pillow and accepted that the rest was earned. He closed his eyes, not to sleep but to shut out any distractions. His mind was a whirl of unaccustomed activity, all of it the activities of old, violence and conflict, duties and obligations, things he'd hoped he'd left behind forever in the hands of younger men.

When he'd become a policeman he'd imagined his job was to protect society from murderers, thieves and madmen. He'd soon learned that his job was to protect society from itself. There'd been times when he couldn't help wondering if society deserved protection. He'd spent a lifetime dragging violent husbands away from battered wives, violent parents from battered children, violent drunks from each other. He'd pulled lifeless, broken bodies from wrecks of cars because some damn fool drank too much and drove too fast.

Pulled out bodies of wee bairns, still warm and seeping blood, that lay limp in his hands like broken dolls.

He'd caught the whiff of corruption and manipulation, seen the guilty set free and the innocent jailed. Dealt with murderers, rapists, sodomites and pedophiles. He'd seen the side of human nature that makes mockery of notions of decency, and learned a simple fact of life: the closer he got to people, the more they disappointed. He'd done his duty and thought it enough, but had somehow allowed himself to be dragged into the madman's private war. There was no sense to it. The madman could never win and could only get himself beaten up in the process. The events of the day were ample proof of that. And Rosie! He clenched his teeth when he thought of the changes she'd wrought upon him. Had any grandfather sacrificed more for the sake of a grandchild? There was a limit, and she pushed him to it at every opportunity. He longed for the quiet days when all he had to concern himself with were his writing, his basic needs and the odd feral cat.

But some good had come of it all, he had to concede. He'd abandoned his story of how the boy, Hamish, had pacified the two fractious Maori tribes and become their leader. Instead he'd begun a new Hamish story, set during the Second World War. It told of how the boy had become a volunteer coast watcher for the Royal Navy on the wild and bleak island of Stornaway, after his uncle the lighthouse keeper had fallen and broken a leg. (Hamish had devised a splint using his cricket bat and two stumps and set the bones.) Hamish looked out for U-boats while Angus scanned the seas for foreign trawlers. Every time he climbed the ridge with the radio, he lived Hamish's adventures and gathered material for his book. The radio had become a treasured possession. Gradually his exertions and his generous gift of blood took their toll. He fell asleep wondering who would bring Red's pharmaceuticals around from Fitzroy, Col or some unwilling fisherman? It didn't matter who came, he decided. Neither would be welcome.

Thirty-two

M ickey sat in the lobster boat and watched the Shoto Maru ease around
the headland into Tryphena Harbor. He'd ordered the amphibian back
to Auckland the moment it had dropped them off. Shimojo's request
for an aircraft to fly his injured seamen to hospital had taken on the
form of a demand, but Mickey had refused. Instead he instructed the
Shoto Maru to make for Tryphena, where he'd meet them with a doctor and translator. Mickey derived a grim satisfaction from his obsti-
nacy. The tables had turned. Once Shimojo had frustrated him with a
long, slow crawl into Auckland Harbor, now it was payback time.
Mickey had no doubt that Shimojo was not the least concerned for
the welfare of his injured crewmen but for the lost fishing time.
Mickey intended to make sure he lost as much of it as possible.

"Christ, look at their lifeboat," the young doctor said contemptu-
ously.

Mickey followed his gaze, saw the splintered timbers and side
scored with black paint from the trawler's hull, noticed the bent
davits. Whatever the lifeboat had been carrying must have weighed
many tons more than the designers had allowed for, and Mickey
reckoned he knew what the load was. Snapper. Clearly Shimojo was
hedging his bets and using his lifeboat as a longline dory. Mickey
couldn't begin to imagine what drove a man to be so contemptuous
of the safety of his crew.

The lobster fisherman brought his boat parallel to the Shoto Maru and stood off while its crane lowered a platform for his passengers. Mickey looked at the swaying cradle and wondered if they were in for the same sort of ride that had banged up the lifeboat. But the crane operator was a professional and as skilled as any Mickey had seen. Once aboard the trawler, he sent the doctor and interpreter below to the ship's infirmary, ignored the hands that grabbed his arm and tried to guide him elsewhere, and strode purposefully up to the bows. He leaned over the rail, looked down toward the waterline and found the confirmation he was looking for. The port bow was scored and streaked with white paint from Red's boat. Hardly evidence to convict, but justification for harsh words. He swung around suddenly and looked up at the bridge. Shimojo was too slow moving from his line of sight. Mickey pointed his finger at him and over the railings, leaving Shimojo in no doubt as to what was on his mind. Let the captain sweat, he decided, let him worry about what evidence they had on him. Grim faced, Mickey allowed himself to be escorted below to the infirmary.

The doctor greeted him sourly. "What did you expect me to do here, Lieutenant Commander?"

Mickey knew he was in trouble the instant the doctor called him by rank.

"The old bloke's okay, but the other two should be in hospital now! Particularly this one. He's a bloody mess. He mightn't make it. You should've let the amphibian take them."

"If only I had the foresight to match your hindsight."

"Don't give me that, Mickey. Anyone else but Shimojo and you would have bust a gut to help. Aren't you letting it all get a bit personal?"

"Just do your job." Mickey slumped down in a chair. Truth had an undeniable ring to it. But why should he show more concern for these crewmen than their captain did? It was a spurious argument, and Mickey knew it. He held no grudge against the men who were only carrying out their orders, and they held no grudge against him, yet one of them could well pay with his life.

"Did you get anything out of the others?"

"Like what?"

Mickey ignored the tone of the junior officer's voice. The doctor was under stress, trying to stabilize his patient and monitor his vital signs. "Did they say anything about how the accident occurred?"

"Not a word. It was all the interpreter could do to get them to tell him their names."

"I'll have a word with the captain when you've finished with the interpreter. Tell him he can find me up on deck."

Mickey wandered up onto the stern deck, stared brooding into the dark, tossing waters swirling past the hull as the trawler made full speed to port. All he had to fire at Shimojo were accusations and a threat that he might not be able to carry out. He felt helpless and frustrated. He'd left Gloria behind to beg and plead for permission to have the old minesweeper *Kotaku* made ready for sea so that it could escort the *Shoto Maru* out beyond the twelve-mile limit, and maybe even sit there awhile to frustrate Shimojo. Would Phil listen for once, put the split peas he liked to call his balls on the line with the commodore and pull off this modest miracle? Mickey smiled ruefully. Phil Scriven was many things but hardly the stuff of miracles.

He decided to let Shimojo stew a little before he confronted him. He had no grounds to impound the trawler or delay its departure, but Shimojo wasn't to know that. Let him fear the worst. Mickey's thoughts returned to the injured seamen below. He dreaded the prospect of any of them dying, knowing a measure of the blame would rest squarely with him. They were still five hours from port. The amphibian could have had them there in twenty minutes. What the hell were a few fish when lives were at stake?

"Bugger it!" he said softly but vehemently. He decided to have his conversation with Shimojo then and there. Bugger tactics! Bugger courtesy! The three seamen below weren't the only ones with their heads split open, there was Red to consider as well. He went back to the infirmary, grabbed the interpreter and set off purposefully for the bridge. He just hoped like hell there'd be some activity around the *Kotaku* when they passed Devonport.

322

BOOK FOUR

Thirty-three

Another day. Red woke at dawn as he always did and, for the first time in weeks, eased himself out of bed to begin his ch'i kung. He tiptoed quietly so that he wouldn't wake Rosie. Despite the bed rest and Rosie's tender care, his body was still stiff and sore. The headaches had gone, along with most of the swelling, but he still had broken ribs and deep bruising to contend with. He was not healing as quickly as he expected and believed his body needed the stimulation of his exercises. He crept slowly out onto Rosie's veranda and turned eastward to face the spot on the ocean where he expected the sun to appear. He tentatively set his feet in their familiar positions and bent his knees. He raised his arms slowly, carefully, waiting for the pain to hit him as the weight of his arms transferred to his battered ribs. It didn't keep him waiting long. He dropped his arms back to his sides and relaxed, eyes half closed. Something cold and wet nuzzled his hand. Automatically he ruffled Archie's ears and neck.

He concentrated on his breathing, drawing in slow, deep breaths that reached right down inside his body, then exhaling with a similar lack of haste. Muscles that had tensed to support others that had been injured slowly eased their grip. His shoulders slumped, and his arms hung as loosely as rope. The muscles in his lower back began to relax. Hamstrings, which had contracted through inactivity, began to stretch tentatively. His anger and hatred dissolved. For the first time in weeks, Red was no longer aware of his body. He let the calming effect of his deep breathing infuse every cell of his body, let them absorb oxygen from his newly enriched blood. He was almost ready to begin. Patiently he emptied his mind and slowly raised his arms. This time there was no pain, or if there was, it failed to register. He flowed into his warm-up exercises just as the first rays of the sun lit upon his naked body. If he was aware of the fact, he gave no acknowledgment.

An audience of tuis and kakas looked on curiously as they waited patiently for Rosie to bring them pieces of bread dipped in water and honey. A couple of chooks warbled softly in their throats, hinting of freshly laid eggs. Archie kept a watchful eye on them all, daring them to squawk. The only human eyes to catch Red's solitary performance were Rosie's. She'd guessed where he'd gone and followed him out onto the veranda. She watched in awe, marveling at his balance and poise and the fluidity of his movements, all this from a man who the previous night had not been able to pull a cork from a bottle of wine. Urgings from her bladder reminded her of the real reason she'd risen from bed, and she made her way up to the outhouse.

Red exercised for twenty minutes, then sat cross-legged on the veranda deck. He sat motionless, concentrating on the feel of each breath as it reached deeper and deeper into his body, healing, regenerating. He surfaced slowly, taking time to regather his wits. The sun's warmth came as a revelation even though it had been beating down on him solidly. The tuis and kakas saw him stir and decided it was time to remind him of other duties. He looked slowly around at a world freshened by overnight showers and as sweet as the first morning in Eden.

"Tea?"

He smiled and raised a hand to take hers. His ribs protested immediately. His ch'i kung could speed up the healing process but not work miracles. Without the protective shield of meditation his ribs were still spiteful. Rosie placed the mug of tea alongside him.

"Could you do me a favor, Red?"

He smiled in reply, not yet ready to talk.

"No fish this morning, please. How about toast and honey, or toast and Vegemite? Eggs if you must, but please, no fish."

"Toast will be fine." He had an overwhelming desire to smile. He

326

could feel his body respond to his mood and imagined he could feel the healing within accelerate. He knew he had to let other things rest for a while until he was stronger. He had to put aside his anger and forget about the Japanese. He dragged himself to his feet and put his steaming mug of tea on the veranda table.

"Can't the birds wait?"

"They've been waiting all morning, Rosie."

All morning? Rosie looked at her watch. Two coughs and a sparrow's fart past six. But she knew better than to try to deflect Red from anything he'd set his mind to do. He hadn't been a bad patient at all. He'd just wanted to sit up two days before he was capable of doing so and had entertained similar ambitions toward standing and walking. On each occasion, when he'd become insistent, she'd simply withheld his painkillers. It was amazing how quickly he'd seen the light. She watched him carefully as he came back outside with a bowl of honeyed bread. His legs were no longer as sure of themselves, and he seemed glad to sit down. Pretty much as he'd been the day before. It puzzled her how he could do his ch'i kung.

"Come on, then." Red placed pieces of bread along the rail and on the table. The birds swooped down immediately and had enough confidence not to fly off with their prize. "Two more days," whispered Red, "and they'll be eating out of my hand."

"Figures," said Rosie dryly. "That's how long it took me."

Red pretended not to hear, but the lines around his eyes creased.

"After breakfast you can help me find a site for a proper clay pit. Today's going to be a big day for pottery."

"It's not hard to work out, Rosie. Do you want to carry clay uphill to your wheel or downhill?"

"You know, Red, sometimes I think I liked you more when you didn't have so much to say."

"Do you want to dig straight down or carve into an embankment?"

"Are you being deliberately annoying?"

"Just past the lemon tree would be a good place to start."

"Thank you. I had no idea you were such an expert."

"There's no shortage of experts, Rosie." The levity drained from his voice. "Just ask anyone who worked on the railway. I'll go make breakfast."

"Better make another pot of tea while you're at it. Here comes Baden Powell."

The old Scot appeared at the head of the track in his khaki shirt and shorts and with an old, knitted, navy-blue beanie on his head. The straps from the radio and binoculars crisscrossed his chest. With Red out of action, Angus had taken to his observation duties with uncharacteristic enthusiasm. Every morning at sunup, he climbed the heights of Tataweka Hill and scoured the seas for the enemy before reporting his sightings to whichever sleepy radio operator was on duty. He repeated the process every evening, making use of the last light of the day. He only ever wore his khakis. Rosie thought they made him look more ridiculous than military but wasn't prepared to spoil things by saying so.

"Anything suspicious?" asked Rosie.

"The summer sailors are keeping the Japs at bay during daylight hours. They'll have to come at night. I'm thinking perhaps of setting up camp on the hill for a few nights."

"Come on up and join us. We're about to have breakfast."

"Perhaps a cup of tea. I've a way to climb and no stomach for rice this early in the day."

"It's okay." Red shifted his chair around to make room. "Neither has Rosie. It's strictly toast, honey and Vegemite this morning."

"Toast is it, now?" Angus's eyebrows shot up, and he looked hopefully at Rosie. She ignored him and marched off into the kitchen. He eased the radio off his shoulder and lowered it to the floor. He propped the binoculars against it and sighed as he settled awkwardly into the chair next to Red's.

"How's Bonnie?"

"Oh, fine. Caught a rat, you know. At last she found one that was fatter and slower than she is. How's Archie?"

"Never changes. He'll be happy once he gets his breakfast, even if Rosie doesn't want to warm it."

"Why's that, do you think?"

"She's not keen on the smell."

"Oh, aye."

They sat staring into the bush and out to sea, each pursuing his own thoughts.

"That's a good idea of yours," said Red unexpectedly.

"And what might that be?"

"Staying overnight on Tataweka. He'll be back, you know. Before Christmas is my bet. Before all the holidaymakers come. Shimojo's been here before. He knows what happens."

"You think so?"

"Know so."

Angus digested this information for a while. "Seems to me there's not a lot we can do about it if he decides to come back. Other than just keep watch and report what we see."

"We're going to have to do a bit more than that, Angus."

"Now don't you go involving me in your schemes. The lieutenant commander has been quite specific about that. Shimojo's shown how ruthless he is, and we're under strict orders to stay clear."

"We can't count on the navy. Mickey's been quite specific about that as well."

"Then we'll just have to accept what happens. Maybe Mickey can station a boat nearby."

"Angus, we have to assume that no help will be forthcoming. It's our territory. We have to protect it ourselves."

"There's nothing we can do, man, other than inform the navy. For God's sake, use your brains! Hasn't that good blood of mine you've got brought you any sense at all?"

"Angus, on your way back could you help Rosie dig out her clay pit?"

"Don't tell me she thinks she's going to dig a clay pit. A woman in her delicate—"

"Angus!" Rosie shoved her head out through the door and cut him off midsentence.

"What I mean is—"

"Yes." Rosie glowered. "What *do* you mean, Angus?"

"I just meant it's not work for a woman. It's too heavy. I thought we'd agreed to help you with the heavy work?"

329

"Ah, so you're offering to dig out a clay pit for me? Is that it?"

"Aye . . ." Angus looked around uncomfortably, seeking an avenue of escape. He'd planned to radio the navy, then spend the day with Hamish, writing about the German submarine that tried to ram the boy. "I suppose so," he said reluctantly. He turned unhappily to Red. "This clay pit, is it urgent?"

"Yes, Angus, it is." Talk of the clay pit had revived memories and given birth to an idea. "Will you do it?"

"I have plans for the day. You know very well there's no place for idle hands here. But I suppose there's nothing that can't wait."

"It's either you or me, Angus, and right now I couldn't dig potatoes."

"All right, I said I'd help! But will you not tell me why it's so almighty urgent?"

"A surprise, Angus. I'm planning a surprise for Shimojo. The more clay you bring down here, the bigger the surprise will be."

"What's going on?" Rosie placed a tray of tea and toast on the table.

"Red is planning a wee surprise for Shimojo."

"Great!" Rosie tipped a little milk into each cup. She'd got used to the taste of powdered milk and no longer gave it a thought. "Am I included in this?"

"Very much so," said Red. He turned and looked over at Rosie's potter's wheel as if inspecting it for the first time.

"Fourteen miles due north of Cape Runaway and still running away."

"Confirmed sighting?"

"Positive, with pictures to prove it." Gloria smiled and waited for the compliment. It didn't come. She'd left her hair down and worn a brighter shade of lipstick. Mickey looked her straight in the eye and didn't notice a thing. "The air force scheduled an Orion training flight over the Bay of Plenty," she said, stalling to give him a second chance. "They picked up the *Shoto Maru* an hour ago." She swished her hair from side to side. Nothing. "Coffee?"

Mickey slumped down behind his desk and wondered why Gloria rolled her eyes as she left. Definitely has a bit of her old man in her, he thought grudgingly. She'd reached the stage where she seemed able to anticipate his every move and even his thoughts. It unsettled him. That sort of thing normally only happened between identical twins and couples who'd been married too long, and there were some thoughts he desperately wanted to keep to himself. Even though he and Gloria had only been going out together for a couple of months, their relationship had acquired a stamp of inevitability about it. He would have already popped the question but for the possible complications with Rosie. Every day that passed with no news of any change in her condition brought with it a lessening of his dread. But no news wasn't necessarily good news. The more he'd thought things over, the more he'd come to appreciate Rosie's true nature. If she'd decided to have a child and fallen pregnant, she was just as likely to regard the natural father as no more than a biological necessity, one long past his usefulness, and keep the news to herself until concealment became impossible. He knew Rosie wouldn't give a damn if he chose to ignore her. But he couldn't ignore his own flesh and blood. He couldn't begin a life with Gloria withholding such a secret.

"One coffee. Freshly filtered."

He looked up in surprise.

"Well, it's no secret you don't like instant."

Actually, Mickey didn't mind instant. It was what Gloria did to it that he objected to. He raised the cup to his mouth and sipped. It wasn't bad, in fact, it was pretty good. "Well done. This is the best coffee you've ever made. Excellent."

"Well, I didn't actually make it. Sublieutenant Zoric made it for me. But now that I know how, I'll make it in future."

Mickey smiled bleakly at the prospect. Filtered coffee from a girl who couldn't make instant. It didn't bear thinking about. Reluctantly Mickey turned his attention to his real problem, the *Shoto Maru*. He knew there was very little he could do until the fisheries protection squadron's new instructions came into force on New Year's Day. Commander Wainscott had succeeded in having the squadron's tactics revised against ministerial opposition and in the face of obvious reluctance on the part of Lieutenant Commander Scriven, whose

331

only input had been to delay the adoption of Mickey's ambush tactics until January. The delay served no purpose. Nonetheless the lieutenant commander had been quite proud of his contribution.

The two nearest patrol boats were on station north and south of the *Shoto Maru,* but neither was within one hundred miles. Mickey knew the *Kotaku* was back at its berth outside his window but didn't fancy his chances of commandeering the old minesweeper again. It had been a miracle the first time, and Mickey didn't think Shimojo had believed a word of his threats until the old tub had tucked in behind him. His only hope of holding Shimojo at bay lay with the air force and sustained groveling.

"Gloria," he yelled, waited for her to come running, ever eager. "Send our friends in the air force a thank-you for this morning."

"Already done that, sir, under your name."

Mickey sighed. "Yes, I suppose you would have." The irony in his voice was lost on Gloria. "Any word from Great Barrier?"

"Able Radioman Press thinks I've got a lover there."

Mickey winced.

"Angus McLeod calls up every morning and night, rain or shine."

"Anything to say?"

"Nothing much happening during the daytime. He's going to do a couple of overnighters at what he calls his observation post."

Mickey laughed at the image of the old Scot camping up on Tataweka Hill, but it didn't lighten his mood for long. "Shimojo will try again, you know. If he's not getting the catches he wants, he'll be back."

"What about your warning?"

"Words. Shimojo can count and knows the score. He knows where our patrol boats are and he knows our tactics. Only two things can stop him. A change of tactics and the Orions. Until both things come into play, he can laugh at us. I just hope Red and Angus will be smart enough to keep out of his way."

"Haven't you warned them, too?"

Mickey looked up dolefully. "Gloria, do you ever get the feeling that nobody takes a blind bit of notice of what I say?"

Thirty-four

❧

"What the heck are you going to do with these things?" Rosie had asked the question a dozen times and got nowhere. She didn't expect this time to be any different and wasn't disappointed.

"I'll tell you in good time."

"Listen, Red, if you want me to keep pumping out these bloody vases you'd better tell me what they're for before I go out on strike."

Red ignored her and kept shaving and sanding the cork net floats he'd salvaged from the beaches. Every now and then he'd check on Rosie's production, making sure the corks were a tight fit in the flared necks of the flat-bottomed oval vases she made him. She'd already made eighteen, all around ten inches high, although Red had told her not to be too fussy about the height. But Rosie was nothing if not meticulous in her work. She took pride in her skills, keeping the shape, height and the thickness of the walls uniform. Red insisted that she make the walls half an inch thick, which annoyed her because she'd become very skilled in making them thin. If she'd known how Red intended to use her vases, she would have been downright furious. If nothing else, the work was bringing her rusty hands back up to their former skill. She watched Red fitting the corks to the necks of her vases.

"You're a bit premature. The clay will shrink in the kiln, you know."

Red smiled. "Then I'll just have to shave the corks a bit more."

"How many more do I have to make?"

"How about half a dozen? I'll go fire up the kiln." Red rose and strolled off to choose suitable firewood from the supply under the house. The previous few days had brought a marked improvement in his condition. His ribs still hurt, but nowhere near as fiercely, provided he didn't try to lift or carry too much. Earlier that morning he'd managed to swim a slow and uncomfortable length of the beach. Still, it was a good start. Archie had certainly enjoyed the exercise, dog-paddling just off Red's shoulder and barking encouragement. He chose tinder-dry pieces of hakea and carried them out to the kiln a few pieces at a time. He picked off the wetas and put them on the timber supports. The repulsive-looking, heavily armored insects did him no harm, and he could see no point in harming them.

"This reminds me," he said, turning to Rosie. "I'm out of smoked fish. Fancy a spot of fishing this afternoon?"

"Sure." She watched Red go back to the task of lighting the kiln. Since the brush with the trawler he'd begun to relax in her company and even engage in small talk. She saw this as something of a victory. However, she'd studiously avoided any mention of Burma and changed the subject whenever his memories had surfaced. She'd decided to wait until he'd moved back to his own place and back into his routine before she started questioning him again. The key parts of his self-administered therapy were his ch'i kung, his routine and his work. Not all the parts were back in place, and she realized that if she was going to make any progress, she needed everything working in her favor. There was so much she wanted to investigate. Important things like what happened at the one-oh-five? What happened to Archie? Why was Red so riven by guilt and despair? Silly things like why his vegetable plot was protected like Fort Knox, and why he walked around naked? She wondered if she could ever free him from his anxieties, if she could ever bring him home from Burma.

Another blessing of his recovery was that he made breakfast for her less often. When he slept with her, she'd lie in bed and wait until he went to feed his chooks, then jump up and preempt him. Eggs were another problem. She couldn't face them scrambled nor smiling back at her, sunny-side up with the rooster's signature in the middle.

She didn't mind them boiled or poached. Toast and jam, toast and honey, toast and Vegemite, they were her staples. But there were the mornings when he'd keep the chooks waiting and let the snails have an extra half-hour nibble at his lettuces while he cooked his fish rice. Then the bach would fill with the pungent, oily aroma, and Rosie would have to rush out to the lavatory. She wondered whether it had even occurred to Red to speculate on why she spent so long in there.

She placed another vase on the ground and carved off another lump of clay to throw on the wheel. For the life of her she couldn't imagine what Red wanted them for, or what possible relevance they could have to the *Shoto Maru*. She decided that the time had come to insist on a proper answer from Red. Her hands were willing, but they'd become a darn sight more willing once she knew what she was doing. She made up her mind to question him again on their afternoon fishing trip.

"Red, where the hell are we going? I thought we were just going to the pinnacles."

"Secret place, Rosie." Red steered his boat due north, taking his bearings from Aiguilles Island and Miners Head. "The last resting place of Bernard Arbuthnot."

"Why now?" A four-foot swell was running, with steep pointed waves kicking off the top. The lifeboat rode the swells easily, but even so its rolling motion was making her feel queasy. "At least the pinnacles would be sheltered."

"We want big fish for smoking, Rosie. We're more likely to catch them out here. Right, Archie?" Archie barked on hearing his name. He stood with his front legs propped up on the foredeck, alternately searching the water to port and starboard for a sign of his playmates. "Nearly there."

"I'm relieved to hear it." In fact Rosie was anything but. She knew the rocking and rolling of the boat would be three times worse once they were at anchor. There again, maybe she'd be okay. At least she'd have a fishing rod in her hands and something to do. Big fish had a way of concentrating the mind.

Red checked his bearings, looked critically at the waves and how they steepled. He turned into the wind and cut the motor. "I'll do the anchor."

Rosie settled back and reached for the bait bucket. She took out two pieces of salted-down yellowfin and baited both lines. They had fresh trevally for bait but Red insisted that they use the salted-down bait first. He didn't like anything to go to waste. She handed a rod to Red, smiled as he unthinkingly adjusted the bait on his hook. She couldn't see anything wrong with the way she'd baited it but guessed she still had a lot to learn. "Whoever catches a fish last empties the lavatory can."

"You'll regret saying that." Red released his line and watched it disappear into the depths. It had hardly hit bottom before he began reeling it in.

"Don't look so smug, Red O'Hara!" Rosie struck hard and un-necessarily, because the fish that had grabbed her bait had bypassed the formality of a bite and simply swallowed. She groaned as her fish made a powerful run, stripping line off her reel, groaned again as Red effortlessly swung a four-pound snapper aboard. Her fish chose to make another desperate lunge for freedom at precisely that moment. Rosie held on as the fish took more line. "I think I've caught your fish's grandfather."

"Take your time," said Red innocently. "Game's already over and won. Save your strength for the lavatory bucket." He released his line and waited for it to hit bottom. Almost immediately the rod doubled over. "Told you they were big out here."

Rosie finally dragged her struggling fish to the surface and sank a gaff into its head. She lifted it one-handed into the boat.

"Nice fish, Rosie. It'll go twelve pounds." Red gaffed his. It was marginally bigger and both knew it.

"You're a bastard, Red O'Hara."

"We'll quit when we've got a dozen."

It took them just on ten minutes to reach their bag limit. Rosie sat back and watched Red drag the last snapper on board. They'd caught well over a hundred pounds of fish. "Well done, Mr. Smart Ass. Ready to clean out the toilet, are you?"

"I thought we'd already settled that," said Red amiably.

"Learn to listen, Smart Ass. I said whoever catches a fish *last* empties the toilet bucket. I believe you just qualified."

Red rolled his eyes and raised his arms in surrender. "I'll get the anchor." He grabbed hold of the anchor warp and made a big show of trying to haul the anchor up. He had a lesson for her as well. He dropped the rope and clutched at his ribs.

"What's the matter?"

"Anchor's caught."

"Motor over it."

"No, it's on solid. I'll dive down and have a go at freeing it."

"You're kidding! It has to be at least a hundred feet deep."

"About seventy." Red steadied himself and began to draw long, deep breaths, felt them push down on his diaphragm and fill his chest. He repeated the process five or six times, picked up his fishing knife and dived over the side. The waning afternoon light hardly made for ideal conditions, but the water was clear enough. He followed the anchor rope to the bottom and pushed aside the seaweeds and grasses until he found what he was looking for. He pulled on the anchor warp until he had enough slack to make half a dozen loops and slipped a five-inch shell through them. He cut the reef anchor free and finished tying the shell on with a couple of half hitches. He grabbed the anchor and set out lazily for the surface, slowly exhaling as he went.

Rosie watched the quicksilver bubbles break apart on the surface, wishing Red would hurry up. Without fishing to occupy her mind, the motion of the boat was getting to her. Twice she thought she was going to start puking. There was nothing like vomit for bringing the trevally around. She gazed intently at the spot of bubbling water until Red's head broke clear. "I was about to send Archie down to look for you."

"Hang onto this, Rosie." He handed her the anchor.

"Eh? What's going on?" She took the reef anchor from him and put it on the deck behind her. She turned to Red, puzzled. "If this is our anchor, what's holding us on the bottom?"

"A surprise. Shimojo's surprise." He hauled himself on board and gave her a wry smile. He made his way forward and started pulling on the anchor warp. "Might just surprise you as well."

Thirty-five

~~~~~~~

When Red had told Rosie what he intended to do with the old naval shell, she'd been stunned speechless. His scheme smacked of insanity, and she regarded the risks as unacceptable. She wanted to tell Angus what Red was up to so that the old Scot could try and talk some sense into him, but Red had sworn her to secrecy until he'd finished making his prototype bombs. And that depended upon how successful he was at dismantling the five-inch shell.

She hunted around and gathered up eggs from the new hiding places the chooks had found to lay them, trying to occupy her mind so that she wouldn't have to think about what Red was doing. What was the point of her new escape-proof henhouse, she wondered, if she forgot to lock the stupid chooks in at night? They followed her around, pecking at whatever took their fancy, clucking to one another as if sharing a private joke at Rosie's expense. She nestled the eggs in her pinny, using both hands for support, and opened her screen door with her foot. She froze when it slammed shut behind her. All morning she'd been on edge, fearing a bang coming from Red's place signaling the end of Red's little scheme, the probable end of Red and the end of a friendship that had grown beyond the usual boundaries. Her hands shook as she placed the eggs on her egg rack. Red had shown her how to store them for months on end without refrigeration simply by turning them over once a week. Now she had more than five dozen. Red had told her not to worry, that she'd work her way through them all once the hens took their annual break from laying. Not for the first time, she wondered how she'd have managed without Red, how she'd cope if the silly bugger blew himself up. She felt close to tears, which was silly, but over the past few days her tears had seemed to have a mind of their own.

"Damn you, Red O'Hara!" she said softly. She ripped her apron off and strode purposefully out onto her veranda. She sat and pulled on her gum boots. The suspense and her apprehension had got to her. What was the point of hiding at home when her mind was elsewhere? She simply wasn't used to worrying about other people. At the last moment she remembered the old squeezed-out toothpaste tubes Red had asked for and went back inside for them. She had no idea what he wanted them for this time, but he always found a use. He'd used the aluminum tubes as flashing when he'd repaired a rotting window frame. He made shapes and suspended them on string over his garden to keep the birds off. He made windbreaks for seedlings. Red found a use for everything, so nothing was ever wasted. But she couldn't imagine what toothpaste tubes had to do with making bombs. Red was working at his veranda table when she burst into the clearing below his bach.

"Hi, Rosie."

"Still in one piece, then?"

"Yeah. So far, so good. I wouldn't come any closer though if I were you."

Rosie stopped dead in her tracks, eyes blazing. "Red O'Hara! If it's too dangerous for me to come any closer, it's too dangerous for you to do whatever you're doing. So stop it this instant!"

"It's not so dangerous, Rosie. I've unscrewed the priming charge. It's in that brass rod over there. If it goes off it won't affect what I'm doing here." Red pointed over toward his outhouse. Rosie spotted the brass tube resting on a nest of burlap bags by the shed door. She looked back at Red.

"What if it blows your toilet up?"

"It won't."

She hesitated, uncertain of her next move. She watched Red carefully. He appeared to be sawing with almost surgical delicacy. His caution screamed risk. "What are you doing?"

"I'm cutting into the shell casing so that I can get the cordite out."

"Isn't that dangerous?"

"Shouldn't be so long as I'm careful not to let the hacksaw blade heat up."

"Red, stop it!"

"It's something that has to be done."

Rosie bit her lip. Something that had to be done. Just as the track through to Tataweka had to be cut. The man was programmable and once programmed, utterly inflexible. She realized there was nothing she could do to stop him and turned her attention to finding a way to make sure he took no unnecessary risks.

"It's okay for you to get blown up but not okay for me, is that it?"

Red stopped sawing and put the hacksaw down flat on the table. "You can come up and give me a hand if you like, Rosie. I was thinking more of the baby."

Rosie was about to take the first step toward him when the significance of his words hit her. They struck home like a sledgehammer, made even more forceful by his calm, matter-of-fact delivery. They didn't invite a denial. They were simply a statement of fact. But how had he found out? She thought she'd been so careful. She tried to gather her wits together but it was already far too late. Red was watching her, had been ever since he'd spoken. "H . . . h . . . how did you know?" she stammered.

"I had two brothers much younger than myself. I know what morning sickness is, Rosie. You went up to the outhouse to be sick."

Rosie hung her head. "I was going to tell you, Red. It's just that the right time hadn't come along. I didn't know how you'd feel about it." She looked up at him steadily. "How do you feel about it, Red?"

"Is the baby mine?"

Rosie felt her blood turn cold. She was overwhelmed by feelings of guilt and shame. Standing at the foot of the clearing talking up at Red on his veranda only made things worse. It made her feel vulnerable and isolated. Like a schoolgirl made to stand in the corner, except that she wasn't facing away with her head cupped in her hands to hide her shame and her tears from the world. At school she'd found comfort in the corner. There was no comfort for her here.

"We live on an island, Rosie. People like to talk. One of Mickey's crew talked, or Captain Ladd. It doesn't matter." There was just a hint of hurt and accusation in his voice and it stung her. Enough to make her feel sick and weak at the knees.

"I'm sorry, Red. I really am." Rosie could no longer help herself. She was sorry for him, sorry for herself. She began sobbing soundlessly. She wanted to turn and run away down the track but fought the impulse. Her shoulders slumped, and her arms dropped by her sides. She stood staring at the gray dirt, watching dust encase her tears as they hit the ground. Her shoulders heaved. Recriminations hammered at her brain. It took her a moment to realize that Red's strong arms had wrapped around her, were hugging her and pulling her forward until her head rested on his chest. She had a thousand things to say, a thousand apologies. Her mouth worked, but words refused to form. Her arms came up, slowly wrapped around him and held on tightly for comfort. She felt him flinch and let go. She'd forgotten about his ribs.

"Jesus, Red. I forgot. I'm sorry." Her voice was thick and halting.

"Come and have a cup of tea."

"What about the bomb?"

"I'll put it out on the grass."

Red led her up to the veranda and sat her down at the table. She barely had time to see the saw marks on the shell casing before Red picked it up and carried it away. Her mind reeled. What could she tell him? The time for lies and glib dismissals had clearly gone. All she had left was the truth and a plea, if not for forgiveness, then perhaps for a little understanding and a partial absolution. Red walked past her into his bach. She transferred the tears from her streaming eyes to her sleeve and looked around to see how the world had changed. Red's chooks were eying up the shell suspiciously, probably hoping that it contained chicken pellets instead of cordite. Sparrows checked the grass to see if it was beginning to seed, and goldfinches nosed busily into blossoms. It amused her that the most momentous event in her life had come and the entire world apart from Red didn't give a damn. Archie came up and nuzzled into her hand as if to assure her that he, at least, was on her side.

"Here you are. Water was already hot."

"Thanks, Red." She sipped her tea while Red pulled out a chair and sat beside her.

"The birds and the bees don't care if I'm pregnant or not." She smiled weakly. "I thought that was their line of business."

Red attempted a smile, but it lacked conviction. "You didn't answer my question."

"No, I didn't, you're quite right." She took another sip of tea, stalling, wondering what the best reply would be before deciding that she needed more information. "Do you want the child to be yours?"

"Yes."

The simplicity and honesty of his response stunned her. Again she felt an upwelling of shame.

"I've thought about it quite a bit." Red looked away from her, out over the canopy of trees where the hill fell away toward the broad sweep of ocean. "I kept waiting for you to say something."

"It was going to be your Christmas present." Rosie took her time deciding what was fair and what wasn't. She didn't want to build his hopes up beyond their entitlement nor cause him further hurt. "You're probably the father, Red. The odds favor you for what it's worth."

"Yeah?"

"But I can't rule Mickey out entirely. I'm sorry, Red. I wish with all my heart I could. Sometimes I think my father was right. I am stupid, thoughtless and willful. Sleeping with Mickey was pretty dumb."

"I don't own you, Rosie."

"It was still a dumb thing to do. Okay, I was lonely. Okay, you weren't exactly beating my door down. It was still dumb. I want to have a child by you, Red. By you!"

"Then you probably will, Rosie. The odds are in your favor for what it's worth." He smiled wryly. "If not this time, then next time, and anyway, who's to know?"

"We'd know, Red."

"Would it matter?"

"Not to me."

"Nor me."

"What if the baby's Mickey's? What'll I tell him?"

"Tell him he can be godfather."

She stared at him incredulously, almost as if seeing him for the first time. In some ways she was. She'd never seen him in such a mood. "Red, you're really happy about this, aren't you?" His eyes shone, and every line on his weathered face was creased into a smile. "You're really, really happy!"

"Yes, Rosie. I've thought about this for a while and I'm happy about it. I know it'll take adjustments, and you'll have to be patient while I learn to manage. But now it all makes sense, doesn't it? It all makes sense."

"What makes sense?"

"Surviving. Having a baby. That's the whole point of survival."

Rosie held the shell casing for Red as he patiently cut around it, believing her presence and the child she was carrying would caution him against taking risks. Besides, she just wanted to be with him. Rosie had never been in love before, wasn't entirely sure that she was but suspected she was displaying the symptoms. She didn't care. She just did as she was told and tried to stop smiling.

"Let go now."

Rosie pushed her chair back as Red stood and gingerly began pulling the shell apart, lightly sawing the threads of metal that still held. Black dust spilled onto the newspaper covering the table as Red finally separated the two pieces.

"Pass me two of your pots." He took the top part of the shell with the projectile still attached and placed it by his feet, then emptied the black spaghettilike cordite from the casing into the clay pots. He ran his finger around the inside to dislodge the last strands. "The other bit's the business end. It's probably packed with TNT. It's going back into the ocean."

"Is it safe?"

"Pretty safe. It needs a detonator to explode, and this one's probably set to explode on high impact. If you drop it over a cliff it might go off."

"Doesn't sound an entirely unattractive option," Rosie suggested dryly, as Red picked up the shell and carried it away from the bach to the edge of the clearing. She sat quietly as Red patted down the cordite in the two pots. "What about this stuff, is it safe?" she asked dubiously.

"It would burn if you threw a match on it but that's about all. Cordite has to be confined to explode."

"That's why you wanted the corks to be a tight fit."

"Right."

"What about the hole in the middle of them?"

"That's for the fuse."

"The fuse?"

"Yeah, the tricky bit. Might be better if you moved away a touch."

"No way, Red. If it's dangerous for me, it's dangerous for you. If it's dangerous for you I'm not going to let you do it. I'm going to stay here."

"Suit yourself."

She watched in awe as Red split open the tube of priming mixture and crumbled the powder onto cardboard salvaged from a soap-powder box. He took a small amount and sprinkled it in a thin line down the center of a strip of old toothpaste tube. Rosie could still see part of the label and wondered if the Colgate company had any idea of the uses Red had found for their packaging. He opened a tobacco tin that had been sitting on the table. It was full of match heads, which Red interspersed along the line of priming mix. He then rolled up the aluminum, as if rolling a cigarette, and crimped the loose edge tight with his thumbnail.

"Should do the trick."

"Red, where did you learn how to make bombs?"

"In Burma. Sometimes we had to make explosives so that we could blast out rocks and tree stumps. They had to work in rain and underwater. They weren't very effective but made our lives a little easier. In theory the aluminum keeps the fuse waterproof, and hopefully, heat from the combustion of the matches and priming mixture will keep water from getting in the open end. The idea is to float our little bombs, so the fuses need to be pretty watertight."

"How long before the fuse burns down to the cordite and it explodes?"

"That's the tricky bit, Rosie. I'm going to make a number of fuses of different lengths to see how long each one takes to burn. I want them to last close to a minute. We'll just try this fuse first to get an idea." Red walked over to the generator shed, reached in and dragged out a four-foot length of corrugated iron. He filled a Vegemite jar with cordite and jammed the fuse through the punctured lid. He lit the fuse, dropped the sheet of corrugated iron over the jar and ran toward the veranda. "Start counting!"

Rosie had barely counted to ten when the iron sheet leaped into the air and every bird within three hundred yards took flight. She could clearly see the hole blasted through the middle of the sheet.

"Bloody hell!" She started laughing uncontrollably. As a kid, Guy Fawkes night had been one of the highlights of the year, when they'd lit bonfires and set off skyrockets and firecrackers. This was better than any crackers she'd ever had. Better than the Mighty Cannons and Double Happies. Even better than the Thunder Flashes one of her army uncles had once brought along. But a disturbing thought crossed her mind. "How big an explosion are you planning on making, Red? You're not going to try and blow up the *Shoto Maru,* are you?"

"All I'm going to do is make a loud bang, a bright flash and a big splash. Like I said before, the idea is to warn them away, not blow them away."

"Will a minute be long enough for us to get away?"

Red calculated the ratio of match heads to priming powder and tried to assess the effect of a reduction in both. Clearly his fuses would have to be longer and slower burning. He looked Rosie squarely in the eye and watched her mouth tighten. "You can come to the rehearsals, Rosie, but understand this: When I go after the trawler, I go alone. I don't want you in the way."

"And you hear me, hero. If I don't go, you don't go. I don't trust you. I've patched you up twice already, and it's getting boring."

"It's not a game, Rosie."

"It's not a war, either, Red."

"Have the two of you gone mad? I've never heard such foolishness in all my born days! And you, Rosie! I expect such stupidity from him! But you! I thought you were smarter. Obviously I was mistaken." Angus stood shaking with anger and outrage. He'd heard the explosion and raced uphill to find the cause. Red told the old Scot his intentions and tried to enlist his help.

"All I'm asking you to do is help me bring the shells up from the rise," Red persisted.

"I'll have no part of it, I'm telling you."

"Oh, I think you will."

"I'll not, Rosie. It's illegal, dangerous and downright foolhardy, and I'll not change my mind."

"I'm not asking you to help make the bombs or deploy them. I just need a hand to get the shells off the bottom." Red pushed on doggedly. "The way my ribs are, it's hard enough for me to pull up just one shell."

"No, no, no! Do you have trouble hearing? Can you not get it through your thick skull that I'll have no part of it? You're mad! You're both stark, raving mad, and I'll have no part of it, you understand?"

"If you help me, I can use a scuba tank. All I need is ten shells. I'll make a cradle, and we can pull them up in one go."

"Can't you use your winch, man?"

"I want you to operate the winch. I'll stay in the water and guide the cradle."

"Why not use Rosie? She can work the winch."

Red sighed. "Sooner or later we have to manhandle the shells on board. They're heavy, Angus, too heavy for Rosie. And I can't do it by myself."

"I suppose you also expect me to carry them up the trail for you. No way. I'm telling you, the whole scheme is madness."

"No, Angus. I'll make the bombs down on the beach. The less fetching and carrying the better."

"I'll still not help you."

"Oh yes you will," Rosie cut in.

"I'll not, Rosie, and there's not a thing you can say to change my

346

mind. Besides, I'll not stay silent on this matter. I intend to call up the lieutenant commander first thing this evening and tell him what you're up to."

"I don't think you'll do that, Angus."

"Ohhh? And what makes you so sure?"

"It's politic to be nice to the father of your grandchild." Rosie smiled sweetly.

"What?"

"Rosie and I are going to have a baby."

Angus looked from one parent to the other, his face mirroring a conflict of emotions. He wasn't sure whether to congratulate them or berate them. There they were, about to produce the baby he'd wanted all his adult life, and the two of them were playing around with explosives! They were waiting for him to say something, both staring at him, the madman grinning like the fool he undoubtedly was. One thing at a time, he told himself. First congratulate them, then make them see reason. He smiled finally. The fact was they were going to give him a grandson! That was reason to celebrate!

"I don't know what to say. Congratulations, man! That's tremendous news!" He thrust his hand at Red and shook hands vigorously. "And you, Rosie. I can't tell you how happy you've made me." He put both hands on her shoulders and for a moment looked like he might kiss her on the cheek. He pulled back embarrassed. "I can't say I've not suspected something. A drink! We must drink to the young fellow!"

"Red, do you have anything to celebrate with?"

"Bernie's sherry, Rosie. Use it for cooking."

"Sherry it is," said Angus unenthusiastically. He turned to Rosie as Red went to the kitchen. "Rosie. . . . does he know?" Angus nodded toward Red, who was inside busying himself pouring.

"Know what?"

"About the lieutenant commander?"

"Of course. I told him."

"You told him?"

"Yes. Why not?"

"Did you tell him it might be Mickey's baby?"

347

"It isn't, Angus. And don't you go saying otherwise to Red or to Mickey. As a matter of fact, there's no need for Mickey to even know I'm pregnant."

Angus's eyes narrowed suspiciously. "You're not sure, are you? You want it to be Red's, but you can't be sure."

"A mother knows, Angus," said Rosie but she could see the old Scot was unconvinced. He had the crafty look back in his eyes. "I'm warning you!"

"You can't deny a child the right to know who his real father is!"

"Angus!" Rosie hissed a warning.

"Sherry."

Rosie and Angus turned to Red, who was holding three glasses, both suddenly smiling, their unfinished conversation pushed aside.

"To Hamish!" proposed Angus.

"To Archie!" countered Red.

"To the baby, whoever he or she may be." Rosie used the tone that both men had come to know and be wary of. "Well?"

"To the baby, whoever he or she may be," they echoed dutifully.

Red had only half-filled the glasses, and they were quickly drained. He immediately refilled them.

"Now, Angus, tell me how you intend to let the mother of your grandchild risk a miscarriage lifting five-inch shells." Rosie smiled sweetly.

"It's probably not the right time to be discussing such matters."

"It's precisely the right time, Angus."

"For mine, I don't believe any of us should be handling those shells. I think we should just notify the navy so they can dispose of them."

"Wrong answer, Angus. Your grandchild, should you ever have the opportunity to speak to him or her, would undoubtedly express disappointment in your attitude."

"That's blackmail!"

"Absolutely."

"Have you no shame, woman?"

"No. Just a fetus who would like to be proud of his or her grandfather."

"Are you going to help me, Angus?" Red asked the question quietly and sincerely. "I'm asking for your help. Just help me get the shells back to the beach. That's all you have to do. Will you do it?"

Angus realized Rosie had left him no choice. He set his jaw to leave them in no doubt as to where he stood. "It's madness, sheer, bloody-minded madness, but you leave me no option. Aye, I'll help you. But in return, the child must be called Hamish!"

"Funny name for a girl," Rosie said evenly. "I thought something like Scarlett. Red, Rosie and Scarlett. Scarlett O'Hara has a ring to it."

"Scarlett O'Hara." Red started laughing, but Angus stood his ground. "I'm not asking to be mocked, Rosie. I'll not be made a fool of. If it's a boy child do you agree to call him Hamish?"

"Well, let me put it this way, Angus, I don't think you're in any position to make any demands. As you admitted yourself, you have no choice but to help us. I'll agree to consider Hamish just as I'll agree to consider Archibald. Along with Bernard."

"Bernard!" Both men reacted at once.

"Then it's agreed?"

"No, it certainly is not!" Angus cut in hotly. "I'll not have Bernard!"

"Actually you'll have no say in the matter. I owe everything I have to old Bernie, God rest his soul. Be a nice way to remember him. But I'll keep an open mind. Both of you can work out what that means. In the meantime, the only things that are agreed are that you'll help Red bring the shells ashore, and we'll keep the news of my pregnancy a secret between us. Won't we?" Rosie narrowed her eyes at Angus. "Hamish might grow on me, given the right inducement."

Angus began scheming the instant he set off back down the track to his bach, walking as quickly as he could as if trying to keep up with his thoughts. A hawk rose rapidly and silently in front of him, ghosted over his head, angry that Angus had disrupted its hunt right at the moment of kill. Angus's only acknowledgment was to duck. He was too occupied by his thoughts to worry about birds or bush rats. Rosie had failed to close the door. She hadn't entirely discounted the possibility that the lieutenant commander might be the father. He was delighted that Rosie was going to have a child, but the circumstances could be better. He'd waited too long to accept half measures if full measure was still a possibility.

If Mickey turned out to be the father, would he want the child or give up his career in the navy to live at Wreck Bay with Rosie? No! On both counts. Angus was sure of that. But would Mickey want his son brought up by the madman? No, again! Angus was nearly chortling with glee as the hypothetical scenario unfolded in his mind. Red would have no claim on the boy, and Rosie could hardly deny the natural father's wishes. Angus imagined positioning himself as the boy's kindly grandfather, charged with the responsibility of raising the child on Mickey's behalf. That was an altogether more attractive proposition than playing a distant second fiddle to Red.

He heard a cat yowling ahead of him as he rounded the old pohutukawa, and quickened his step. Bonnie was no match for the feral cats, who'd have their way, then rip her apart. He nearly stumbled in his hurry, slowed as he recalled seeing Bonnie curled up tight in the corner of the sofa as he closed the door gently behind him. He decided to write to the lieutenant commander. There were some things that couldn't be said on the radio.

Thirty-six

~~~~~~~~

Shimojo fished out deep for fifteen days. Once the attentions of the Orions were no longer directed at him, he turned north toward Great Barrier Island, running at full power by day, trawling in close by night. Sometimes when he encountered dense schools of snapper, he adopted a normal zigzag trawl and crossed and recrossed the target. But schools large enough to justify the tactic were infrequent. For the most part, he steamed northward. His freezers were clear and his crew was primed. Snapper was fetching record prices at the Tokyo fish markets. He had the opportunity and means to return the sort of profits the company—and his career prospects—demanded.

Thirty-seven

"Who do you know on Great Barrier Island who would write you a personal letter?" Gloria asked archly as she dropped the plain white envelope with the copperplate handwriting onto his desk. She watched closely for a reaction, but there was none. The truth was, Mickey was too paralyzed to react. He stared dumbly at the letter, immobilized by dread and foreboding. Gloria laughed. "It's from my boyfriend, Angus. He's probably asking you for my hand in marriage. Time somebody did."

Mickey watched Gloria march primly out of his office before picking up the envelope and reading Angus's name and address on the back. He didn't mind that Gloria had played games with him. He would have minded less if she'd come in and told him she had a sexually transmittable disease. Everything else paled into insignificance alongside the plain white envelope. He didn't have to open the letter to know its contents and that the thing he most feared had happened. He flicked open his pocketknife and slipped it under the flap. At least Angus had shown enough wit to write "Personal" on the envelope, otherwise Gloria would have opened it when she'd opened the rest of his mail. And probably read it, too. He didn't discourage her from reading his mail. Quite the opposite. She was his filter, protecting him from everything he didn't need to concern himself with, and familiarizing herself with everything she needed to know. Mickey had never seen the point in withholding information from his assistant but was beginning to.

"Dear Lieutenant Commander," the letter began. "I am writing to inform you that Rosie is expecting a child. She has made it perfectly clear to me that under no circumstances are you to be informed of this." Mickey groaned. Normally he appreciated directness, but these were hardly normal circumstances. "However," the letter continued, "as you may well be the child's father, I feel you have a right to know. My advice is that you contact Rosie yourself, but I urge you not to admit any foreknowledge for my sake. If I may be so bold as to make a suggestion, you should indicate to her that on the occasion of your last visit, I intimated to you her intention to have a child. Insist on your right to know the outcome. Yours sincerely, Angus McLeod."

"As you may well be the child's father . . ." Mickey pondered the significance of the statement. Angus was nothing if not precise, reflecting years of preparing statements of evidence. If Mickey was the father beyond doubt, or even the likely father, Angus would not have hesitated to say so. But all Angus had admitted to was the possibility. The news wasn't good but not catastrophic. What he couldn't understand was Angus's role in the whole affair. Why had he written? Why would he care? One thing was certain, Angus hadn't written out of consideration for Mickey's rights as possible father. It slowly dawned on him that Angus wanted him to be the father, not Red, which opened the possibility that the letter might owe more to wishful thinking than substance. Yes, it was a possibility, but supposition was no basis for comfort. What worried him most was the fact that Rosie had not wanted him to know. He could only think of one reason for that.

"Well?"

Gloria stood provocatively in the doorway. Whatever had happened to the formal protocol, Mickey wondered? It wasn't regulation navy conduct for personal assistants to pose in doorways and stick out their hips. "You guessed right," he said. "I refused Angus permission to marry you on the grounds that he was too old and that you had a career to consider, Third Officer Wainscott."

Her smile vanished instantly, and she stood upright, giving her skirt a quick straighten on the way. "Yes, sir!"

"See if you can get an update on the position of all foreign trawlers and longliners in North Island waters, and see if there have been reports of any of them misbehaving overnight."

"Sir!"

Mickey watched a suitably chastened Gloria set off on her appointed task. He knew it was a largely pointless exercise, and so did she. But there again, most of what they did was pointless. At least it would keep Gloria out of his hair for a couple of hours and give him the chance to think. There was no cause for panic—yet—he told himself. No need to take Gloria aside and confess his dirty deeds. So why did he feel such an overpowering need to punch holes in his wall?

Obviously he had to write to Rosie. But if the news was bad, did he really want to know before Christmas? Then again, did he want to go through Christmas with the shadow hanging over him if he was in the clear? He had a feeling that Rosie would not be able to add to his knowledge. And there was another complication that he couldn't ignore. Gloria clearly wanted to formalize their relationship, and he knew the pressure would be on for Christmas Day or New Year's Day, when the family was all together. But how could he go ahead and propose without first discussing Rosie? He was adamant that he wouldn't build a new life on deceit but wasn't thrilled by the likely consequences of his confession, either. Reluctantly he picked up his pen and began to write. Bare the soul, he told himself. Truth invites truth. He didn't want Rosie to lie to him, as he knew she was quite capable of doing.

Red and Rosie set up their workbench under a gnarled and sprawling pohutukawa. Their workbench wasn't much to look at, just an old door fastened on top of two trestles, but no one could fault their choice of workplace. The stream that ran down from the ridges to seep into the white sands of the beach also kept Wreck Bay's one patch of grass glowing with verdant good health. It made a cushion for the shells and a soft mat for their bare feet. Overhead, the pohutukawa was a blaze of crimson, one of a dozen or more lining the shore that couldn't wait until Christmas to bloom. The trees were alive with bees, white-eyes and fantails. Out in the bay pairs of blue penguins tooted to one another each time they surfaced, announcing their position and the whereabouts of the juvenile sprats they feasted on. This was the paradise Rosie had dreamed about, only in her fantasies she'd made pottery instead of bombs.

"Remember, there's no hurry," cautioned Red. "Saw slowly and make sure the blade doesn't heat up."

Rosie sighed and said nothing. Red issued the same warning at least twice a day. He'd agreed to let her help simply because of the amount of time it took to cut the shell casings open. But he watched her like a hawk and justified his actions by maintaining that they'd watched each other just as carefully in Burma. Rosie knew better than to argue with anything that happened in Burma.

"It's tiring, boring work. Sometimes it's tempting to take shortcuts and saw in one spot too hard and for too long. That happened to some of the blokes in Burma. They grew too weary to care and paid the penalty."

Red's cautions became a litany as familiar to Rosie as her father's constant admonitions to grow up.

"Remember, cordite is an explosive. Be patient with it. If it doesn't come away easily from the casing, leave it there."

Rosie worked diligently, following his instructions to the letter. Sometimes in the midafternoon, when even the bees were becoming drowsy, she thought she understood the reason for Red's caution. It was easy to forget that she was making bombs as she soaked up the filtering sun, the comfort of their togetherness and the close, intimate smell of the mossy soil. She'd begin to get lazy and saw one place for too long. When that happened she downed tools, stripped off and ran naked into the sea. Archie always joined her, eager to instruct her in the finer points of chasing mullet, and sometimes Red joined in. Rosie put the bombs out of her mind and the coming confrontation with Shimojo, and joyfully played Eve to Red's Adam. She couldn't recall being happier.

Her morning exercises and her daily work regime had changed her. She no longer fitted her skin as well as she had. Stretch lines had appeared at the top of the cleft between her breasts even though they'd shrunk in size. When she held her arms up there was a telltale fold of loose skin beneath them. Her eyes, she decided, were like

Rome. Many roads led to them, not as the result of laughter but of overexposure to the sun. She didn't care. She was fitter and stronger and happier than she'd ever been and over a stone lighter, although she knew she'd soon put the weight back on in the months ahead. What made their Eden even more special was that Angus had decided to pay the widow an extended visit and had taken Bonnie with him in a cardboard box. He'd helped raise the shells but wanted no further part in the proceedings. At the end of their third straight day as a backyard munitions factory, Red decided they'd made enough bombs for the time being. They'd opened nine more shells and made another twenty bombs.

"You don't think they're still a bit too powerful?" Rosie asked. She'd watched Red's experimental detonation of his first two bombs and had been staggered by the size of the explosion. It had bred doubts that had gnawed at her and that, even at this late stage, she felt she had to air.

Red smiled. "They'll make a big bang and a big splash, and a vivid flash at night. They'll look frightening. But they're not going to blow a hole in the side of a trawler. They won't blow a hole in steel. Shimojo's not to know that, though."

Rosie still looked doubtful.

"Come on. Help me put this lot in the bunker." The bunker was a coffin-shaped excavation in a clay bank that Red had lined with corrugated iron held in place by stakes. The spare shells and the previous days' production were already stored inside. As Rosie gingerly picked up one of the finished bombs, cork and fuse held in place by a plaster-of-paris seal waterproofed by painting, she couldn't help thinking that it reminded her of the round, fizzing bombs anarchists threw in Buster Keaton movies. She waited until Red had wedged the benchtop over the bunker's opening, pulled a tarpaulin over it and weighted it down with rocks.

"I've had a busy day, Red," she said. "I can't be bothered cooking. How about you make one of your vegetable rice dishes?"

"Okay."

"And while you're making it you can tell me why you've turned my garden into a fortress just like yours."

They set off up the trail, Red leading. "They've got to be properly enclosed, Rosie."

"Why?"

"To discourage pilfering."

"By Angus, you mean."

"No, Angus wouldn't steal our vegetables."

"Then who are we protecting them from, Red?"

He went quiet again as she knew he would. At one time in his life there'd been good reasons why things were done a certain way, but many of those reasons no longer applied. Rosie knew she had to break his wartime habits if she was to stand a chance of bringing him home. She waited. Sooner or later he'd tell her she didn't understand or, with luck, start opening up. The fortified vegetable plots might not lead her directly to the camp at one-oh-five, but Rosie was determined to get there eventually.

"After Archie was killed, I couldn't take the beatings anymore. Archie was my strength. I could be lying all broken up and bleeding on my bed, barely able to breathe, and Archie could still make me laugh. Sometimes I was so hurt and exhausted I just wanted to die. I wasn't frightened of dying. I don't think many of us were by then. But Archie had a way of making us feel indignant that we were letting the Japs get the better of us. Indignant, outraged, cheated. It's hard to explain. Not long after he got killed, we were moved back to Singapore. We even traveled on the railway we'd helped build. Let me tell you, Rosie, we'd done a rotten job." He almost started to laugh but choked it off. "Bugger my days! It was bad enough building the bloody thing. It was hell riding on it. Over bridges, knowing how suspect the foundations and pilings were. Along embankments filled with dodgy ballast." Red strode on, pushing himself, quickening his pace. Rosie forced herself to keep up.

"When we got back to Singapore, I scored a job in the vegetable gardens. We were all bloody hungry by then, not just us, but the Japs as well. If any man was caught eating or stealing any of the vegetables we grew he was hauled off and shot. If anyone managed to sneak into the gardens and steal anything, we were beaten up for not preventing him. In fairness, so were the Jap guards. The Japs were hungry, desperate and they knew they were losing. Some of the Asians working in the paddies were beaten to death by four or five guards with pickaxe handles, because they were slow chasing birds away. They beat them right in front of us as a warning. It got so bad they beat us if they found leaves where caterpillars had been feeding. They caught an English sergeant one day, eating a bit of Chinese spinach or something. It was probably worthless. One of the bottom leaves off the stalk. Man couldn't help himself. He was starving and surrounded by food that he couldn't touch. The Japs made him eat rotten green rice, forced a hose down his throat, laughed when his stomach swelled up and burst. Then they jumped on him. Half a dozen of them took turns to jump on his stomach, screaming in high-pitched voices like a bunch of mad women." He stopped talking and slowly turned around to face Rosie. His voice quavered, and even after twenty-odd years Rosie could hear his fear. "It could've been me, Rosie. Just as easily have been me."

"Why?" she asked levelly. His hands had begun to shake.

"We all stole, Rosie."

"The difference is, Red, you were more careful. But keep going."

"We'd suck bits of leaves until they got soggy and started to break down. Bok choy, gai lan, cabbage, it didn't matter. We took anything we could sneak into our mouths, shit-scared the whole time."

Rosie reached up and put her arm over his shoulder. "But you survived. You might not think that was fair, Red, but there's nothing anybody can do about it. War isn't fair. It wasn't fair for you, or for the innocent women and kids sheltering under stairs when a bomb blew their home to bits. War isn't fair. Life isn't fair. You can't blame yourself for that, because you didn't make the rules. Now go on home and raid your garden for me. When you've got all you need, leave the gate open. You may be surprised to learn that absolutely nothing will happen. Nobody will steal your carrots or your beans. You'll still get the odd snail and bird dropping in, but they don't use the gate anyway. Okay? I'm going to run a bath. Remember what I said and leave the gate open."

"It's not right, Rosie."

"It's not wrong, either, hero. Go on. Show me what you're made of. Give the Japs the finger. Leave the gate open."

"Rabbits, Rosie."

"With Archie the fearless bunny biter around, are you kidding? Well, at least leave the padlock off." Rosie turned up the fork that led to her bach, wondering what had happened for Red to speak so freely. She'd hardly had to push him. She'd expected him to hold off until he'd begun to cook their dinner and even then to try to dodge the question. Perhaps she was finally making some progress. To the best of her knowledge he'd had no flashbacks since the night the trawler had tried to ram him, and he was more relaxed than she'd ever seen him. Perhaps the baby had something to do with it. Perhaps it was his ch'i kung exercises. She reached the edge of her section and stopped. The high wire-mesh fence he'd erected around her vegetable plot seemed to suggest a different reason altogether, and it frightened her. It suddenly occurred to her that Red was actually looking forward to taking on Shimojo, as if fighting Japs was his vocation and gave him strength. She vowed not to let him go out against the trawler alone. He might be cavalier where his life was concerned, but he wouldn't be with hers. And especially not with the baby's.

The navy alerted Angus to the coming storms, not that he needed telling to get down from Tataweka before night fell. Years on the Barrier had made him a good judge of weather. The barometric pressure was tumbling, bringing an end to the clear spring skies and gentle westerly breezes. Soon strong nor'easterlies would come raging in and whip up the sea. It meant an uncomfortable few days, but there was some compensation. The rough seas would make it difficult for foreign fishing boats to come in close.

At six in the evening, as the sun dipped below the gathering overcast, throwing one final pyrotechnic warning of the storms to come, Shimojo ordered the *Shoto Maru* inside the twelve-mile limit at full speed. On the aft deck, the new crew quit repairing the net and replacing missing floats and bobbins. Five miles off the southern tip of Great Barrier Shimojo ordered speed reduced to six knots and prepared to shoot the net. The nor'easter would make fishing difficult but also offered compensations. The navy would not be expecting him.

The first trawl disappointed. Shimojo ordered the helmsman to take them in closer, to around three miles. He planned his next trawl in a familiar arc that would swing them wide of Arid Island before dipping in close to Whangapoua Beach once more. This is where he expected the fish to be, where there were reefs nearby for shelter, and thick beds of scallops, pipis and tuatuas. One hour into the second trawl they began to sweep northeast toward Arid Island.

The fish finder began to glow green with concentrations of fish. The trawler immediately began to zigzag. On the net recorder the constant trickle of fish became a flood. The boat struggled against the seas, held captive by the heavy mass of fish that grew heavier by the second, dragging behind them like a monstrous sea anchor. The engine strained once more, changed pitch as it answered the call for more power.

On the stern deck, a young crewman raced to gather floats that the pounding waves had bumped free of their boxes. He was fast and nimble on his feet and didn't bother clipping his safety line back on. As he crossed the opening to the stern ramp he was caught off guard. The propellers bit and the bow rose hard into the swell. He instinctively grabbed for the bobbin bin as the deck pitched violently and corkscrewed, knew instantly it was beyond his reach, felt his rubber boots teeter on the brink of the stern ramp, felt them slip. He managed one desperate, shrill cry before the ramp disappeared from beneath him and he tumbled backward into the water. An hour passed before his absence was noted, by which time any search would have been futile.

Thirty-eight

‸

A ngus was not happy and neither was Bonnie, although for different reasons. Bonnie cried pathetically because she'd been woken up from her
warm place beside the stove and put into a cardboard box without
breakfast or even a saucer of milk. Skipping breakfast didn't worry
her as much as the significance of the box. The last time she'd been
inside a box she'd hardly stopped vomiting long enough to draw
breath. It had been only her second journey in a boat, an experience
that she'd hoped would never recur. The return voyage was not a
prospect that filled her with joy, and her constant, heartrending wail
was her way of letting the world know this. It did nothing to improve
Angus's mood.

Angus accepted that taking Bonnie with him to visit the widow
Campbell had been an error in judgment, but it had not been the
last nor the most serious of the errors he'd made. The motive for his
extended stay had, he felt, been misinterpreted by the other party,
and over the course of the previous days he'd made statements and
whispered endearments that had only exacerbated the situation.
He'd meant the things he'd said at the time, but he'd said them secure in the knowledge of the distance that lay between them—he at
Wreck Bay and avowed to stay there, she at Awana Bay and bound
to it by her farm. How could he have guessed that she was prepared
to give up the farm for his companionship and his little cottage?
Had he even suspected the set of her mind he would probably have

stayed at home. In her aspirations and his half-promises he saw an end to his solitude and his selfish, orderly ways, and every nerve fiber in his body jangled with alarm. Fiona Campbell was as fine a woman as Scotland had produced, but he didn't want another woman at Wreck Bay. One was enough, more than enough, and the cause of his predicament. The widow would never have contemplated a life at Wreck Bay if she thought she'd be the only woman there.

"I'll be away, then."

Fiona reached up and embraced him then and there on the beach. She turned her head up for a kiss, and he could not deny her. He glanced northward up the length of Awana Bay toward the smattering of tents in the campground, relieved that not a soul had seen fit to rise early and bear witness to their public display of affection. But Angus well knew that seeing nobody didn't necessarily mean nobody saw them. Not on Great Barrier Island, where unseen eyes always observed anything anyone ever did and gleefully passed on everything they witnessed.

"It would appear the wind has risen before you. You'll not stay dry for long, Angus McLeod. Best leave the pussy in the box inside the cabin, poor thing."

"Aye," Angus said sourly. He'd stayed too long, and now the nor'easter was up and building. He'd hoped for a dawn calm, which hadn't eventuated. In truth it was no more than he expected. When nor'easters settled in they gave little respite and the saw-toothed horizon left him in no doubt as to what the run north would be like. Cold, wet and bone jarring. He eased the widow's arms open and took a pace backward. "Once again I thank you for your company and hospitality."

She laughed at his awkwardness and formality. "Away with you, now! I'll see you on Christmas Eve. Now take care, mind, and keep an eye out for crayfish pots." She watched as he waded out to his half-cabin, Bonnie caterwauling in the box held chin high, his canvas-and-leather carryall balanced on top of it. Gingerly he lowered both onto the transom and made sure they couldn't fall. He hauled himself upward and aboard, grateful that the low tide had saved him a swim.

Nevertheless he was soaked up to his waist. He stowed both bag and cat securely in the cabin, fired up his diesel and cast off. Fiona Campbell waved, and he responded automatically. She was a fine woman and grand company. But why on earth couldn't she leave it at that? Why did she want to go and change things?

He looked up toward Red Bluff, trying to calculate how much sea room to allow before he rounded the headland to Overtons Beach, and headed for the temporary shelter of Arid Island. The wind and waves were already challenging the helm and pushing the bows out to sea. Angus sighed. Christmas was the peak season for crayfish, and the crayfishermen would be out in force with their pots and barely visible floats. He had no desire to repeat the indignity and discomfort of his last brush with the pots. But going wide meant he'd have to take the swells and steep-rising waves head-on, and these were precisely the sort of conditions his boat labored in. He decided to risk the crayfish pots and run parallel with the shore, trusting his knowledge of the habits of the crayfishermen and his eyesight. At least this time he wouldn't be caught by surprise.

He watched a flight of cormorants head out on patrol, wings squeaking in the morning air, then returned his attention to the sea. The wind whipped raw and cutting around his dripping shorts and bare legs. He considered changing into dry clothes but was reluctant to take his eyes off the water ahead. So he did what his father had urged him to do so many years before when he'd complained of the wind whistling through the cracks in the walls of their croft. He endured, and took comfort in thoughts of people worse off than himself. Gradually he ceased to be Angus the retired police inspector and became instead a sharp-eyed Scottish boy, alone on the North Sea, bravely scouring the water for telltale signs of U-boat periscopes.

Shimojo handed over command of the bridge just before the six o'-clock shift change. He went to his cabin well satisfied. The last trawl had come aboard shortly before five, and he'd known without looking that the catch was the equal of the others. The codend was jammed to bursting with snapper, bringing the night's haul to over sixty tons. He'd had no hesitation in ordering the *Shoto Maru* to make full speed due east, beyond the twelve-mile limit, and away from prying eyes. He knew where the school was, knew the speed with which it was moving north, knew exactly where to intercept it come evening. His last act before leaving the bridge was to send a message to company headquarters and the Japanese embassy in Wellington, informing both of the loss of a member of his crew.

Angus spotted the large, bell-shaped mooring buoy more than two hundred yards ahead of him and turned farther east to run wide of it. Amateurs, he thought to himself, and wondered how many more pots he'd come across. At least whoever had laid the pot or pots had made sure he'd find them again. Angus had no time for the cowboys who used old tins or plastic bottles as buoys. Half the time they couldn't find them themselves when they came to collect them, even though they knew where to look. What chance did he have of spotting them once the wind was on the water? He looked again at the old mooring buoy in grudging appreciation. Nobody would have trouble spotting that, though in all probability the people who'd left it there had considered no one but themselves. He was surprised at how large it was. How was a crayfish pot supposed to anchor that, he wondered? The thing had probably been dragging all night. He thought of the shiny motorboats that now sat on the moorings out from the campground. Holidaymakers hadn't a clue.

"What in the name of charity . . . ?" He asked the question out loud in disbelief, in shock at what he now clearly saw. He swung the bows toward and below the buoy so that he could approach it upwind. "Dear God!" The figure wasn't moving, just dangling in the water, supported by the buoy and his life jacket. "Ahoy there!" he called, but there was no reaction. As he throttled back to coast up alongside, the wind and waves tried to tear the bows around. Angus fought to hold his boat steady. He'd hoped the man would offer an arm so that he could haul him aboard, but saw at once that he had tied himself to the buoy and was unconscious. Or dead. Without thinking, Angus grabbed his boat hook and slipped it under the rope fastening the man to the buoy and pulled hard against the wind. What next, he wondered, and wished fervently that the madman were with him. The force of the wind on his boat threatened to pull his arms from their sockets. He heaved hard to regain valuable inches, leaned over and took a firm hold of the man's life jacket with his left hand. He released the boat hook and threw it behind him onto the deck, grabbed his fishing knife from the side pocket and began chopping and sawing at the rope. The wind caught his boat, which reared up and away. Angus grabbed hold of the man with both hands, cursing his impatience and stupidity for not anchoring and backing down to the buoy. His arms shrieked with the strain, and he felt the sharp pain of a muscle tearing in his left shoulder. He was about to let go and try again when he heard the man groan. He redoubled his efforts and felt the rope give a little where he'd been sawing. He cursed his fishing knife and the bluntness of it. Chopped once more. But knives left on boats never stayed sharp, and it was all he could do to cling on as strand after strand of the rope slowly gave, unable now to let the man go in case he slipped from his makeshift harness and sank. He ignored the burning pain in his shoulder until the last strands separated and the man broke free. Angus dropped his knife in his desperation to hold on to the life jacket, braced his legs and dragged the man up onto the gunwale. By the time he'd wrestled him aboard, the boat had drifted more than two hundred yards. He dropped the limp body onto the deck, heard the man groan once more on landing, then engaged gear. He swung his boat back into the wind and fed it full throttle, backing off only after it had begun to gain headway. Angus was so exhausted he was sorely tempted to lie down on the deck himself.

Bonnie coughed wetly and continued her plaintive cries. Angus glared through the open door into the tiny cabin. Bonnie's cardboard box had vibrated off the padded bench seat and lay on its end in the footwell. Too bad. She'd have to stay like that for the moment. He flexed his aching arms and rotated each of his shoulders in turn. He knew it would take more than a hot bath and a good rub with liniment before they'd come right. He turned to look at the man he'd saved and noticed the Japanese characters on his life jacket. He smiled grimly at the irony. Still, a man in need was a man in need, and it didn't matter a whit what country he was born in. He needed help, warmth and shelter, but Angus could offer nothing until they reached calmer waters.

His first thought was to put in to Homestead Bay and seek help. The family living there had an airstrip of sorts and could call in assistance. But that could still take hours, and the man looked like he needed a doctor urgently. There was only one doctor nearby that Angus knew of, though he dreaded to think what Red's reaction would be.

As soon as he'd anchored up in the lee of Arid, Angus attended to his patient. He was surprised by the youthfulness of the face before him. He found a pulse, weak and slow, and breathed a sigh of relief. Angus had seen all the corpses he wanted to see in his life. He stripped off the boy's life jacket and clothes and half-carried, half-dragged him into the cabin. Bonnie let him know she was singularly unimpressed to have company. The man born on the shores of the Minch knew exactly what he had to do. He'd been raised in the shadow of hypothermia, where a few minutes in the Minch, even in summer, extinguished the life spark in the strongest. He recalled the relay of women who attended the bedside of a fisherman from Achiltibuie who'd fallen into the harbor while painting his boat. The women had taken turns to massage life back into the frozen flesh, vigorously rubbing his body, legs and arms with rough towels. They'd rubbed through an entire day and night, patient, serious women who drove the cold from men who had every reason to die or lose limbs to frostbite. But the women had persevered, and so would he. Angus forgot his own pain and did what duty required of him, vigorously massaging every part of the boy's body, rubbing his blue-tinged skin until it flushed burnished pink. He rubbed and rubbed until sweat formed on his forehead and dripped down onto his patient. Occasionally the boy's eyelids fluttered and he attempted to speak, but he lost grip on consciousness just as quickly. Angus knew he should keep rubbing but was torn between that and the need to get the boy to a doctor. He took his own dry clothes out of his carryall and dressed the shivering youth, finally wrapping him in his wet-weather oilskins to trap in any body heat the boy could muster. He secured Bonnie's box between the hull and the tightly wrapped boy so that it wouldn't tumble back down into the footwell. Bonnie showed no gratitude and maintained her wailing.

"I just hope the boy doesn't wake up to hear that," said Angus to his cat. "What on earth would he think had happened to him?"

Thirty-nine

Red rose before sunup, anxious to resume his familiar and trusted routine and reassure himself of its rightness. Rosie had begun to question everything he did. She queried his need for a mosquito net in the absence of malarial mosquitoes. Perhaps it *was* a hangover from his Burma days, but Rosie had yet to pass a summer at Wreck Bay, when the air was thick with both mosquitoes and sandflies. She queried the need for a closed gate on the fence around the vegetable plot. Perhaps the gate didn't need padlocking, but it did need closing. He'd left it open, knowing that it was wrong, but did so only for Rosie's sake. When the wind had picked up during the night he'd had to get out of bed and close it to stop it banging off its hinges. There were reasons, good reasons, why he did what he did that he believed had nothing to do with Burma. He exercised, made his fish rice and shared it with Archie. It felt good, just the two of them, just doing what they'd always done.

After breakfast he set about scrubbing the counters, table, floors and the square of linoleum that was Archie's personal dinner mat. He cleared his kitchen shelves, scrubbed them, and scrubbed his bathroom out as well. He checked the walls, ceilings, cornices and window frames for spiderwebs, but the spiders had learned not to bother making webs anywhere where Red could reach them. Satisfied, he checked his garden for snails and slugs and extracted the odd impudent weed. It all felt so very satisfying. He was about to throw himself beneath his summer shower, when a little tug alongside his ribs, an annoyance he mostly ignored, reminded him of his need to get his body back into shape and fully fit. He grabbed a towel and set off for the beach, pausing when he reached the fork in the track that led to Rosie's bach. It seemed selfish not to give her the opportunity to join him. Archie led the way, tail wagging, eager to feel the hand that spoiled him and slipped him little treats. Red stopped when he saw Archie suddenly break into a sprint, was glad he'd thought to make the detour.

"Hello, Archie. Did you bring my penis with you?"

Red stood his ground and waited for Rosie to appear around the bend in the track. He couldn't help smiling.

"Ah . . . there's the little fellow. And how are you, Red?" She kissed him perfunctorily. "I missed you last night, but at least I could sleep in."

"Morning, Rosie."

She bounced past him, towel over her shoulder, her T-shirt barely keeping her breasts in check.

"You're getting tough, Rosie."

"What do you mean?"

"Wasn't long ago you wrapped up at the slightest sign of a breeze and pulled a sweater on if the sun went behind a cloud. Now look at you. Soon you'll be like me."

"I'll try to take that as a compliment."

"Now you're even going for a swim on a day like this."

"It's your fault I've got energy to burn off, and anyway, I want to listen to the penguins. We'll have to make some more bombs, I'm beginning to miss them."

"I'll take you to the penguins' caves one night, if you like."

"I'd like."

"Low tide tonight?"

"Thought I'd go out fishing at the pinnacles."

"Wrong tide, wrong wind. Besides, they're probably surrounded by crayfish pots.".

Rosie stopped dead in her tracks. "What?! What are we going to do about them?"

"Nothing, Rosie. Every Christmas boats come over from Leigh. They're pretty good and spread their pots around. Whenever they overfish, I empty both crayfish and bait from every trap I find. Those guys don't like working for nothing. They soon get the message. Had a chat with them one year and explained the rules. They spread their pots all the way down from Aiguilles Island, out and around Bernie's Point. They follow the reefs a fair way out, too, which is pretty good of them. They don't just take the crayfish close in."

"I'm surprised you're so tolerant."

"People eat crays at Christmas, Rosie."

"Okay, so we'll go penguin spotting tonight. Listen! Hear that?" They'd almost reached the bottom of the track, where it broadened out. They stood silently, listening to a blue penguin calling for its mate out in the choppy waters of the bay. "Isn't it great?"

"It's all great, Rosie. Now come on."

Red walked straight down the beach and swam out to his boat to check the mooring lines, which were always secure, and his storm cover, which was always properly fastened and had only once lifted in a blow. He dived under the boat, looking for barnacles and weed, but he scrubbed the hull too often for any organisms to settle. He checked the chain and swivel attached to the concrete mooring and confirmed what he already knew. Both would need replacing before winter. It was important not to let equipment go, and he kept a constant eye on it, just as he'd inspected his weapon and kit every day in the army and his pathetic few possessions in Burma. What use was a mess kit allowed to rust or a cup with holes? By the time he'd finished his inspection, Rosie had already stripped off and swum past the main beach to the bay's third little stretch of sand. He set off after her, careful not to overreach and aggravate his ribs. Archie dog-paddled between them, unwilling to leave his master but anxious not to abandon Rosie, either. It was a predicament that guaranteed Archie more exercise than Red and Rosie combined.

Red was first to spot Angus's boat, out wide, giving Bernie's Head and the pinnacles a wide berth. He called to Rosie, who was plowing the water ahead of him on their return leg. He thought she'd want to put her shorts and T-shirt back on before the old Scot had a chance to remonstrate. She stopped swimming and began to wade ashore.

"You might have to help him onto the beach, Red," she said. "The widow's had him for five days."

Red followed her up the beach and dried off while they waited for Angus to come in. "He's in a bit of a hurry."

"Probably forgot to go to the little boys' room before he left."

Red took no notice of Rosie. He couldn't remember when he'd last seen Angus cranking so many revs out of his old diesel, and the conditions were hardly ideal. He watched the red-and-white half-cabin as it lined up for the beach with the wind and waves dead astern. Saw it catch a swell, ride with it before slewing to the left and falling off its back. Odd, he thought, not like Angus at all. "I think he's in some kind of trouble, Rosie."

Rosie squinted at the boat heading toward them, suddenly serious. She expected the Scotsman to throttle back so that he could glide up to his mooring, but it soon became obvious that he had other intentions. Red started running down the beach, Rosie and Archie hard on his heels.

"He's going to beach her! Stand clear."

Angus cut the motor, judging the moment to perfection so that he set the bows firmly into the sand with no more of a jolt than necessary.

"What's the problem?" Red was at the side of the half-cabin in seconds.

"I've picked up a hitchhiker. More drowned than alive. He'd tied himself to a buoy."

"I'll help you get him out."

"Before you do, Red, there's something you should know. He's Japanese." He looked Red straight in the eye to gauge his reaction. "A Japanese fisherman."

Red's eyes narrowed. "You rescued a Jap fisherman?"

"Aye, that's what I've done."

"How is he?"

"Not the best. Not good at all."

"Then we'd better get him out of there!"

"It doesn't worry you, him being Japanese?"

"I don't know!" Red leaped over the transom and opened the cabin door. An unearthly wailing came from within. "Christ! Is that him?"

"Away with you! That's Bonnie."

Red stuck his head into the cabin and fought hard to ignore the stench saturating the enclosed space. He saw the figure bound up in Angus's oilskins, head down, feet up. All he saw was a boy, a hurt boy who needed help. *"Konichi-wa,"* said Red. *"Daijobu, daijobu anzen desu.* Everything is okay, okay. You're safe." Angus and Red picked up the crumpled form, lifted him and carried him onto the beach.

The boy struggled back into consciousness, aware of voices and people and being carried. His mind was filled with fragmentary recollections of vile odors and the tortured screams of the spirits of the dead. He forced his eyes open just as Red laid him gently down on the sand. He saw the flaming red hair and flaming beard and recoiled. He heard a stifled scream, his own, but failed to recognize the source.

"Daijobu, daijobu . . . " Red said soothingly. "Everything is all right, everything is okay." He put his hand on the boy's forehead and stroked it, just as he'd stroked the heads of his mates in the death house at Thanbyuzayat and Aungganaung. *"Zenzen daijobu ne?* Everything okay, understand?"

"Let me look at him, Red."

"It wasn't his fault, Rosie."

"What?"

"It wasn't his fault."

"Of course it wasn't. Now, out of my way."

"He's too young, you see?" Red moved aside so that she could examine the boy. He turned to go and checked himself. There was another patient to attend. "Angus, you'd better get Bonnie out of the cabin. Smells like she's puked all the way from Awana."

"She has, Red, take my word for it. From both ends."

Red volunteered to piggyback the sick boy up to Rosie's bach while Angus put his boat out on its mooring. Rosie made up a bed in her spare room, covered it with every blanket she had, filled a hot water bottle for good measure and left the boy to sleep. When she rejoined Red, he'd begun making a fish soup for the boy to eat when he woke up. A pot of tea and two cups waited for her on the dining table. She slumped onto a chair.

"You know, Red, I've practiced more medicine here in the past eight months than I did in the previous eight years."

"How is he?"

"He'll live. Give Angus a lot of credit for that. Did you see how chafed the poor bugger is? Rubbed raw in places. Fortunately there doesn't appear to be much water in his lungs. Angus had laid him down so that his head was lower than his feet once the boat was under way. Whether Angus intended it or not, that probably helped drain saltwater from the boy's lungs."

Red sat down opposite Rosie and poured the tea. "When do you think I'll be able to talk to him?"

"What's your hurry?"

"It's time, Rosie, don't you see?"

"Don't play games with me, Red! See what?"

"A Japanese fisherman picked up half a mile from shore," Red said patiently. "How do you think he got there?"

"Oh, shit . . ."

"I've got to talk to him, Rosie, the sooner the better."

"I understand, Red, but I'm not going to wake him for you. Why don't you take the radio and alert Mickey?"

"What will I tell him? We don't know if we're looking for a long-liner or a trawler."

"You could see if he's got a patrol boat available."

"No!" Red said vehemently. "First we find out who we're dealing with."

Rosie took no notice of his sudden explosion of temper. She put it down as another symptom of his inability to cope. "What difference does that make? You should still alert Mickey. If he's got a boat, he'll send it."

Red shifted uncomfortably on his seat. "You don't understand, Rosie."

"I understand perfectly, Red O'Hara. You're just looking for an excuse to use your bombs. You're hoping it's the *Shoto Maru,* and you don't want the navy getting in the way! That's right, isn't it? Isn't it, Red?"

"Angus has the radio." Red wouldn't meet her eyes.

"Well, go and get it from him!"

"All right!" Red stood angrily. "But if anyone's going to send a message to Mickey it'll have to be Angus. I'm coming back in case the boy wakes up. And let me tell you something, Rosie. Angus will also want to know what boat the boy's from—for two reasons. One, so that he can tell Mickey when he asks, so that he doesn't look stupid. And two . . ." Red's eyes clouded for an instant and she could almost see his mind flick back to Burma. His voice turned bitter. "And two, because they—whoever they are—owe him sixpence!"

When Red called in on Angus he found the old Scot unusually subdued, gazing around emptily like a vacating householder taking a final look at what had been his home.

"What is it you want now?" The Scotsman's voice was flat, detached, uninterested.

"Rosie wants you to contact Mickey and tell him about the Jap."

"Aye, it's my duty, I suppose."

Red was caught by surprise. He'd expected an argument or to be told to go call up Mickey himself. But the Scot just acquiesced with a sigh. "How's your shoulder?"

"I'll survive."

"Anything I can do?"

"Nothing! I don't need you or anyone! I'm not senile, you know."

"Sorry."

"Ah. . . . away with you. It's me who should be sorry. It's just that I don't like all these changes that are happening. Nothing's the same anymore."

Red shuffled with embarrassment. "I know what you mean, but things'll get back to normal."

"I wish I had your faith. Soon we'll have the wee bairn and . . ." He hesitated as he contemplated a life shared with the widow Campbell and sighed heavily. "And God only knows what then!" He noticed Red looking at him strangely. "Ah . . . enough of this mawkishness! You go about your business and I'll go about mine."

"Ask Mickey if he knows where the *Shoto Maru* is."

"The *Shoto Maru?*" Angus stiffened, and his interest quickened. "Do you think the lad's from the *Shoto Maru?*"

"It's a possibility, and if he is, we have to know."

"Dear God! Don't you go doing anything foolish, now!"

"Find out if Mickey has a patrol boat on standby."

"Aye, I'll do that. I hope for your sake that he has."

"How's Bonnie?"

"Fine. I gave her some food and she's sleeping. How's the boy?"

"Asleep. And doing fine, thanks to you. I'll ask him a few questions when he wakes up."

"Aye, and let's hope the *Shoto Maru* isn't one of the answers. I'll drop by Rosie's on the way back. Don't you go involving her in your madness!"

Red turned away without bothering to reply and set off for the beach. He didn't believe in patrol boats on standby any more than he believed in fairies at the bottom of the garden. The wind had strengthened and pushed the white-capped waves hard in on the beach, where they backed up and crashed like surf. Wreck Bay had little protection when the nor'easters blew. He watched Rosie's and Angus's boats dancing wildly on their moorings and thought momentarily of winching them up onto the sand. But he had another job to do first, a more important job, one that he couldn't put off. He swam out to his boat, stripped off the storm cover, fired up the diesel and maneuvered the boat over to the jetty. The tide was high, almost full, which gave him some satisfaction. He topped up his fuel tanks and walked purposefully over to the bunker he'd made. Rather than fight the tarpaulin, he took it off altogether and folded it up, using stones to stop it blowing away. Then he turned his mind to the serious business of transferring his homemade bombs to his boat. He'd intended to make racks for them so they wouldn't bump against each other, or anything else for that matter. He knew how easily the vase-like casings could break or crack, but time had beaten him. His eyes wandered to the stands of flax and toi-toi and saw a solution beckoning. For the next hour and a half he sat and wove individual baskets for his bombs and packed them out with handfuls of grass. Then he attached three large glass floats to each bomb, enough to keep them on or close to the surface. When he'd finished, he tied lengths of rope between the gunwales and suspended the bombs far enough apart so that they wouldn't bang against each other as the boat pounded through the waves. He took a step back to admire his handiwork. Four rows of five bombs suspended in a cat's cradle of rope and fishing line. Though not a perfect system, and one that would force him to crawl between bow and stern when he cast off, it was good enough to enable him to control the boat and deploy his bombs single-handed.

When Signals rang and said Angus was on the radio and needed to talk to him personally, Mickey immediately feared the worst. He assumed Rosie had received his letter and confessed to the truth. He expected to hear a gloating Scot publicly proclaiming his imminent parenthood.

"Hello, Angus," he began tentatively, regretting the fact that he hadn't thought to order his faithful assistant elsewhere. Gloria looked on expectantly. The Scot's first words brought a surge of relief, but Mickey's pleasure was fleeting as he digested their significance. He instructed Angus to come back on air in the evening for an update and raced back to his office.

"Coffee!" he bellowed. "And bring me the movements and last known position of every foreign vessel within one hundred miles north and south of Great Barrier."

He slumped down in his chair, certain that it was Shimojo up to his old tricks, and equally certain that Red would not sit idly by. The problem was, they'd lost contact with Shimojo once he'd moved out wide. The air force had lost interest and found other things to occupy its Orions. No domestic pilots had reported sightings, but that was only to be expected. There was a limit to how far they could safely stray from their flight paths. He'd ordered the *Cormorant* up from its patrol around Hawkes Bay, but it had only reported a blip on its radar wide of the Mercury Islands and had been unable to identify its source. They'd had reports of phantom trawlers from positions a thousand miles apart and had been unable to find a pattern in the sightings. The reports had become too widespread and unreliable to interest even the newspapers.

In the meantime, longliner dories were wreaking havoc along the northwest beaches. Mickey cursed under his breath. There were too many games being played and too few resources at his disposal. In a sense he felt relieved at finally discovering Shimojo's whereabouts, but it was only the relief of a cancer victim receiving confirmation of the disease. Waiting could be worse than actually knowing, but knowing was hardly something to shout about, either.

He was concerned at how earnestly Angus had pleaded for naval intervention and had pressed the old Scot for details of "the dire consequence" he'd alluded to. But Angus hadn't been forthcoming. What on earth was Red O'Hara up to, he wondered?

"Coffee."

Mickey looked up as Gloria plonked a mug of unidentifiable gray liquid on his desk. He sipped it tentatively and stifled a grimace. Gloria's instant was bad, her filtered was atrocious. "What have you got for me?"

"Not much, sir. The demersal longliners on the east coast are still working farther south between the Bay of Plenty and Great Barrier."

"Get on with it."

"The Russian and Taiwanese trawlers are still working the same grounds well wide of the twelve-mile limit. Last we heard, the two tuna longliners had moved farther out to sea, and we've no reason to think they've moved back in close, though the Egret did report large schools of tuna in the gulf. We've had no reports at all of the Shoto Maru. There've been sightings of an unnamed trawler working wide between the Bay of Plenty and the Mercuries. In all probability it's the Shoto Maru, but we can't assume it. Nor can we assume that the sailor Angus rescued was from the Shoto Maru or was even from a fishing boat."

Mickey winced. She was right, of course. Apart from her, they'd all been guilty of assuming that the sailor was a fisherman. He tried to recover lost ground. "I'm aware that assumptions are being made here, Gloria. However, no Japanese vessels have left port in the last forty-eight hours and only one has arrived. The arrival, a cargo ship, came from the north." The *New Zealand Herald* always reported arrivals and departures, and Mickey had been reading the paper when Angus's call had come through. For once he was ahead of her, but only just.

"Do you think Angus could tell the difference between Japanese, Chinese or Korean characters?"

"Ah." She'd got him again.

"A boat from Hong Kong arrived this morning."

"Thank you, Wainscott," Mickey said frostily. "I'm pleased to know you also read the paper. But let's just assume for a moment that our man is a Japanese fisherman. If you had to wager your future career on the identity of the vessel he fell from, what would be your guess?"

"The *Shoto Maru.*"

"Thank you. Now can we get on with the job?" Mickey knew he was being unreasonable. All Gloria had forced him to do was consider other possibilities. Normally he'd have complimented her, but he didn't normally get women pregnant, nor live with the threat of exposure. He felt he'd earned the right to be irritable. "What have we got available?"

"The *Kotaku,* sir. Yesterday I overheard Lieutenant Commander Scriven discussing the possibility of having the *Kotaku* permanently attached to the squadron."

"Did you? Who with?"

"Don't know, sir. The lieutenant commander was on the phone." Gloria looked fixedly at a spot above Mickey's head, but her cheeks were slightly flushed.

"Gloria . . . ?"

"His assistant had a dental appointment, sir. You may recall he asked me to stand in."

"But did he ask you to listen in? Never mind. Get onto it, Gloria! Let's hope the crew hasn't been sent home for Christmas. Ask the *Kotaku*'s commanding officer to stand by. Tell him what's up and that we might need him to sail as soon as possible, tonight at the very latest."

"Sir!"

"And Gloria . . . well done!" He smiled ingratiatingly, but she was already out the door and out of sight.

Forty

"*Dozo tabete kudasai,*" *Red urged gently. Eat, eat. At Rosie's request he'd put on some old gray boxer shorts and a red-and-green tartan* flannel shirt with buttons that shared neither color nor size with one another.

The boy sat propped up in bed and allowed the woman and the strange red man who spoke snippets of his language to feed him. The soup was good and the pieces of fish floating in it delicious. He'd been overjoyed to discover that he was alive, but he still had no idea what to make of the unearthly, high-pitched keening that had chilled him more than the long hours in the water.

"More?" Rosie asked encouragingly, but the boy shook his head weakly and allowed it to fall back against the pillow.

"*Domo arigato gozaimasu.*"

"He's saying thank you," said Red.

"So I gathered." She patted the boy's hand and stood up to take the spoon and bowl back to the kitchen. "All yours, but keep it brief. You can see how tired he is."

Red sat on the edge of the bed and smiled. "Do you speak English? *Eigo-o hanashimasu-ka?*" Red's Japanese was rusty and barely remembered. That he remembered any of it at all surprised him, but then again, how could he forget?

"*Hai!* Small . . ."

"*Namae?*"

380

"Matsui Kuraishi."

"Red O'Hara."

"Ohira?"

Red looked away. It was such a simple mistake and an obvious one. It had saved his life and cost Archie his. A simple mistake that had caused him more pain than he'd ever imagined possible. But he couldn't hate the boy. What was there to hate? Matsui hadn't pulled the trigger, and he wasn't one of the guards who'd tormented and beaten them. But Red's mood changed, and with the change came a grim reminder of the purpose of his interrogation. *"Namae boat?"*

"Wakarimasen."

Red sighed. Matsui clearly didn't recognize the word in English. He hadn't wanted to confront the boy directly with the name of the *Shoto Maru*, given that the boat had been fishing illegally. He was worried that he might deny it. But with no other option, he decided to take a chance. *"Shoto Maru?"*

"Hai!" The boy's eyes bulged large with surprise.

"Shimojo Seiichi?"

"Hai!"

Red rose and went out into the living room and returned with a map of Great Barrier. He pointed to a spot just offshore from Awana Beach. He wanted the boy to confirm that the *Shoto Maru* had been there the previous night. *"Yube?"*

"Hai! Yube."

Yesterday accounted for. Red moved his finger to a spot just north of Arid Island and asked the sixty-four-dollar question. *"Kyo?* Today?"

"Hai!"

"Konya? Tonight?"

"Hai!" Matsui took the map from Red and ran his finger along the shoreline from Arid Island to Aiguilles Island. *"Hai, konya, konya!"*

Red took the map back and bowed toward Matsui. *"Domo arigato!"* The boy's eyelids had begun to close. Red turned and wandered out onto the veranda. He ignored Rosie's quizzical looks as he walked past her. He leaned against the rail and gazed out toward the horizon, noting the deep furrows that crept ashore almost indolently and the slow, lathering foam. Distance deceived, but Red wasn't fooled. He could hear the wind bending back the giant totaras, kauris and puriris, hear it beat down the scrub and palms and roar in its ascendency. He thought he could hear the sound of distant artillery, the crashing and thundering of surf hurling itself in on Aiguilles Island. The light level dropped as the cloud-filtered sun dropped behind Tataweka ridge and late afternoon gloom engulfed their side of the island. The time had come, but he felt no sense of excitement, only a deepening sense of foreboding. It was madness to fish close in on such a night, even madder to try and stop them. Any reasonable skipper would stay wide. But would Shimojo? He felt Rosie's hand on his shoulder.

"Well?"

"He's from the *Shoto Maru.*"

"Oh dear."

"No problem, Rosie. He thinks Shimojo will run back south out wide."

"Really."

"Yes really, Rosie." Red fought back the sudden flash of temper that would reveal his hand. He hated the way she'd assumed he was lying. "Work it out for yourself. He's had a good night's fishing and can afford to cut and run. He's lost a man overboard who may have been picked up or washed ashore. If so there'd be a good chance that somebody would be looking for him. Lastly, take a look out there, Rosie. When you first came here I brought you around from Fitzroy in waves one-fifth the size you see out there. Plus the wind was blowing from the west. Now it's blowing from the northeast and gusting over forty knots, I'd say. If you had a trawler and your trawl speed was four and a half knots and you knew the coast was studded with reefs and pinnacles, would you risk your boat in close?"

Rosie rubbed both of his shoulders, a peace offering for her unwarranted suspicions. "Poor Red," she said. "I do believe you're disappointed."

Just before evening, Angus dropped by on his way up to call Mickey. He seemed burdened by more than the weight of the radio.

Red broke the news to him that the boy had fallen from the *Shoto Maru,* and that only deepened the Scot's air of doom.

"Why don't you let Red call up Mickey?" Rosie suggested. "You've done enough today. Stay here and have dinner with us. Red won't mind going. Besides, he's convinced that Shimojo won't show tonight and thinks he's probably headed back south."

Angus looked over at Red and understood immediately. "It's kind of you to offer, but we all have our jobs to do. I promised the lieutenant commander that I'd call, and I'll stick to my word. I'll pass on Red's point of view. The sea's getting up, and out there is no place to be, whether it's Shimojo or anyone else. I dare say they've fished worse, but I doubt they'll have done so in close. Nevertheless I'll press Mickey for some kind of presence. It wouldn't hurt them to do a run out to the island."

"I'll walk with you as far as my place," said Red. "There are some things I want."

"The offer of dinner still stands, Angus."

Angus thought of the eggs and tin of baked beans that were all he had to make his dinner with. He'd hoped for a snapper from Red, but Rosie's proposal was by far the better option. Besides, he thought she might need some calming down if Red took off after Shimojo. "Thank you, Rosie. I'll not say no to your kind offer. But excuse me now."

The two men walked in silence until they reached the fork up to Red's place.

"Will you not tell me your plan, man?" Angus asked bluntly.

"It's wait and see. There's no point in going out unless he shows himself, and that won't be until he brings his first haul aboard. Then he has to be in range. If he's south of Arid, up by Aiguilles Island or more than four miles offshore, he'll be beyond reach. His lights will be out by the time I clear Bernie's Head. In these conditions if he's more than four miles away I'll never find him."

"What do you intend doing if you do find him?"

"Warn him off, Angus. Why, what did you think?" Red stopped by his bach. "It'll be dark by the time you're back. Do you need a torch?"

"No, I have all I need." Angus stared at the ground for a moment. "I've cut a track from my house out onto Bernie's Head. I go there sometimes to think. It has the best views up and down the coast."

"Thanks, Angus."

"You're a bloody fool, man, but take care of yourself." Angus set off up the hill to Tataweka ridge, not at all sure why he was being so cooperative. Times were changing, and that was a fact.

"I need a good reason, Angus, give me one!"

The radio operators had discovered an hypnotic fascination with their VU meters. Gloria looked down at her notepad. Mickey's face was flushed, and he'd banged the tabletop so often it was a miracle it wasn't dented.

"I've given you reason enough, man, what more do you want? We've identified the trawler the boy fell from, and he's confirmed Shimojo's intentions. The seas are rough but not too rough for the likes of him. Now you tell me you're just going to sit back there and let Red do your job for you. One man in an open boat to do the job of the navy. There'll be repercussions, I'm warning you."

"What repercussions? Give me a clue. Give me something to work with." Mickey thumped the table again with frustration. "Let me explain it to you once more. There are probably a dozen foreign vessels fishing inside the twelve-mile limit while I speak. We can't send a patrol boat out to watch every one because we don't have a dozen patrol boats. So it's not enough for us to know that a boat is fishing illegally. All our patrol boats are committed. We have an old minesweeper on standby, but my superiors, in their infinite wisdom, require more reasons than the ones you've given me to send it out. Its crew is due to go on Christmas leave tomorrow. Now give me a reason to hold them over! Tell me there's potential for conflict or an international incident. Tell me Red's going to start shooting at them again. Tell me there's a risk that lives will be lost. Tell me that something might happen that could embarrass the government!"

Mickey's diatribe was greeted with silence from the other end.

"Angus! Are you still there?"

"Aye! Hold your horses, I'm thinking."

"There's no time to think, Angus. Tell me what you know!"

"It's not easy, man. I've been sworn to secrecy."

"Give me a clue. What's at stake here?" Mickey glanced over to Gloria. He sensed a weakening in the old Scot's resolve. "What is it, Angus? Help me so that I can help you. Is it risk of life, an international incident, are you and Red going to make our politicians piss their pants, what?"

"Probably all three, truth be known."

Mickey's blood turned cold. "What's he up to, Angus?"

"Do you promise to send a ship?"

"Yes yes yes! Get on with it!"

"He's made bombs."

"What?!" Instantly all eyes were on Mickey. Faces appeared in the doorway. Mickey's brain trust, which had been discreetly eavesdropping in the corridor, threw discretion to the wind.

"He's found some old five-inch shells and extracted the cordite and primers. I watched him and Rosie detonate one off Bernie's Head, and, man, you should have seen the fountain of water it threw up."

"Angus, are you telling me Red's going to try to blow up the *Shoto Maru?*"

"Perhaps. Or maybe just warn them off."

"Angus, how many shells did he find?"

"Thousands. But he's only cut up about a dozen."

Only a dozen! Mickey had begun to sweat. He could feel it on his upper lip and on the palms of his hands. "Angus, we'll have to leave you now. Thanks for being honest with us, but you should have told us hours ago. It'll be midnight at best before we can reach you. Try to stop Red going out. Tell him we're definitely coming and to leave it to us. Tell him I order him not to interfere again. Remind him that he let Shimojo get away once before. Tell him we won't tolerate it happening again. Tell the stupid bastard anything, but make him put his bombs away! Now listen carefully. I want you to be our eyes and tell us exactly where Shimojo is when he lights up. I'm going to hand you back to Able Radioman Press to work out a method of relaying messages to us until we come around to your side of the island. I want you down off the ridge and close to Red.

Keep your radio open, and we'll use the same relay to get messages to you. Stand by."

Mickey handed over to the radio operator and drew a deep breath. He'd needed reasons and he'd got reasons. Boy! Had he got reasons! He turned to pass on instructions to Gloria, but she was already gone and more than likely already getting into Lieutenant Commander Scriven's ear. He allowed himself a grim smile. The news would put Phil the Pill right off his Pimm's. He looked around at his brain trust. "I need a volunteer for an immediate assignment."

"Sir, sir!" The brain trust nearly tripped over one another in their eagerness.

Mickey picked out the youngest. "You. Good man. Nick over the road and get us some hamburgers. It's going to be a long night."

Shimojo completed the last daylight trawl at five forty-five and immediately ordered the *Shoto Maru* to make full speed toward the coast. He expected to relocate the snapper school north of Arid Island, over the shellfish beds off Whangapoua Beach, or even north of Waikaro Point. The school had been large and slow moving the night before, but things could change quickly. Rough weather might have pushed them back south or farther out to sea. It might even have split the school, with some making a run for shelter behind Aiguilles Island. Shimojo picked up his pencil and drew a line from southeast of Arid Island to Waikaro Point that roughly corresponded to the curvature of the coast. By starting so far south he allowed for the possibility that the fish had turned back the way they'd come and covered himself in the event that the snapper had gone deep. He took careful note of the islands off Waikaro Point and the pinnacles off Wreck Bay. They were too close in to be of any real concern, but a good captain took all risks into consideration. With the nor'easter blowing, they were hazards deserving of caution. He checked with radar. There were no other vessels or aircraft in the vicinity. He drew a second line north of Waikaro Point to Aiguilles Island.

The first hour brought little reward, less than two tons. But as they passed the eastern side of Arid Island and moved in toward Waikaro Point, they began to encounter snapper in good numbers, though still nowhere near the density of the previous night. Shimojo instructed the helmsman to sweep within half a mile of Waikaro Point and head northeast. The quantity of snapper flowing into the net was encouraging but not conclusive. He watched the bows of the boat come around slowly into the wind, fighting against its force and the rush of the swells. He ordered more power. The fish finder was beginning to light up. The pattern was similar to the previous night's, the edges not clearly defined and irregular, but becoming denser by the minute. He held his course. He needed to ascertain how far out the school extended, whether it had split or stayed intact. The fish finder showed a solid mass, and he began to feel the drag of the giant net holding the *Shoto Maru* back as it tried to hammer through the swells. His net filled with fish that would soon tumble down the chutes into the holding tanks for the workers below to process while the boat pitched and wallowed. It would be a miracle if they all greeted the dawn with thumbs and fingers intact.

The density of the school began to fall off before the *Shoto Maru* had gone much past the two-mile mark. The fish were closer in than he expected, which made working the school difficult and downright hazardous with the nor'easter blowing. Shimojo shortened the run inshore and swung back northeast. He could see Waikaro Point and its guardian islands clearly on the radar screen and knew that if he stepped outside he'd hear the surf pounding in on the cliffs. He concluded that the school had spread out in a cigar-shaped stream reaching up the coast, which left him little option. When he reached the outer edge of the school he'd have to trawl northward. Over the course of the night they'd gradually work their way in closer, where the concentration of fish would be most dense. The night would be rough, uncomfortable and dangerous, but certainly productive. He checked his watch. It was approaching nine o'clock. Midshift. Time to bring in the net. It seemed prudent to complete their eastward run and empty their net at the farthermost point from shore.

Over dinner, Angus explained to Rosie what the navy required of them. "In the unlikely event that Shimojo decides to risk fishing in close, they need us to tell them where the *Shoto Maru* is so that they can sneak up and nab him. If Shimojo doesn't show, they're going to overnight in Tryphena harbor until tomorrow night."

"What can I do?"

"You can make us up a flask of coffee."

"Terrific. Thanks for including me in your adventure." Rosie's eyes narrowed. She couldn't get used to seeing the two men together, almost matey. It didn't seem right, in fact seemed dead fishy. She looked from Angus to Red and back again. "Promise me you two aren't cooking something up."

"There's nothing to cook up, Rosie," said Red evenly. "We're going to take turns to sit out on Bernie's Head and listen to the radio, that's if we can get reception. If the boy's lying and Shimojo shows, we tell the navy where to look. It's hardly my idea of adventure."

Rosie was still not completely convinced.

"It's not my idea of adventure, either, Rosie. It's not something I look forward to. It's a hot water bottle my shoulder needs, not a heavy radio." Angus spoke sharply to make his point. But in fact he could hardly wait to get down to the headland. The night promised precisely the sort of experiences he needed for his book. He was convinced his new book would be his best, a rare event in itself as he was usually beset with self-doubt and only believed he'd written something worthwhile once his publisher had said so. The only aspect of the night's duty he didn't embrace enthusiastically was the task of dissuading Red from taking his boat out. He was sure he could make the madman see reason, he just wasn't looking forward to the process.

"All right, but before you go you can both look in on our patient. It would be nice if he could meet his rescuer. Well?"

"Aye, I suppose so." Angus stood and Red followed.

"I'll go in first," said Rosie, "and make sure he's awake. The way he put his dinner away I reckon he'll be up and about by morning."

Angus glanced at Red, who simply shrugged. They both wanted to get to Bernie's Head as soon as possible but had no choice. Through a combination of Japanese, English and mime that had Rosie shaking her head in wonder, Red managed to communicate to the boy that it was Angus who had pulled him out of the water. He lifted his head and shoulders from the bed as if bowing and thanked

Angus in halting English. Angus shook his hand and backed away embarrassed.

The boy looked up at Red, concern on his face. *"Terefonu!"*

"What does he want?" This time it was Rosie asking.

"Telephone."

"He probably wants to let his family know he's safe. Can't you get Mickey to contact the Japanese embassy?"

"There's a wee problem," said Angus awkwardly. "The lieutenant commander is withholding the information. If we tell the embassy about the boy, they'll tell Shimojo. That could ruin everything."

"But what about his parents?" Rosie was aghast.

"We have to be patient, Rosie," said Angus unhappily.

"You're prepared to let his parents believe their son is dead just so you can play your little games?"

"Only for twenty-four hours, Rosie. I have the lieutenant commander's word."

"Well, let me tell you something. First thing in the morning I'm walking over to Fitzroy and I'm bloody well going to ring the Japanese embassy myself!"

"We'll speak in the morning, Rosie. We have to go now." The two men edged out through the doorway and began to pull on their warm clothing and wet-weather gear. Archie joined them, ears flattened and tail between his legs, as they opened the door onto the veranda.

"One more thing, Angus!"

They both turned at Rosie's voice.

"You can make your own bloody flask of coffee!"

Neither man spoke until they reached Angus's place and stopped to collect his propane lamp, binoculars and a thermos of coffee.

"You know Mickey wants you kept out of the way, don't you Red?"

"We'll see."

"What's there to see, man? Orders are orders, and they don't want you getting in the way of their operation like you did last February up at Aiguilles."

"I'm not yet convinced they have an operation."

389

"Don't be a fool, man. They're sending the old minesweeper, the *Kotaku*. I told you that."

"Yes, you did. But we don't even know if they've left port yet. And in these conditions, we don't know how long it will take them to get here."

"Away with you. I promised the lieutenant commander. It's their job to arrest those poachers, not yours. I'll not stand by and let you interfere. Remember the Sunderland, Red! Your meddling has already cost the navy dearly."

Red stared sullenly at his feet. It wasn't just his fight. Perhaps it wasn't his fight at all. "Okay, if the *Kotaku*'s on its way, I'll keep clear."

"Good man!" Angus was pleased at how easily Red had given in and did nothing to hide it. "The best thing we can do is be their eyes. Come on. I have some whisky, for the coffee you understand. The wind will be fearsome."

Red took the radio and let Angus lead, carrying the rucksack. The track rose sharply toward the lookout, and Red could sense Angus beginning to struggle. Why wouldn't he? The old Scot had been up at dawn, saved a drowning man and climbed Tataweka ridge twice. Red simply adjusted his pace. The roar of the wind let them know when they were approaching the seven-hundred-and-sixty-foot-high summit. It roared like Eden Park football stadium when the All Blacks went over for a try. Angus had cut a clearing to open up the view, but by doing so had left the summit exposed to the nor'easters and southerlies, which was why the scrub had been slow growing back. But it afforded the sort of view that made their labors worthwhile. They could see past the tip of Aiguilles Island and all the way east and south across Waikaro Point to Overtons Beach and Arid Island.

Angus reached the top and continued over the brow onto the southern side to escape the wind. He slumped down on the ground. Red joined him and began to set up the radio.

"What's the procedure, Angus?"

"Let a man get his breath back! Have you no patience at all?" Angus exhaled noisily and coughed. "First, we try our luck and see if we're high enough to get through to Devonport direct. If we can, they'll put us on relay to the *Kotaku*. Otherwise we have to call up Police Sergeant Milne at Claris Airfield to relay messages. The sergeant will have to act as intermediary."

"Let's hope you can get them direct." Clutching the binoculars, Red climbed back up to the top of the rise and lay flat on his belly so that the wind would pass over him. Archie lay alongside, one front paw touching Red's elbow, letting him know he was there. If they had to go via Claris, everyone on the island with a ham radio would be listening in and adding their twopence worth. He listened to Angus calling up Devonport and breathed a sigh of relief when he heard them respond.

"Ask them what time the *Kotaku* left," Red called down. He scanned the night in front of him, but nothing was visible beyond the looming presence of the first line of trees.

"They're just casting off now."

"What?!" Red shone his torch onto his watch. It was almost nine o'clock. Almost time for Shimojo to show himself if the game was on. "Find out what time they expect to get here." Red did a quick calculation, trying to figure what speed the old minesweeper could muster running head-on into the sea. It didn't look good.

"They expect to round Aiguilles at about two-thirty, that's if Shimojo has put in an appearance. Anything else?"

Two-thirty! Red clenched his fists in dismay and tried to imagine the havoc the *Shoto Maru*'s gaping net would have caused by then. There'd be precious few fish left and the sea bottom ripped apart. He began to hope with all his heart that he was wrong, that the boy was wrong, that Shimojo wouldn't show. He'd just settled back when Archie emitted a low growl. He looked up, and his skin prickled into goose bumps. No ghost could have startled him more.

"Bloody hell, Angus! The bastard's right on our doorstep!"

Without warning the *Shoto Maru* had suddenly lit up just southeast of them, little more than two miles out from Waikaro Point. Red heard Angus shouting into the radio but couldn't drag his eyes away from the apparition. He grabbed the binoculars and held them to his eyes. He could clearly make out the yellow-jacketed crewmen with their orange helmets scurrying around the stern ramp, see their safety lines and the signals they gave each other. Judging by the angle of the deck, the catch was good. It had pulled the stern down so far that the bows broke clear of the water as they crested each swell. How many snapper did it take to weigh down the stern of a two-and-a-half-thousand-ton trawler, he wondered? How many breeding snapper that would never live to breed? His face flushed with sudden anger. He could feel his anger surge through his system, boiling, roiling, building in force. His hands shook, and his temples began to throb. The roaring in his ears reached a crescendo. He had to do something! He tried to line the trawler up again in his glasses, but his hands wouldn't hold steady. He had to do something! Had to work! Had to do something! His agitation grew and fed on itself until it became panic, until the pounding in his ears became unbearable and threatened to split his head apart.

"No!" he screamed. "Bastards!"

Angus swung around as Red screamed, saw him leap to his feet and the binoculars fall. Saw him turn and bolt back down the hill, Archie hard on his heels.

"Red! You come back here! Come back here, you bloody fool!" But Angus knew he was wasting his breath. Agreements counted for nothing when Red had one of his turns. "Damn you, Red O'Hara!" He started climbing to the top of the clearing but stopped dead in his tracks as the *Shoto Maru* came into view. "Dear God in heaven!" He picked up the binoculars just as the codend of the net emerged from the water and began to inch up onto the ramp. All around the stern the water foamed pink with blood in the glare of the arc lights. "Dear God!" Angus said again, but this time in little more than a whisper. What chance did Red have against such a formidable enemy? Suddenly he felt scared. Scared for Red and scared for Rosie and her unborn child. What did Red think he could do against the trawler? It was insanity, pure and simple. Suddenly Red's little bombs seemed just that. They seemed puny, pathetic even, and the swirling blood-stained water a chilling warning.

"He's done it! The bloody fool's gone and done it!"

Mickey stared at the speaker in the *Kotaku*'s radio room in dismay. Things had gone beyond his control. He thought of Red alone in his little boat up against the *Shoto Maru*. Surely the man must have learned something from his last encounter with the trawler. What did he hope to achieve? He thought of Red's bombs and the likely consequences. Shimojo was certain to return fire. At worst there'd be loss of life, at best an international incident. Either way the navy would wind up on the rack, and God only knew what would happen to Red if he managed to survive. Mickey felt sick and dismayed. The man was a fool, but in his heart Mickey knew the navy was also partly to blame. They'd procrastinated when they should have acted. It was always the same story. Too bloody little too bloody late.

"Can we get some more speed out of this bloody tub?" Mickey looked around, but everyone studiously avoided his eye. It wasn't his call and they all knew it. The commander of the *Kotaku* was well aware of the situation and doing his best. The *Kotaku* was an old girl, she was old when they took her over from the Royal Australian Navy, and as everyone knew, minesweepers tended not to be sprinters even when young. But she handled the short, steep, pounding chop of the gulf well, carved through waves that made life on patrol boats a misery.

What the hell was Red playing at, wondered Mickey? He'd pressed Angus for a more precise description of Red's bombs and had come away little wiser. What was Red trying to do? What was his plan? If all he intended to do was warn Shimojo off, there was no point in their busting a gut to get there. The bird would have flown. And if that happened, he'd have Red on toast for breakfast. They'd been handed the perfect opportunity, with eyes on the shore reporting on the *Shoto Maru*'s position and Great Barrier providing a radar shield. Shimojo would have had no time to react and no chance to run. They would have him cold if Red kept out of the way.

But Red hadn't kept out of the way, and, Mickey suspected, Red had other plans in mind, but what? Mickey groaned in frustration. He wanted to grab hold of Red with his massive hands and beat some sense into him. Dear God! The man was mad! But the undeniable truth was that if Red hadn't made his bombs, and if he wasn't so pigheaded, they wouldn't have been given the *Kotaku* or be in a position to effect an arrest. He checked his watch. The next five and a half hours would be purgatory and, possibly, the most decisive in his career. A sublieutenant passed him a steaming mug of coffee.

"Sublieutenant Zoric?"

"Yes, sir."

The young officer looked pleased that Mickey had remembered his name. But what Mickey had remembered was the taste of his coffee.

"Give Gloria a few more lessons with the filter, will you?"

Forty-one

~~~

Red raced blindly down the track, his torch swinging so wildly that it was virtually useless. He blundered into scrub, bounced off the trunks of pungas and nikau palms. A root trapped his foot, and he fell heavily, flat on his face. The impact shook him, shook him enough to convince him to stay there until he'd come back to his senses. He tried to steady his breathing and still his mind. But rage flared, fiery and bitter. He wanted to scream and lash out. His mind flipped back to the days immediately after the war, when his sudden fits of rage earned him a stay at Carrington Road mental hospital. When he was considered dangerous, put in straitjackets, fed slops and tranquilizers that left him numbed out and gibbering, when he'd fought those who'd tried to help him and those who didn't care. He remembered his frustration, his tears, his anguish, but most of all he remembered the futility of it all. He'd been helpless then, unable to help himself, unable to change anything. Helpless. Hopeless. He sat up, closed his eyes and began to draw in long, deep, calming breaths. Carrington Road was a long time ago, and there was no going back. He forced himself to release his anger. It hadn't helped him before and wouldn't help him now. He felt Archie's wet tongue lick his hand. Good old Archie.

Red sat cross-legged and motionless until he was sure he'd regained control. He picked up his torch and walked at a quick but steady pace to Angus's cabin, where he helped himself to a bottle of methylated spirits, a box of matches and an empty Golden Syrup tin. He dragged Angus's dinghy down onto the hard sand. He didn't have time to strip off and swim, besides which the night would be cold enough without him being wet. The swells had grown since he'd loaded his boat. They formed a shore break that thundered in onto the sand. He dragged the dinghy to the extreme eastern end of the beach, where there was some protection.

"Stay, Archie!"·

The dog sat, obedient to his master's wish but decidedly unhappy about it. He began to whine and shuffle forward on his bottom. But there was no place for Archie on board. He began to yelp anxiously as the dinghy was swallowed up in the gloom. He wanted to leap into the surf and dog-paddle after his master but was prevented by his instructions. Instead, he began to run in short bursts up and down the beach, barking, pleading, beseeching Red to come back for him. He kept running back and forth long after the sound of Red's diesel had faded away, lost in the roar of the wind and the crashing of the surf. Archie turned and sprinted as fast as he could up the track toward Rosie's. It was too much for a dog to bear alone.

Red headed northeast into the gale and seas, keeping well clear of the shore and the Christmas crayfish pots. He didn't dare use his torch. There'd be alert eyes on watch aboard the *Shoto Maru*, so he had to err on the side of caution. He momentarily regretted the fact that he'd forced the crayfishermen from Leigh to drop their pots so wide. He stared hard to his right. Already the shape of Bernie's Head was indistinguishable in the dark. He held his course. If the *Shoto Maru* still had its lights on, he expected it to swing into view at any moment. He cupped his torch in his hand and held it close to the face of his watch. Nine forty-five. The *Shoto Maru* had switched off its lights and continued fishing. But where? He strained his eyes, peering into the gloom, trying to locate the pinnacles before making his turn south. He was beginning to have doubts that he could achieve anything. If he couldn't find the pinnacles, what chance did he have of finding the trawler? What chance did he have if he had no bearings, no position to fix on, nothing to show him where he was? He felt the first gnawing of despair. Then a weak light flickered into view above and behind him. It appeared, disappeared and reappeared. But the farther out he went, the more constant the light remained. He broke into a smile. The old Scot was lending a hand. Red only hoped he'd shielded the light from his propane lamp from the watchful eyes on the *Shoto Maru*.

Red judged he was a mile north of Bernie's Head and turned east, straight out to sea. If Shimojo was catching fish, Red knew he'd still be somewhere in the area, working the school. The question was whether the trawler was working north or south. He started thinking through his options, something he should have done before. The trawler had been facing north when it had lit up. Logic suggested that the *Shoto Maru* would continue north before turning back over the school. He switched off his engine and listened. The wind roared in his ears, and the waves burst in anger against his hull. His boat creaked and shuddered, but even so, if the *Shoto Maru* was anywhere within a mile or two to the northeast, he could expect the wind to carry the throb of the diesels to him. It took power to drag big nets. Shimojo could turn off his lights, but he couldn't silence his engines. Red heard nothing. He decided to back his judgment and head out deeper. Behind him and away to his right, Angus's light flickered encouragement.

He reduced his speed so that he barely made headway against the waves. He realized there was no point in chasing blindly all over the ocean. If he was over the school, and if there was any merit in his reasoning, Shimojo would come to him, probably from the south. He dropped anchor.

The school of snapper failed to broaden out on the trawl northward, restricting the trawler to working north-south along a narrow corridor less than two miles from shore. Only the length of the school and its density justified trawling so close, but even then a wise skipper would refuse the challenge. Shimojo accepted the risks knowing his only alternative was to quit and run into deep water, where catches would be insignificant. He zigzagged along the outer edge of the school. The first haul had weighed in at just under fifteen tons, almost all snapper, and the second promised more. Midway through the trawl his radar operator drew his attention to a blip on the screen that indicated a small craft half a mile inshore of them. It appeared to be stationary. Shimojo dismissed the contact as a local fisherman, an opinion that appeared to be confirmed by a weak light shining on the headland. A small craft would need a bearing to find its way home in the conditions.

Red wished he'd brought bait with him so that he had something to occupy his mind while his boat tossed and bucked at anchor. At least he'd know if he was over snapper. His first job had been to suspend the Golden Syrup tin with a half inch of methylated spirits in the bottom and secure it. When the time came to light the fuses on his bombs, the tin of burning meths would serve well. Then he'd checked and rechecked the lines from which his bombs were suspended. His lines held fast, and there were no breakages. He thought of Mickey charging out toward them in the *Kotaku,* cursing Red for interfering, but what did Mickey expect? By the time the minesweeper arrived the *Shoto Maru* would've stripped the ocean, swallowed all the fish and ripped apart the shellfish beds. There'd be precious little left of Red's fishing grounds after the trawler had raked over them. A sound reached him, indistinct and definitely out of place. He froze and turned his head slowly into the wind. There it was again. Unseen but unmistakably mechanical, the throb of the massive diesels pushing against both wind and sea, pulling against the deadening drag of the net.

Red listened intently, eyes closed. The sound came in waves carried on gusts of wind, but he gradually worked out the trawler's position. It was working northward, too far out for him to do anything. His anger swelled to cold fury as he tried to imagine the damage the net would be inflicting. The crime demanded punishment! But what? How? Red calculated the trawler was far enough away to pass outside him on its return trawl, close enough for his bombs to warn it off and out to sea. But Red wanted more. That wasn't punishment. That wasn't retribution. Justice demanded retribution, and the time for warnings had passed. He stared grimly into the night as he contemplated a change of tactics. His plan was fraught with danger. But if he was successful, the *Shoto Maru* would never fish in close again.

The school thinned out as the *Shoto Maru* neared Aiguilles Island. Shimojo brought the trawler around to head back south for its third run. Even on the bridge he could hear the sound of the surf. The whole coast was treacherous in a nor'east blow, but the storms reserved their worst for Great Barrier's northernmost tip.

Rosie had washed and dried the dishes and sat down for a quiet read when she heard Archie whining and scratching at her door. "That you, Red?" she called. She dragged herself out of her chair and opened the door. She patted Archie, but there was no sign of Red. "Got too cold for you, did it boy? Come on in." But Archie stayed outside, whining, and feinting to go back down the veranda stairs. He looked up at her, whined, feinted again. Slowly the penny dropped. Archie hadn't left Red. Archie would never leave Red. Red had left Archie. She looked at the dog, first in disbelief, then in anger. "Red O'Hara, you bastard!"

She grabbed her heavy sweater and parka, sickened by the implications. He'd promised and he'd lied. He'd lied to her! She ferreted around in her dresser drawers until she found her woolen beanie and gloves. Hardly Christmas wear, but it didn't feel like Christmas anymore. What else would she need, she wondered? The propane lamp! Hurriedly she fitted a new cylinder and pocketed a box of matches. Her torch. Fortunately the batteries were relatively new. She thought about looking in on the boy to see if he was awake. What on earth would she say to him? "Sorry, have to duck out for a moment. Red's just gone to blow up your ship." She stepped out into the night, unclear of her intentions, having thought no further than to follow Archie.

The dog was clearly anxious, racing ahead, then coming back to make sure she followed. Perhaps Red had tripped and fallen? No, Red didn't trip. Archie led her down to the beach and stared straight out to sea. With the aid of her torch she could make out her boat and Angus's, but there was no trace of Red's. Just the Bronlund and Anderson dinghy hanging off the mooring where his boat should have been.

Where's Angus, she thought furiously? He also had a lot of explaining to do. She retraced her steps back up to the old pohutukawas and took the track to his bach. A single light burned in the living room, but no one was home except Bonnie. The cat purred her pleasure at Rosie's unexpected company, but to no avail. Rosie was gone as quickly as she'd arrived, following Archie up the track that led to the lookout. Rosie was out of breath when she reached the top and saw Angus's huddled figure beside the waning lamp, but it didn't stop her from giving him a piece of her mind.

"Angus!"

The old Scot jumped and spun around.

"You lying bastard! What have you and Red cooked up? Where is he? You tell me or I'll—" The beam of her torch caught his face and held it. Even in the uncertain light she could see that Angus wasn't well. "Oh Jesus, Angus, are you all right?"

"Aye . . . I couldn't stop him, you know. I tried, Rosie, believe me. He promised me he wouldn't do anything. He promised!" Angus was shivering. His shoulders slumped, and he looked every day of his sixty-five years.

"It's okay, Angus. Sorry for yelling. He's gone after them, hasn't he?"

"Aye. One of his moods took him. Got the better of him. God only knows what goes through that mind of his. Help me down with the radio, could you? I need a spell out of the wind. There's no stopping that man when the devil takes him."

Rosie picked up the radio and reached for his lamp.

"No! No! Leave that there. That's for Red. That's for Red so that he knows we're watching out for him and so he can work out where he is. He'll not see his own hand in front of his face out there. Help me down, then keep watch awhile for me. Will you do that, Rosie?"

Rosie helped him down into the lee, found the thermos and poured him a hot coffee.

"Get on up there now, lass, and keep your eyes peeled." Angus added a generous, warming shot of whisky to his drink. "I'll have a word with the lieutenant commander."

Rosie lay down on top of the rise with Archie pressed in close alongside her. She picked up the binoculars and put them down again. Why did she need glasses when she couldn't see anything? Angus's lamp began to fail as it used up the last of the gas in its cylinder. She lit hers, turned it up to full brightness and ran her hand slowly up and down in front of it, wondering if Red would see her signal and realize it was her. She hoped desperately that he would. He had to be reminded that he had others to think of besides himself. She looked at her watch. Eleven o'clock. "Angus, when will the *Kotaku* get here?"

"Two-thirty, from the north."

"Two-thirty!" Rosie bit her lip. Three and a half hours of waiting and fearing the worst. She put her arm around Archie and pulled him close to her for comfort.

"Don't worry, Rosie." Angus tried to sound reassuring. "You know Red. He's a survivor."

Shimojo began his return run a third of a mile in from his northerly run, using the sweep of his turn to execute the first zigzag. Once again the dense glow of the fish finder indicated they were over the school. He turned to his radar operator to check that the contact they'd identified earlier would not interfere with his trawl. He was surprised when his radar operator reported the contact to seaward of them, yet still apparently stationary. By rights, the contact should have been four to five hundred yards inshore of them. He was surprised but not alarmed and took no action other than to instruct his radar operator to keep a close eye on it.

The net recorder reported a thick river of fish flowing into the net. Shimojo's decision to continue fishing despite the nor'easter was vindicated. Being a third of a mile closer to shore made all the difference. The school was consistently dense. His intuition, his knowledge and his daring had paid off. He checked the position of the contact a quarter of a mile ahead of the trawler, and turned sharply southwest to make certain they passed well inside it. He didn't want whoever was fishing there to panic as the trawler drew close and inadvertently move into his path.

He stared through the bridge window to see if he could spot the contact's anchor light or running lights. It took him a moment or two to realize that the contact wasn't showing any lights. Shimojo knew why he wasn't showing lights, but why wasn't the contact? Surely whoever was out there could hear the *Shoto Maru's* engines and would want to make sure they weren't run down? He glanced at the taped-up bullet holes and felt a knot tighten in his stomach.

"Angus! I think I can hear something. A motor." Rosie lifted onto her elbows and peered into the blackness. Sometimes she thought she could hear it clearly, but at other times there was nothing.

"You're imagining things, Rosie. Nobody would be fool enough to come in so close that we could hear them. Not on a night like this."

But Rosie wasn't convinced. "Look at Archie." The dog was staring straight into the wind, sitting up, alert. "Look at his ears. He can hear it, too."

"It's possible, I suppose," said Angus. He was cold and too tired to argue. "If they're not too far out the wind might carry the sound to you."

Rosie was staring into the darkness in front of her, to where she thought the sound was coming from when the first of Red's bombs exploded.

"Angus!"

"What?"

Rosie thought she saw the flash bounce off the trawler and off a white shape nearby. But then it was gone, over in an instant, swallowed in the darkness. But where was the sound? That was the thing she remembered most from their trial detonations. She was beginning to doubt her own eyes when it reached her. A solid, thunderous boom. "Angus . . . !" she screamed again. Then even louder in a voice charged with anguish and fear. "Angus!"

But she'd no need to call out. Angus had missed the flash, but there was no escaping the bang. He bounded up to the top of the rise. Rosie was on her feet, the binoculars jammed to her eyes.

"Did you see where it was?"

"Right where I'm looking, Angus! And close in."

Angus peered intently into the gloom. He followed the angle of the binoculars and shook his head. Nobody would come in so close to the pinnacles with the gale blowing. Another explosion ripped the night, proving him wrong.

Forty-two

Red's heart raced faster than his straining motor as he surged ahead of the Shoto Maru to deploy his next bomb. The pinnacles were looming up in front of them, unseen in the night but no doubt glowing in warning on the trawler's radar. Shimojo would have to turn and Red had to make sure he turned the right way. If he detonated the next bomb too far ahead, he'd open a gap behind him and allow the trawler to escape to sea. He pulled back on the throttle. Where was the trawler? Had it already turned away, risked the bombs and cut through his cordon? He could hear the pounding of the Shoto Maru's diesels, the raised voices of the crew, but see nothing. There is a decisive moment in any battle, and Red was well aware that the moment had arrived. The outcome hinged on the next thirty seconds. He lit the fuse and lowered the bomb into the water.

The beam from the spotlight stabbed the water behind him, tracked him, found him. Red slammed the throttle forward, turned and raced back along his wake. The spotlight had found him but it had also enabled him to find the trawler. He doubled back to position his boat between it and the open sea. The spotlight clung to him, stayed with him despite the pitch and roll of both vessels. He turned away from the glare to preserve his night vision. Soon Shimojo would recover from his surprise and make a break for open water. Red swung around viciously, lining up to cut back across the trawler's bows once more, waiting, counting, praying that the bomb he'd just deployed wasn't a dud. The ocean erupted ten yards in front of the *Shoto Maru*'s port bow. Red wrenched the wheel hard over to seaward, away from the blast. Which way would the trawler turn? The spotlight swung off him, swung forward, touched gently on the pinnacles as it swung in an arc. Red nearly shouted with relief. Shimojo had turned away from him, turned to starboard, turned into the bay. Now all Red needed was a little luck.

Shimojo realized he'd sailed into a trap. The glimpse he'd caught of Red's boat left him in no doubt as to the identity of his enemy. The Red Devil was no vengeful spirit guardian, but a determined man of flesh and blood who had once fired on them with a rifle and now used bombs. Shimojo had no way of knowing what the bombs were or what they were made of. But the flash, the bang and the amount of water they threw up convinced him he had to do everything in his power to avoid them.

Their escape route was risky, but not too risky provided they completed their turn quickly. He ordered full power. The *Shoto Maru* turned so sharply that it began to wheel around its own net. Shimojo knew the loss of forward momentum would cause the net to settle and snag and ordered the helm to straighten. A wise man would have abandoned the net then and there, cut through the hawsers and made his escape to sea. But Shimojo was loath to give away his fish so easily. The bay wasn't large, but there was enough room to widen the turn. The question was, would the lunatic in the lifeboat try to block their exit? And if he did, what could they do about it? The captain took a set of keys from his pocket and unlocked the emergency cabinet, which housed the ship's distress flares, signal rockets and the rifle used when large sharks became entangled in their net. The bridge crew's eyes widened in surprise when he removed the rifle and a box of ammunition.

The spotlight caught Red again as he prepared to dash in close, off-load another bomb and force the trawler to widen its turn even more. He pulled back on the throttle and lined up the helm so that he could use both hands to steady the fuse against the flame. Just as the fuse began to fizz he saw a flash from the *Shoto Maru*'s bridge and heard the sharp crack that followed. He knew the tossing seas and the wind made him a difficult target, but the grim reality was that it would only take one lucky shot, one bullet to strike one of his bombs, and all of Rosie's painstakingly turned vases would be blown to smithereens, and him with them. He gritted his teeth and ducked in beneath the cover of the trawler's bows, dropped another bomb and sped away. He glanced over his shoulder and saw the trawler straighten to avoid the coming explosion. Two more bombs, two more perilous forays across the bows, and he could stand off a safe distance from the rifle and pray that his plan succeeded. But if the *Shoto Maru* completed its turn too soon and began its run to sea, he had little choice but to allow it to escape. He didn't have enough bombs to keep the trawler bottled up all night.

Shimojo realized he was being manipulated. His enemy had wanted him to turn into the bay, had maneuvered him in and begun to dictate the radius of the turn, but he didn't know why. He couldn't understand why his adversary didn't just save his bombs and block their escape to sea. The madman had little to fear from a rifle. The constant pitching and rolling made it ineffective as a weapon. Nevertheless he handed it over to the first officer in the hope that its presence would at least make his adversary think twice about coming in close, giving them a chance to straighten and run out to sea. He caught a glimpse of reefs and rocks on the depth recorder and wondered how many tons of snapper would be lost to snags. Another explosion blasted water over his bows.

The *Shoto Maru* staggered momentarily under the weight of the fish trapped in the net. His second officer stood waiting for the order to cut the hawsers. Yet Shimojo hesitated, still not ready to surrender the catch. He was a man unaccustomed to doubts. He did what lesser men always did in similar circumstances. In the absence of will to make the right—though painful—decision, he made no decision, made no attempt to seize back the initiative. He completed the turn and waited for the *Shoto Maru* to surge forward and produce the rush of speed that would enable him to escape. The spotlight had his adversary in its beam off to starboard, held at a distance by the threat of the rifle. The way seaward was open, and suddenly all the risks he'd taken seemed justified. The massive diesels roared, but the surge didn't materialize. Instead he was almost thrown off his feet as a harsh vibration ripped through the ship. Before he had a chance to grab the intercom, the engine-room alarm assaulted his ears. Shimojo grabbed the phone. Another bomb exploded to starboard of them. He screamed down the phone, stood stunned as the engineer relayed the news. The *Shoto Maru* had fouled its props.

Shimojo rushed out onto the observation platform, grabbed the spotlight, panned it left and right over the water, looking for clues. A round, white object bobbed up by the stern, followed by another, and another. He flashed the spotlight in front of him and up toward the bows. Floats. He realized instantly why the lifeboat had shepherded him inshore, but the knowledge gained him nothing. Without power the trawler was helpless before the wind and waves, and began to slide backward over its net into the bay. He raced back onto the bridge to order the anchors lowered, pulled up with the sickening realization that he was too late. The *Shoto Maru* had already drifted back over its net. His hesitation had cost him dearly. He should have ordered the anchors lowered and the hawsers severed the instant the props had fouled.

Red spun around as the *Shoto Maru*'s alarm sounded and the trawler suddenly lit up. He'd noted the change in the sound of the big diesel engines, hoped his plan had succeeded but was nevertheless overwhelmed to receive confirmation. But his elation rapidly turned to dismay and bewilderment as the trawler swung around broadside-on to the swells. Why hadn't Shimojo dropped his anchors? The stern of the trawler lit up blue as crewmen attacked the steel hawsers with acetylene cutters. The trawler kept turning, pushed by wind and wave. What would happen when they cut the net free? For the first time Red grasped the full extent of the trawler's plight. He'd schemed to foul the *Shoto Maru* on the Christmas lobster traps, not to run it aground on the rocks. But that seemed the most likely outcome.

The boy awoke the instant he heard the ship's alarm sound. He swung his legs over the side of his bed, feeling for the bunk below before jumping to the floor. But there was no bunk beneath him. He remembered where he was, the woman who tended him and strange red man who spoke his language. Why then did he hear the ship's alarm? He stumbled blindly through the darkness toward the glow that outlined the front windows. He looked down toward the bay and gasped out loud, spun around and went searching for clothes. Unbelievably his ship was lit up right in front of him. Even more unbelievably, it was foundering.

"My God! The fool's done it! He's done it!" Angus stared at the sight of the *Shoto Maru*, exhilarated, relieved, incredulous. Rosie grabbed hold of him and hugged him tight. She wanted to celebrate but still wasn't sure what they were celebrating. Below them they could see the crew of the trawler running to their emergency stations. The *Shoto Maru* rolled heavily as it took the sea beam-on. Its powerful lights lit the bay, and Angus didn't need the braying alarm horn to tell him the ship was in serious trouble.

"Let me have the glasses, Rosie. Ah . . . just as I thought. Red's run them into the crayfish pots. Bloody genius!"

"Where's Red? Can you see him?"

"Aye! He's still patrolling the mouth of the bay. No doubt he'll stay out there away from their riflefire till the *Kotaku* arrives."

"Thank God for small mercies. You better get in touch with Mickey and tell him what's happened."

Angus looked down at the *Shoto Maru*. "I don't like the look of that." His concern was justified. The trawler had completed its one-hundred-and-eighty-degree swing so that its bows now faced directly into the shore and the stern straight out to sea, into the teeth of the gale. The weight of the net was the only thing keeping the *Shoto Maru* from being swept inshore, but it also had the effect of pulling the stern down so that the swells and waves crashed over it. Dead fish and spare net floats washed free by the seas littered the water around the stern. "She'll not last long like that."

Rosie looked at her watch. It had just turned midnight. "Will she last another two and a half hours?"

Mickey listened in amazement. Everyone in the radio room and the corridors outside wore Cheshire cat smiles. Shimojo Seiichi was finished, that much was clear. But the *Shoto Maru* might be finished as well, and lives lost. Mickey wasn't smiling. If the *Shoto Maru* was in trouble, so was Red, and it was a toss-up which of them was in it the deepest. Mickey could see a major international incident looming. LOCAL FISHERMAN USES EXPLOSIVES TO FORCE JAPANESE TRAWLER ONTO ROCKS. He shuddered. Poaching was a serious matter, but it didn't warrant the sinking of ships or deaths among their crews. He realized he'd have to act fast to have any hope of saving Red's neck. He decided to take on face value Angus's claim that the bombs Red had made were all sound and no fury. HERO FISHERMAN SCUTTLES JAP POACHER WITH FIREWORKS, had a much nicer ring to it. That was a story the media would love to run with. Little bloke defies the might of the Japanese fishing fleet. The whole country except the wool and beef lobbies would rally behind him. No one would dare prosecute Red then, provided no lives were lost. Mickey realized he had to set the agenda and preempt the official view. He pulled out his wallet and rifled through for the business card of a friendly *Herald* reporter to whom he owed a story. With Gloria as go-between, it was time to deliver.

Red motored back and forth just beyond the spill of the stricken trawler's lights. He thought they'd be too busy attending to other problems to bother firing at him. He watched the trawler turn sideways-on to the sea as the stern crew severed the hawsers, held his breath while he waited to see if the anchors would bite and hold. He knew the bottom well and didn't hold out much hope unless the anchors snagged on a reef. The trawler's bow snapped around as the anchors bit, faded as they let go. He wondered if he should motor up and offer to take a rope and anchor out into deeper water, but hesitated, unsure of the reception they'd give him. He held off, saw the bow snap around once more, fade and kick back. His hopes sank as he saw the trawler drift backward, lifted when he heard the clanking of chain and realized they were laying more slack. It was a maneuver that won Red's approval. Perhaps they had a good hold. But the crew gathering by the lifeboat, preparing to abandon ship, suggested otherwise.

Red reacted the way the digger from Melbourne had so many years earlier. He moved into position astern of the trawler where he'd be able to assist if the launch of the lifeboat went awry. He could not stand by and let men drown, even if they were the enemy.

Shimojo elected to remain aboard and do whatever he could to save his ship. He still held hope that the anchors would snag and hold before the trawler bottomed and was rolled over by the swells, or washed up onto the rocks. He was prepared to pay the ultimate price for his mistakes until Red moved astern. He didn't see Red as a potential rescuer, poised to scoop up desperate seamen if their lifeboat capsized, but saw instead a predator moving in for the kill.

"Captain." Abe, the oldest man aboard, had volunteered to stay with him and called for Shimojo's assistance in launching the lifeboat. Shimojo obliged although his mind was elsewhere. The old man was a superb judge of the sea, timed the launch to perfection and set the crew safely on their way to shore. Shimojo wheeled about and returned to the bridge. He broadcast one final distress call and heard a longliner respond. Their words of hope brought a grim smile to his face. They informed him that help was on its way, little more than two hours off, in the form of an old minesweeper, the *Kotaku*. His enemies were gathering like wild dogs around a stricken calf. His anger stirred, surged and shaped into a desire for revenge. He spotted the rifle the first officer had left propped against the emergency cabinet. He still had use for it.

Forty-three

※━━❦━━※

Red watched the *Shoto Maru's* lifeboat swing out on its davits, saw the anxious crewmen crouching within, white knuckles showing over the gunwales. He was glad he wasn't among them. The wrong wave at the wrong time and the lifeboat would roll over. He took out his knife, cut the floats off his remaining bombs and tossed them overboard. If their lifeboat foundered, he'd need all the deck room he had. The two men who'd stayed aboard the trawler made the launch seem child's play, and Red acknowledged their skill. With little fuss the lifeboat powered away from the stricken trawler and made a sweeping turn toward the sandy strip at the northwest end of Wreck Bay.

Red flashed his torchlight at the two men remaining on board and moved in close so that they couldn't mistake his offer of assistance. Under the circumstances it seemed the responsible thing to do. One man responded, the other had disappeared. Red assumed he'd gone to collect the ship's log. He stood off until the second man reappeared, flashed his torch briefly once more and moved in beneath the gap in the railing where the trawler's crew had boarded the lifeboat. Without warning he found himself blinded, caught in the spotlight. He swung the wheel and rammed the throttle as far forward as it would go. The light wavered, went off him. He risked a quick look back at the ship and saw the two men confronting each other. He throttled back. To his utter amazement the taller man be-

411

gan flailing at the shorter man with what appeared to be a stick. The shorter man reeled backward, clutching his head. Red could see what was about to happen and spun his boat around. The shorter man continued to stagger backward, groping for a railing that was no longer there, overbalanced and toppled through the gap. Red gunned the throttle. He took his eyes off the trawler to scan the water, looking for the man who'd fallen. There! Red saw him struggling on the surface about forty yards from him. He glanced back up to the ship's rail and realized his mistake. They hadn't been fighting over a stick, but a rifle.

He headed for the trawler's stern and powered in close, where the ship's sloping sides made it hard for the remaining man—Shimojo?—to get a shot at him. He crouched to make himself less of a target, trying to draw comfort from the knowledge that the pitching of the *Shoto Maru* and his own boat's wild gyrations would make him a nearly impossible target.

He skidded sideways back into the wind, saw a flash of yellow in the water, an upraised arm. Sixpenneth of Jap. Either the trawler had drifted right, or the man had floated left, because he was a good twenty yards away. Red turned toward the drowning man, knowing he'd be exposed in the spill of the arc lights. He gave himself only one chance for the pickup, fed the motor full throttle, aimed slightly upwind of the bobbing splash of yellow, then throttled back and slammed the diesel into neutral. He threw himself against the port gunwale and reached down toward the water, met eyes staring urgently, desperately into his own, felt a hand grab his wrist, grabbed with his other hand and pulled. He gasped aloud at the explosion of pain from his ribs and heaved with all his strength. He let the injured seaman drop onto the deck, left him lying there as he engaged gear once more and gunned for the shore. Red braced both feet as the bow rose under power and briefly held sway over the tossing sea. In that fleeting moment, Red's luck turned. Shimojo saw his enemy hold steady in his sights and squeezed the trigger.

Crack! The bullet thudded into Red's right buttock and slammed him hard against the console. His mind reeled, stunned by the unbelievable force of the impact. So that's how it felt! So much harder, so much more brutal than he'd ever imagined. Was that what Archie felt in the last instant of his life? Poor Archie. Red's right knee buckled, and he collapsed backward onto the engine housing. Searing pain stabbed up his back and into his brain. He forced himself to sit up, to steer, to try to take a bearing from the fast-closing dark mass that was the lower slope of Bernie's Head. He tried to spot the jetty and failed. Every bounce of the boat, every wave brought a surge of pain and nausea. He managed to turn the helm slightly to the right, but the effort of reaching for the throttle and pulling it back was beyond him. He braced himself. Running up onto the beach under full power would be bad enough. But at least he wouldn't ram his jetty.

"Red's been hit!" Rosie screamed. She'd watched through the binoculars, not daring to breathe as the wind carried the reports of the rifle to them. Red's boat had ducked and dived, but she'd known he was in trouble as soon as he'd stopped to pick somebody or something up from the water. She'd seen him pitch forward then slump back, loose as a rag doll. "Angus! Red's been hit!"

Angus clambered back up to the top of the rise. "Where is he?"

"He's headed for shore. I saw him fall, Angus! I saw him get hit!"

"Steady, lassie! Is he still driving the boat? Tell me! I can't see him."

"I think so." The tears in her eyes blurred her vision. She thrust the binoculars at Angus. "You take them. You stay and tell Mickey we need help. I'm going down to the beach to find Red. Come on, Archie!"

"Be careful!" Angus called after her. "You might run into the rest of the crew. They mightn't take too kindly to what has happened!" He could hear her crashing into the bushes and ferns as Red had done, but he doubted she'd heard him or that it would make the slightest bit of difference even if she had. "Bloody madness!" he said aloud. "Bloody madness!" He wrung his hands and hopped from foot to foot in frustration. He thought of Rosie tripping, falling, losing the child. Running headlong into the trawler's crew, being beaten up and losing the child. Losing the child! His eyes watered but not from the wind. Losing the child! He didn't know what he'd do, how he'd ever recover if he lost Rosie and the child as well. "Red, you bloody madman! Don't you realize what you've done!" He sent a final message to Mickey, swung the radio and binoculars over his shoulders and set off down the track. He had a feeling he'd be more useful closer to the action.

Rosie slowed. She'd already scared herself badly with two near falls, saw the faint light still glowing in Angus's bach and detoured. She found his medicine chest in his bathroom, grabbed two clean towels as well and a facecloth. She was close to panicking but still thinking, still a doctor as well as a terrified lover, still in control despite her galloping heartbeat. She found a milk bottle under the sink and filled it with water. Bonnie sat up, alert, watching her, wondering what on earth was going on. Rosie made sure she shut the door properly behind her.

Shimojo saw the white boat pick up speed and surge beyond the range of the arc lights and lowered his rifle. He made his way back up to the bridge, checked the depth recorder and found he'd drifted into around fifty feet of water. The question was, was he still dragging anchor? The bow faced head-on to the wind, which was a good sign, even though the ship tossed and pitched wildly. The anchors appeared to be holding. But as quickly as hope flared, the wind dispelled it. The wind caught the bow and swung it wickedly toward the beach. The trawler rolled heavily, throwing Shimojo against the bridge wall. Just as quickly the anchors bit once more and snapped the bow back. His fingers gripped tightly around the rifle stock, turning white at the knuckles. It was over. He was finally convinced his ship was lost.

He fought his way back to the stern deck, made straight for the life raft, a buoyant, airtight box covered with cork and canvas and looped with rope for survivors to cling to. He used his pocketknife to saw through the ropes lashing the raft to the rail and tossed it overboard. He followed immediately after, grabbed hold and let the wind and waves carry him toward the shore. Seawater washed over his rifle and flooded the barrel. There was nothing he could do to prevent it. Shimojo only needed the rifle to fire one more bullet, the bullet which would end the life of the man who had destroyed his ship, his career and everything he'd worked for.

Forty-four

Red's boat fluked the back of the shore break, which softened the impact of the hull hitting the sand. It bounced twice before coming to rest, well clear of the high-water mark, motor screaming. Red had been pitched forward, unable to stop himself, and lay gasping for breath, waiting for the pain to subside, waiting for his head to clear. Someone turned off the diesel and leaned over him. A hand touched his neck, searching for a pulse. He sensed the dark presence of someone looming above him.

"I'm okay, okay . . ."

The hand reached beneath his shoulders, another behind his knees. He felt himself being lifted, felt foolish in his helplessness.

"*Domo arigato,*" Red said weakly. "Thank you."

"*Un!*" More a grunt than a word.

Red heard the man hissing through his teeth at the effort of lifting him over the gunwale and onto the beach. The man laid him down on the sand, then collapsed alongside him.

"*Domo arigato gozaimasu!*" An exhausted whisper. The Japanese trawlerman thanking him.

"*Namae* Red."

"Abe."

Red reached out and found the man's hand. He gripped it weakly, resisted the temptation to follow up with *konichi-wa* and instead lay still, waiting for the pain to dull. His body stiffened and warned against any movement. He could just make out the shape of Abe alongside him, trying to sit upright, head in his hands. Red recalled the blow to the man's head and speculated on the damage. He heard an excited yelp, a familiar snuffle, and felt something wet across his face. Good old Archie! He lifted a hand to ruffle his mate's ears.

"Red! Red!"

Red tried to turn and look toward the track, but the pain discouraged him. It didn't matter. He could hear her feet on the sand, see the beam of her torch flicking from Abe to him. Hear Archie whining excitedly.

"Red! Are you all right?" She was by his side, kneeling, another hand reaching for his pulse.

"I'm okay, Rosie."

"Where were you hit?"

How did she know he'd been shot? "Right buttock."

"Tasty. Roll over."

"Roll me over."

Rosie pulled him toward her, rolled him facedown and shone the torch on the sickening mixture of sand, saltwater and blood. "Bloody hell, Red!" she said, but the relief in her voice was evident. She shone the torch at Abe, pulled his hand away from his face, saw the pulpy mess of his right ear, the split above his right eye. "Oh Christ, Red, your mate's no better." She poured water over the facecloth and handed it to Abe so he could start cleaning his wound while she attended to Red.

"The bullet's ripped right through the cheek. Damn you, Red, I'm getting tired of patching you up." She made him swallow some aspirin, began to clean his wounds and tried to staunch the flow of blood. She wished she had more water. Out of the corner of her eye she saw Abe stagger to his feet and stumble around the bow of Red's boat, back toward the sea. He obviously needed more water as well.

"Move over, Archie! Give me some elbowroom!" But Archie had rejoined his master, and his master was in trouble. It didn't matter what Rosie said, there was no way he was going to budge.

•   •   •

Shimojo saw two lights on the shore, one far to the right, on the third of Wreck Bay's little beaches, which was where his crew had landed in the lifeboat. The other was virtually straight ahead, a single torch, attracting him like a magnet. He could hear the shore break clearly, feel it sucking him toward it. The life raft was designed to support the weight of many men and scudded along the top of the waves, pushed by wind and sea. It didn't require much imagination to know what would happen once it caught the shore break. The tumbling life raft would announce his arrival as surely as a ring on a doorbell. Shimojo let go. It could serve as a decoy while he washed ashore farther down the beach.

Without his weight holding it back, the life raft galloped away, bucking and tossing on the waves like an unbroken pony. Shimojo did his best to kick his way farther down the beach, rifle held high.

"What's that?" Rosie heard the life raft thud into the sand and tumble in the rush of the wash. She spun around and shone her torch at the sound. She held the beam as steady as her shaking hands would allow. "It looks like some kind of big box with rope."

"Don't worry, Rosie. It'll just be something that's washed off the trawler. I've got a feeling we're going to see lots more."

Rosie turned her attention back to Red's wounds. The exit wound badly needed stitching, but she lacked the means. She poured antiseptic directly into it, saw his buttock spasm involuntarily as it registered the sting. She dried the surrounding skin and began pulling the wound closed with strips of adhesive tape. Red didn't complain, but then she didn't expect him to. All she could do until Mickey arrived was make Red as comfortable as possible.

"That'll do for now," she said. "You'll live. You won't be able to lie on your back for a while, so you'll have to lie on me instead." She thought she heard Red snort. "I'm going to tend to your mate with the sore head." She went to stand, but Archie beat her to it. He leaped to his feet, snarling, charged two yards and stopped, forelegs rigid, rear legs bent, ready to spring.

"What is it, Archie?" Her blood turned cold. Whatever had worried Archie had to be bad news for them as well. She saw a shape silhouetted against the glow from the trawler's lights and aimed her torch at it. She saw a man pointing a rifle at her, no more than fifteen yards away. She screamed but had the presence of mind to kill the torch.

"*Ugokuna! Ugokuna!*" Freeze! Don't move!

Rosie froze. She didn't speak Japanese but knew hysteria when she heard it. "Oh Christ, Red," she sobbed. She tried to drag Red away but he immediately cried out in pain. What else could she do? She thrust both hands under his arms and heaved. Archie snarled, leaped and retreated, darting one way and then the other, trying to draw off the attacker.

Shimojo was confused and disoriented. He no longer had the light to guide him, and when the torch had shone straight at him it had deprived him of what little night vision he had. He rubbed away seawater that had dripped into his eyes, stinging them and blurring his vision. He wasn't accustomed to dogs, and Archie worried him. He realized he'd have to deal with the dog first. He pointed his rifle at the sound of the snarling, the scuffing sounds in the sand, but the beast wouldn't stay still. It circled to his right, growling, snarling. Came closer. Charged. Shimojo fired in desperation. Archie's sudden yelp split the night.

"Archie! Archie! Nooooo!" Red couldn't bear it! Not again! Dear God, not again! It was happening a second time. How many times did Archie have to die for him? How many times! "Nooooo!" he screamed. "No! Shoot me! Shoot me! You're supposed to shoot me!"

Shimojo stepped closer to his target, slowly raising the rifle to his shoulder and concentrating on the direction of Red's voice. Saltwater mixed with sweat stung his eyes and caused him to blink involuntarily.

"*Iie! Iie! Watashi! Watashi!*" Red screaming, Archie whimpering. "No, no! Here! Here! Shoot here!" All the suffering, all the years, and it was all going to end as it had begun in Burma at the one-oh-five. The little man with the long rifle. His namesake.

Shimojo was surprised to hear his enemy speak Japanese. But it didn't make any difference. He took a deep breath, exhaled, began to squeeze the trigger.

Red flinched at the explosion. Rosie screamed.

"Red! Red!"

In the moment of stillness that followed, Rosie switched on her torch and pointed it at the prostrate form of Shimojo Seiichi.

"Damn you, Red! Damn your foolish hide! See what you've gone and made me do, you damn fool!"

Rosie heard Angus's voice and spun around. Angus crept cautiously up to them, stood shaking over them, his old Lee Enfield still jammed hard against his shoulder.

"See what you've made me do, you bloody madman!"

Forty-five

~~~~~~~~

Mickey stood on Angus's veranda, drinking strong black coffee generously fortified with the Scotsman's whisky. He watched the movement of lights below him as the *Kotaku* towed the stricken trawler into the safety of deeper water. Personally, he would have been happier if the *Shoto Maru* had foundered, but he had Red and Rosie to consider. No amount of PR, no matter how cleverly contrived, could counter the loss of the trawler. But the fishing company back in Japan had retained its asset minus one net and the fish in the trawler's freezer holds, which would be confiscated. Both countries would treat the incident as regrettable, exchange protest notes, and return to their trade negotiations. Briefly, New Zealand would have a new hero.

Angus's bach had become a casualty ward, with both the *Kotaku*'s doctor and Rosie tending the wounded. Captain Shimojo Seiichi's shoulder was shattered, but at least he'd live to explain his actions. Again Mickey was relieved for all of their sakes. The ship's doctor had finished with his human patients and turned his attention to Archie. The dog's foreleg was smashed beyond hope. Mickey glanced back indoors to see if Rosie had finished patching up the old trawlerman's head. He wasn't squeamish, but watching wounds pulled open, cleaned and sutured wasn't his idea of a pleasant evening. The boy Angus had rescued was helping her. Theoretically, these two Japanese were both under guard, but Mickey was happy to leave it theoretical. They posed no threat to anyone and were clearly overjoyed just to be in each other's company. He'd have to take them both over to Auckland for questioning, but he foresaw no problems. Angus's and Rosie's statements were clear and unequivocal, and the interpreter had indicated that neither the old man nor the boy disagreed with their version of events.

Mickey turned his attention back to the bay, where the *Kotaku* and the trawler's crew were fully occupied saving the *Shoto Maru*. He shook his head at the irony, took another swig of coffee and wondered if there was a divine being somewhere having a laugh at his expense.

"Hello, sailor." Rosie came out to join him and leaned heavily on the veranda rail.

"How are the patients?"

"Which ones? I'm thinking of opening a practice. Red and Archie are asleep. Both need a spell in hospital. That bullet made a right mess of Red's bum, and the dog will probably need the whole of its shoulder removed. Your MO was wise to leave that to a vet. Pity it was his front leg. I have this vision of him toppling over every time he lifts a leg to pee."

"What about Shimojo and the crewman?"

"Shimojo is heavily sedated and unconscious. The crewman will need plastic surgery. Did you get a good look at his ear?"

"Enough. Where's Angus?"

"He came and gave me a big hug, so I knew immediately that he wasn't well. He's quite convinced he's going to jail. At the very least he knows that Wreck Bay will be overrun with police and reporters. He's not sure which he fears most. I gave him a jab to stop his whinging. He should've gone bye-byes by now. Well, that's everyone accounted for."

"Not quite, Rosie . . ."

"What's the problem?"

"Did you get my letter?"

"What letter?"

"This probably isn't the right time."

"Which means it probably is. Let me guess. Angus has told you I'm pregnant."

Mickey nodded, held his breath.

"Did he also tell you that you might be the father?"

Mickey winced, closed his eyes. "He alluded to it."

"Well, Lieutenant Commander, you can relax. I had my period ten days after you left. Sorry, stud, you put up a good show, but you might just as well have been firing blanks."

Mickey exhaled, sighed, couldn't stop himself from smiling. "Is that God's honest truth, Rosie?"

"Absolutely," she lied.

"'You're supposed to shoot me,'" said Rosie. "That's what you said on the beach. Care to explain?"

"Not now, Rosie." Red lay on his stomach on crisp white sheets. The hospital had given him a bed at the end of a long public ward, with a vacant bed alongside. With the side curtains drawn, they achieved at least an illusion of privacy.

"You're going to be here three days."

"Three days!"

"That's what the doctor said, Red. Now you can either lie here feeling sorry for yourself or tell me about the one-oh-five. If you want to feel sorry for yourself you can do it on your own. I'll go down to the vet's and sit with Archie."

"Don't go, Rosie."

"If I stay, you have an obligation—not just to me but to our baby." She reached over and took Red's hand. She held it against the slight swell of her stomach. "See? We're running out of time. Our child is starting to make its presence felt."

"What do you want me to do?"

"You know what I want you to do. Our baby is entitled to a father who lives here, Red, here and now in the same place and time!"

Red lay silent. Rosie couldn't tell if he'd slipped away from her or was gathering his thoughts. She decided to give him ten minutes to respond, and if he didn't, walk out. As it turned out, she barely had to wait thirty seconds.

"I failed, Rosie, I failed. When it came to the crunch I wasn't good enough. *Nogoodenah! Nogoodenah!*"

"I'm the doctor here, let me be the judge of that."

"I let everyone down. Archie was killed because I let everyone down." Pain and anguish infiltrated Red's voice, and the hand Rosie still held against her stomach began shaking.

"Right. That's what you felt. I guessed as much. Now stop that, Red, or I'll go! Do you want me to go?"

"No, Rosie!"

"I don't want to hear how you felt, Red, I don't want you to drown me in buckets of guilt! Besides, I'm not convinced you have any reason to feel guilty anyway. From all that you've told me, you guys were prepared to die for each other, would willingly die for each other. Right?"

"Right." Red's voice was barely a whisper.

"So Archie died for you. Doubtless if the tables had been turned, you would have died for him. Right?"

"Right."

"So just stick to the facts. Go back to the beginning and tell me what happened the day Archie was killed. What was the weather like?" She snapped the question.

"It was raining."

"Hot or cold?"

"Hot. Humid as hell."

"What were you doing?"

Red told her, told her of the drumming of the rain on leaves, of the knee-deep mud and rain-slicked rocks, of the *banga* he and Archie carried, of his exhaustion, his desperation, his ultimate failure. Rosie turned her chair away so she wouldn't see the tears running down his cheeks, and he wouldn't see the tears running down hers. He told her of the Big Bash Artist and the little man with the long rifle, of the silly banter between them over the similarity of their names and how it had cost Archie his life. He told her of his despair afterward, the numbness, the grieving, the self-loathing and the blur of weeks when his mates helped him through his unwillingness to survive. He showed her the full extent of his nightmare, but more than that he showed her the burden of his guilt, held it up for her to weigh and share.

When he'd finished, Rosie turned and buried her face in his hair and smothered his cheek with kisses. "Thank you," she said. "Thank you for both of us."

Postscript

Wreck Bay never returned to normal after the police and press lost interest in it. The incident with the Shoto Maru had put the bay on the map, and it became a summer destination for day-trippers in boats and bushwalkers. A well-meaning Barrier Council set up picnic tables, which were promptly destroyed and consumed in a Stanley slow-combustion range. No attempt was made to replace them. The permanent population doubled nevertheless.

On the fifth day of May, 1967, Rosie gave birth to Archibald Hamish, who delighted both parents with his shock of red hair. The three of them forged a mutually dependent unit, which suited Red right down to the ground and gave purpose to his survival. The unit was strengthened when Archibald Hamish acquired a sister, whom Rosie could not resist calling Scarlett. Rosie moved into Red's bach and adopted his regime because it was easier for her to change and she was already heading his way. Red still needed every part of his therapy, his exercise, his routine and his work, while Rosie concentrated on dispelling his nightmares and feelings of guilt.

In addition to a doting grandfather, Archibald Hamish also acquired a grandmother, in a quiet ceremony at Awana Bay, and never wanted for love, a slice of cake or cup of cocoa. Angus kept up his writing and continued his regular patrols in search of foreign trawlers and German U-boats. However, the highlight of his days was telling stories to his adoring young audience and reveling in the childhood that had been denied him.

Mickey Finn announced his engagement to Gloria Wainscott on New Year's Day, 1967, and married her five months later. When Phil Scriven was promoted to a staff position, Mickey took over the fisheries protection squadron. He tried to give it the edge and impact needed to control incursions but was frequently frustrated by lack of funds and political will. Nevertheless the foreign fleet recognized the need for greater caution, and the rate of incursions halved. Every summer he and Gloria took leave and stayed as guests in Rosie's cottage. Angus even adjusted to that.

Paullina Simons

Red Leaves

On a New England college campus, the naked body of a beautiful student is found frozen in a bank of snow. Why had she not even been reported missing by her friends?

Spencer O'Malley, the police detective assigned to the case, is soon drawn into the strange world of four friends, Jim, Conni, Albert and Kristina. O'Malley finds that these children of privilege who played, studied, and occasionally slept together also kept secrets of their own, secrets that must be pieced together to form an entirely new picture.

O'Malley is a stranger in this Ivy League environment, yet he feels an affinity with the victim. In her death, he gradually discovers the truth of her mysterious and complex life, and each revelation is more shocking than the last.

Suspenseful, claustrophobic and utterly compelling, *Red Leaves* puts Paullina Simons in the very front rank of contemporary writers

ISBN 0 00 655057 6

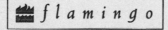

Nothing Lasts Forever
Sidney Sheldon

In the frenetic world of a big San Francisco hospital, events catapult three women doctors into a white-hot spotlight:

Dr Paige Taylor
She swore it was euthanasia, but when Paige inherited a million dollars from a patient, the District Attorney called it murder.

Dr Kat Hunter
She vowed never to let a man too close again - until she accepted the challenge of a deadly bet.

Dr Honey Taft
To make it in medicine, she knew she'd need something more than the brains God gave her.

Racing from the life and death decisions of the operating room to the tension-packed fireworks of a murder trial, *Nothing Lasts Forever* lays bare the ambitions and fears of healers and killers, lovers and betrayers in a heart-stopping story you wish would never end . . .

'Of all the popular novels I've read this summer this beats the lot for sheer storytelling mastery'   *Today*

0 00 647658 9